EVER WITH ME

ANNABELLE MCCORMACK

Published by Annabelle McCormack

Edited by Marion Archer

Cover by Kari March Designs

Illustrated Cover by Patrick Knowles

www.annabellemccormack.com

Brandywood, I love you. Thanks for being there when I needed you.

EVER
WITH
ME

1

MADDIE

"No, no, no . . . don't do this to me," Madison Yardley breathed, feeling the blood drain from her face.

Across the small table from her, Josh Hawkins refused her eye contact, his fingers curling around a paper coffee cup.

Josh.

Who, until three weeks ago, she had been certain would put a ring on her finger any day.

Sure, it had been a whirlwind relationship of four months. They'd moved in together after two weeks, and Mom had freaked out about that fact, but—*when you know, you know*.

Or something like that. Maddie had been sure she'd "*known*."

"I'm in a really hard position, Mad, you know that. Gina's family is sponsoring the main stage on Friday night. And Luke is my cousin, after all. She just—"

"Doesn't want her boyfriend's connections going the way of his ex? Yeah, I get it," Maddie managed. She wrinkled her nose, the smell of the stale brew Josh had grabbed from the coffee cart making her feel physically ill.

It had been his idea to meet here at the town hall—in "neutral" territory—before the fall festival committee meeting. Here, where Gina wouldn't get jealous about their meeting. She was one room over, already waiting in the main hall, while Maddie had to endure the humiliation of being spotted talking with Josh in an awkward corner near the entrance by everyone arriving.

Maddie breathed as calmly as possible. "I understand that it's your cousin who's in River House, but I'm the one who scheduled them to play for the last night of the festival. If they play on Friday, who the hell am I supposed to get for Saturday night? The festival is a month away, Josh. Booking a musical act bigger than River House would take months, not weeks."

He shrugged. "No one says Saturday night's act has to be bigger than Friday's. That's just your family wanting their sponsored event to be the biggest and best." A guilty streak of red crawled up his face despite his words.

She clenched her fingers into fists. "You're completely screwing me with this. All because the Stricklands can't let go of their hatred of my family. Everyone knows the last night of the fair is the biggest night. What the hell am I supposed to do?"

"I don't know. Get a local act?" Josh stood abruptly. "It's not my problem. Figure it out yourself. I'm just the messenger." Josh slid the envelope across the table. "This is the deposit back from Luke. Gina's family has paid him for Friday night instead."

Maddie resisted the urge to shred the envelope to pieces. *Seriously?*

"Deposit or not, I should sue Luke and River House for breach of contract."

Josh shoved some of his blond hair out of his eyes. "I guess it's a good thing you didn't make him sign one, then." He smirked smugly, then tossed his coffee cup in the nearby trash can. "See you at the meeting."

A fresh wave of tears stung in Maddie's eyes as he disappeared.

Dammit. He *would* know she hadn't officially signed a contract with River House. Maddie had been so excited about getting such a big-name country band for the festival that she hadn't worried they'd screw her over like a lesser-name band might.

But none of that hurt as much as the way Josh had done a one-eighty.

And here I am. Still half in love with him.

God, she wanted to hate him so much.

Maddie pushed a strand of honey-blond hair behind her ear, cursing at the perfect wave she saw out of the corner of her eye. *Why did I put so much effort into my hair tonight?*

But Josh's callousness toward her was unexpected. He never would have done something like this to her—or her family—before.

She stuffed the deposit into her purse and searched for a tissue. After dabbing the tears from her eyes, she swiped her nose. Somehow, she needed to compose herself so she could go into the meeting tonight.

What the hell am I going to do?

She already imagined the triumph on Gina's face when she'd announce to the committee that River House would take the main concert stage on the Stricklands' sponsored day. All for what? To make Saturday's concert look less important?

The pettiness of it all was sickening. Gina wanted a win.

But damn if I have to let Gina know how defeated I feel.

Maddie sniffled, then stood. She found her way to the bathroom to take a minute and calm down. Make sure her expression didn't read *on the verge of tears.*

She wouldn't let Gina see a single tear on her face.

Checking the time, she took a few deep breaths. The committee meeting would start in five minutes. She'd slip in after it had already started to avoid any of the small talk that took place beforehand.

Maddie paused in front of the mirror and pulled out a tube of lip gloss, then reapplied. Her face looked blotchier and more pinched than she wanted it to—a side effect of how red she got every time she cried.

There would be time for her tears later when she got back to her place.

Not now. Right now, just get through this meeting.

She concentrated on breathing deeply, thankful no one else came into the bathroom. When enough time had passed, she hurried back out to the foyer, then found her way into the main hall.

The group had gathered toward the front of the hall. Usually, the main hall was packed for town hall meetings, as Brandywood wasn't a town content to have a few octogenarians running things. Everyone wanted a say.

However, at committee meetings like this one, the groups that gathered were considerably smaller. Josh didn't need to be here—but he'd come with Gina to represent the Stricklands. Maddie had always taken town fair committee duty for her family, a fact she now regretted.

Luckily, TJ was chair of the town fair committee this year. As a transplant to Brandywood, he was neutral on the most divisive issues in town. Friendly and funny, TJ was easy to get along with.

"Did you get the handwashing station rented from Larson's?" TJ was asking Dottie Perkins.

Dottie, a sixty-year-old Black woman who'd handled the petting zoo for years, smiled politely. "I told you I did last time."

TJ scratched his beard. "Sorry about that. We're mostly down to crossing T's and dotting I's at this point." He struck through a line item on a paper attached to the clipboard in his hand, then grinned at the group of eight. "In the interest of saving everyone's time, is there anything new we need to add to the agenda today?"

Predictably, Gina raised her hand. "I have a change to announce in the lineup for one of the main events. It turns out River House isn't available on Saturday night for the fair, so they've agreed to play on the main stage on Friday night. I already spoke to the band that we'd scheduled, and they've agreed to be an opening act instead."

Just breathe.

Maddie's heart ached against her tight chest.

"Oh." TJ furrowed his brows at Maddie. "I mean, I guess that's fine for Friday night—we'll have to edit the website and any associated social posts—but what about Saturday? Who's playing then?"

Maybe if Josh hadn't just sprung this on me, I'd have an actual answer.

Maddie's throat went dry as everyone's gazes trained on her. Conveniently, Gina pulled out her phone and looked at it. *As though anyone has proper service in the town hall.*

"Uh, so I'm working on it still and don't want to make any official announcements until I've got a signed contract in hand." Maddie cleared her throat. The weight of expectation on everyone's faces was clear.

Gina quirked a brow, a mocking laugh on her lips.

Fury rankled Maddie. She leveled her gaze at Josh, then TJ. "I am *very* close, though, to booking a national act that will blow everyone's socks off. Maybe the biggest band that's ever come to Western Maryland and definitely to Brandywood."

Now why in the hell did I say that?

"Really?" Gina said dryly. "And who might that be?"

Shit. She really shouldn't have opened her big mouth.

"Someone huge." Maddie glared at Gina. "But they'd prefer I not make any announcements until it's official. It's an old friend—someone I've known for years."

Dammit, dammit, dammit. This lie kept getting worse and worse. All because—what—she wanted to save two seconds of face in front of Gina now? This would just make her look so much worse in the future.

She should just admit the truth and be done with it.

But that little smirk in Gina's eyes made her temper flare.

Maddie drew a thin-lipped, plastic smile, then flipped her hair over her shoulder coolly. "I should have a confirmation by the end of the week," she told TJ.

"Great. Can't wait to hear more." TJ gave her a thumbs-up, then turned toward Dottie again. "Any way we can get baby kangaroos at the petting zoo?"

As the conversation turned, Maddie's bravado faded.

For his part, Josh continued to stare at TJ's face—as though if he broke eye contact, his head might explode.

But Gina gave her a daring look.

Because she knows I'm full of crap.

Maddie didn't look her way. She might fold if she did.

What the hell am I going to do now?

2

BROOKS

"Smile real pretty. This one's going in the papers, for sure."

The schmuck taking Brooks Kent's mug shot smirked.

Brooks gritted his teeth, restraining the *fuck off* that floated through his head. *Not that the asshole is wrong.*

This was about as far from the evening he'd envisioned when he'd shown up for his concert tonight in Baltimore, Maryland. His buddy, Cormac Doyle, had flown in from Nashville to sub the electric guitar for the night—this was practically Cormac's turf.

Their plan to make a quiet exit to Cormac's small hometown in Western Maryland, then spend the week fishing and boating at a lake, had all gone sideways when Kayla had shown up at sound check, though.

"Follow me, Kent," another cop said, tilting his head toward a doorway.

A doorway that would lead him to jail for the night. Or at least until Darren posted bail for him. Who knew when his manager would show up, though.

Brooks rubbed the torn skin on his knuckles. Would the cops give him ice for his bruised face if he asked? Not that he gave a shit about how he looked. But the split lip was hurting like hell, and the worse he looked when the news leaked about his arrest, the worse the public would view his fight.

Plus, I don't want anyone to think that motherfucker got anything other than one good cheap shot at me.

He decided against asking anyone here for anything. Better to keep his head down. *Shut up. Don't give them any more dirt to bury you with.*

He'd learned that lesson about ten years too late.

The sharp squeak of hinges sounded as the officer opened the door to the jail cell. As Brooks slipped through it, the officer thrust a napkin and a Sharpie at him. "Can I trouble you for an autograph?"

Seriously?

The officer smiled sheepishly. "My wife was headed to your concert. Damn near crushed her when she found out about it being canceled, and she's been texting me for the last hour complaining. I figure this could be a good consolation prize."

Brooks hesitated, then took the Sharpie and signed the damn napkin.

At least they had the decency to put him in a jail cell alone. They'd also let him finish his phone call to his lawyer when they'd shown up to arrest him. Christine had promised to get his manager working on bail.

Not that he expected special treatment. Mike was pressing charges for assault, and the fact was, Brooks *had* wanted to beat the shit out of the prick.

He'd punch Mike all over again, too. He hated Mike Valders more than he'd ever hated anyone—even his own father. *Which says a lot.*

Brooks sank onto the bench, his shoulders drooping.

His bruised left hand was going to hurt like hell for at least a week. And he knew he'd catch all hell from not performing tonight. *Fuck my life.*

The shuffle of a footstep pulled him from his thoughts.

Darren.

"How the hell did you get here so fast?" Brooks asked, rubbing his forehead.

"You pay me to be fast." Darren looked over his shoulder at the officer who'd let him in, as though to dismiss him. Then he stepped closer to the jail cell bars. "Unless you'd like to spend the night here."

"Fuck no." Brooks stood. He just hadn't expected to be here for only two minutes.

Darren smirked, his perfect white teeth shining in the fluorescent lighting. "You can thank me later. Let's go."

Whatever small miracle Darren had pulled to get him out of this place so quickly wasn't something Brooks would question. Not fast enough to save his concert tonight, of course, but nothing could be done about that at this point.

By the time the cops returned his belongings and he walked out to the parking lot to his awaiting car, it was already close to midnight. He should have gone on at eight. What a way to finish the tour.

Darren held out the keys. "You been drinking? That's the last thing—"

"Not unless you count the shots of Jack Daniel's with the cops," Brooks quipped sarcastically. He snatched the keys. At least Darren wasn't threatening to drive him. Brooks had made that rule clear from day one of their partnership. He drove himself everywhere, whenever possible.

"Straight to the hotel, you hear? We'll be having an emergency meeting to see about damage control. Ava already knows, so save your breath if you're expecting me not to shoot straight with you here. It's bad, Brooks. Worse than ever."

"It's one fucking concert. One stupid arrest. Mike's charges won't hold water in front of a judge, but I'm not going to even let it get to that. I already told Christine to settle it out of court. Mike loves nothing more than money, so that should keep him happy for a while." Besides which, when he'd talked to his lawyer, she seemed to think that a settlement would be the way to go. Less noise.

"If you think I'm on your side with this, you've got another thing coming," Darren snapped, glaring at Brooks.

"Think."

"Huh?" The lamppost above them threw a shadow onto Darren's features.

"The expression is, *'you've got another think coming,'*" Brooks said dryly.

"No, it's not. And who cares?"

He wouldn't normally correct Darren about something dumb like this, but it proved the point for him. "Because you're wrong. You *think* you know, but you don't." Brooks crossed his arms. "Just like you haven't heard my side of what happened tonight."

"I don't have to." Darren pulled out a pack of cigarettes and lit one. "I've heard it all before with you. And this time, you're doing it my way, kid. Because if you don't, we'll both be fired."

Brooks winced at the moniker. Darren was maybe ten years older than him. He rubbed his dark beard, his face itching from the discomfort of just about every damn thing that had happened today. Instantly, his neck felt hot, the watch around his wrist too tight, the damn black T-shirt too constricting. His jeans dug in around his waist, and he nearly ripped his flip-flops off.

Taking a calming breath, he managed, "And what's your way?"

The tip of the cigarette glowed in the dark. "You know. I suggested it to you last fall after the Vegas—"

"*Abso-fucking-lutely* not." The words spilled out of Brooks's mouth faster than he could even react. *Hell no.*

"Yes, Brooks. We tried it your way. And your image is shot to hell. You want the public to think you're doubling down on being a narcissistic asshole star who's out of control? Then you better start looking and acting sorry. You need to recoup your reputation—which is barely salvageable, according to Ava. The studio isn't happy with you, especially after that last album didn't do so hot."

"Maybe that has something to do with all the sampling shit you all pulled when my back was turned," Brooks growled. *Enough already.*

"Samples or no, it wasn't your best work, Brooks."

Ouch.

But tell me something I don't know.

"Yet . . . I'm still selling out shows, aren't I, dickhead?" Brooks's eyes narrowed. "You know what, Darren? You don't have to wait to find out if Ava's going to fire you. You're done." His hand enclosed around the key fob. "I've had just about enough of your bull—"

"I already floated the idea to Ava, and she loves it, by the way. Thinks it's the best PR move you could make. It did wonders for that actor from *Turntable*. Ava wants to go for it."

Of course she does. Brooks leveled his gaze at his manager, strongly considering decking him, too. Then again, when had punching anyone ever gotten him anywhere?

Darren's proposed plan was infuriating . . . but a sad commentary on public perception of his life, too. Who wouldn't believe that Brooks Kent needed to check into rehab, sex therapy, and whatever other so-called *treatment* Darren planned? No one would bat an eyelash. A few loud apologies, some groveling, sorry-faced social posts where he admitted his *addictions* had taken him to a bad place—hell, it might even get him some interviews and sympathy.

The public gobbled that shit up. Darren was right.

No way, no how.

"Then tell Ava to come up with something else. Because I'm not doing that bullshit plan. Ever." Brooks unlocked the car and slipped into the driver's seat. "See you around."

"Straight to the hotel or—"

Slam. The door silenced Darren, who clearly hadn't taken his firing seriously.

Brooks started the car with a push of a button and pulled out his phone.

Cormac picked up on the first ring. "What the fuck happened to you?"

"Long story." Brooks adjusted the mirrors on the car. "Quick question. You still heading back home tonight?"

"I'm halfway there. I figured you'd be, ah . . . otherwise occupied."

"You mean you figured I'd be in jail for at least the night?"

"Yeah, man, I mean, I'm glad you're not unless I'm your phone call, in which case, I gotta tell you, I'm a terrible lawyer."

Brooks chuckled. "No, don't worry, I'm not that stupid." He cleared his throat, glancing in the rearview mirror. Darren appeared to be heading across the parking lot. "Mind if I still come crash at your place?"

"Yeah, sure. I'll text you the address. It's a few hours away, though."

Brooks pulled out of the parking spot, not bothering to wait for the text to come through. When it finally did, he opened it in his Maps app and glanced down.

Brandywood, Maryland.

Could be Podunk, Maryland, for all he cared. He just needed to get out of here.

Fast.

3

MADDIE

"Madison Yardley, open the damn door."

The knock on Maddie's bedroom door was loud, annoying, and insistent—and somehow oddly endearing.

"Come on, Mads, we know you're in there," her younger sister, Lindsay, called from the other side.

"I have a key," Naomi chimed in, using a singsong voice that Maddie swore she'd heard her older sister use on her children.

Maddie sat up from her bed, squinting one eye at the back of the door. This was the problem with having moved into the attic apartment above their grandfather's Country Depot store that she and Naomi ran on Main Street. Naomi *did* have a master key.

Groaning, Maddie flopped back down onto the bed. "I'm changing the locks as soon as you leave today," Maddie said into the pillow.

"Do you even know what time it is?" Naomi asked, concern in her voice.

"Knowing her, she's probably wearing Josh's Virginia Tech

hoodie, eating Little Debbie cupcakes, and has been listening to 'All Too Well' on repeat," Lindsay said.

Maddie cringed, swiping the cupcake packaging off her bed as she sat and pushed back the orange hoodie off her head. Her sisters meant well, but she wasn't ready to leave the bed.

Maybe not for the whole next day.

But Naomi had a point. She checked her phone for the time. *Yikes.* Almost eleven p.m.

Biting her lip, she trudged toward the door and opened it reluctantly. She crossed her arms and rolled her eyes at her sisters, who were illuminated by the yellowish light in the hallway. "What do you want?"

"Do you really think this is the healthiest way of dealing with this? We've been trying to get ahold of you for hours. The news about River House and the town fair is all over town." Naomi wrinkled her nose.

Ugh. Dammit. Maddie cringed. Leave it to her lovely little hometown, where every teeny thing that happened spread like wildfire within hours. Except it was always like a terrible game of telephone, where fifteen different versions would circulate, no one quite knowing the right version.

Lindsay set a hand on Naomi's arm. "Maybe we talk about that another time? She's clearly having a rough time."

"I get that, but this isn't healthy. Josh is a douche who doesn't deserve your tears. He's gone too far this time in stabbing you in the back—he stabbed all of us Yardleys. Don't waste your tears on him."

Maddie sighed impatiently. "That's easy enough to say when you have the perfect husband and she"—she gestured toward Lindsay—"has the perfect boyfriend. Meanwhile, the guy I was desperately in love with completely pulled the rug out from under my feet."

Lindsay and Naomi exchanged a look. Lindsay brushed

past her, flipping on the lights. "Number one, you're completely overestimating the so-called *perfection* of our partners." She collected scattered food wrappers from the floor. "And number two . . ." She appealed to Naomi.

Maddie raised a brow. "Number two?"

Naomi gave her a chagrinned expression. "Maddie, it's not like you were with Josh that long. You fall in and out of love pretty easily, sweetheart."

Ouch.

She'd always suspected they thought that about her, but hearing Naomi put it so bluntly hurt. In the gut.

Maddie glared at Naomi. "Low blow, Na—"

"We're not trying to hurt you, babe." Lindsay came over and tugged at her elbow. "You just feel things hard. And that's a good thing sometimes. But you dated Josh for like four months and were already talking about long term. I know he's a shitbag for moving on so quickly—"

"He practically cheated on me, Naomi." Maddie set her hands on her hips. "And now this? You should have seen him at the damn meeting. He was so cold." Also, her sisters knew nothing about how it had been with her and Josh when they'd been together. They'd both fallen hard and fast. Gone from a first date to moving in together after two weeks. Josh had been just as vocal about forever as Maddie had been.

And then he'd gone on that work retreat with Gina, and it had been over in a blink.

"We're not saying he's anything other than a total loser." Naomi frowned. "But we care about you. And the fact that you're letting him get to you like this worries us."

Maddie rubbed her swollen eyelids, then twisted her hair back into a messy bun. "Seriously. Go home, guys. I'm not ready to move on and prove how happy I am without him. Not tonight. I'm completely heartbroken tonight." She'd even rearranged the schedule for tomorrow so she didn't have to work the next day in the store.

Naomi grimaced. "He doesn't deserve your tears, Mads. But if this is how you want to spend the night, let us at least stay here with you. We can hang out. Drink some wine. The kids are asleep, and Jeremy won't mind if I stay over with you."

Maddie considered their offer as Lindsay continued to straighten out the room. Ever since Lindsay had moved in with Travis last year, she'd become appallingly neat and organized, leaving Maddie as the wild and crazy "messy one."

Wild and crazy. Exactly what they think about you. Crazy to fall in love so quickly. Crazy to still be hung up on Josh.

Maddie sniffled, hating feeling sorry for herself. Naomi was right. Josh was out there with Gina, happy. A happy ending that hadn't included her after all.

No matter how much that made her chest ache, she couldn't change it.

She flung the sweatshirt into the corner of the room into a pile of laundry. "Did I mention I effing hate him?" she moaned, not meeting either of her sisters' gazes.

At once, Lindsay and Naomi enveloped her in a hug. She said nothing, soaking in their warmth and friendship. *God, I'm so lucky to have them.* Her siblings, including her eldest brother, Logan, and her younger brother, Jake, had always been tight-knit. There for each other. Now that Lindsay and Logan had smoothed the friction that had formed between them when Logan had found out she was dating Travis Wagner the year before, they were all closer than ever.

Maddie's closeness to her siblings had actually been a point of contention with Josh, come to think of it. He'd grimace when she "overshared" details about their relationship with her sisters.

Deep down, she knew she was better off without him—*but why does it still hurt so much?*

It wasn't like she was the only single one in her family—both Logan and Jake were, too, and heaven help the woman who dared to date Logan.

She stopped trying to psychoanalyze herself and sighed, pulling away from the embrace. "I'm fine, you guys. Really. Go home. I'm really okay. I didn't realize it was so late. I just . . . needed a good cry after the meeting."

"Can you try to make that the last cry?" Lindsay asked with a worried expression. "We want you to be happy."

Maddie gave her a half-hearted smile. "I'll try. I promise."

And she meant it, really. Or she thought she did.

She could make it through the night without crying. Or worrying about what she was going to do about the town fair when morning came.

But as she walked Lindsay and Naomi through the attic apartment to the door, she considered having them stay, watch *Gilmore Girls*, and eat too much chocolate. God knows she'd already done that enough the last few weeks since the breakup, though, and it hadn't helped. Their company would be nice, but the best thing to get them to stop talking about everything for now was to convince them she was fine and then do whatever she wanted when they left.

Naomi seemed to sense it. "You're not just trying to get rid of us still, are you? We really want to help."

Maddie forced a smile. "No, really. I'm good. You're right. It's ridiculous for me to be mourning someone who's clearly happy without me."

"That's not what we said." Lindsay looked chagrinned. "I was just—"

"Really, it's okay. I'm just tired at this point. Maybe if it wasn't almost midnight, we could do something, but I don't want you guys out all night on my behalf."

"We tried calling and texting earlier, but you didn't answer," Naomi said.

"You know how bad cell service is at the store." *And also, I put my phone in Do Not Disturb mode.* Maddie held the apartment door open. "I'll call you guys tomorrow. Maybe we can grab brunch at the pub. If I'm still heartbroken by then, I'll drown my sorrows in Orange Crushes."

Somehow, the attic apartment felt even smaller once they'd gone.

Maddie turned, resting her back against the doorway. This wasn't meant to be a long-term living solution—she'd just moved in here three weeks ago after Josh had broken up with her. She and Naomi had designed the place when Pops was still coming up with plans for the Depot—a little functional apartment complete with a tiny kitchen, a bedroom, and a full bath in case either of them wanted to crash here after a long day.

At first, they'd both used it a lot. Getting Pops's store off the ground had been a ton of work, considering his level of national fame from his cable television show on the Happy Home Network, which owned the *This Charmed Life* magazine that had discovered her grandfather. The Depot had become *the* destination for any tourists coming to Brandywood to get the "Peter Yardley experience"—so popular, in fact, that half the town had lobbied to kick it off Main Street at one point.

But now that Naomi and Maddie had been at it for a few years, they'd been able to delegate many of their responsibilities to their employees. They were both still at the store almost every day—Pops insisted on a personal level of involvement for any of the family businesses he'd established—but the apartment had lain unused for almost a year until Maddie had moved in.

She hadn't considered at first how it might be to have her home and work be at the same address. Maybe it was part of why she'd felt so suffocated lately.

Maddie sighed and smoothed her hands over her T-shirt. She needed a shower, but she was tired and grouchy and ready to jump back into her bed.

Naomi and Lindsay were right.

It was time.

She needed to move on from Josh.

Not shed another tear over him. Especially after the stunt he'd pulled with his cousin's band.

Maybe tomorrow she'd wake up ready to face her problems head-on. Tonight, though, a little sulking wouldn't hurt anyone. Sleep would help her feel better anyway.

She shut off the lights in the living room and headed for the bedroom.

Convincing her brain to sleep was easier said than done. Doubts crept around the edges of her racing thoughts, frustrating her with everything she should have said to Josh. Comebacks that were several hours too late, and she'd never get out of her system.

An hour after lying in bed sleeplessly, she pulled out her phone and started scrolling. That didn't help either, though.

When it was finally past three in the morning, she threw the covers to the side.

This is ridiculous.

No more.

I'm not letting Josh rob me of one more second of sleep.

With a sigh, she headed to the bathroom.

A half hour later, she exited into her bedroom, a towel wrapped around her torso. She'd taken the time to linger in the hot water and exfoliate and *damn* if it hadn't made her better than all the sad love songs and cupcakes.

She hadn't gone far when a loud, hideous screech sounded in the store below her.

Maddie steadied herself onto the wall, yelping.

What the hell was that?

She ran to the small window, heart slamming against her rib cage.

Had something exploded in the store? She could have sworn the floorboards and wall had shaken.

Clutching her towel to her chest, Maddie ran through her apartment and flung open the apartment door. She was down the stairs in a minute, the thought that she should probably get dressed barely registering as she made it to the ground floor. If there had been an explosion, there might be a fire, and she might need to get out immediately. Clothes be damned.

The stairs led to the back hall of the store. Nothing there.

She headed to the door that opened to the main area of the store. Opening it, she threw the lights on and blinked.

Then she gasped.

Where the main display window normally was—the one that faced Main Street—there was a crashed car instead.

4

BROOKS

Brooks blinked dazedly, his eyes adjusting to the harsh glare of electric lights as he pushed back against the steering wheel.

Holy fuck.

His car was sitting in the middle of a store. *A store.*

Glass shards glittered from his windshield and hood, a metal display rack of handmade cards lying against his driver's side window. *Why didn't the airbag deploy?*

He peeled his hands from the steering wheel.

It had all happened so fast.

One minute, he'd been pulling on Main Street in the sleepy Maryland mountain town Cormac had given him directions to, and the next, a deer had leaped into the road, inches from his bumper. He'd swung out of the way on reflex, hopped the curb, and landed in the store window.

Going through a window was actually lucky. If he'd gone into a wall, who knew what shape he'd be in now?

His legs were stiff as he pushed the door open, the card rack clattering to the floor with a metallic thud. He winced and stepped out onto broken glass and debris, surveying the damage.

"Hey! What the hell?"

Am I seeing things, or is a woman in a towel yelling at me?

He rubbed the back of his neck, hoping to God she wouldn't recognize him immediately. Or at all. "Uh, deer jumped in front of my car and—"

"Are you drunk?" The woman marched up to him, fearlessness in her blue eyes, her wet blond hair bouncing on her bare shoulders, then halted. She retreated a step as though thinking better of approaching him.

"No." Brooks scowled. "And I'm fine, thanks for asking."

She wrinkled her nose, then scanned the store. Hurrying toward a display of sweatshirts with *Brandywood, Maryland* emblazoned on the front, she grabbed a pink one and a pair of gray sweatpants, then disappeared into a back door.

She must own the place—which, from the looks of it, meant she was a successful small business owner. His eyes narrowed at a table of beer mugs etched with *Yardley's Country Depot.*

Why does that name sound familiar?

Before he could figure it out, the woman had returned, wearing the sweats. She hurried toward him. "Sorry about that. *Are* you okay? You're right—I should have asked. Your face looks bruised on one side. Did you hit it on the steering wheel?"

"I'm fine." He didn't feel like explaining that he'd already been wearing a shiner before he'd gotten in the car.

"You sure? I can get you some ice if you need it. Or call 911."

Hell no. He pushed the driver's door shut and winced at the outside of the car. He'd have to get Darren to take care of that . . .

Shit, I fired him.

Dammit.

It'd been a long time since he handled anything like an insurance claim himself.

What he needed was an assistant and—

The woman continued to stare at him, but she'd raised her eyebrows by now.

"Uh, yeah, great." He released a long sigh and rubbed his neck again. Maybe he had a bit of whiplash.

"All right, well, I'm calling the cops anyway." She turned toward the register.

The cops?

"Whoa, whoa, whoa." Brooks took a few long strides to reach her. "Hang on now. Do we have to do that?"

She whipped a suspicious look at him. "You don't want me to call the cops?"

"Not really. If possible. I'm happy to take care of fixing all of this for you."

She set her hands on her hips, arms akimbo. "Do I look like an idiot to you? You just drove your car into my store. I'm *absolutely* calling the cops." She continued past him.

His hand shot out reflexively, grabbing her by the elbow. "Please, miss."

A divot of consternation formed between her brows, and her gaze traveled down to his hand, then back to his eyes. "First, I'd appreciate you not touching me. Second, if you try anything with me, I will scream. I also have a gun and know how to use it."

Of course she does.

He dropped his offending hand, his fingertips burning. "Sorry." Taking a step back, he pinched the bridge of his nose and tried more peaceably, "Listen, I know it sounds suspicious as all hell when I ask you not to call the cops, but it's a privacy thing for me."

"Privacy?"

"Yeah, I . . . really rather not have this get out."

"Not get out? Your frickin' car is in my store. The window is gone. In three hours, all of Brandywood will know about this." She scanned his face. "Besides, why would it make a difference if it gets out . . ."

A flash of recognition lit those pretty eyes.

Damn.

"Holy shit, you're Brooks Kent."

And there it is. He grimaced. "Yeah, I am."

She bit her lip, an unreadable look on her face. "You have proof?"

He guffawed. "Proof?"

She crossed her arms. "You could just look like him. Be using that to your advantage."

"You're right, I could." He reached into his pocket for his wallet and pulled out his license. "Here."

She examined it, then handed it back with a dubious shrug. "Could be a fake."

Good God, this woman is maddening.

Sighing, he took out his phone, then opened his Instagram. Holding it out to her, he asked, "How about this?"

She brought the phone closer to her face. After a moment, she paled and looked back and forth from the screen to his face. "Damn, you really are him, aren't you?" Redness crept into her cheeks as she returned his phone.

"In the flesh," he said in a dry, flat tone. "And you are?"

"Madison—Maddie. Kent. *I mean Yardley!*" The last phrase burst out of her mouth, and her cheeks grew scarlet. "Yardley. Maddie Yardley. I-I don't know why I said your last name. I'm just exhausted. I swear I'm not like a creepy groupie or anything. I don't even think I've listened to anything by you in, like, maybe four years. It's just late, you know? Or I guess early. Shit. I'm so embarrassed." She face-palmed.

Brooks did his best not to chuckle. It was strangely cute, the effort she was putting into explaining away the innocent slip. "No big deal. So . . . Maddie, maybe you can see my predicament? Honestly, your little town knowing is the least of my worries." *Especially after last night.* "But I can pay for the damage."

She tucked a strand of wet hair behind her ear, her eyes fixed on the car. "Brandywood might be a little town, but news around here travels like wildfire. If one person finds out Brooks Kent crashed his car into the Depot, you can count on pretty much the whole town gossiping about it, and then it just taking on a life of its own from there. Also . . ."

Noted. "Yes?"

"This isn't exactly *my* store. It belongs to my grandfather. Much as I might want to help you out, it's not really my call to make. But I also don't really want to call him and his wife at four in the morning. Pops has some heart issues, and I don't want to give him a scare if I can avoid it."

Maddie let out a long breath between puffed cheeks. "Maybe . . ." She tapped her foot with nervous energy. "Okay, so my future brother-in-law is a mechanic. I can probably get him to tow your car back to his shop within the hour—that's the easy part. And I have the contractor who built this place basically on like speed dial—he's a family friend—so I might get him to come out here and put up plastic or something. But the cops . . ." She massaged her temples.

No wonder she runs a successful business. Whatever other quirks she might have, Maddie seemed remarkably adept at thinking on her feet.

Her face lit. "I got it. My sister's best friend's brother is a cop. I don't know if he's on duty, but if I call him, he'd probably come out here and take a report. I can ask him not to turn it in unless it becomes necessary."

"You mean if I somehow renege on my promise to take care of the damage."

She gave him a steely-eyed gaze. "Yeah, I mean, you might be famous but I don't know you."

Smart woman. "That's fair," he said in a low tone. Of course, that didn't solve the problem of him getting to Cormac's place tonight, but he could deal with that later.

"If I go upstairs to get my phone to take pictures and make those calls, you're not going to leave, right?"

He released a sigh. "I'll be right here."

"I do have security camer—"

"I get it." This time, he couldn't keep the annoyance out of his voice. Maybe his reputation preceded him here.

Her lips set to a line, then she gave a quick nod and left again.

Brooks ground his teeth. Considering he'd been in jail only a few hours earlier, the phrase *from the frying pan into the fire* didn't quite sound right.

But damn if coming here doesn't feel like a massive mistake.

5

MADDIE

TRAVIS WAGNER, Lindsay's boyfriend, frowned at Maddie as he came inside from loading the wrecked car onto his tow truck. "Did Dan give him a breathalyzer at least?" Travis asked Maddie in a low voice, his gaze traveling over her toward where Officer Dan Kline was talking to Brooks Kent.

Brooks Kent. *As in massive rock star Brooks Kent who is in my store at five in the morning.*

Maddie had done everything in her power not to freak out when he'd revealed it. She should have recognized him sooner, but he'd grown a dark beard, and she hadn't seen pictures of him recently.

And, of course, I blubbered on and made a fool of myself in front of him.

Back in the day, she would have been totally star-struck by him. She'd liked his music and had only stopped listening to him when Hank—one of her former boyfriends—had sent her down a country music rabbit hole.

But she never, ever would have expected that she'd run into

him in the wee hours of the morning in her store while wearing *a towel.*

Oh God. If Linds and Naomi find out, they'll never let me live it down. But they wouldn't find out. She'd promised Brooks not to tell anyone and to store the security footage from the crash somewhere for her eyes only.

As much as she hated to lie to her family about the whole thing, those were the terms he'd set when he'd promised to pay back the damages plus any estimated revenue losses from the crash. She wouldn't get that good of a deal from an insurance company.

Maddie's attention went back to Travis. "I honestly don't think he was drunk. Dan knows what to do anyway, but Brooks seemed pretty okay with it. Besides, he's not the first city person who comes into town and doesn't know what to do when a deer jumps in front of them."

Travis appeared skeptical. "I may have fixed up my fair share of cars thanks to deer, but I've never heard of anyone driving into a store. He's lucky he hit the window."

"And we're not so lucky. Naomi is going to freak when she sees this mess."

Travis nodded. "She sure as hell will. You might want to warn her before she hears it from someone else."

Maddie whirled toward him and wagged a finger. "Remember your promise. Not a word about Brooks to anyone. Not even Lindsay. He doesn't want anyone to know, and I don't want him to have any reason not to pay immediately for this damage."

Travis rolled his eyes. "I remember. I better get back to the shop before sunrise, then."

Maddie watched him go, then headed outside to where Garrett Doyle was stapling thick, opaque plastic sheeting over the broken window. Garrett glanced up with a grin. "Only the Yardleys could get me out of bed this early on a Sunday."

"You know we love you, Doyle." Maddie crouched down beside him. "What's the likelihood of repairing this sometime soon?"

Garrett took out a box cutter and sliced at the plastic. "Honestly? It's gonna be at least three weeks at minimum to even start. Maybe more. I'm booked solid, but I might be able to squeeze in some hours before and after to get things going. But this window's going to have to be special ordered."

She could barely remember a time when Garrett hadn't been everyone's first choice for home repair and contracting—his business had grown so large that she doubted he even took on smaller repairs like this personally anymore. Yet it always made her proud. Pops had always liked Garrett Doyle, even when other folks in Brandywood had seen only the worst in him. Naomi once told her that Pops had suggested she date Garrett when he'd come back into town, which made sense, considering they'd been in the same class through high school.

But for all the success Garrett had found, it didn't make this current situation any easier. She needed to get the Depot back in shape as soon as possible. Three weeks or more—especially when the fall festival was at the beginning of next month—would mean the Depot might not be ready for the influx of tourists at peak fall.

That was terrible news for the Depot. Their location in a small, mountainous Appalachian town meant they relied on those seasonal tourist drops for income.

"We'll take any time you can spare for us, Garrett. And bill accordingly. We're not paying the tab, and my guess is that asshole in there can afford it."

"What do you figure Brooks Kent is doing here?" Garrett's

brown eyes were curious as he continued stapling the plastic sheeting into the wooden window trim.

"No idea. Somehow, I don't think it was to visit the Country Depot." A snicker left Maddie before she could help it, a fresh wave of exhaustion hitting her. She must be more tired than she realized.

"I'm wondering if Cormac coming into town has anything to do with it," Garrett said with a thoughtful look.

Maddie raised her brows. "Cormac's in town?" Garrett's older brother, who'd moved to Nashville long ago, only came home occasionally. Like all the Doyles, he was friendly and easygoing. He'd been good friends with Logan in high school.

"Yeah, he got in late last night. Texted me to see if I wanted to meet him at the pub, but it was like one thirty in the morning. I think he ended up meeting with one of my brothers, though."

"You think Brooks Kent might be one of Cormac's friends? That would be crazy." She'd known Cormac had made it far in the music world, but not *that* far.

"Could be." Garrett shrugged and finished cutting the plastic. "Come to think of it, Cormac said something about fishing with a buddy for the week. I hope he wasn't planning on using Dad's old cabin—the place got infested with carpenter bees and is on my to-do list for repair when I have time." He squinted at the battered storefront. "Sorry it's not more attractive of a solution."

"Don't apologize. You're doing me a huge favor. And it's not like you drove *your* car into the store." Maddie opened the main glass door, the familiar scent of cinnamon wafting to her from a display of fall candles. She held the door for Garrett as he gathered his tools. "Want a cup of coffee or anything? I can get one brewing."

Garrett hesitated and lifted the thick roll of plastic. "Normally, I'd take you up on it, but I should get back to Sam and the girls. The baby was up with a fever last night."

"Still hard to believe that you've got two girls." Maddie winked at him. "Say hi to Sam for me. Tell her to come by as soon as she's feeling up for more work. Naomi wants some new product photos for the website."

"I'll tell her." Garrett nodded a goodbye, and Maddie left him. She wrinkled her nose at the sight of the mess beyond the window. They would have to open late today. Thank goodness it was Sunday. Nothing on Main Street opened before ten in the morning on Sundays.

She approached Brooks and Dan, doing her best not to watch Brooks too closely. Even though she'd talked to him, there was an awkwardness there with him being a celebrity. No doubt he was used to being noticed in public—and let's be honest—gawked at. The man was hot, even with the scruffy beard. He had dark gray, brooding eyes befitting of a rock star, chiseled features, and a strong jaw, and he clearly worked out. Maddie had hung a poster of him years ago in her college dorm, but thankfully, he didn't have to know that.

And she'd greeted him fresh from the shower in a towel.

Which he clearly noticed.

The internal cringe made her want to run away.

"Where are you heading after this?" Dan was saying to Brooks. The blond, blue-eyed officer was taller than Brooks—who was tall himself—but the Klein brothers were known for their stature.

"My buddy has a place somewhere around here." A tired expression crossed Brooks's face. "But I haven't been able to get a call out to him."

"I can take you there if you like," Dan offered, his gaze flicking to Maddie momentarily. "My wife and I also run a B&B, though, if you need a place to crash."

"I think he already found that here," Maddie quipped before she could stop herself.

Both men looked at her, and she smiled. "Sorry. Couldn't help myself. Too soon?"

Is that a hint of a smile on Brooks's lips?

Brooks turned his attention back to Dan, hesitating. "Uh, thanks for the offer, Officer, but I'm good. I'll figure it out."

Maddie studied his handsome face. There was that desire to stay away from the police again, too. And the fact that he'd referred to Dan as "officer" meant he viewed Dan that way, even if Dan wasn't wearing a uniform or on duty.

Why does he not like cops?

"Need anything else, Maddie?" Dan asked. His gaze traversed the damaged displays. "Looks like you're going to need a few sets of hands to clean all this up."

"It's fine. I'll put a sign on the door that we're opening late and try to get ahold of a few people scheduled to come in this morning. Hopefully, we can get it all done."

She almost regretted not asking Dan to stay and help. Moments after he'd walked out the door, the awkwardness of Brooks's presence flooded her. She stuffed her hands into her pockets, feeling the weight of his proximity even though he was at least an arm's length away. "So . . . um, do you want me to call you a ride or something?"

Brooks didn't answer, bending over and picking up the stem of a shattered, hand-painted wineglass. Grace Wagner would cry if she saw her gorgeous creations broken on the floor. They'd just put the fall collection on display a week ago. "Actually, I'd like to help you clean this up if you don't mind."

What now?

Brooks Kent wanted to help her clean?

Unexpectedly nice as he might intend that to be, she just

wanted him gone already so she could crawl into bed and try to salvage a couple of hours of sleep.

"Um—no, you don't have to do that," she said flatly and snatched the stem from his hand.

Reflexively, he closed his hand around the stem as she pulled.

A bright burst of blood came from his palm, and he drew his hand back. "Christ!"

Oh shit. She gasped, dropping the stem to the floor, where it cracked into several pieces. "Oh my God, are you okay? I'm so sorry."

He sucked in through his teeth, a hint of irritation on his face. "Consider this the cherry on top of the best night of my life. I'm just thankful I chose to come to this hellhole over a week in the Maldives."

Arrogant son of a bitch. She glared at him. "You don't have to be an asshole about it."

"Sorry," he said in a voice that was anything but.

She rubbed her temples, which throbbed with exhaustion. "Follow me," she grumbled. She couldn't believe she was considering taking him upstairs to her apartment, but she'd stashed the first-aid kit up there—and he could sit down more comfortably in her living room.

"Where are you taking me?"

"Upstairs. I have an apartment up there. I'll clean that up for you."

He clenched his fingers into a fist. "You don't have to do that." Blood dripped down to his wrist.

"Actually, I do. Or at least give you the first-aid kit. I *am* sorry, believe it or not."

He opened his mouth but then said nothing as though thinking better of it. "Lead the way."

She took him through the back hallway and up the stairs,

her brain spinning. Maybe she'd wake up and find out this had all been a weird dream. She could practically imagine herself seeing Travis, Garrett, and Dan at something around town and telling them about the strange nightmare with the *Wizard of Oz's "... and you were there ... .and you were there ..."* line.

Brooks was oddly quiet as he followed her. His cheap shot about how much this sucked compared to his celebrity lifestyle stung—not that it didn't make sense. But it also made her embarrassed to bring him up here. He was wealthy and had traveled the world.

Something about that made her feel like a country bumpkin from the backwoods.

She held the door to the apartment open. "Right through here."

Thank goodness the door to her room was mostly closed. She could just barely see the mess through the slit in the door—she'd have to sneak over there and close it.

She flipped on a light in the living room and pointed at the couch. "Have a seat. Can I get you something to drink?"

"No, I'm good, thanks."

He sat, and she avoided looking at him once again.

This is just too weird.

She needed to stop acting like a star-struck dope and get on with it. The sooner she patched up his hand, the sooner he could get out of here, and this whole strange episode would be over.

The first-aid kit was under the kitchen sink. She washed her hands and grabbed it, along with a bottle of peroxide. Going back toward him, she sat and unzipped the case, then set it on the coffee table, reaching for his wounded left hand. "Let me take a look."

"I can clean it up."

"It's your dominant hand," she said with a frown.

Brooks scanned her face. "How do you know that?"

She bit her lip, hoping she hadn't given her former fangirl self away. She'd always liked the fact that she shared the lefty trait with someone famous like him. "You play left-handed guitar, don't you?"

His eyes met hers, and he nodded.

He didn't protest further and, instead, extended his hand for her. She took it gently. The cut wasn't terribly deep, but it crossed most of his palm. *Ouch.* "I'm so sorry again," she murmured as she started cleaning it with peroxide.

"Accidents don't require apologies."

Really? What an odd life philosophy. She frowned. "That's not true. Just because something wasn't done purposely doesn't mean there wasn't hurt inflicted. Or fault. Otherwise, how do you explain manslaughter sentences?"

His expression darkened. "I was just saying—"

"No, you were just excusing. You didn't mean to ram your car into my store, did you? But that doesn't absolve your responsibility for wrecking the place."

The space between them filled with tense silence once again, and she kept her head down, focusing on cleaning the cut. It was too long for even a large Band-Aid, so she pulled out some pieces of gauze and the tape instead.

Maybe she'd spoken too harshly. But something about his statement had unsettled her. Disappointed her. Not that she'd expected much out of him—she'd seen in the tabloids over the years that he had a reputation for partying hard and leaving a trail of broken hearts.

When she'd finished bandaging his hand, he sat back and rubbed his eyes. "Thanks. You really didn't have to do that. I wrecked your place, after all."

Her eyes narrowed at him. Was he mocking her?

She didn't have the energy to deal with another jerk. Not

after spending the past couple of weeks mourning Josh. She was ready to swear men off altogether.

She checked the clock on her wall. Wow. Almost five thirty. She needed sleep.

For that matter, Brooks probably did, too. He looked just as tired as she felt.

She nodded stiffly and stood. "I'll be right back. Just going to wash up. You sure I can't get you a cup of coffee or something?"

"Yeah, I guess coffee would be good. I need to call a friend who has a family cabin nearby, but my service keeps disappearing."

She was tempted to ask him if Cormac was his friend, but that just seemed too nosy. It had to be, didn't it? Brandywood has its fair share of people who'd gone out and done some big things after high school, though.

"Welcome to Brandywood," she said with an eye roll. "Service is spotty all over town. But we do have Wi-Fi in the store, so if you hang on a minute, I can grab one of the cards we hand out downstairs with the passcode. I think I have some in my room."

"You don't know the code?"

She shrugged. "My sister changes it monthly. I don't bother to keep up with it."

She stood and grabbed the first-aid supplies, dropping them off in the kitchen. After washing her hands again, she started a pot of coffee, then went down the hallway to her bedroom. Her limbs were oddly jittery—probably a combination of her tiredness and the fact that Brooks Kent was in her living room.

That was a mind trip all by itself.

She slipped into her room as discreetly as she could, hoping Brooks wasn't watching her and seeing what a disaster her room was. Catching her reflection in the full-length mirror on the wall, she grimaced. Her hair had dried wavy and messily, and she wore sweats.

Yikes—and it was clearly obvious she didn't have a bra on despite the sweatshirt dampening the effect.

She plucked a bra off the floor, then dug around for a clean T-shirt. Clearly, she needed to do laundry soon.

Finding an old college shirt at last, she yanked it on and then traded the sweats for leggings. She brushed and tied her hair back quickly. Her features were drawn and tired, but she couldn't do much about that now. Besides, she didn't want Brooks to think she was trying to impress him. An outfit change could be explained because she'd shown up in a towel before. Makeup would be ridiculous.

She tugged a pair of socks on, then grabbed a Wi-Fi card off her dresser. The delicious, warm scent of coffee greeted her as she opened the door once again. The living room was still only lit by the warmth of a yellow lamp, and her window curtains were tightly shut. Brooks had nestled into the corner of the couch, his head resting against the back cushion. His eyes were closed and . . .

He's asleep.

She hadn't been out of the room that long, had she?

Maddie bit her lip.

She should wake him up, give him the cup of coffee, and send him on his way. The last thing she wanted was a strange man sleeping in her living room, no matter how famous he was.

But something about him resting there made her feel bad for him. He *had* just been through an accident and—apparently—not slept for a while either.

Dammit.

Considering the amount of trouble he'd caused her, she didn't feel like being nice to him. His attitude wasn't great either. He was standoffish and sometimes even rude. Clearly not interested in being friendly.

Then again, he offered to stay and help clean up the Depot.

He must be exhausted if he'd fallen asleep so quickly. And what harm could really come from letting him take a nap? She sighed, then headed back into her room, locking the door behind her. Let him nap. She could use one, too.

I just hope I don't regret this.

6

BROOKS

SNEAKING out of some random girl's apartment hadn't been on Brooks's list of activities for the day, but here he was, doing it anyway.

Even though the last time he'd done this, he'd been a lot younger, and it had been after a much better night, damn if the guilt wasn't similar.

Maddie seemed nice enough—hell, she'd let him stay asleep on her couch—but waking up here had startled the shit out of him. He wanted to be at least a few miles away before this sleepy town woke up and anyone else discovered him here.

He found his way out of the apartment through that hallway in the back of the store, grabbed the guitar and duffel bag he'd taken out of his car before it'd been towed, and then went out a back door that let him out into a small parking lot.

After checking that the door locked shut behind him, he reached into his pocket for his sunglasses. Not the best way to remain incognito, but it was better than nothing. All he needed was to find a pocket of cell service, call Cormac to pick him up, and he'd be fine.

Except I'm out of a car and my life feels in shambles.

He'd come here to get away from the mess he'd created in Baltimore, but the truth was the mess had started long before that.

Heavy pressure enclosed his chest, like a belt wrapped too tight, and he started forward. It didn't take long for him to find the street. Draped in blue-toned early morning light, the collection of brick and stone shops on Main Street was strangely bleak. Flyers on the window fronts spoke of community events —including a charity festival—all so small-town stereotypical and saccharine that he rolled his eyes.

People in places like this were all the same. *Busybodies, cliquish, insufferable.* They'd smile at outsiders and then turn right around and gossip about them as soon as they walked out the door. People who weren't born here never truly broke into the so-called community.

He'd seen it all before in his hometown of Fountain Springs in North Carolina.

He saw the way they'd pretended to rally around his family.

Nothing but a bunch of fakery.

Hands stuffed into his pockets, he tore his gaze away from the buildings, dripping with their attempts at charm. Just like that Depot he'd crashed into. It had more cinnamon-scented, plaid-toned knickknacks than a Cracker Barrel Country Store.

He'd walked for what had to be at least a couple of miles when he gave up on the concept of cell service getting any better. At the sound of a car approaching, he turned to the road and threw his thumb in the air. He couldn't remember the last time he'd hitchhiked—maybe as a teenager—but this seemed as good a time as any.

An old man in a truck slowed and rolled the window down.

"Don't think I've seen a hitchhiker round here in twenty years." He laughed, his blue eyes twinkling. "Where you heading?"

Thank God the man was old. Old people didn't tend to recognize or give a rat's ass who he was.

"I'm trying to get to"—he searched for, then rattled off the address Cormac had texted him—"but my car broke down. Any chance you know where that is?"

The man nodded. "Sure do. Want a ride? I was heading into town, but I can take you over there if you'd like. Short drive from here."

"Sure you don't mind?" Brooks didn't mention how much *he* minded getting in the passenger seat of any vehicle, but he had to accept his situation.

He smiled again, his face pleasant. "Would I have stopped if I minded?"

Fair enough. Brooks set his bags in the bed of the truck and climbed into the passenger seat. The man shifted a hand-tied bouquet of what appeared to be wildflowers from the seat into the back. "Sorry. I just picked these for my wife."

Brooks raised a brow. "You serious?"

The man pulled back onto the road. "Absolutely. She loves flowers. Always has. And I love to see her smile."

It was almost enough to make his cynical heart thaw *slightly*. Almost.

But not really.

The man was clearly a kook.

"You're not from around here, obviously," the man said, his eyes focused on the road. "Just passing through or staying for a while?"

"Passing through for a few days." His palms started sweating as he jerked his eyes from the steering wheel. He didn't want the man to think he was studying his every movement on the wheel intently—even though he was.

He hated, *hated* not being in control of a car.

"Where're you coming from?"

"LA." How hadn't he gotten the clue that he didn't want to talk yet? "I'm not staying in town, though."

"That's too bad. The lake is nice, but the town is better." The old man reached over into the side pocket of his door and pulled out a can of Pringles. "Want one?"

"I'm good, thanks." He couldn't think of anything less appetizing.

The man winked, then popped one in his mouth. "The wife thinks I eat too much salt. So I have to sneak them in the car." He gave an obvious glance at Brooks's left hand. "You married?"

Of all the people who had to pull over, it had to be someone chatty. "Nope."

He put another chip in his mouth and chewed slowly. "Let me guess. You don't have a good woman in your life, either."

Brooks snorted. "Come again?"

The man grinned. "Don't take this the wrong way, but you wear that look on your brow . . . of a man who's spent too long having to take care of himself without a soft place to land. A good woman gives you that."

Ridiculous bullshit.

"You mean you think I look miserable?"

"Well, yes, but that's not what I meant."

"I've seen plenty of marriages that make men—and women —miserable." Brooks checked his phone and started scrolling through his apps. Maybe the man would take the hint and quit the chatter.

"That's because they didn't marry a good person." The old man shifted in his seat. "Believe me, I know. People have always told me their stories and secrets. What troubled them. Whether or not I wanted them to. That's what you get when you tend bar for forty years. My wife says I have a gift for listening."

Right now, the only gift this old geezer seemed to have was a gift for talking. "Huh," Brooks muttered, keeping his gaze down.

"While you're here, think of heading into town sometime. You never know. You might find a good woman there."

This *good woman* talk was getting old fast. "I'll keep that in mind." Brooks cleared his throat.

"I'm Peter, by the way." He gave Brooks another glance. "Happy to take you fishing while you're up at the lake, if you want. No problem that a few early morning hours in a fishing boat can't solve."

Brooks couldn't keep the sardonic chuckle out of his throat this time. "I doubt that."

"I'm serious." Peter had a kind smile, even if he was clearly a dimwit.

Brooks crossed his arms. "So you're telling me that if I spend two hours fishing, my massive career problems will magically disappear, my niece's deadbeat dad will stop trying to use her existence for more money, and my car will fix itself?"

A few beats of silence followed, and Brooks almost bit his own damn tongue. *How did this guy get me to spill all that?*

Maybe he did have a gift for getting people to tell him their secrets.

Peter eyed him thoughtfully. "I didn't say fix. I said solve."

"Same difference."

"No, that's not true. Language has nuance."

Brooks didn't respond. He of all people should know the latter part, though. He was a lyricist. Maybe not with his last release, but even a few years back, he'd been considered the best at his game. No one dared argue with his sense of musicality, his compositions, or his lyrics.

A lump formed in his throat, and he took the break in conversation gratefully. The brief nap on Maddie's couch had kept the beginnings of a migraine at bay, but his tiredness was overwhelming.

For his part, Peter didn't say much more. He'd clearly gotten the hint, and he hummed to himself as he drove, the occasional crunch of a chip punctuating the silence, a slight smell of grease in the air each time he popped the can open.

The car slowed, and Brooks frowned as Peter put on his hazard lights and stopped. They were in the middle of the woods on a two-lane road.

His shoulders grew taut, his senses alert. "Are we almost there?"

"Almost."

Was this the part where the kindly old man turned out to be a murderous psycho?

Peter opened his door and slipped out onto the road. Brooks watched as the man limped toward a blackish lump in the middle of the road, then bent over and lifted it. He carried it to the other side of the road, then wiped his hands on his jeans, smiling down as he said something Brooks couldn't hear.

When he returned to the car, Peter settled into his seat. "Box turtle. The road's not the best place for him to be." He chuckled, his eyes lit with amusement. "Guess they like life in the fast lane sometimes. Damn things think a hard shell's all they need to protect them."

Oh.

Brooks said nothing as Peter started driving again.

After a few minutes, they turned into a gravel driveway, and Peter stopped in front of a small cabin in the woods. "This is it," he said with a nod. "The Doyles' fishing cabin."

Brooks tilted his chin at Peter. The man really did know this town inside and out, didn't he? That was probably how it was with locals around here—especially old men like Peter. He opened the door. "Thanks for the ride."

"Not a problem. I was on my way to my granddaughter. She'll probably be glad I didn't wake her up." Peter smiled, then reached into his seat console and pulled out a pad of paper. Taking a pen from his pocket, he wrote a phone number and held it out to Brooks. "If you change your mind about going fishing, give me a call. And get some cream of crab soup from Bunny's Café if you go to town. I know the owner. She's a gem."

Thanks, but no thanks.

The man had given him a ride, though, so he couldn't be a complete asshole to him. Brooks took the paper and folded it, then slipped it into his pocket. He nodded a goodbye, then closed the passenger door and grabbed his stuff.

The truck turned slowly in the driveway, and Brooks watched as the lights faded. He rarely had genuine interactions with people these days, especially people who clearly had no clue who he was. Once upon a time, he would have found it refreshing, but the one thing he'd learned about having a bad reputation was that it kept people at arm's length.

He'd even seen that wariness on Maddie Yardley's face this morning. That hesitation to even consider granting him the favor of privacy. *Distrust.*

Brooks went to the front door and did a cursory search for a doorbell. None. He knocked instead.

A minute of silence passed, then Brooks knocked again, more loudly this time.

Silence.

Maybe Cormac was still sleeping?

He squinted at the driveway. Come to think of it, he hadn't seen a car in the driveway.

He knocked one more time.

What if he's not here?

Yet why wouldn't he be? It was just past seven in the morning, and Cormac had said he was coming here.

Brooks double-checked his text messages from Cormac against the address on the metal mailbox beside the door. He couldn't be 100 percent certain that the street was the same, but the house number seemed to be.

With a sigh of frustration, Brooks went around the side of the small cabin to the patio. He set his hands on either side of his face, trying to peer inside the sliding glass door.

The inside was dark . . . and a mess.

The furniture appeared to be piled, the ceiling drooped, and insulation poked through the rafters.

What the hell?

Cormac had mentioned it was a rustic place, but surely, he couldn't have meant this?

Brooks sat with his back against the sliding door and stretched his legs in front of him. Taking out his phone, he checked for service once again.

What type of fucking town was this? How was his ability to communicate with the outside world suddenly so truncated? He had no car, was now in the middle of nowhere, and couldn't get a phone call in or out.

The urge wasn't so much to feel sorry for himself as it was to throw something, which he nearly did—the useless cell phone in his hands. He caught himself at the last second, cooling his brewing temper.

One . . . two . . . three . . .

Deep breaths.

Focus.

The soft, dappled light hitting the rime of the forest floor around him sparkled. Enough to distract him, to settle the pressure on his chest somewhat and let his fingers uncurl.

The sort of thing he should have done when Mike threw that goddamn punch yesterday.

Kayla.

His heart tugged at the memory of his sister finding him with tears in her eyes. She always drove anytime he was performing within a couple of hours of Alexandria, Virginia, where she'd settled after Audrey had been born. He'd wanted her to come live with him in Los Angeles, but Kayla hadn't wanted to tear Audrey away from Constance, who lived in Virginia.

Crazy to think that a piece of shit like Mike could come from someone as kind as Constance Valders. She'd been like a mother to Kayla after Audrey's birth, taking the role that their own mother would have happily filled if she'd been alive. She watched Audrey when Kayla needed childcare and brought Kayla diapers and formula despite her fixed income. Protected both Kayla and Audrey from Mike, too.

And Audrey loved her Mom-mom. Kayla couldn't tear her daughter away from the only other family Audrey had besides Brooks. Especially when Brooks did so much traveling.

"Mike is suing for custody."

The words still made a shiver go through him.

Brooks had fired off an angry text, and Mike had responded by showing up at the concert venue, then snuck back before the band went on. Got mouthy and confrontational.

And the rest was history.

Except this time, Brooks's temper had cost him more than ever.

He needed to call Kayla as soon as he could. Apologize to her, too, because this wouldn't help Kayla in a courtroom. Mike would spin it to his advantage—about how Kayla was using her celebrity brother to bully him and "keep him from his daughter."

Kayla had been there when it went down, begging Brooks to cool it.

Drawing one knee up, Brooks rested his elbow against it, then covered his face with his cut and bruised hand.

Dammit.

This time, his problems felt unfixable.

He sucked in another deep breath.

He hadn't gotten to where he was in life by crumbling and giving up when things got rocky. Maybe Cormac hadn't been able to get in touch with him, but this was ridiculous. Plenty of houses had dotted the side of the road on the way over here—if phone service was so unreliable around here, then people probably had landlines. He'd just have to walk.

He stood and wiped his hands on his jeans. The thought of lugging his expensive guitar along as he searched for help didn't appeal, so he tucked it and his duffel bag under a tarp covering a pile of firewood.

Then he started back down toward the road.

He couldn't remember the last time he'd been out in the woods like this. Much as he'd claimed he'd loved the abundance of trails near him when he'd moved to LA, he rarely went into nature. Work beckoned him to cities, both here in the States and all over the world.

He went the opposite direction from where he'd come in. The old man who'd brought him here seemed to have taken some backroads, and that wasn't what he needed right now. Main roads were more useful to his search.

He had only been walking for about ten minutes when a barrage of notifications chimed in his phone. Standing off to the side of the road, he scrolled through them. Several texts from Kayla, Cormac—who was wondering where the hell he was and who said he was, supposedly, at the cabin—and even Darren.

Also, a message from the president of his label—Ava Peterson.

***Ava**: Call me immediately.*

Shit. Maybe it had been better to have his phone out of service.

He groaned and dialed Ava's number.

"Where are you?" Ava answered without bothering to say hello.

"At a friend's place."

"You need to come back to LA immediately. We need to have some serious discussions about cleaning up your image. Our phones have been ringing off the hook with this mess you created."

Brooks rubbed his eyelids. "What, so you can send me to sex therapy and rehab? Darren already floated his crap-tastic idea to me, and I fired him. The charges against me are for assault, Ava, not sexual assault. And the charges aren't going to stick. I punched the guy, not beat him up with a baseball bat."

"What difference does it make? You think people won't start pulling all sorts of stories about you out of the woodwork? If you have any better ideas, then please, enlighten me. Because you're costing us a lot of money right—"

"Surely not more money than I've made for you, Ava. Let's get that straight."

"No, you get this straight. Your new contract says you can't go anywhere else for three years. You know it, and I know it. We pull the plug on you, and three years from now, you'll be even more irrelevant than you're already becoming. Any move you make, you'll be slapped so hard with a lawsuit your eyes will be permanently stuck to the back of your skull. We own you, Brooks."

Brooks clenched his jaw, resisting the urge to tell her to fuck off.

"I'm not coming to LA right now," he said at last in a voice that sounded much calmer than he felt. "Or following Darren's ridiculous idea. I'll get my new assistant to send you a PR plan by the end of the week. Until then, I'll be lying low."

"One week is too long."

"Tough. I need time to come up with a solid plan."

He hung up, his head pounding.

Ava wouldn't call back right away. Despite her no-nonsense, hard-ass approach, they'd had a good working relationship for years. He'd only signed on with the label again recently because of that. But he didn't want to think about Ava or the label right now.

He had no idea what the hell he was going to do.

First things first, find Cormac.

He headed back to the cabin. Cormac hadn't mentioned in his texts that he was leaving the cabin, so maybe he'd just gone out?

That didn't explain the state of the cabin, but who was he to judge?

This time when he got to the cabin, rather than going to the front door, he banged on a few windows on the way to the back again.

A CLICK, followed by a soft metallic sliding *whoosh* sounded as Brooks approached the back door.

Cormac stepped out onto the patio, a look of bewilderment on his face. "What the hell are you doing out here?"

Thank God.

"I knocked a few times on the door." He scrambled up from the ground. "But you didn't seem to hear me."

Cormac blinked at him. "Sorry, the place is an absolute wreck. I ended up having to rough it in an old sleeping bag I found in the closet and was curled up inside it. You must have been out here for hours. Why didn't you call?"

"No service." He didn't bother correcting Cormac's ideas about how long he'd been here because that would mean an explanation about the accident and lots more he didn't feel like getting into. "Where's your car?"

"Shed." Cormac grimaced, his dark brown eyes lively. "Yeah, I should have warned you about service and the smallness of things around here. Why do you think I wanted to get the hell out of this town as a kid?"

"I'm seeing that."

"So it turns out that my parents had some issues with carpenter bees this past summer, and no one told me about it—but I don't think we can stay here. I slept here so you wouldn't show up and think I'd bailed on you, but we may need to find another place. Unless you really feel like roughing it."

As Brooks squinted at him, some early morning sun poked through the treetops and hit him square in the eye. *At least someone still tolerates me. Understands me.*

But, no, he didn't feel like roughing it.

After the night he'd had and Ava's phone call, the sound of a sleeping bag and a wrecked cabin was the last thing he wanted. Hell, he'd worked too hard in life to deal with that anymore. He'd never really been the type to throw his money around, but maybe it was time for him to start living the way people thought he did.

Embrace the asshole persona everyone had boxed him into.

He grinned, a carefree feeling curling through him. "Actually, I have another idea."

7

MADDIE

"This is bad. So bad. I can't believe you didn't call me immediately," Naomi said from behind her fingers, which still covered her mouth.

"I don't know. It looks like she jumped right on taking care of the bigger problems." Pops squeezed Maddie on the shoulder gently. "Did Garrett say how long it'll be before the window can be replaced?"

"A month at least. Maybe more. He says it's gotta be custom ordered."

At least Pops seemed to be taking this well. He'd shown up early this morning—someone in town had seen the plastic on the window and called him. Predictably. Nothing in Brandywood happened without Pops knowing about it. It was a small miracle that Brooks had crashed when he did—on a Sunday a few hours before dawn might be the *only* time he would have been less likely to be seen.

Not that Maddie was fully confident someone hadn't seen *something*. After all, Travis had needed to tow the wrecked car away. But fortunately, for as many businesses as there were on

Main Street, only a handful of them had residents living on the upper floors. Retail space on Main was a premium, and most of the buildings near the Depot in the last few years had become purely commercial.

Naomi was clearly agitated. "This is a disaster." She directed a sharp look at Pops. "We'll need to close for the day."

Pops's normally pleasant expression darkened. "We can't do that. Some people have traveled here just to see the Depot. That's not fair to them."

"Not everything in life is fair. Just ask Maddie about what happened last night at the fair committee meeting." Naomi flicked her annoyed expression at Maddie.

Maddie squirmed. Naomi wasn't intending it as an attack, but somehow Maddie couldn't help but feel defensive about the whole thing. Like she'd lost the big act for the town fair concert by dating a jackass. "I know, I know. I should have signed a contract." She couldn't keep the defeat out of her voice. "I got the deposit back, though."

Naomi raised her eyebrows, a flare of surprise lighting her expression. "Wait a minute. You mean to tell me you never had them sign a contract?"

Maddie shifted her weight back, crossing her arms. "I didn't think I needed to. It never occurred to me that Josh would dump me and then have his cousin switch the dates on us. I just thought—"

"Always get a contract, Maddie. *Always.* Even with people who are legit and you don't think would break their word." Naomi shook her head. "I can't believe I'm having to tell you this."

Guilt spilled into Maddie's throat with an acid clench. *Oh shit.*

Naomi is really going to flip when she finds out about my handshake deal with Brooks Kent.

"Well, lesson learned," Pops said. "But it needs to be taken care of right away. The festival is a little under a month away. Though I heard Maddie assured TJ she's got another act lined up." He gave Maddie a curious look.

Great. The last thing she wanted to do was continue that stupid lie.

Thankfully, Naomi spoke up. "Speaking of another act, we could also consider getting quotes for the repairs in here by someone other than Garrett. I know we all love him, but there are other contractors in the world."

Pops shook his head. "I don't just love Garrett. He's one of our own. The whole point of all I've done and built is to give back to Brandywood. After all the ill will from the Depot last year and with the tourist center about to open, I want our town to know how much I will support every one of them."

A lump formed in Maddie's throat. Pops had been through so much in the past few years. The highest of highs—a random appearance on a cookie recipe special for the magazine that Sam Doyle had worked for—had led to an unexpected career and fame. He'd gotten a television show on the Happy Home Network, a line of branded products, built the Depot, providing careers for all his grandchildren to manage his mini empire.

And he'd reconnected with his former flame, marrying Bunny Wagner the year before.

But the work had taken a toll on his health, forced him to retire from bartending at the pub he'd built and worked in most of his adult life, and turned half of the town against him. Many of Brandywood's residents had disliked the changes and tourists who now came for Peter Yardley and his Country Depot.

Even though Lindsay and Travis had worked out a solution

that had pacified those angry residents, Pops still carried the weight of so much on his shoulders.

Maddie was so proud of him. He always did the right thing, trying to see the best in everyone and lending a listening ear to people who came to him for help.

Even if they don't always deserve it.

She couldn't lie to her grandfather about the fall festival. "I don't really know if I'll get a bigger musical act than River House," she said, returning the conversation back to his earlier question. "But I'm working on it."

"We need to be realistic." Naomi frowned. "River House was sheer luck. It's not like we'll have another band that big just walk through the front door."

Maddie straightened.

Actually . . .

No. She couldn't even consider it . . . could she?

Brooks Kent wasn't just a singer. He was an enormous star, with all the arrogance of one, too. If she asked him to sing at the charity festival, he'd probably laugh in her face.

But he owed her a favor.

Even if he skulked out the door this morning when I was asleep.

Whatever reason Brooks had for wanting his privacy, she'd granted it to him. Naomi and Pops didn't know the full extent of things, and Maddie wasn't sure she could keep it a secret if any more people knew. Between Dan, Travis, and Garrett, too many people knew already.

Instead, she'd told her family that the accident had been a hit-and-run and she'd turned the security footage over to the cops. If her family knew the truth, they'd be furious. She already felt horrible lying to them, but as long as the bills for the damage were paid, she could live with it.

Which is exactly why I should take full advantage of the

situation and get something out of it I really need. She wasn't beneath blackmail, especially for a jerk like Brooks.

Still, the idea made her stomach turn. No wonder Brooks wanted privacy. She barely knew the guy, and she was already thinking of getting him to do something for her.

He probably got that a lot.

She had his cell phone number, but he'd slipped out of her apartment without a note of thanks or any attempt to say good-bye. She doubted he intended—or wanted—to return. Or to talk to her about anything other than the damages.

"I'll come up with something for the festival." She plastered on a smile full of fake confidence. "Just give me a couple of days." Even if she had to devote every waking hour to it, she would do her best.

Pops nodded, then checked his watch. "I should get back home. Bernadette will wonder what happened if I'm not back to get ready for church."

That Pops had a wife now was still something Maddie hadn't fully wrapped her head around—or that the wife was Bunny Wagner. It had to be weirder for Lindsay, though, considering that Travis was Bunny's grandson. She'd already gotten some comments about love running in the family.

Maddie kissed his cheek. "Sorry to bring you out here so early on a Sunday."

"I'll always take an excuse to see my girls." Pops hugged her tightly. "Walk me out to the truck, will you? I have a bone to pick with you."

Maddie nodded, then followed him out the main door onto Main Street. The town was already coming to life, alive with the colors of the coming fall. Maddie loved the yellows and reds that popped up everywhere this time of year—it made everything feel more vibrant.

Pops's truck was on the curb, and he stopped by the tailgate, then scanned her face. “I understand you came home from that meeting quite upset yesterday.”

She squirmed. “Yes, and I know I messed up by not having River House legally—”

“I don’t care about that. You could have a one-man band with a harmonica up on stage for all I care.” He brushed his knuckle gently against her cheek. “I don’t enjoy hearing that one of my grandchildren is hurting so much she can’t get herself out of bed. That Josh really did a number on your heart, didn’t he?”

Maddie’s breath caught as she searched Pops’s eyes.

Josh.

Funny how she hadn’t thought about him at all this morning. After Brooks had crashed into the Depot, it was like her brain had refocused.

She swallowed hard, then nodded. “Yeah, but I’ll be okay.” The last thing she wanted was any more unwelcome advice about how she needed to get over Josh already.

“You know, some of us Yardleys just feel things harder than others. Look at me—I never forgot my first love, no matter how many years had passed.”

“If you’re telling me I need to wait fifty years for Josh until Gina is dead, I’m gonna say no right now.”

Pops chuckled. “No, that’s not what I’m saying. And even I didn’t spend my life waiting around for Bernadette. I wouldn’t have my wonderful family if I had. I just wanted you to know it’s okay. I understand. So you fell in love quickly with Josh? That doesn’t mean it wasn’t real. Genuine love takes time to heal from when it’s gone.”

She sighed, her heart squeezing. “That’s the thing, Pops. I’m not even sure it was so much Josh I was in love with. More like . . . the idea of him.”

Pops raised his eyebrows skeptically.

"I'm serious." She tucked her hair behind her ears. "Think about it. So many people we know—including you—have the most amazing love stories. You married your lifelong love after forever. Travis and Lindsay are practically Romeo and Juliet. Even Jen Cavanaugh. Her love story is like something out of a book, including the part where she married a multimillionaire."

Pops frowned. "And that's what you're looking for? A fairy-tale romance?"

She drew in a slow, deep breath. It sounded so silly when he said it that way. "Maybe? I mean, would it be so terrible if a handsome and dashing Prince Charming came into town and swept me off my feet?"

"The problem with the fairy tales isn't that love doesn't happen that way, it's that you don't get to pick the one you get. You might be looking for the wrong sort of prince."

She smiled halfheartedly, knowing that he meant well by trying to indulge her with the conversation. "Or there's no prince." Heaviness clouded her thoughts. "My love story just might be more ordinary. Fewer fireworks."

"There's no such thing as ordinary love. Being in love is a wondrous thing. Nothing ordinary about it."

"You're too romantic for your own good, Pops."

"That's the pot calling the kettle black." He winked at her. "Didn't you just say you wanted a prince to ride in on a white stallion? You may as well have sung that you wanted more than this small-town life."

"Oh, stop." Somehow, his ribbing made her feel better. Strangely, this also seemed like a conversation she could only have with her grandfather. Like he was the only person who would understand.

He hugged her again. "Just keep your eyes—and heart—open. You never know. Your prince might not be so obvious."

He turned to go. "By the way, I hear Cormac Doyle is in town. He might know a band or two willing to play at the fair."

True.

And he's probably hanging out with a rock star who owes me.

She needed to banish the manipulative thought. Was she really considering blackmailing Brooks?

"Doesn't hurt to ask, I guess. It would be good to see Cormac anyway."

"I think he might be up at the Doyles' old cabin with a friend." He patted the back of his truck, then climbed on inside.

It wasn't until Pops had pulled away from the curb that Maddie processed his words. The cabin? Hadn't Garrett said something about it not being usable?

But if Cormac *was* there with a friend, it had to be Brooks, didn't it?

She pulled out her phone. Maybe a quick Google search could tell her if Cormac and Brooks were friends. There might even be pictures of them together. Or she could stalk Brooks's Instagram and see.

But when she typed *Brooks Kent* into the search engine bar, a headline caught her attention:

BROOKS KENT ARRESTED FOR ASSAULT IN MARYLAND.

Maddie's eyes widened.

What the hell?

The headline was from . . . *just a few hours ago.*

Wait. What?

She opened the article and scanned it, trying to keep the butterflies in her stomach from whipping into a roiling nausea.

The article was damning.

Brooks had been arrested the night before, apparently,

before a concert in Baltimore . . . for attacking a man who had ended up in the hospital with his injuries. And witnesses claimed he'd been drinking—maybe even on drugs—beforehand.

Shit.

Shit.

No wonder his face was bruised.

And she'd let that creep sleep on her sofa?

How was he out of jail already? And *what. The. Fuck?* Why had he been *driving?*

No wonder he hadn't wanted her to call the cops.

Asshole.

Still, he hadn't seemed drunk. Maybe he was just that good at hiding it.

His sudden, unannounced departure this morning—slipping out like a thief—now seemed more ominous.

What if he intends to screw me over with paying for the damages?

Sure, she'd had Dan take a report, but it wasn't official.

Her family was going to kill her.

Maybe she was too naive and trusting. Emotional. Whatever the hell else Naomi and Lindsay had called her last night.

She had photo evidence, though.

Photo evidence that could be used in more ways than one.

Seething, she stormed back inside. Naomi's head shot up from where she was bent over a broken display table. "We have so much inventory to figure out—where are you going?"

Maddie breezed past her, heading to the back of the store. "I need the day, Naomi. I have some important things to take care of." Thank God she hadn't told Naomi about the deal she'd made with Brooks Kent to take care of the damages.

I can still fix this.

And maybe even get Brooks Kent to solve another problem for her. He owed her. And now she understood just how much.

She had to find Cormac Doyle.

8

BROOKS

SITTING on a dock in an Adirondack chair with a beer in hand wasn't a bad way to end what had started as a goddamn awful day.

Brooks took a long pull from his beer, then leaned back into his chair, his gaze lazily sweeping over the red-hot flames licking the logs in the firepit a few feet away.

See? He didn't need an assistant or manager or anyone else handling his every movement. He'd run into trouble and had solved it. The wreck this morning was well in hand, and now the cabin situation was too. He'd found the most expensive, luxury-filled short-term rental near here, and he and Cormac had headed over there by mid-afternoon, when the rental began.

While waiting, he'd even snagged some sleep in Cormac's cabin on an old cot. Not enough, but at least his eyelids weren't burning now. Cormac had gone out for supplies and steaks for them to grill tonight, and Brooks planned to find a private chef to take care of meals for the week.

Another problem solved.

The best part of it? This place had five full glorious bars of cell phone service.

He had even called Kayla to see if she and Audrey wanted to come and spend the week with him. With Audrey starting school next year, their ability to visit him for last-minute trips would be hampered.

Now all he had to do was come up with a reasonable plan for Ava, and he'd be set.

Brooks stretched his long legs in front of him.

"Hey, I'm back," Cormac said from behind. "Brought a family friend with me."

Brooks turned to see Cormac standing on the gravel path that led from the driveway, two paper bags in his arms.

Beside him was a stunning blonde wearing a plaid minidress and knee-high boots. Her hands were on her hips as she stared boldly in Brooks's direction.

Maddie Yardley?

Stunning didn't quite describe her . . .

And she had daggers in her eyes.

"Brooks, this is Madison Yardley. Maddie, Brooks Kent. Feel free to grab a seat," Cormac said to Maddie, nodding toward the dock. "I'll grab you a beer."

Cormac made his way inside, and Maddie's lips curled into a sneer as she approached him, her hips swaying naturally as she walked.

"Hi, asshole," she said, her voice dripping with anger.

Well, at least she'd lost any sort of flustered fangirl embarrassment. Brooks pushed his sunglasses off his eyes and leaned forward. *So much for a nice evening.*

"You missed me so much you stalked me down? I'm touched." His eyes narrowed. Just why had Cormac brought her back here?

She laughed without humor and stopped near his chair.

"Stalked? No. Turns out, you're not that hard to find. Especially when you rent out a good friend's property. She called my sister, freaking out about it. Then, when I heard Cormac Doyle was in town and staying here, too, it was easy to snag an invite." She smiled prettily.

"Should I tell him you only came back with him to see me?" He took another pull from his beer. "He might not like that too much." She'd clearly dressed up. Probably flirted with Cormac.

"Should I tell him how you wrecked my family's place and failed to mention you'd been in *jail* the night before?" She sat in the chair next to his, making herself comfortable.

Too comfortable.

He shrugged. "My personal business is none of yours."

"Unless the news outlets are saying you were under the influence last night when you *assaulted* someone. Do you honestly think I would have let you step foot in my place—"

"Oh please. I punched my niece's deadbeat dad in the face. That's not assault. It's him getting what he fucking deserved."

Whatever retort she'd had coming stayed stuck in her throat. She blinked at him a few times, then said, "Still doesn't excuse you for driving after being incapacitated. No wonder you crashed into my store."

"Well, see, that's a simple answer too. Because I wasn't. I don't drink. Or smoke. Or anything else."

She gaped at him. "You're literally holding a beer."

He turned the label toward her. "Nonalcoholic. I've been sober for five years."

"But the news—"

"You honestly think the media tells the truth about anything? You probably believe in Santa Claus, too, don't you?"

She scowled. "They can't just publish straight-up lies. That's called libel."

"That's called *life*. If I had a nickel for every lie that's ever been published about me, I would have more money than I've ever made with any record." Brooks pinched the bridge of his nose. "Look, what do you want? I'm about ten seconds away from getting up and throwing your ass out of here, whether or not Cormac invited you."

Maddie sat straighter, not an ounce of remorse on her face. "You walked out this morning without settling anything with me about payment or otherwise."

"I gave you my *cell phone number*. You think I just hand that thing out to anyone? You're welcome to call me. Better yet, text me. I'll pay the bill. What else were you looking for? A goodbye kiss? Did I hurt your feelings by sneaking out of your apartment first thing in the morning? Don't worry, no one saw me, princess. Your reputation won't be tainted by me."

"Hope you like IPAs," Cormac said from the end of the dock.

Both Maddie and Brooks turned to look at him. A flush lit Maddie's cheeks. No doubt she was wondering the same thing as Brooks—*how long had Cormac been standing there, and what did he overhear?*

Cormac's gaze traveled to Brooks, and he raised a brow, just slightly, but said nothing. He'd clearly heard *something,* and Brooks's last statement was damning—especially if Cormac liked this girl.

Maddie stood from the chair, abruptly. "IPAs are great," she said with an unfaltering smile. She accepted the beer as Cormac held it out. "You know me. Good beer is part of the family business."

"That's true." Cormac clinked his beer against hers and winked. He turned back toward Brooks. "I've known Maddie since she was practically born. I used to play Little League with her eldest brother, Logan."

"Eldest? How many siblings do you have?" Brooks asked Maddie in a tone that almost sounded congenial.

"Five. I'm in the middle of the pack."

"How old does that make you?" Cormac couldn't know Maddie that well. He had to be a lot older than her if he'd played with her eldest brother. "You must have been in pigtails when Cormac left town."

Maddie cocked a brow at him. "Are you asking my age? I'm thirty, thanks for asking."

Oh. She was only four years younger than him. For some reason, that gap had seemed wider.

"Don't pay any attention to this jackass." Cormac settled into one chair near the firepit "You'd think he'd know his way around women, but he's got the social grace of an elephant."

"I couldn't have put it better myself." Maddie rolled the rim of her bottle against her full lower lip, and Brooks's stomach lurched. He tore his gaze away as she went on. "He's awkward. Likes to crash into things. Sounds like Brooks Kent, the ladies' man, is just another *media fabrication.*"

He choked back a laugh, avoiding looking at her. She wasn't shy, that was for goddamn sure. But maybe she hadn't realized how sexual that might sound, considering what Cormac might have overheard.

He should just tell Cormac that this girl was using him and explain how they knew each other.

But, then again, he'd have to explain why he'd lied about his car breaking down and being in a local shop.

He didn't even really know the answer to that.

The lie had just come easily. Naturally. He had few good friends, and Cormac was one of them. Unlike a lot of other musicians who'd worked with him, Cormac was a steady, honest guy. Responsible. Someone he could count on to be sober after a show when the rest of his band was stoned. He'd tried recruiting Cormac to play for him regularly, but Darren had shot the idea down.

Whatever the reason, Brooks would have to figure out a way to tell Cormac he'd lied about the car and admit that he'd crashed into the store. No doubt that was better than him thinking Brooks had hooked up with Maddie—especially if he cared about her somehow.

"You two act like old friends," Cormac observed with a guarded look. "Speaking of Logan, is he still on his way?"

Jesus, how many people did Cormac invite over here?

Then again, if it were any other person than Maddie, Brooks wouldn't have given a damn. This was how things went whenever he went to anyone else's hometown. He'd hang out with them and meet their friends, their family. Always the outsider.

But it *was* Maddie, and Brooks was sure she'd orchestrated this.

"I think so. He was just going to grab some crab cakes from the pub."

Cormac nodded. "I'll get the grill going for those steaks. I haven't had steaks from the Pearsons' place in forever."

"I can do that. Where's the grill?" Maddie said.

Cormac scratched his head. "It's up on the deck. But you don't have—"

"I'm already standing." She waved her hand. "And I'm used to grilling. I'll get it." She grinned and hurried down the dock again.

She must be rattled.

Brooks finished his beer as tense silence settled between him and Cormac.

"Well, that was fast," Cormac said at last, his gaze focused on the lake.

Brooks cut a look at him. "What was?"

"You snuck out of her place this morning?" Cormac cocked his chin, his lips curling with a smile.

Yup. He overheard. Still, Brooks broke eye contact. "It wasn't like that."

"Wasn't it? I guess it should have surprised me when Maddie practically dragged Logan over to say hi while I was at the butcher. Just figured she was being friendly. But she clearly already knew you and I were hanging out."

"Man, I really am not trying to get between you and a woman you like—"

"No, no, there's nothing between Maddie and me. I haven't seen her in a few years." Cormac chuckled. "I'm not trying to find a girl from my hometown to drag me back. How did you meet her, though?"

"Hey, Cormac," a male voice called.

Both men looked up to see another man standing near the driveway. From the similarity in their appearance, he must be Maddie's older brother, Logan.

But why in the hell did Logan have a suitcase with him?

"Uncle Books!"

Audrey's voice pierced the quiet of the yard. Then he saw her, dark brown ringlets streaming in the air as she barreled through the grass toward him, dropping her stuffed gorilla.

He barely caught sight of Kayla as she stepped up beside Logan, then Audrey was on the dock. Brooks stood, and Audrey flung herself against him as he scooped her up. "Uncle Books, I missed you," Audrey said, her arms tight against his neck as she clung to him.

"Hey, baby girl," he said with a smile, settling her into his arm. It felt like ages since he'd seen her because of the tour. The sight of her angelic face, her dark chocolate-brown eyes that were just like Kayla's, instantly lightened the strain on his heart.

Kayla made her way across the golden-hued, sun-drenched lawn, a grin on her face. "Audrey didn't stop talking about how excited she was to see Uncle Books the entire drive up here." She waited by the end of the dock as Brooks carried Audrey over toward her.

Brooks stopped, and Kayla's expression shifted, her lips turning downward in a frown as she sized up the bruising on his face. "Audrey, why don't you go get Mr. Fluffy from where you dropped him? You don't want him to get lost."

Audrey nodded enthusiastically, then scrambled down from her perch in Brooks's arms.

When she was out of earshot, Kayla set her hands on her hips. "What the hell, Brooks? You said your face was fine."

"It is fine. Just a little bruise. No big deal. You should see the other guy."

"That's not funny, and you know it." Kayla's eyes glistened. "Dammit, you shouldn't have let him get to you. Mike is going to juice this for everything it's worth. Even if the charges don't stick, he's gonna sue you. Then use this in the custody hearing."

Brooks's gaze traveled over the top of Kayla's head as he caught sight of Maddie's brother coming their way. Audrey was beside him now, chatting happily while she held the gorilla that she usually carried everywhere. She'd never been afraid of strangers, unfortunately, and would talk the ear off anyone she met.

"Let's talk about this later," Brooks said gruffly.

Cormac's footsteps approached from behind, and he arrived beside Brooks at the same time as Maddie's brother and Audrey joined them. "Hey, Kayla. I see you met Logan. Logan, this is Brooks."

"We pulled up at the same time," Kayla said, offering Logan a smile. "He offered to grab my suitcase."

Brooks extended a hand to Logan, who had that look of

discomfort he'd seen on so many people's faces when they were introduced. It had taken him a year of being a known celebrity to get used to that look—the awestruck glimmer while trying to play it cool and pretend he was just any other stranger. "Nice to meet you. If you don't mind not mentioning to anyone else you know that I'm staying here, I'd appreciate it."

"No problem." Logan shook his hand. "Hope you don't mind my sister and me crashing your party. This is a beautiful house you're staying in."

Crashing. There was that word again, and Brooks winced.

"Yeah, it really is," Kayla said, tossing a silky lock of dark hair over her shoulder as she turned to gawk at the lake house. The house was massive, with several decks on three levels overlooking the water. Each room seemed to have a balcony, and one deck had a hot tub, while a main deck had a comfortable seating area and grill.

The living room was distinguishable by an A-framed enormous picture window, which reflected the reds and pinks of the sky now that sunset approached.

"It's not really a party," Brooks said with a shrug. "But you're welcome. I just hope we don't bore you."

"Speak for yourself," Kayla said with a roll of her eyes. "I am not boring. Neither is Cormac."

"Mommy, I'm hungry," Audrey said, tugging on Kayla's shirt.

"Don't worry, we're going to eat soon," Cormac said. "I should see what happened to Maddie. She might have gotten lost trying to figure out what deck the grill was on."

Logan lifted a bag in his hand. "I brought some crab cakes, too. From the pub. And some wine."

"I like cab cakes!" Audrey said with a hop. "And wine!"

"Sorry, kid, no wine," Kayla said with a roll of her eyes.

"Also, maybe don't go announcing that, please. I give her sips occasionally," she explained sheepishly to Logan.

"I'm not judging. I have a couple of nieces who like to 'share' my beers."

The entire group started across the yard toward the house, then the string lights above the porch came on, and Maddie leaned over the rail and called out a hello. She looked too comfortable, which bothered Brooks. This wasn't his place, really, and Maddie was Cormac's guest.

He still wouldn't mind sending her away. She'd shown up here, acting like now that she had the dirt on him, she *knew* him. Why the hell would she go to so much trouble to come here tonight?

The care she'd taken with her appearance was noticeable. He hadn't really noticed how tanned she was, and that plaid skirt was short on her well-toned thighs, barely covering the curves of what appeared to be a *very* nice ass.

He let his gaze skim every inch of that delicious figure of hers. Maybe he'd been too tired to notice it before, but Maddie was gorgeous in a natural, girl-next-door way. The sweatsuit out-of-the-shower look just hadn't done her any justice.

"Who's the girl?" Kayla asked in a whisper beside him.

"Cormac's friend. Logan's sister," Brooks grumbled back, pulling his gaze away from Maddie.

Kayla bit her lip, giving him a knowing glance that made him feel like he'd been caught in the act. "Cormac's *lady friend*?"

Brooks put a bit more space between him and Cormac as they went up the stairs.

"Who knows? I don't really give a damn."

"Okay. Just, you know. Be careful. She's cute."

Brooks quirked a brow. "When have you known me to be stupid about women?"

"Fair point. You're practically dead inside." Kayla jabbed a finger in the side of his ribs. They reached the deck where Maddie stood, and Kayla kept walking past him. She held out a hand to Maddie. "Hi, I'm Kayla."

Brooks hung back, a knot of tension in his gut. Kayla had said similar things in the past, and it didn't really bother him normally . . . except there it was. That perception of him as heartless. Cold.

He'd always accepted it and moved on.

Why the hell was it getting to him so much today?

Logan was still carrying Kayla's suitcase, and Brooks took it from him. "I'll take this inside," he said. "Can I get anyone a drink?"

"Can I have a Coke?" Audrey asked brightly.

"Sure thing," Brooks said.

"No, you may not." Kayla broke away from talking to Maddie and gave him a sharp look. "She cannot have Coke an hour before bedtime, Brooks."

"Pweeeeeeese?" Audrey batted long lashes at him.

Brooks simply winked at her, then started inside.

"Brooks, don't you dare!" Kayla called after him.

He chuckled as the door closed. As if he could tell that little girl no. Although he wouldn't tell Audrey he'd watered it down. *A lot.*

He set the suitcase down near the living room, then pivoted toward the kitchen. The house had come fully stocked with all staples and drinks in their own refrigeration, including a wine fridge. He grabbed another nonalcoholic beer for himself, and Maddie's reproach about drinking went through his head.

The coldness of the bottle seeped through his palm as he rummaged through the drink fridge for a soda for Audrey. He found one, then closed the door and flinched, startled.

Maddie was coming in through the back door.

"Need something?" he asked, not bothering with a hint of friendliness.

She reddened. "Bathroom."

"In the hall, third door down on the left. I think."

Maddie nodded a thank you, then started in the opposite direction.

Brooks straightened. She'd caught him off guard when she'd shown up, but it might be a good time to establish some boundaries with this girl. Let her know that, while her nerve was almost admirable, it wasn't acceptable either.

"Hold on one sec," he said, setting the drinks on the counter. "I want a word with you."

9

MADDIE

MADDIE FROZE IN PLACE, her heart beating a little faster as Brooks came up behind her. She turned to face him, slowly. When she'd looked for Cormac earlier today, her plan to find Brooks and raise hell with him seemed so solid. So justified.

Then she'd found him sitting on the dock looking so . . . *normal*.

Not Brooks "the rock star" Kent. Just a guy. Drinking a nonalcoholic beer. Which, unless he liked punishment, was a good sign he probably *was* five years sober because those things were terrible.

He'd even cracked the door about personal business that, if true, she probably shouldn't have pried into. And then his sister and niece were here, and *dammit* if he didn't seem like just another guy with a real life.

A gorgeous guy, at that, with a silky, velvet-toned voice that she'd listened to for hours at a time before.

She held his gaze as he came closer. "Is there a reason for this little visit tonight?"

The contract she'd printed and folded in an envelope in her purse seemed so ill-conceived.

Stop. Don't chicken out. Just because he tells you a sob story and drinks a near-beer doesn't make him a good person.

She'd spent enough hours reading up on his activities the past few years to make a solid judgment.

Raising her chin, Maddie gave him a fake smile. "I've come to make a deal with you."

"A deal?" Brooks raised his brows.

Maddie gripped the strap of her purse tighter. "You have a lot more to lose if that news about the wreck gets out than I realized. And you're not exactly trustworthy."

His expression darkened. "What's that supposed to mean?"

"You can say whatever you want about your personal habits, but isn't it true that you and your band were all busted in Vegas last winter at a party that got out of control? And that the model you were dating three years ago, Paulette Stevens, claimed you slapped her during an argument?"

His eyes narrowed. "I don't remember you being there to know the facts of either of those situations."

"Still, it doesn't look great when you get arrested for assault, then get out of jail and wreck your car into a store at four in the morning, does it? You owe me a favor for covering your ass."

His jaw clenched so hard that she saw the muscles of his temples bulge. She almost backed away at his stare. "Follow me," he snapped coolly, then turn and strode down the hall, not bothering to wait for her.

Shit.

He was clearly furious. If he was violent, putting herself in a vulnerable position alone with him wasn't smart.

She glanced over her shoulder toward the deck. Logan was here. So was Cormac. Even if Cormac was Brooks's friend, he'd step in and help her if she needed. And from the way Brooks had behaved around his niece, she doubted he'd do anything extreme with her around.

Swallowing her trepidation, she followed Brooks down the hallway. He slipped into a room with French doors and shut them behind him.

Maddie released a slow breath, then went into the room.

Brooks was over by an enormous bed in a decadent room with its own sitting area and balcony—this must be the primary bedroom.

He lifted a black duffel bag onto the comforter, then unzipped it, and fished out a black leather case. Without a glance at her, he opened the case and pulled out a pen. "How much do you want?"

"What?" She blinked at him, leaning back against the door.

"For your silence. How much?"

He was offering her a check?

She bit her lip. That look in his eyes was dead and cold, the simplicity of the business transaction making it clear that he'd be willing to pay well for her silence—and could afford it.

"I don't want money," she finally said, trying to keep her voice from wavering. "I don't need your money. I need your . . . *talent*."

He jerked his chin up, his gaze roving over her with spurious admiration. "I don't put out in exchange for anything, sweetheart."

Sex? Her eyes widened. *Does he really think I'm asking for sex?*

Had women tried to manipulate him into sex before?

She coughed back a startled laugh. "No. I'm not asking for *that*." A fresh wave of embarrassment trickled through her. "Our town is having a fair in a little less than a month. And someone like you would be normally impossible for us to book for the main stage. We can't pay what you're normally used to, I'm sure but—"

"You're seriously asking for a *concert* in exchange for your silence?" He flipped the check ledger onto the bed. He tilted his head, staring at her as though dumbfounded.

"You owe me, Brooks. And I need this because—" She paused. She wasn't about to spill her guts out to Brooks about Josh and Gina and the whole stupid mess with River House. He didn't care, and it wouldn't likely influence him. "This would be great for our town. The fair is a huge deal, and we get people from the whole tristate, not to mention tourists. It would be well-attended."

He continued to stare at her in disbelief. "You're blackmailing me for a concert," he repeated. "I don't care how fucking *attended* it is."

She sensed she should hurry before this got ugly. Reaching into her purse, she grabbed an envelope. "This is a contract I drew up. It assures I'll be quiet, that you'll pay for the damages, and that you'll do the concert. My dad is a lawyer, so I know a thing or two about contracts and—"

"Leave it on the bed, then get the fuck out of this house."

Her breath caught. She hadn't really planned on staying for dinner, but the way he was dismissing her was rude. Not that she didn't probably deserve it. What did this mean, though? He wouldn't make a deal with her? The image of him ripping up the contract as soon as she left floated through her imagination.

She avoided his gaze as she edged closer to the bed, then set the envelope down.

Brooks didn't move, every muscle under his shirt taut as he stared at her with feral, intense scrutiny.

She turned and started back toward the door.

"Wait."

Looking over her shoulder, she met that burning gaze of his.

"Come back tomorrow. Noon. Sharp. I'll give you an answer then."

10

BROOKS

"It's too bad your friend didn't stay last night," Kayla said to Cormac as she leaned over her morning coffee at the long farmhouse-style table in the kitchen. "She seemed really nice."

"Yeah, well, you sure seemed to get along with her brother." Cormac winked. He snuck a glance at Brooks, who was frying an egg at the island stove nearby them. "Just don't let Brooks see you flirting."

Brooks held Cormac's gaze with a mock scowl. "Am I supposed to jump in like a Neanderthal and threaten to beat him with a club if she sleeps with him?"

"Hush. Audrey might hear you," Kayla scolded, looking over her shoulder at her daughter, who was lying on the couch, snuggled against a pillow, watching cartoons.

"If I know my niece, nothing can take her attention away from *Bluey*," Brooks grunted.

Kayla smiled, then shrugged. "You have me there."

"In all seriousness, Logan's a good guy. You could do worse," Cormac said, then picked a piece of bacon off a plate.

"I have done worse," Kayla said with a chuckle, then gave Cormac a knowing look. "And so have you."

Brooks transferred the egg to his plate, then grabbed his toast from the toaster, content to settle into the background of Cormac and Kayla's conversation. Cormac had always gotten along well with Kayla and treated her with respect and friendship. In a way, it was easier for him to have both here—it meant Brooks could talk a whole lot less. They could just talk to each other.

"So why did Logan's sister haul out so quickly?" Kayla gave Cormac a curious look. "I figured she was here to hook up with you."

"Don't know. But I don't think she's on the market for a hookup. Logan was telling me she just went through a nasty breakup with some guy in town. Guy was a real asshole to her, apparently. Really screwed her over with some typical small-town drama."

Kayla laughed, then sipped her coffee. "What's small-town drama? Mrs. O'Leary's cow being accused of starting shit again?"

Brooks sat beside her, ignoring what Cormac had said about Maddie. He didn't want to waste an extra second thinking about that bitch. "Nah, it's mostly gossip and backstabbing. You're lucky we left Fountain Springs before you started high school. That's when it all gets a thousand times worse."

That was one of the few things he'd been proud of. Because Kayla was seven years younger than him, he'd been able to assume guardianship of her when Mom had died. As soon as he'd signed his first contract with a label, he'd moved them away from Fountain Springs and gone to Raleigh so he could still attend classes at Duke.

The money hadn't been as substantial at first, but a year

later, he'd graduated and started making more by getting a full-time job. LA hadn't come until Kayla had graduated from high school and started at the University of Virginia.

He'd gotten her away from Fountain Springs.

Kept her from all the ugliness there.

You weren't able to stop her from meeting Mike at UVA, though.

The voice in his head was ugly. Condemning. He should have been around more. Done more to step in as Kayla got more and more involved with Mike.

"That's too bad," Kayla said, interrupting his thoughts. "Logan says she's amazing with their family business. Brilliant with PR and marketing and sales. It's always the smart ones who men treat like crap."

"It's because insecure weenie men can't handle their women shining." Cormac shrugged. "A real man has no problem looking like second best beside the woman he loves. Women need to look for the guys with actual balls."

"I like balls!" Audrey said, popping her head off the couch just then. She slid out from under the blanket and came over to them, her bed hair sticking out in a thousand directions. "Can I get a new ball, Uncle Books?" She gave him a wide grin.

"You need to stop spoiling her. Notice how she skips right past me and goes straight to you?" Kayla said dryly. She plucked Audrey over toward her and pulled her onto her lap. "Stop asking Uncle Brooks for things. You have more toys than any one kid can even play with."

"What type of ball do you want?" Brooks said with a wink, taking out his phone.

"Brooks August Kent. I will kill you if you keep buying her things. We're going to need a new house to fit all the crap you send her."

Brooks smirked and gave her a look. "What type of new house do you want?"

Kayla rolled her eyes. "You know, you can't use your money that way. It's not like an endless supply that will never dry up. Money won't buy away every problem that comes along."

"Has she seen your house?" Cormac grimaced at Brooks, then looked at Kayla. "It's practically a shack. I've never met a famous musician that lived in a smaller place—even the poor struggling ones in Nashville."

"A shack on the beach, though," Kayla countered. "That's probably over one million dollars because of its location. And yes, I've seen it. Audrey and I have to take his bed since he insists on sleeping on the pull-out couch when we visit."

Brooks shrugged. "Location was all I wanted. Why do I need a big house when I'm one person?"

"You have a nice car, though," Cormac said.

"Because he insists on driving himself everywhere," Kayla said, bouncing Audrey on her knee. "Because he's weird and neurotic."

"What's noo-ro-tic?" Audrey asked.

"It means your uncle Brooks is smart." Brooks dug into his egg with the edge of his fork. "But enough about me. What should we do while you guys are up here this week?"

"Hot tub!" Audrey smiled, continuing to bounce exaggeratedly on Kayla's knee.

"We can do that. What else?"

"Wait, hold up. Four is too young for a hot tub." Kayla cut a look at Brooks. "And we don't need to do anything crazy. Just spend time with you. Maybe Cormac knows of a good playground around here."

Cormac chuckled. "I can ask my one billion nieces and nephews for recommendations. Maybe even ask for a playdate. A couple of the kids in my family are Audrey's age."

Audrey's eyes lit up. "Can we? Pwease?"

Kayla's phone rang beside her. She lifted it and frowned. "Hold on. I'll be right back." She transferred Audrey to the floor, then hurried away. "Hello? Hey, Stephanie . . ." Her voice faded as she shut the door down the hallway.

"Did you get some breakfast?" Brooks asked Audrey. He tried to ignore the curiosity that had arisen in his mind as Kayla had left. If he didn't know any better, she'd looked worried.

She shook her head. "Can I have a popsicle?"

This kid. "I might be gullible, but I'm not that gullible. Your mama isn't going to say yes to that one. Plus, I don't have any. How about a scrambled egg?"

Audrey shook her head. "Dip egg?"

Brooks exchanged a look with Cormac. "What the hell is a dip egg?"

"Hell if I know." Cormac chewed on his bacon.

"Mommy says hell is a no-no word," Audrey said sternly.

Brooks swallowed. The private chef would be arriving for lunch and dinners, but breakfast was on him. "She's right. Don't say it." He stood, then went back toward the island. "So what does a dip egg look like?"

"Like a dip egg!" She settled into the chair he'd just vacated, her little legs swinging as she held on to her stuffed gorilla.

"What color is it?" Cormac tried, helpfully.

"Egg color." She picked at her gorilla's fur.

"Of course it is." Brooks lifted his head as the sound of footsteps approached. Kayla returned to the kitchen, a strained expression on her face. "Hey, what's a dip egg?"

"Over-easy," she said distractedly and gathered her plate. "That was my boss. I changed shifts with one of the other nurses so I could be out until Friday, but Stephanie didn't approve it. She's furious and wants me to come in right now."

"Even though you covered your shift? Haven't you always been allowed to change shifts pretty easily? That's part of why you took that job."

"Yeah, but Stephanie is new. She doesn't love the amount of flexibility we had before and has really cracked down on it." Kayla ran her fingers through her hair. "This is so stupid. Jenna is already there, covering my shift. By the time I get there, it will be almost noon." She tugged at Audrey. "Come on, kiddo. We have to get going."

Audrey looked stricken. "Where?"

"Home. Grandma will watch you."

"No!" Audrey clutched her gorilla tightly. "I wanna stay with Uncle Books!"

Kayla rolled her eyes and attempted to lift Audrey from the chair. Audrey flopped herself over, making herself a dead weight. "No!" Audrey wailed again.

"Uncle Brooks is busy. He doesn't have time to watch you by himself."

"Yes, he can!" Audrey shot him pleading eyes. "Uncle Books can watch me by hisself!"

Brooks caught his breath. How hard could it be? He'd watched Audrey for a couple of hours at a time before when Kayla came to visit.

Brooks came over toward them and took a wiggling Audrey from Kayla. "I got her. It's no big deal."

"Yes, it is a big deal because I've got to work on Wednesday, too. I can't be back and forth from here every day." Kayla reached her arms out. "I can't leave you with Uncle Brooks until Friday. That's too much work for him. You don't even like to sleep by yourself."

"I stay with Uncle Books!" Audrey's little arms clung to his neck as Kayla tried to pull her away.

"If you don't mind her staying with me, I can watch her," Brooks said, trying to keep Audrey from falling.

"Yay! I can stay!" Audrey beamed.

"These are conversations we have without the four-year-old present." Kayla gave him a hard look, then threw up her hands. "Fine. You want to babysit? Go ahead. But when she's freaking out in the middle of the night because I'm not there, I'm going to tell you I told you so. I'm going to go pack my stuff."

Cormac let out a low whistle as Kayla stormed off. Audrey continued to smile triumphantly, holding on to Brooks. "You're a brave man. Even I wouldn't volunteer to watch my nieces and nephews for the better part of a week. Four is a tough age."

"I got nothing planned."

Except dealing with Madison Yardley. The thought made his stomach churn.

Brooks set Audrey down on her feet, then ruffled her hair. "Why don't you go watch some more cartoons while I make you that dip egg?"

Audrey bounded back toward the couch, the tutu on her pjs swishing as she ran.

He didn't know what Kayla was so worried about anyway—he'd practically raised his sister, and everything had turned out fine. "Hey, speaking of your nieces and nephews, can you possibly do me the favor of taking Audrey to the park maybe to hang out with some of them around noon? I've got one thing I need to take care of, and I'd prefer Audrey not be around for it."

Cormac raised his brows. "And what's that?"

"None of your business." Brooks smirked.

What Cormac didn't know wouldn't hurt him.

But the burning question?

What am I going to do about Maddie and her ridiculous "favor"?

11

MADDIE

Maddie had been less nervous about pulling up to the place where Brooks was staying the night before. But now, staring at the enormous lake house, her fingers tightened around the steering wheel, her gut in knots.

What the hell did I get myself into?

Brooks hadn't ever been nice during their interactions. Maybe civil. At best.

But nice? She wasn't sure if he was capable of that.

Last night, though, he'd shown a harder edge. Maybe she should have expected that, considering she was blackmailing him.

She checked her reflection in the mirror, trying to put on a mask of calm before she killed the engine to her car. She could handle Brooks Kent, no matter how nasty he got. She'd dealt with plenty worse before. Her family considered her to be the angry customer whisperer—somehow, she always defused sticky situations better than everyone else. Pops claimed she got it from him, and she probably did.

She opened the car door and slipped out onto the paved

driveway. Jason Cavanaugh sure knew what he was doing when he'd bought this place and fixed it up. The house was one of the prettiest on the lake now. She'd checked the rental fees for it after Lindsay had told her Brooks had rented it. Not something she would even think of renting for a week.

No doubt Brooks didn't have any problem spending per night what would be someone else's monthly income to stay here.

Maddie hurried to the front porch, then rang the doorbell. She was early, but that was normal for her. She always got everywhere fifteen minutes early, at least. Today, it was almost twenty.

When no one answered, she pressed it again.

Could he be out back? He might not hear her if so.

She went around to the back of the house. "Brooks?"

Nothing.

"Hello?"

She made her way closer to the back deck, seeing the sliding glass door to the living room open.

He must be here.

Then she spotted him. He was in the hot tub, leaning back with his eyes closed. He'd shaved, which surprised her, and appeared to be relaxing. Clearly not in a rush to get ready for their meeting time.

She started up the stairs, lifting her long, flowy skirt as she walked. Just as she got to the top of the stairs, Brooks shifted, then stood out of the hot tub, dripping wet . . .

And naked.

She stopped short, staring at him.

God*damn,* he had a nice body. Well-toned muscle carved his skin, his arms both covered with tattoo sleeves. His stomach was perfectly chiseled, a trail of dark hair dipping to a deep-V that led—

He turned toward her, then gave a start. "Holy fuck!" He grabbed the edge of the hot tub, tumbling out of it with a yelp.

As he fell to the deck, Maddie took an involuntary step toward him, then stopped again. She turned in an embarrassed circle as he stood, fig-leafing himself with his hand. He yanked an earbud out. "What the fuck are you doing here?"

"Why the hell are you naked?"

"Because I don't have a bathing suit and thought I was alone. Why the hell are you so early?"

A flush heated Maddie's cheeks. "I'm sorry. You didn't answer the door and—" She turned away. "I'm sorry."

She could feel his stare—man, was he angry.

"Will you toss me my towel? It's on the bench beside you."

Maddie grabbed the gray-striped towel beside her, then flung it toward him.

It landed in the hot tub with a splash.

"Nice shot," Brooks said wryly, a hint of red on his throat. Probably from the hot water. He fished the soaking towel out, and it landed against the deck with a slap.

"I can go get you another towel," she offered, looking down.

"No, I'll get it myself. And get dressed." He turned and left her there, not bothering to cover his naked ass.

Man, he has a nice ass. For a guy.

She could practically imagine the hardness of that muscular behind, how it would feel to rake her fingers against his hips, and—

What the hell am I doing?

She moistened her lips, a fresh wave of embarrassment creeping through her. Had she really just been fantasizing about him?

If she was honest, though, it wasn't the first time the man had been involved in her fantasies. Maybe she hadn't imagined *him*, but she'd lain in bed before, listening to that silky voice, lowering her hand between her legs, and . . .

Her core turned to liquid at the distant memory.

Okay, enough. Get ahold of yourself, you idiot.

This was Brooks the Asshole. Not some fantasy man who'd play the guitar for her.

She curled her arms around her waist.

Josh had once written a song for her. *"This is for you, beautiful. And someday, I'm going to record it and have it played for our first dance as husband and wife."*

A stab went through her heart.

She sat on the bench, turning away from the house and looking out over the lake. Swiping a tear from the corner of her eye, she sighed. Did Josh still play that song? Would he sing it for Gina, too?

Here at the lake, she'd always found a sense of solace. That was the nice thing about Brandywood. If you wanted company, you could always find someone to share a conversation in town. If you wanted to be alone with your thoughts, there were a ton of beautiful, serene spots to let your soul be at ease.

A heron dove over the sparkling water and flapped its long wings, gliding smoothly. The first hints of fall were showing on the surrounding trees. Soon, everything would be golden and red and breathtaking.

Brooks cleared his throat from behind her, and she stood. He was on the deck again, this time fully dressed in a pair of jeans and a gray T-shirt. Flip-flops completed the outfit. His hair was dark and wet, revealing a hint of curl at the top. He looked like a different person without the beard but also . . . not.

He looked like Brooks Kent.

The one who had graced the poster in her bedroom.

A dry lump formed in her throat.

"I'm sorry," she said. "I didn't mean to intrude."

"We'll call it even. I caught you in the shower yesterday, and now it's my turn to be caught unaware. Care to come inside?" Brooks gestured toward the house.

She nodded, tempted to keep her hands curled around her stomach. She was so nervous she might throw up.

He held the door open for her, and she went past him into the living room. The place was as immaculate as it had been the evening before, without a trace of anyone having been there. "Are Cormac and your sister out?"

"My sister had to go back home for work. Cormac took my niece to the park so I could talk to you." Brooks went over to the fridge. "Sparkling water?"

Maddie shook her head. "No, thanks." Did that mean Cormac knew about her attempt to blackmail Brooks?

Brooks shut the door and uncapped his water. He ambled over to the couch. "Have a seat."

No way she was about to protest or argue with him when he was being polite, so she went over and took the loveseat across from him, crossing her legs at her ankles. He stared her down, a frankness to his perusal that made her shift with discomfort.

"You've never blackmailed anyone before, have you?" Brooks said it without a hint of irony or amusement.

"Are you saying you don't believe I'll go to the press?" Maddie tilted her head, holding his eye contact. If he didn't believe *that*, then she was screwed. *Act tougher.*

His mouth turned into a slight scowl. "I'm prepared to believe the worst about you, Madison. I haven't gotten to where I am in life by being naive."

Something about the way he said her name made her heartbeat speed up. No one ever called her by her full name—just her nickname. It had always been that way.

Yet the sound of her name on his lips felt oddly . . . *natural.*

Sexy.

Dammit all to hell. *Enough, already.*

He leaned forward, resting his elbows on his knees. "The thing is, I'm not at liberty to commit my band to a concert without talking to the powers that be. I'm not the only person involved, and my band would have to be available. And it's a big ask. I can't exactly explain to them why I want to play at some backwoods town fair when I usually play at international venues."

That wasn't a no, though.

Dare she hope? "I'm sure you could pull the right strings to make it happen."

"Maybe." He sipped his drink. "But it doesn't exactly feel like an even arrangement. You can't guarantee me no one will find out about the wreck. And . . . let's say they did. Let's say you go to the press. You can't prove anything other than that I had a car accident—which *is*, by the way, exactly what happened. Sure, they might spin it, but there's not any evidence that I was anything other than tired."

"There's the fact that you tried to hide it, though, isn't there?" Maddie kept her shoulders thrown back. "That doesn't really sound innocent."

"The only thing I'm guilty of is being famous." His mouth drew to a line. "Why do you want this favor so bad? What's in it for you? You could go to a concert of mine anytime you choose. Hell, I was supposed to play a few hours from here just the other night. You weren't there, and you're not a fan, so why the interest now?"

Would a little honesty hurt?

Maybe. He might think she was weak and stupid.

Then again, their relationship was already fringed with enough lies on the outside. She had even lied to her family for him. Asked others to lie for her.

She twisted a ring on her finger. She didn't have to tell him the *whole* story. Just enough that he would understand the need.

"Until about a week ago, I had River House on the books for the concert. Then they pulled out from the day I'd scheduled them for—which is supposed to be the 'big night' for the fair—and were moved to the day before. I'm in charge of filling the spot for Saturday's musical act now because my family's business is sponsoring the main stage that night."

Brooks furrowed his brow. "River House, the country band?"

"Yeah, the one and the same." Her posture relaxed slightly. He wasn't being aggressive at all. If anything, he seemed genuinely curious.

"They suck." Brooks rubbed the bandage on his left hand that he still wore from the day before. "You should consider yourself lucky they pulled out."

"But they didn't entirely pull out. They moved to Friday. And now I'll be lucky if I can find a local band to take that slot."

"So?" He crossed his arms. "What's the big deal? It's just a town fair."

"The town fair *is* a big deal. We might be a small town, Mr. Kent, but that doesn't mean we don't excel at what we do. I'm not kidding when I tell you we draw a sizable crowd, especially after my grandfather put Brandywood on the map in Maryland a few years ago."

"You can call me Brooks, you know."

"Can I?" Her eyes narrowed. "We never went through the formalities."

Something roguish danced in his eyes. "I suppose we skipped to the part where I nearly saw you naked, I wrecked your store, you cut me with broken glass, blackmailed me, and then definitely saw me naked."

"Don't forget I tended to your wounds."

He smirked. "We should sell our story to River House. They'd make a terrible bro-country song about it."

Our story. Her diaphragm dropped. He had a way of disarming her that was unexpected. Just like the day before, when she should have been angrier at him. Yet he'd talked her into calling three people to cover his tracks, asking them to lie, then lied to her own family and concealed the evidence of his crash.

Come to think of it, how did he get me to do all that?

He seemed to sense the tension dissolving between them and stiffened. "Like I said, I can't make any guarantees. Which means I can't sign your contract."

She shrugged and stood. "Fine. Then I'll go to the press."

His fingers curled around the neck of the bottle. "But then neither of us gets what we want, Madison."

She stepped toward him. "At least if it's public, I'll have more of a guarantee that you'll actually pay for the damages you inflicted on my business."

"If it's about trust, I should warn you that this stunt you're pulling is doing the opposite of building trust between us." Brooks set his bottle down on the coffee table and stood. He was several inches taller than her—had to be over six feet—and she had to raise her chin to look him in the eyes.

"Admit it, sweetheart, you need me. River House might suck, but you're right—you've got no chance of booking a bigger band than them in a month. Not for some country fair in Appalachia. And maybe I'm not so dishonest that I won't pay for the damages to your store, but I sure as hell can take my time doling that money out to you, given your bad behavior."

"My bad behavior?" She spat a laugh out. "What are you going to do, put me in time-out? Give me a good spanking?"

Oh God, did I just say that out loud?

"Don't tempt me," he said, taking a step toward her.

That intense look in his eyes from the night before returned, and this time, it burned right through her chest. "Don't throw your weight around with me, Brooks. I may not have many cards to play, but I will play that ace all day if I have to. Either you sign the contract or I walk."

He edged closer still, using every inch of his body and posture to bear down on her, intimidating, raw . . . *masculine* energy.

And dammit if her body didn't seem to betray her when he was this close to her. Her panties were fucking wet.

Damn him.

He scanned her gaze, his gray eyes fierce in their scrutiny. "I'll sign the contract under one condition."

Her mouth grew dry as he focused his attention on her lips. "And what would that be?"

"Ten hours of your time this week, whenever I want, no questions asked."

Huh?

Her brows drew together.

What on earth did he mean by that?

"What for?" She swallowed hard.

"I haven't decided yet. Don't worry, I won't ask for anything illegal. But something about you intrigues me. Most women, hell, most people, are more afraid of me than you are. You've got guts. I might find a use for you. Deal?" He held out his hand.

She hesitated. "The fact that people are afraid of you doesn't make me feel better."

Ten hours to be at Brooks Kent's beck and call for god-knows-what?

A wicked gleam lit his expression. "Are you still worried I

want to spank you? This isn't one of those types of deals. There are no safe words with me."

"I'm not going to sleep with you." She stared at his hand.

"That was never on the table." He continued to hold his hand out. "I won't make you an offer again."

Her mind raced. She hadn't expected him to turn the tables on her like this. "But you said you can't guarantee your band will be there."

"You let me worry about that. Five seconds or no deal, Madison."

"Wait, but—"

"Five . . . four . . ."

Shit. He wasn't even letting her think about this.

What's the worst thing he could ask me to do? She knew nothing about him, after all.

". . . two . . . one."

She thrust her hand into his. His fingers enclosed around hers, a sizzle of electric current seeming to leap through his touch. A smirk played on his lips. "Good girl."

"You're a real ass, you know that?"

"I'd be offended if you thought otherwise. You know how long it's taken me to spread that rumor?" He released his grip. "You can go. I'll call you when I figure out what I need you for."

She drew her hand back, suddenly drained of all confidence.

Did I just make a deal with the devil? Something I now doubt I'll win?

12

BROOKS

Audrey's cry pierced the silence of the night.

Brooks sat in his bed, listening. After a long wail sounded, Brooks tossed his sheets to the side and hustled to the room beside his. Audrey had insisted he lie down with her to fall asleep, but he'd left once she was solidly out.

Now she was awake and sitting up in the bed, crying.

Brooks flipped on the light on the bedside table, and she covered her eyes and tear-streaked cheeks. "What happened?" he asked, sitting on the edge of her bed.

Damn. His heart pounded in his chest.

"You left," Audrey wailed, throwing herself into his arms.

Brooks gathered her into his arms and kissed the top of her head, holding her close. Lying back against the pillows, he reached over and flipped the light back out again, then rubbed her back.

She was so much like Kayla it wasn't funny.

Mom had started leaving Kayla alone with him at the house when he was eight and Kayla was just one. North Carolina didn't have a legal age for babysitting, and Mom needed all the help she could get. So it was Brooks's bed that Kayla slept in more often than not. He'd learned to change diapers, make formula—all of it—while most other kids his age were playing outside or on their gaming systems.

Sports weren't an option, mostly because Mom had no extra money to spend on registration. She needed him home anyway. So he'd found a hobby in his dad's old guitar and library books on how to play.

Kayla had loved to hear him play.

When she had nightmares, it was the one thing that calmed her down more than anything else.

But that was then, when playing the guitar was something he shared just with Kayla. She was his only audience, the only one who listened. Kayla's rapt attention made him want to play better, sing better, and eventually, write songs.

Now that he'd played for more people than he could ever count, he rarely picked up the guitar if he didn't have to. *When did I stop loving what I do?*

When Audrey's sniffling and breathing deepened again, Brooks peeled her away and stood. He started back to his room, but what was the point? Insomnia had plagued him for years, so he wouldn't be able to sleep now.

He headed out to the back deck. Cormac had been out there when he'd gone to bed, hanging out by the firepit. Maybe he was still there.

The seat Cormac had occupied was empty, though, and the last log on the fire had nearly burned through. Brooks found a small pile of wood near the pit and threw on another log, then settled into the chair.

The night air chilled his skin through his shirt and pajama pants. He should have grabbed a sweatshirt on his way out the door. Still, he let the cold seep in, leaning his head against the tall back of the chair. This sort of thing was what he'd come here for, after all. Peace and quiet. Time away.

He just hadn't known when he'd agreed to come out here with Cormac how much peace and quiet he'd need.

His problems continued to grow, and he wasn't sure how to stop the rolling snowball from becoming an avalanche. First, the legal issues with Mike, and the subsequent fallout with the label. Then the car crash.

. . . and now Madison Yardley.

He had to give it to her. She'd taken her shot and practically *swished* with victory.

And maybe he could have told her no. Maybe he *should have* told her no. What was one more scandal in the tabloids at this point?

Except he was so damn tired.

He'd spent years thinking that if he ignored what they printed about him, he could walk away from it, and it wouldn't make a difference. In some ways, he enjoyed the reputation. The more people thought of him as a temperamental jerk, the less likely they were to mess with him.

Most of the whispers didn't really bother him—though the stuff about Paulette had infuriated him. He'd considered legal action that time, but Darren had convinced him a drawn-out court case of he-said-she-said would only do more harm than good.

Maybe he should have dumped Darren a long time ago.

He sighed, letting his gaze wander over the stars above the treetops.

For whatever reason, he couldn't get Madison's expression out of his mind as she'd repeated back to him the stuff about Paulette.

He shouldn't care what she thought. She was a stranger . . . no one to him.

Yet the words had bothered him to his core.

He took out his phone and dialed Maddie before he could overthink it.

"What?" She didn't sound amused to hear from him.

He smiled, cradling the phone against his ear. "Is that any way to say hello?"

"Sorry, majesty. I just can't seem to remember my manners around you." She yawned. "You do realize it's almost midnight?"

The log he'd thrown on the fire caught at last, and a bright burst of flame and warmth radiated from it. "Weren't you the woman who was taking a shower at four in the morning the other day?"

"How do you know that's not when I get up every morning?"

I just know. He could picture her as the type of person who stayed in bed as long as she could. But picturing her in bed wasn't the best idea either. He hardened at the mental image, those tanned legs bare against soft sheets . . .

"Brooks?"

"What?" *Shut that image down.* It had been too long since he'd had sex, clearly. One semi-nude encounter with a beautiful woman, and he was suddenly horny as fuck.

"I said maybe I get up at four every morning."

"I don't buy it."

"You know what? It doesn't matter. What the hell do you want? I'm going to bed eventually here."

"How is it you can receive my call with your shitty service, by the way? Are you not home?"

He could practically hear her smirk.

"My, my, someone's a little nosy tonight. There's this thing called Wi-Fi calling. You really should think about adopting twenty-first-century technology, old man."

Right. He should know that.

Why am I calling her? The whole idea seemed ill-conceived. Foolish.

Yet outside of Cormac, he didn't know anyone else around here.

"I was hungry. You know of any good places for takeout around here?"

"At midnight?" She laughed. "My grandfather's pub is still open. I might get the kitchen to make something for you, but how will you pick it up?"

"You can bring it to me." He leaned into his chair with a self-satisfied smile.

"I'm not your errand girl." Her voice was flat.

"You are now. You can deduct it from the time you owe me."

Maddie groaned. "You're the worst, you know that? Fine. What do you want?"

"Surprise me. I'm on the back deck . . . not naked this time."

"Good. I think I'm still half blind. Be there in like a half hour."

He hung up with a smile on his lips. Had he really just called her and demanded she bring him food? He wasn't even that hungry.

But there was something inherently thrilling about having her at his disposal.

True to her word, Maddie pulled up about a half hour later and climbed onto the back deck, a paper bag in hand, scowl on her face. "I brought you a pit beef sandwich and fries. The kitchen was closing. Also, Travis told me to tell you that you should come by his shop tomorrow. He wants to discuss the car repair with you." She thrust the bag into his lap. "Good night."

He hid a smile. She wore leggings and a white crop top, a zip-up fleece hastily thrown on top of that. Despite the casualness of her outfit—it was a far cry from that breezy skirt she'd worn over here today—she looked cute.

And she's already leaving.

"What's pit beef?"

"It's a Maryland thing. It's good. Like a roast beef sandwich, but way better." She kept walking without looking back.

"How much do I owe you?"

"On the house. I got it for free." She was already approaching the stairs.

"Care to join me?" he asked, gesturing to the other empty chair beside the firepit.

"Are you serious right now?" She glared at him. "Some of us have businesses to run. Lives to live. We're not all on vacation this week." She turned to go down the stairs.

A strange, desperate feeling floated through him. "I just wanted you to know . . . about Paulette. It's not true."

She froze in place. Slowly, she glanced his way over her shoulder. "It's not any of my business."

Brooks stared at her figure in the moonlight. Why did it matter to him that she know the truth? She didn't care, and he shouldn't either.

But he pressed on. "You asked me about it, and it makes a difference. I have never, not ever, lifted my hand to a woman. I never will, either. I never slapped Paulette."

She turned toward him with a frown. "Then why would she say that?"

Why indeed? He'd wondered so many times.

He reached into the paper bag and pulled out a foil-wrapped sandwich that smelled heavenly. The chef made beef bourguignon for dinner, and while it was delicious, Brooks spent so much time trying to convince Audrey to eat her food that his own plate had gone cold while he played airplane with her fork.

"Dating in Hollywood or as a celebrity is hard. My manager thought it would look good for me to find someone to settle down with, so he set me up with a celebrity matchmaker. She paired me with a few different women and eventually Paulette."

Evidently curious, Maddie came back over and sat. "There are celebrity matchmakers?"

He chuckled. "Sure are. And they make a small fortune for their lovely service." He took a bite, nearly groaning. *God, this is good.* Maybe he had been hungrier than he thought.

"Anyway, Paulette really wanted things to work. She'd just broken up with a movie star who had cheated on her, and she wanted him to see how happily she'd moved on. She leaked our 'relationship' to every outlet she knew. When I realized things between us were going nowhere fast, I told her I was done, and she was infuriated. She didn't want to be broken up with publicly again after what she'd gone through, so she asked me if she could tell the media that she'd dumped me. I just didn't know she'd get so carried away with her story."

Maddie stared at him, unblinking. "Wait. So let me get this straight. You *let* her tell the press that you'd slapped her?"

He took another bite, thinking about his answer. "I didn't like it. Actually, I hated it. I asked her to change her story, but she refused. Anyway, the damage was done. I just never spoke to her again."

He'd also only told a handful of people the truth about it. Most people just assumed it was true, and his casual friends didn't ask. *Moments like those are when I've felt the loneliest. What sort of creep do those so-called friends think I am?*

"That's . . . terrible. Like super shitty of her to do." Maddie leaned closer to the firepit. "Why did you let her get away with something that damaged your reputation so much?"

"People look at me and see what they want to see." Brooks

shrugged. "Apparently, I look like an abusive ass who'd hit a woman. No one really seemed to think it was out of character for me."

"I doubt that. You have to have dated women who could speak up in your defense."

"Like I said, dating as a celebrity is hard." He dug around the container for some fries. "Sure, I could hook up with women after every concert if I wanted—and believe me, I did my fair share of that when I was young and stupid. But those weren't relationships. They were one-night stands."

"What about before then? Don't you have a high school or college sweetheart who could sing your praises?"

The hoot of an owl from the woods beside them made him look away, his gaze piercing the dark. He didn't need to tell her what his life had been like back then, but he was in a sharing mood for some reason. "I didn't have time to date in high school or college. My mom died in a car accident when I was eighteen. Kayla was only eleven, so I became her guardian."

Her eyes widened. "I'm sor—"

"Don't be. Everyone always says that, but it's sort of meaningless." That phrase had always bothered him. *"Sorry for your loss." No, you're not. You just want to fill the awkward silence.* "The point is, I don't think anyone will step forward as a character witness anytime soon. Anyway, people have spread worse lies about me."

She stared him down, then scooted her chair closer, plucked a fry out of the container, and ate it. "You're crazy. If someone had said something like that about me, I would have been shouting from the mountains about what a liar they were."

"So you believe me?" He raised a brow. She'd been surprisingly easy to convince.

She took another fry. "I guess I do."

"That's not too persuasive." *And why does it make me nervous that she might not?*

"I mean, I do." She chewed slowly. "I don't know why." She was quiet, then picked up the bag. "Didn't they give you any ketchup?" The lid to a small container of ketchup popped, then she plopped it on the arm of his chair.

"I didn't know we were sharing food now."

"You have no idea how many fries I already stole out of that bag on my drive over here."

He threw back his head with a laugh. "Why can I picture you doing that?"

She smiled mischievously. "At least I'm honest with you. We'll both go to hell lying to everyone else, but you and me? We're in it together now."

"Trust me, you don't want to be seen in public having anything to do with me. Everyone you know—and don't know—will assume the worst." He handed her another fry.

"God, you're negative. Do you only see the awfulness in people?"

"No. There are a couple of people I like."

She rolled her eyes. "Your sister and niece don't count."

"Of course they count. They're the only ones who count, as far as I'm concerned."

Maddie shook her head. "I don't know if that makes you a psycho or surprisingly human and sweet."

He finished the sandwich and crumpled the wrapper in his hand. "You're safer believing the first. I've been called a lot of things, but sweet isn't one of them. Not sure human is either."

She pursed her lips. "You know, for someone whose songs have sometimes brought me to tears, you're surprisingly closed off to emotion."

He grinned, oddly pleased with the backhanded compliment. Maddie had gone out of her way to tell him she didn't listen to his music. "I thought you weren't a fan."

"That's what you got out of what I said?" She took another fry and dipped it in the ketchup. "So what are you, like this tortured soul who can only do feelings when he sings? Is that where you get your outlet?"

"Maybe." He was growing alarmingly comfortable around this woman, something that rarely happened. But she was forward in a way he wasn't used to.

Not forward. *Earnest.*

He almost chided himself. The woman who blackmailed him . . . earnest? Maybe he was getting dumber the older he got. Still . . . "I don't sing that much anymore when I'm not actively doing something for the label. I barely even write my own songs these days. Honestly, I can't remember when I took out my guitar for an outlet . . . or for fun."

"That's . . . sad, Brooks."

"Eh. I'm over it. The whole songwriting thing. You can only write so many songs about being empty inside. People want love songs."

Her lips parted with surprise.

Time to change the subject.

He didn't like where this was headed.

No more.

He held out the remaining container of fries to her. "What about you? What's your story? Just a small-town girl who got stuck running her family's business?"

She froze for a minute, then licked the salt from her fingers. The action sent an unexpected shiver through him.

"I'm not *just* a small-town girl, thanks. But do I want to stay here? Yeah, I do. My family's here. They mean everything to me. Plus, Brandywood is a pretty great place to live."

"You never get the urge to see other things? To me, living in the same place your whole life would get old quick. Dealing with the same people's idiosyncrasies."

"Fancy word." She wiped her hands on her thighs. "I've traveled. And I plan to do a whole lot more of it. And, sure, there can be a negative side to living in a place where everyone knows who you are *and* your business. You'd die here. You think as a celebrity you lack privacy? That's nothing. The rumor mill here works even when people are sleeping. The morning you crashed into the store, my grandfather got a call about the window from at least five different people before seven o'clock."

"You're totally selling the whole experience here," Brooks remarked dryly. He glanced over his shoulder. "I need something to drink. You want something to swallow those fries down with?"

"If I didn't know any better, I'd say you were lonely and called me for company, not food." Her eyes bored into his.

He was tempted to kiss the smirk off those full lips, but if he was honest, her words also hit close to home. He'd lowered his armor a bit too much for comfort, and she was looking at him like she knew him now. "You got me. Who needs friends in high places when I've got enemies who blackmail me? You want a drink or not?" He stood and stretched.

She chewed on her lower lip, then gave a nonchalant shrug. "Whatever. You're the one who's on the clock." She checked her phone. "As far as I can tell, I owe you only nine hours and ten minutes now."

Right. This is a business arrangement.

The reality check was all he needed.

She's just another person who wants whatever she can get from me.

"Don't worry about it, then." The desire to play his own card and shift the power dynamic came hurtling back to him.

"Why don't you come back tomorrow afternoon? Say four o'clock?" He started the walk back toward the house.

"I have to work."

He glanced over his shoulder to find her standing there, hands on her hips.

"Not my problem." Then he went inside, leaving her alone on the deck.

She might be gorgeous, but I'm right to keep my distance. Unfortunately.

13

MADDIE

Naomi was in the back of the Depot getting a bag of flour to make waffle cones when Maddie found her. "Hey, got a minute?" Maddie asked, unexpectedly nervous.

It wasn't like Naomi was her boss. When Pops had first pitched the idea of the Depot to them, they'd agreed that they would run it like co-owners. Maddie had gone to school for marketing, so it fell to her to do more of the administrative and marketing parts of the business while Naomi did more of the day-to-day operations.

But since Naomi was her older sister, there was always that feeling there that, somehow, Naomi was in charge.

"Sure." Naomi set the flour down, then brushed her hands on her apron. "What's up?"

"I need to take off this afternoon." Maddie crossed her arms. "It's for the business."

Naomi gave her a curious look. "You know you don't have to ask me about that."

A guilty feeling went through her. "I just wanted to let you know."

Naomi smiled as she tied her light blond hair back with an elastic hairband. "As long as you've got Lars covering you, I'm good. But thanks for telling me."

Maddie nodded, then moved to go back to the front.

"Out of curiosity, where are you heading?"

The part of her that wanted to tell Naomi all about Brooks burned a hole through her gut. Naomi was her best friend. She was only a year older than Maddie and closer in age to her than Lindsay, so they'd always done everything together, including the Depot.

Not breathing a word about Brooks was killing her.

Especially after he was acting so human last night.

So nice, really.

Until she'd killed it by calling him sad and lonely and pointing out she was only there per their arrangement.

She'd long had a habit of not knowing when to shut up, and it had bitten her in the ass last night. Clearly, Brooks was lonely —why else would he call her up randomly like that?

Maybe as a flex.

But, no, he'd opened up. Told her personal things she got the feeling he didn't share often.

Naomi must have read the tension on her face because her brows furrowed, and she stepped closer to Maddie. "Everything okay?"

"Yeah, I'm fine. Just tired. Overwhelmed. Trying to find someone to play for the town fair. I think I'm close, but I just have a little extra work to do to make sure it happens." That was practically the truth.

"I still want to punch Josh in the face for doing what he did. Did you hear he and Gina registered as a team for the Applepalooza this weekend? They're signed up for every event."

Maddie groaned. She'd nearly forgotten that was this weekend. Brandywood loved its fall events, and Applepalooza was one of the bigger ones besides the fair.

Her stomach clenched when she remembered that she and Josh had signed up a month ago for everything. He must have crossed out their names from the sign-up board in the middle of the town square.

"Guess I won't be going," she said with a nonchalant shrug. Well, as much as she could muster.

"Don't do that. Don't let him push you out of things you've always loved doing. Just find someone else to partner up with. There's no way he's going to win things anyway. Pops and Bunny, or Jen and Jason will win the apple pie contest again. That's a given. And I think Pops has a good chance at cutest couple again, too."

Maddie sighed. "Who am I going to sign up with? Jake? Logan?" She gave Naomi a tired smile. "Brandywood's contests don't favor the single."

Naomi shrugged. "It doesn't have to be someone you're dating. You could ask one of your girlfriends, too. Maybe Amanda?"

"Nah, she doesn't like to compete against Jason in anything." Maddie wrinkled her nose. She'd become good friends with Jason Cavanaugh's ex-wife a few years ago through a book club they were both in. She had to hand it to Amanda—she and Jason did an amazing job co-parenting their son together. But Maddie was certain that part of the reason it worked so well was that Amanda did her best to avoid any situation that could be tricky, like a competition.

"Well, do some of the solo events. Like the singing competition. You usually do pretty well in that one."

"Maybe." The thought of seeing Josh gave her anxiety. But she could at least *sing* better than Gina, right? Josh had told her he loved her singing, and their shared love of music brought them together.

Maybe if Josh hears you singing, you can at least show him what he walked out on.

She drew in a breath and shrugged. "We'll see. Anyway, I better get moving. Let me know if you need anything at all."

Naomi smiled. "Yeah, yeah. Go. I'm not your boss."

Maddie removed her apron and hung it on a locker. She didn't have time to change before heading out to Brooks's place.

Hopefully, he'll be dressed when I get there this time.

She hurried to the back employee parking lot and got in her car. Taking out her phone, she looked for a playlist to download for the drive before she left the comfort of Wi-Fi, then paused, her thumb hovering over the search bar.

Brooks's face, those soulful eyes, flashed in her mind.

"Wildfire" was her favorite of his songs. She typed it in.

The cover art, featuring a younger version of Brooks, filled her phone screen, and her heart lurched.

The man really was hot.

Hot. Rich. *Yet miserable.*

Turns out money and fame couldn't buy friendship.

The sound of a piano filled her car as she drove. She knew he played that instrument in addition to the guitar—was this him playing, too?

As his deep voice started on the first verse, she slid deeper into her seat, relaxing back. Whoever he was now, young Brooks had been soulful. She'd cried to this song more than once. Maybe even made love to it—a slightly awkward thought.

". . . love is the flood she drowned in . . . washing me away. Taking all my feeling, until I couldn't stay. You want me to give, but there's nothing left . . . lost in the water . . . and molded by the flame . . ."

The words were sad. Haunting.

Like he'd written them from something deeply personal.

MAYBE LISTENING to his songs would give her a better insight into who he *really* was.

She gripped the steering wheel harder.

"What difference does it make?" She flicked her gaze at the rearview mirror. Brooks was here for the week, but then he'd leave, and she'd never see him again.

Except, hopefully, for the concert.

That he'd asked her to come out to his place again today was only because he wanted to waste her time like he'd done last night. Because he could. Not because he really wanted her around.

She shut the music off and drove in silence instead.

When she pulled up to the lake house fifteen minutes later, she was in an irrationally bad mood and feeling feisty. She slammed the car door, then practically stomped her way up to the front door. As she got closer, she heard a deep male voice call, "Come on in."

"You'd better not be naked aga—"

Maddie tumbled into the doorway and stopped short. Cormac stood a few feet away from the door, Audrey beside him. Heat flooded Maddie's face. "I mean—"

Cormac raised a brow at Maddie.

"You were naked?" Audrey stared at Cormac with big eyes.

Brooks rounded the corner, his face expressionless. "Audrey, you remember Miss Maddie, right? Why don't we go grab a popsicle?" He grabbed his niece by the shoulders and guided her away, leaving Cormac and Maddie alone in the foyer.

Maddie pushed her hair behind her ears. "It's not what it sounds like," she blurted.

A smile played on Cormac's lips. "It's none of my business. What you and Brooks do is between you and Brooks."

"Cormac, seriously." She crossed her arms.

"Listen, it's cool. He's a good guy. I got the feeling after Sunday that you running into me at the butcher wasn't entirely accidental. But I had the chance to catch up with Logan, and that was great."

Brooks . . . *a good guy?*

She stepped closer. "Whatever it is you think you know, just imagine something else. And for God's sake, don't say anything to anyone about me being here. Especially not to someone in your family or my family."

Cormac laughed. "How about I promise not to imagine anything at all? The not saying anything goes without saying. Brooks is weird about his privacy, not that I can fault him for it. I already swore I wouldn't tell anyone he was here."

She set her hands on her hips. "Then why did you invite Logan and me back the other night?"

Cormac offered her a wide smile. "First, honey, you invited yourself. And second, because I trust the Yardley clan. I didn't think Brooks would mind so long as you all were cool about keeping it to yourselves."

She cringed. Had she really invited herself on Sunday?

Maybe I did. And Cormac is too nice to tell me no.

"Isn't your family wondering who you're hanging out with this week?"

Cormac shrugged. "They know better than to bug me. Mom is afraid I won't visit if they try to dig into my business too much."

"Must be that stoic Irish side. My family would be like bloodhounds during a hunt."

Footsteps approached again, and Audrey came running

back with a red popsicle. Brooks was a few steps behind her. "Cormac, can we go to the playground now?"

"We should probably eat that in the kitchen, Audrey," Brooks said with a worried glance at the rug near the door.

"Actually, I think Miss Maddie is going to take you today. I promised my dad I'd go to a family dinner tonight." He winked at Audrey, then ruffled her hair. "Don't worry, I'll be back tonight. Probably past your bedtime, though."

Wait, what? Brooks was putting her on babysitting duty? Why? Because she was a woman? Ire spilled through her.

Cormac pulled a key fob from his pocket and winked at Maddie. "Have fun."

An awkward silence descended between Maddie and Brooks when Cormac shut the door behind him. Maddie tapped her foot, trying to figure out how to tell him to screw himself, when Audrey gave her a hopeful smile. "Can you take me to the playground with the big slide?"

"Um . . . maybe?" Maddie grinned at her, then set her hands on her knees and leaned down toward her. "Why don't you go back to the kitchen to finish the popsicle while your uncle Brooks and I talk?"

Audrey hurried off, her curls bouncing as she ran.

Maddie straightened and glared at Brooks. "I'm not babysitting, Brooks. I don't want to be responsible for a whole child who doesn't know me."

He gave her a mocking smile. "How about a half a child? I hear they're so much easier."

"Shut up. I'm serious."

"I believe our arrangement was no questions asked." He crossed his muscular arms, and she tried to ignore how good his forearms looked when he did that.

She sighed. "Yes, but I have an aversion to being put in a

position of responsibility to children I'm not related to. Why can't you and your sister take her?"

"Kayla's back home. She had to go in to work yesterday, so I'm watching Audrey for the week."

He was taking care of his niece for an entire week? Somehow, she didn't picture Brooks as the child-friendly type. Still, she didn't want to get off-topic with that. "But why don't you take her to the park, then?"

"I wasn't planning on sending you off on your own with her. But since my car is in the shop and you know where the playgrounds are, consider yourself my guide. Also, I want to go by that mechanic's. He told me he closes at five, so I want to get there as close to closing as possible."

She gawked at him. *His guide?* "Haven't you ever heard of rental car companies and GPS?"

"Nope, never." He smiled with perfectly white teeth. "But I have heard of a certain woman who owes me nine hours and ten minutes of her time."

She stepped closer, pointing her finger at his chest, right in the center. "Eight hours and twenty minutes. I'm charging you driving time."

His eyes narrowed. "Maybe you should keep a log."

"Why, you don't trust me?" God, he was so close that she could smell his aftershave. Tempted to inhale deeply, breathe in the masculine scent radiating from his skin, she held her ground and set her shoulders back.

"Nope."

Maybe it was just her, but a current of electricity seemed to pulse between them, charging the atmosphere. *Maddening prick.*

Those sexy forearms were too close to ignore now. What would it be like to run her fingers against them, feel the soft dark hair, the tightly corded muscle underneath? Her gaze traveled to his throat, where she swore she could see his pulse beating as hard as her own heart sounded in her ears.

"We go now?" Audrey seemed to materialize beside them. Telltale red stained her lips, but how in the hell had she eaten the whole popsicle that fast?

Maddie stepped back. "Yup." She took a step forward, then stopped. "Shoot, though. I don't have a car seat."

"Dammit." Brooks swore in a low voice. "Kayla put it in Cormac's car."

"Why don't we just call him? Ask him to bring it back here?"

"I'll try." Brooks slid his phone out of his pocket, then dialed.

He has surprisingly long lashes. She looked away. Any admiration—physical or not—on her part was foolish.

A moment later, Brooks shook his head and hung up. "Voicemail. I'll shoot him a text in the meantime."

"Can we gooooo?" Audrey asked, clearly not understanding the situation.

"Is there anywhere close by that sells car seats?" Brooks asked.

"Yeah, there's a Walmart about twenty minutes away. But I'm not taking her there without a seat."

"I wasn't asking you to. Kayla would kill me. Hell, I'd be mad at me." Brooks pulled out his wallet and held out a credit card. "Could you go buy one for me and then come pick us up?"

She took the credit card from him, her palm slick. Why did this make her feel so nervous? "I really *am* your errand girl, aren't I? Which one do you want?"

"Hang on, I'll check the safety ratings on the ones they have in stock." Brooks was on his phone again in an instant. He flicked his gaze over the edge at her. "Make yourself at home in the meantime."

Safety ratings? Who the hell even are you, Brooks Kent?

And why was it ridiculously endearing?

Audrey watched Maddie with a frown. "Can I have mac and cheese?"

"From the store or from your fridge?" Maddie asked.

"Store. I don't have any mac and cheese," Brooks answered tonelessly without looking up.

"And hot dogs!" Audrey gave an exaggerated smile, then swiped her red mouth.

Maddie glanced at Brooks. "You want me to pick those up too?"

"You don't need to. I have a chef coming at . . ." He nodded. "Yeah, all right. She'd probably prefer that to whatever the chef is making tonight."

Maddie reached into her purse and took out a tissue, then held it out to Brooks. "You might want to use this on Audrey. Text me a list, and I'll grab what you need while I'm out."

His look was hesitant, and when his fingers brushed hers as he took the tissue, goosebumps rose on her skin. "All right." His hand didn't move, though. "Thank you, Madison."

He has to stop calling me that.

She nodded wordlessly, then stepped back. "Just let me know. Whatever you need." And before she could overthink anything else, she fled back to the safety offered with each footstep she took away from Brooks Kent.

Eight hours. I can make it to eight hours.

What Maddie couldn't work out was why she had to do this in the first place when *he* was the one who crashed into her store . . .

14

BROOKS

"I THINK SHE'S OUT," Brooks said as he rejoined Maddie in the kitchen. She was putting the last of the dishes in the dishwasher despite him having told her many times that she didn't have to clean up.

But she'd apparently done it anyway while he'd put Audrey to sleep.

By the time Maddie had returned from the store with a car seat and the two of them had installed the damn thing, Audrey had complained about being hungry. So instead of going out to the playground, they'd made her mac and cheese and hot dogs.

Maddie and Brooks had eaten the cedar-grilled salmon and mushroom risotto the chef had prepared while Audrey played with a bubble maker Maddie had surprised her with. After dinner, they'd made s'mores—another Maddie surprise.

Audrey had chased bugs on the lawn while the sun had set, then Brooks had taken her in for bedtime, which had been quick, considering it was late, and she'd played outside so much. *And loved every second.*

For that matter, Brooks had enjoyed it, too. And Maddie's company.

A little too much.

Maddie glanced up from the dishwasher and shut it. "I'm not surprised she fell asleep fast. She's four, right? I think my four-year-old niece is ready for bedtime by like seven."

"No wonder you're so good with her."

She shrugged. "I have practice, but honestly, I don't really think of myself as great with kids. It doesn't come naturally to me."

"What does come naturally to you?" Brooks asked, genuinely curious. Because she seemed to interact with Audrey effortlessly.

She stretched, the barest hint of her midriff showing, a slip of her tanned, flat belly. He tore his gaze away. "I don't know. I'm not really sure I'm *great* at anything. My family thinks I'm good at running the business, but it's not hard, either. Anyway, marketing and admin are boring. Numbers are boring. Optimizing is stab-me-in-the-eyeballs-with-forks boring. But it's what I signed up for, so I guess that's on me."

She set her hands on the counter and leaned forward. "And now I'm being boring. Sorry. I don't know why I told you all that. I talk too much."

He could tell. And it was . . . *cute.*

No, you fuckwit.

But he couldn't seem to help it.

She was smart. Pretty. Natural.

Effortlessly good at things.

Humble. Which is both rare and refreshing.

Anything but boring.

And you're lonely and tired.

Brooks leaned against the wall near the entrance to the kitchen, casually hooking his fingertips into his pockets. He couldn't remember the last time he'd been curious about anyone. But the more she talked, the more he wanted to know about her. Which wasn't smart, considering she'd shown she had a dishonest side, too.

"Thanks for doing the dishes. You don't have to stay any longer." He glanced at the clock. This afternoon's debacle had cost him another four hours of her time. Somehow, ten hours didn't seem long enough now.

If he didn't know any better, a flash of disappointment filled her face as she stepped back, lowering her hands to her sides as she nodded. "Yeah. No problem. I'll just get going, then."

"We never got to the mechanic. Think you can come tomorrow at four again?"

She gave him an odd look, then nodded.

Stay.

He bit the edge of his tongue, keeping himself from talking.

He was leaving in a few days.

Loneliness was a bitter drug.

It almost made him believe she *wanted* to be here.

She'd only come because he'd coerced her.

He walked her to the door, his chest tight.

Come on, Brooks.

Don't do it.

Don't be an idiot.

"I think the fire's still going . . . if you wanted to stay."

She tilted her head, the whisper of a smile on her lips. "Are you asking me to hang out with you off the clock?"

"I just didn't want you to feel like I was kicking you out."

Amusement danced in those blue eyes. She dropped her purse by the door, then shrugged. "Okay, Brooks. I'll stay. Off the clock."

"Don't be like that." He crossed his arms, instantly irritated with himself. Why had he gone and opened his mouth? "I don't need your pity, you know."

"Maybe I do pity you. What do you care what I think?" She moved to walk past him.

His hand shot out, settling at her elbow, dragging her to a stop. "Well, I do care. Stupidly. Probably because I'm an arrogant son of a bitch who doesn't entirely love being called pathetic."

Her thumb curved up the inside of his forearm, brushing it with the barest touch. She said nothing, but her eyes locked with his, her chest rising and falling slowly. "You keep contradicting yourself. Either you care about what people think about you or you don't. Which one is it, Brooks?"

Shit. How did she keep digging deeper under the walls he'd spent so long constructing?

When he didn't answer, she dropped her hand. "Thought so. It's not so black and white, is it?" She didn't go toward the outside, though. Instead, she strode toward the game room, where he'd been hanging out with Cormac earlier in the day.

He followed her, intrigued as she ran her fingers over a pool cue, then kept walking. She stopped in front of his guitar case, then dropped to her knees beside it.

"Whoa—hang on." He rushed to her side and squatted. He set his hand over hers. "What are you doing?"

"Taking out your guitar. As your prospective employer, I figure it's probably a good idea for me to hear what you've got." She raised a brow. "Especially if you don't play much anymore."

She'd somehow come back to their conversation the previous night.

Dig, dig, dig.

But piece by piece, he felt the bricks on his walls loosening around her.

He smirked. "Nice try."

"How about you just play a song on the guitar? It used to be your best friend, right? You don't have to sing." She leaned closer. "Or has Brooks Kent lost his spark?"

He glared at her. "You're not as clever as you think you are, Madison."

"And you're not as hard and bad as you think you are, Brooks."

She was too close for comfort.

He had a flashback to an hour earlier when she made s'mores. A tiny bit of marshmallow had clung to her lip. He'd imagined licking it off.

However, nothing could be as sweet and alluring as those lips looked right now.

She was only a few years younger than him.

But she was from a completely different world.

This country, small-town-loving sunshine woman.

God, we couldn't be from more different worlds.

Any closer, though, and he might just have to see for himself what those lips tasted like.

"I should have just let you leave me to quiet while I had a chance," he growled irritably.

"Yet you didn't. Now play. Before you force me to beg."

He grinned wolfishly. "Begging might be interesting."

Stop.

Fucking stop it.

He couldn't keep flirting with her.

The pupils in her eyes widened, and she moistened her lips.

Painful.

Dragging the guitar case closer, he opened it to stop that line of thought. The familiar wooden scent greeted him, and he breathed in deeply because he needed it to slow his erratic heartbeat and because it was the closest thing to the scent of home to him.

Pulling out his guitar, he threw the strap over his shoulder, grabbed the case, and stood, then left the game room without bothering to say a word. She'd follow.

He needed a moment away from her to get his head on straight anyway.

Apparently, so did she because she took a full minute to join him outside on the deck near the firepit.

Even at home near the beach, he couldn't get far away from the lights of the city to see stars like this. The quiet wasn't lonely here, either, even though it should be. Maybe that was because of Cormac and Audrey. *Maddie.* But even when he'd taken his coffee alone out on the deck this morning, he'd relished the way his mind could be blank here, without the cloud of anxious thoughts pressing in.

Nothing was lonelier than feeling alone while surrounded by people, anyway.

The tour had been a whirlwind of cities all over the world, blinding lights, stadiums, crowds of tens of thousands, sweat, and noise. Deafening noise. For months.

Hotel rooms, strangers, foods prepared by different people all the time. Interviews. Celebrities. Flashes of cameras.

All the time.

Here, the simple crackle of a burning log, the hum of tree frogs, cicadas, and crickets were . . . food for his aching soul.

He was quickly falling in love with the spot.

He strummed the guitar, tuning it as he went, watching her out of the corner of his eye as Maddie sat in the Adirondack chair beside him. It still had a blanket on the seat—she'd brought it out for Audrey earlier.

Maddie wrapped the blanket around her shoulders now, then curled her legs onto the seat beside her.

They didn't have to speak. She leaned back and closed her eyes as he continued to strum, not saying a word. The melodies of several of his songs blurred together, a continuum of the notes that had defined the last decade of his life.

But something about sitting here outside by the fire, with just her as company, was . . . oddly freeing. Like he was just a teenager sitting on the carpet of Mom's apartment.

The carpet.

His fingers tumbled over the strings.

He tore himself from the image and focused his gaze on the fire. The memory he'd worked so hard to forget was pressing closer.

The guitar had also been Dad's favorite way of relaxing in the evenings. They'd been too poor to live in a house with a fireplace, but one year, Mom had scrimped and saved and bought one of the standing units with an electric heater that looked like a fireplace so they could have it for Christmas.

"For Santa to come in," she'd said.

His last clear image of his parents together was the three of them sitting in front of that red electric glow while Dad strummed a Christmas tune.

Bloodstains on the carpet.

He sucked in a deep breath, feeling like he'd been punched in the gut.

Maddie opened her eyes, her brow furrowing. "Why'd you stop playing?"

He set the guitar down like it was burning his palms. "That's enough."

"You were really playing bea—"

"I said I'm done," he snapped.

Hurt flashed on her face.

Good. She needs to leave.

She stood, staring down at him. The log of the fire sizzled, sending sparks in the air.

Here, they were surrounded by all the symphony of nature and more beauty than seemed fair, and he'd gone and thought of *that*.

Maddie sat on the arm of his chair unexpectedly, then slipped her hand into his. "Brooks, you're trembling."

Am I?

He hadn't even realized it.

He swallowed hard, pulling his hand from hers. "You should go."

"I know it's not my business—"

"You're right. It's not. Go."

She didn't budge. "You know what I think? I think this tough-as-nails shtick is just an act. You're a softy deep down. Just look at the way you treat Audrey. As though she were your own daughter."

"That's because her father is a piece of shit. And she deserves—" He scowled, his throat feeling tight. "Just go, Madison."

"Why? Because you're going to growl and snap at me like a wounded animal? You've already promised there's no bite to that bark."

He leaned forward, glaring. "How do you know I wasn't lying?"

"I just do. You're not what people say you are."

"Or I'm exactly what people say I am, and you're playing with fire?"

She crossed her arms. "Aren't those the lyrics to 'Wildfire'? Is that what it was? Your anthem? A declaration of what damaged goods you were? Telling everyone to stay the fuck away from you, right?"

He lifted his chin sharply, his breath catching so hard that it sent a piercing pain through his chest.

Never once in all his life had anyone looked at him and seen so much.

He said nothing as she lifted a hand, stroking the curve of his temple with the back of her index finger, then tracing it down his jawline. The gesture was fascinatingly intimate, shivers going through him. As though she was speaking, *"I see you,"* without saying anything at all.

"Audrey deserves better than what Kayla and I got." He closed his eyes, breaking the spellbinding eye contact. "My father committed suicide when I was seven. Two months before Kayla was born," he whispered in a voice he could barely even hear.

He'd never told anyone but his therapist.

Yet he couldn't stop himself from saying, "I was the one who found him lying face down in my parents' bedroom."

Her arms were around him in an instant, and despite his urge to resist her, Brooks pulled her against him instead. He tightened her in his embrace and buried his face against her neck.

"That's horrible, Brooks," she whispered. "I can't even imagine."

"It's why I've never wanted kids. Why I try my best to protect Audrey." He pulled back. "Because parents fuck their kids' lives up all the time—sometimes on purpose but so often by mistake. *Every. Damn. Day.* And I never want to do to anyone what my father did to me."

She leaned away, holding him by the shoulders while she scanned his face. "What your father did wasn't about you. You know that, right, Brooks?"

"Yeah, but that's the point. He had his demons, sure, and probably even got them from his old man. People in town used to gossip about what a piece of shit my grandfather was. But my dad didn't think about stopping the cycle. He just kept it going. He didn't think about Kayla or me at all."

Maddie touched his cheek again, then leaned forward and kissed his forehead. Not the hot, sexy kiss he'd imagined earlier in the evening, but this was much better. *Needed.*

Hell, he might have just torpedoed her desire to be around him at all. If anyone came at him with something so heavy, he'd probably tuck tail and run. Maddie had asked for him to play the guitar. Instead, he'd unloaded on her.

"I'm sorry," he said with a groan and pulled away from her. "This . . . I didn't mean to . . ."

She watched him, patiently waiting for him to continue, her eyes filled with compassion.

He struggled for a breath. "For so long, I just wondered why. Why did he do it? Why couldn't he just . . . *try* a little harder? For the rest of us? One day, I woke up and realized I'd never know the answer. And I've never known how to move forward since."

Maddie took his hands in hers. "Why is a natural question. Trust me, I've asked myself the same question before. I think we all do when we're hurt. But, Brooks, . . . you don't have to know why to heal from what was done to you. You are whole. You're not a half a person because of what happened to you when you were seven. You're still whole. And you're worthy. What haunted your father will only control you so long as you allow it to."

He swallowed hard, his mouth drying.

I see you.

He'd cracked open the deepest, darkest part of his soul, and she hadn't run away.

She'd embraced him.

Who on earth is this beautiful woman?

He cleared his throat, exposed under her gaze. "Sorry. I know you weren't asking for my sob story. Normally, I just shut up and sing instead."

"You still owe me a song. But I'll let it slide for tonight." She smiled sadly, then stood. "Unfortunately, I don't have that many skeletons in my closet to share with you, so I can't even the score."

He appreciated the out she offered him from continuing to discuss his sordid past. She was clearly intuitive, and he needed the respite.

"Let me guess. You have two parents, still married, a large, extended family with lots of kids, and you all get along *and* get together for holidays."

"I can do you one better. My mom still has us all come over for family dinner every Thursday. It's pizza night. She grills pizzas and we all talk late into the night."

"So you're like the Brady bunch without the blended family bit."

"Basically." Rather than leaving as he'd expected her to do—as she probably should do—she sat in the chair she'd occupied before.

"Sounds disgustingly perfect."

Her musical laughter filled the air. "Like I said, I have no reason to leave Brandywood. Everything I could ever want is here."

"Yes, now all you need is your own perfect happy ending, a little farm, some chickens, a couple of kids—"

"Don't forget the handsome man dressed head to toe in flannel—"

"Who'll give you only the best of wood in Brandywood?"

"Oh my, Brooks Kent, you are a rascal!" she exclaimed mockingly, clutching imaginary pearls. She laughed, then rolled her eyes. "Wow, you've just described my nightmare. Do

I look like I'm trying to audition for a Christmas movie romance?"

He smiled. "Maybe. Not sure if the girls on those shows wear crop tops. Get a few more turtlenecks, and then come back to me."

Actually, now that he thought about it, Maddie seemed to have a different side of her. A sexy side that he could see being a bit more . . . *wild.*

That was the thing, though. For as much as she'd been able to pull out of him each time they talked, he barely knew anything about her. Amazingly, she was doing a better job of keeping her cards closer to her chest than he was. No one had ever flipped things on him like this.

"Tell me something about you." He set his hands behind his head, leaning back. "You keep making these conversations one-sided, and I'm going to have to quit having you come over here."

"It is antithetical to your supposed need for privacy."

"Nothing supposed about it. I don't like people knowing my business."

"Hmm . . . I'd argue that you just don't like people knowing *you,* but fine." She played with the fringe on the blanket. "Nothing is interesting about me to share. I'm not shy. Just boring."

"You're anything but boring."

She reclined in her seat. "Yeah? I'm so interesting that you quickly made me your errand girl, right? I'm just good at listening. My grandfather says I get it from him. Secretly, I'm one of his favorites, but that's because we're similar in personality. He likes that one of his grandchildren turned out like him."

Even when asked directly, she still redirected the conversation and talked about someone else. "So what's he like?"

"My grandfather?" Her eyes seemed to sparkle. "He's

perfect. Like honestly. The best man I've ever met. He's like our whole town's grandfather—everyone knows him. A few years back, he had an unexpected brush with fame and ended up with a cable show . . . sort of a home reality show where he talked about his best recipes, daily life, garden tips—you know the type. More people started coming to Brandywood just to see him. So he opened the Depot, and my sister and I run it."

"So he's building a family empire, then?" Not exactly the mom-and-pop shop he'd imagined she was involved in.

"Basically. He started the Depot a couple of years after I graduated from college, and the rest is history."

He grabbed the fire poker and shifted a log. "You know that doesn't tell me anything about you, though. Just your grandfather."

A smile played on her lips. "Speaking of the Depot, I really should get back. I've got a ton of work to catch up on tonight since I spent the afternoon with you. Cormac will probably be back soon, and he won't believe I'm not messing around with you if I'm still hanging around here."

And just like that, he'd chased her away.

"He already thinks that." Brooks quirked a brow.

"I'll have to set him straight, then." She pushed the blanket aside and stood. "Good night, Brooks. Thanks for dinner."

He started to stand, and she held up a hand. "Don't worry about it. I can see myself out the door. I have the past couple of times I've been here, remember?"

She smiled and then left quickly, not giving him a chance to protest.

Just let her go.

She wants to go.

Besides, look what happened when he'd asked her to stay before. She'd just made him reveal more, while she remained a mystery.

Yet that empty chair made the whole backyard feel instantly lonely. *Isn't that how I like it? The solitude?* Perhaps, but something Maddie said came back to him . . . before his emotional diarrhea.

"How about you just play a song on the guitar? It used to be your best friend, right? Or has Brooks Kent lost his spark?"

She wasn't wrong. His guitar used to be his place of solace.

Brooks hesitated, then pulled out his guitar again. Maybe he just needed time with his old friend.

15

MADDIE

Stop thinking about him.

All day long, Maddie had caught herself listening to Brooks's music. And now that four o'clock was rapidly approaching, it was all she could do to keep herself from racing out the door.

Brooks Kent was becoming a problem.

She hadn't intended to have fun playing house with him and his niece.

But it was.

And he'd been so normal. Practically domestic as he grilled hot dogs for Audrey and made mac and cheese on the stove. Put her to bed.

And then he'd opened a window into his dark past, one that made so much sense. Tragically so.

Uncomfortable as she'd been with blackmailing him, it was easier when she'd thought he was just an asshole who jerked people around. Yet the Brooks she'd gotten to know the past couple of days seemed to have an actual heartbeat under that arrogant exterior.

So she'd fled his house, feeling guilty about the fact that he was a *person* and she'd been a jerk to him. A person who'd wanted to know more about her.

Now, here she was, thinking about him nonstop, doing what she did every time she had a *crush.*

God, I'm pathetic. Lindsay and Naomi were right. She did catch feelings too easily.

Actually, Maddie had avoided Naomi all day since Naomi had a way of zeroing in on whatever Maddie was feeling.

Maddie pulled her ear pods out and tucked them away, then left her back office to make a round in the Depot before she left.

Mid-afternoon in the Depot was always one of the slowest times, especially on a weekday. Now that school had started again, they didn't have the throng of customers from the summer, which made the place feel dead. Things picked up on the weekends, and they'd have a few more heavy trafficked days in the fall, especially near the fair and during the holidays.

Yet every September, the pressure of living in a town that depended on tourism for a bulk of its commerce weighed heavily on Maddie. Pops had done a lot with his businesses to bring fresh faces in during the year, but he couldn't even stop the slowdown.

And now they had an ugly, gaping hole where one of their main storefront windows used to be.

She stared at it, her guilt clawing its way through her. She didn't have to close her eyes to imagine Brooks's car sitting there, surrounded by the wreckage.

The man she'd been casually flirting with.

Naomi had done her best to fix the surrounding space, but it was still killing the aesthetic appeal in that section of the store —and, worse still, looked awful from the street.

"I don't know why Pops won't let me call someone else to

see if they can repair it sooner," Naomi said from behind her. She stood beside Maddie. "It looks so hideous. Have the police made any progress on figuring out who was behind it? It's so hard to believe that the security footage didn't get a license plate."

"No, they haven't." Maddie bit her lip. The lie was the worst part of it. Would it really be that bad if she told Naomi the truth? They'd been through this sort of thing before—when Lindsay and Travis had been sneaking around, afraid to tell everyone they were dating. And Maddie remembered how hurt they'd all been about Lindsay's lies.

But this . . . this felt more insidious. Maddie could understand why Lindsay had lied—she'd been terrified about the family finding out she was dating one of the Wagners. The Yardleys had been in a decades-long feud with them.

On the other hand, Maddie was lying just because Brooks had asked her to.

Because, despite what he says, he fears looking worse to the public. He cares about his reputation on some level, even if he tries to pretend he doesn't.

Yet he'd let a huge thing like the accusations Paulette had made go. Why this? Why was he choosing this as the thing he didn't want to get out?

"Maybe I should ask to see if the Stricklands have better footage. They might have gotten something on their cameras across the street."

"No!" Maddie took an involuntary step forward, her hand shooting out toward Naomi.

Why didn't I think of that?

Naomi's eyes widened with bewilderment. "Why?"

"I-I just . . ." Maddie scrambled, her palms feeling sweaty. "You know. Josh is so close with the Stricklands now, and they've hated us since they felt like their ice cream business was threatened by us selling gelato, and I . . . just don't want to owe them any favors. Please?"

"All right, all right, I won't ask them. Calm down." Naomi scanned her face, doubt clear in her expression. "Is there something I need to know?"

Tell her, tell her, tell her.

"No, nope. Everything's good." Maddie glanced down at her watch. Crap. If she didn't leave right now, she was going to be late for Brooks. "I'm taking off, though. So we can talk about it more later."

Naomi followed her as she made her way through the store to the back. "Wait, where are you going?"

"Uh, you know, the band thing from yesterday. Still working on it."

"Again?"

Maddie pushed the door open to the back, wrinkling her nose at the faint smell of stinkbug. They were swarming near the windows and doors, trying to get inside the buildings for winter. She pulled her keys out. "Yeah. It will probably take me about ten hours—the whole process of getting things nailed down isn't so straightforward."

She stopped beside her car and opened the door, then glanced back at Naomi. Her sister's expression was less than thrilled. "I'm sorry if I'm leaving you to do too much around here."

Naomi shook her head. "You're acting really weird."

"No, I'm not."

"Yeah, you are. You're being super weird."

"I'm really not."

"Trust me. I know what I'm talking about." Naomi leaned closer to her car. "And *why* do you have a car seat in the back of your car?"

Shiiiiiit.

Tell her, tell her, tell her.

Maddie grimaced, then closed the door, drawing in a breath. "All right, fine." She covered her face. "I'll tell you. But you have to swear you will not tell a soul."

Naomi crossed her arms. "How can I swear when I don't know what I'm promising?"

"Just do it." Maddie gave her a hard look.

"Fine. I swear."

"Okay." Maddie drew a deep breath, then looked around. She wasn't taking any chances. "Get in the car. We'll talk in there."

She got into the driver's seat, then turned on the car.

Another voice, different from the one urging her to spill, went through her brain as she stared at the car seat Brooks had installed the evening before.

Don't do it, Maddie.

Naomi opened the passenger side and climbed in. "What in the hell is going on?"

She had to tell her. Eventually, it was going to come out. Maddie wasn't capable of keeping this sort of thing from Naomi.

"You know Brooks Kent?"

Naomi looked bewildered. "As in the rock star?"

"Yeah." She drew a deep breath, her fingertips shaking. "He's the one who crashed into our place."

"What?" Naomi's voice reverberated in the closed quarters.

"On Sunday morning. He was coming down Main Street, swerved to avoid hitting a deer, and crashed into the store."

"You're joking."

Maddie shook her head, not really feeling as good about telling the truth as she'd hoped she would. "I wish I was."

"I don't understand." Naomi blinked at the dash, her face drained of color.

"So he crashed into the Depot, then begged me not to call the police but promised to pay for the damages, and I made a deal with him that I wouldn't . . . and now he's going to play in the fair for us. Ta-da." Her weak attempt to end on the good news clearly didn't land as Naomi lifted confused eyes at her.

"I—" She tilted her head. "What?"

"He's in town. Or, really, at the lake. Cormac Doyle invited him to hang out here for the week."

"Wait, isn't he in jail?" Naomi took out her phone, googling his name. "Yeah. Nice try, Maddie. Brooks Kent was arrested on Saturday night near Baltimore."

Maddie closed her eyes. This wasn't going to go well, she was sure of it. Better than if she'd waited, maybe, but not well. "Yeah, I know," she breathed. "That's why he didn't want me calling the police. He got out on bail and then drove here. If you don't believe that he's here, ask Logan. Cormac invited us over to the house where they're staying on Sunday night."

Naomi's face flushed with hurt. "Are you telling me that Logan knows about all this?"

"No!" *Oh God.* The last thing she wanted was to throw Logan under the bus, especially when he had done nothing wrong. "No. I mean, Logan knows Brooks is in town but not about the wreck."

"Brooks?" Naomi quirked a finely chiseled brow. "You're on a first-name basis with that creep now?"

The defensiveness that flared in her stole her breath. "He's not a creep."

Naomi lifted her phone. "He was arrested for *assault*, Maddie."

"I know, I know. It's complicated, though."

Naomi's eyes widened. "Oh my God." Her fingertips rose to her lips. "Tell me you're not sleeping with him, Maddie."

Now it was Maddie's turn to feel hurt. She gaped at Naomi. "Are you serious?"

"Why else would you defend him like this? Make a deal? Hell, *lie to me.*" Naomi glanced back at the car seat. "Is that his? Does he have a kid or something? Wait, is that where you've been going? To spend time with him?"

"No! Well, yes, but not because I *want* to spend time with him. He forced me to. Okay, no, so what I mean is . . ." Maddie ran her fingers through her hair. "Okay, so I made a deal with him that I'd give him ten hours of my time if he played at the concert, no questions asked, and . . ."

The look on Naomi's face was clear: telling her had been a *huge* mistake.

"It sounds worse than it is."

Naomi blinked. "I don't think that's possible. I thought he was a creep . . . turns out he's a *psycho.* Maddie! What the hell? Ten hours of your time, no questions asked?"

"He's not a psycho." She rubbed her temples, trying to think. How had this conversation gotten away from her so quickly? "His car is in the shop, and he's watching his four-year-old niece for the week, so he's needed some favors. Nothing crude or weird."

"What shop?" Naomi's keen gaze nearly eviscerated her.

Shit.

"Uh . . . Travis's."

Naomi was silent for a few moments.

"I'm assuming Travis knows whose car is in his shop."

Maddie nodded slowly. "I made him promise not to tell anyone. Including Lindsay."

Naomi's nostrils flared. "Who else?"

"Who else what?"

"Who else is in on this *secret?*"

She cringed. "Garrett Doyle and Dan Klein."

Naomi nodded slowly. Reaching up, she pulled down the seat belt and buckled it in. “Let’s go.”

Huh?

“Where?” *Please don’t say to see Brooks.*

“To the pub. To tell Lindsay why you’re making her boyfriend lie to her.”

“No, I can’t tell anyone else. I told you. *You* can’t tell anyone else.”

“That was before I found out my little sister is being controlled by a man with the money and means to manipulate her. And that you’ve lost your mind. Now drive.”

“But the store—”

“The store will be fine. Lars is there, and Missy has the register and can serve gelato if necessary.”

That was true. Also the nice thing about having employees.

Maybe it was that Naomi was her big sister or that she felt bad for lying and knew how bad it sounded, but Maddie put the car in reverse and backed out of the parking spot. “I can’t tell Lindsay. That’s too many people. If too many people find out, Brooks won’t play a concert for us. Who knows, he might not even play. I’m technically in breach of contract, having told you.”

Naomi whirled toward her and gripped her forearm. “Tell me you didn’t sign anything.”

“I did . . . but I wrote up the contract.”

The distress on Naomi’s face wasn’t entirely surprising. Maybe more than Maddie had expected, but still . . .

A strange, sad feeling came over her. With a start like this, the chance of Naomi forgiving *or* liking Brooks was slim. She’d never get the chance to know that he had a totally different side. Naomi would just see him as the jerk who had taken advantage of her sister.

“He’s not a bad person, Naomi,” she said in a shaky voice.

"A little rough around the edges, but he's got a really sweet side. He's just been through a lot."

"Yeah, it must be really miserable being a rich, spoiled rock star." Naomi shook her head. "What is with you? I know Josh really messed you up, Maddie, but this isn't like you. You're clearly already emotionally attached to this guy, and you just met him three days ago."

Maddie laughed. "Nothing is going on between Brooks and me. I would barely even call us friends."

Yet that felt like a lie, too.

Brooks had shared some incredibly personal things with her.

And when she'd hugged him . . .

She sighed, hating herself for getting so close to him.

Naomi was right. Not about Brooks—but about the fact that Maddie was getting emotionally attached.

Dammit.

How?

How had she let Brooks in so easily? She'd barely even liked him, and now she was here defending him to the person she was closest to in the world.

He was attractive, of course. *More than that. He's downright sexy.*

Nothing wrong with admitting she was attracted to him. At least to herself. Telling Naomi would be a disaster right now.

But that didn't mean anything. Admitting that Brooks was hot was like admitting that the sky was blue.

Facts.

She said nothing as she drove down Main. They could have walked to the pub from the Depot, so the trip only took a couple of minutes. Maddie parallel parked on the street, then turned toward Naomi, the engine idling. "I know you're mad, but—"

"Mad doesn't begin to cover it. Disappointed? Concerned? All that and more."

"You've always trusted my judgment."

"Maddie, you lied to me. And to Pops. For what . . . some good-looking rock star you don't even know? This is Pops's business—not yours and mine. His. You had no right to make such an important decision without asking us."

"But he's going to play at the fair—"

"Whoopie," Naomi spat sarcastically. "That's supposed to make me feel better about all this? I'd rather have Phil down the street with a banjo than this disaster you've created."

Maddie drew a shaky breath. "I'm sorry."

Naomi's gaze softened. "You know I'll forgive you. I love you. But I am *really, really* worried about what you've gotten yourself into. I think you should tell Lindsay and Pops, at the very least. I may not know Brooks Kent, but he sounds deceitful. Just . . . be careful. You have a good heart, and I worry that he'll stomp all over it and not look back."

A lump formed in Maddie's throat, and she nodded. "I understand." She glanced at the time again. *Crap. I'm going to be so late to get to Brooks.*

Then she breathed out slowly.

Brooks could wait. Because what Naomi said was right. *"This is Pops's business—not yours and mine. His. You had no right to make such an important decision without asking us."*

Time to be wiser, Maddie.

Brooks might require ten hours of her time, but he could no longer be *the only* priority in her life.

16

BROOKS

"WHAT THE HELL did you make in here?" Cormac asked, surveying the pots on the kitchen counter as he entered the kitchen. He set his keys on the counter and a bag of leftovers from his time in town into the fridge.

Brooks lifted a couple of colorful Ziploc bags beside him on the kitchen table. "Play dough." He wrinkled his nose at the mess. He'd told the chef not to worry about coming back to make dinner tonight, which meant he'd have to clean it all, too.

"You know they sell that at the store pre-made, right? Comes in handy yellow plastic tubs, too."

Seated beside Brooks, Audrey was scribbling into a coloring book. Thank goodness Maddie had picked up a ton of supplies for him at the store the day before. He had forgotten how much it took to keep a four-year-old entertained. "Yeah, I know." Brooks shrugged and stood, heading toward the collection of pots.

"I used to do this with Kayla. My mom had a recipe, and it was cheaper than the store-bought one. Lasted longer, too. Plus, making it is a whole activity." He carried some pots over to the sink. "Audrey had fun, didn't you?"

"Wanna see the worm family I made, Cormac?" Audrey asked Cormac.

"Of course I do," Cormac said with exaggerated enthusiasm.

"Yeah, we made all sorts of worms," Brooks said, giving him a grateful smile. He turned the faucet on and started washing one pot.

He really hadn't intended to make a mess, but there had been little time to clean. Originally, he'd hoped he could snag a few minutes to pick up once Maddie arrived.

But she was already forty-five minutes late.

He snuck a glance at his phone.

She hadn't texted him back, either.

Focusing on the task in front of him, Brooks tried not to overthink it. So she was late? She ran a business, after all, and he'd demanded a lot of her time this week.

No reason to let this get to him.

Putting the pot in the dishwasher, he paused in front of the drink fridge on the way to get another pot. His eyes landed on a pack of nonalcoholic Blue Moons Cormac had picked up on Sunday, but then he reached farther in and pulled out a regular one instead. Wordlessly, he uncapped it and took a swig.

Just something to take the edge off.

A beer later, he finished the dishes, feeling remarkably better. More in control.

It didn't matter that Maddie was now over an hour late and hadn't texted.

"Uncle Books, I'm hungry," Audrey said, coming into the kitchen as he dried his hands.

"You want a grilled cheese?" Brooks asked. This he remembered. Little kids always seemed ready for the next meal just as soon as the kitchen was clean. Though, technically, the play dough hadn't been a meal.

Audrey nodded. "Can I have chippies too?"

"Only if you eat the blueberries I bought, deal?"

"What happened to the chef tonight?" Cormac asked. Audrey had abandoned him to the coloring book and he was taking his time coloring a picture of Donald Duck.

"I told him not to worry about it." Brooks wouldn't mention that he'd enjoyed making dinner for Audrey with Maddie the day before. That maybe a part of him had been hoping for a repeat.

Where in the hell is she?

"Why?" Brooks asked Cormac. "You want a grilled cheese, too?"

"Unlike you, Mr. Private Chef, I will never turn down an American classic like grilled cheese," Cormac said.

"My trainer will kill me if I eat that crap," Brooks said with an eye roll. His diet had suffered enough while on tour, but he'd tried to stick to the plan the trainer had outlined as much as possible.

"What your trainer doesn't know won't hurt him." Cormac shot Audrey a glance. "Are you done coloring, Miss Lady? I see a Daisy Duck that wants to be finished."

Audrey scampered toward him, happy for the company in coloring.

Cormac had a point. The trainer didn't have to know. But working out and maintaining his diet were a part of the job he didn't mind so much. Lifting weights had become an outlet for him, even when he was out on the road. A way to keep that pretty mask on an otherwise effed-up interior.

Maybe that was what was going on with Maddie. He'd let her see under the mask too much.

One look at the dark, turbulent part of him and she'd run away scared. Hadn't liked what she'd seen.

Tension squeezed his chest, and quietly, he grabbed another beer while getting cheese to make dinner.

The two bottles were easy enough to shove into the recycling bin as he cleaned up while Cormac and Audrey ate.

And like with the first beer, he felt remarkably calmer after the second one.

Who cares if it's now almost two hours and Maddie hasn't shown up?

He fired off a text, though.

Brooks: *Guess that whole "whenever I want" part of the deal wasn't clear to you.*

His eyes narrowed as the message status went to *Read.*

Still no reply.

What the hell, Maddie?

Audrey came up to him, holding a piece of paper with scribbles on it. "Ahplane wide! Hit this button." She pointed at one squiggle.

Brooks tore his focus from the phone and gave her a half-hearted smile. "What does the button do?"

"Pweess it."

He pushed the squiggle, and she grabbed his hand, then dragged him over to the couch. She repeated the same process with Cormac, then climbed onto the coffee table in front of them. She sat with her back to them, holding the paper like a steering wheel. "Hew we go! Hold on!"

Brooks struggled to concentrate as Audrey continued chatting happily, instead pulling out his phone to check the text messages.

"Oh no, did you hear, Uncle Brooks? We're going to crash into a tunnel." Cormac shoved him.

Brooks snapped his attention back to the game, catching on. "Oh." He covered his head. "Oh no!"

"Don't wowy. We go ova it." Audrey tossed him back a grin.

Focus, Brooks. He couldn't be wasting his time wondering if a woman was going to text him back like a teenager.

Throwing himself fully into the game, Brooks played airplane enthusiastically with Audrey for the next twenty minutes, then scooped her into his arms. "All right, kiddo. I think Cormac has earned a break. Let's go get ready for bed, shall we?"

Thank goodness four-year-olds had early bedtimes.

And that he had a friend as patient with his niece as Cormac had been. He really was the closest thing he had to a brother.

By the time Audrey was asleep and Brooks emerged from the bedroom, the slight buzz from the earlier beers had worn off, though, leaving agitation and anxiety in its place.

He found Cormac in the game room, racking the pool balls into the triangle.

"Thanks for your help tonight," Brooks said.

"No problem. You expecting company tonight?" Cormac asked with a smirk as he lined up a shot on the pool table.

"No. Why?" Brooks tried to appear as casual as possible as he answered.

"You've looked at the clock about fifty times." Cormac gave him a knowing look.

Had he?

Probably.

Then again, it was well past seven, and it was clear: Maddie wasn't coming today.

Maybe something had come up.

But she hadn't answered his texts, either.

Or maybe she just sees you like a weak little pussy who almost broke down last night.

He should have known from the way she'd hightailed it out of here so quickly that he'd freaked her out.

He didn't know why he'd opened his mouth. He'd replayed the scene a thousand times and thought of a thousand different ways he could have handled that situation *other* than telling Maddie about his dad's suicide.

That she hadn't come by or texted was the only confirmation he needed that she probably looked at him like some sort of train wreck she didn't want to be around.

Fuck it. He didn't want to let it bother him. After this weekend, she'd be out of his life other than when he returned for that concert in a few weeks.

It's better that way.

But he'd never told anyone about his dad. He'd been too afraid to. Something about Maddie, though, had brought down that wall though.

Stupid, stupid, Brooks.

You knew who she was when she tried to blackmail you.

Even though she'd said all the right things last night, her actions today spoke volumes.

Volumes that made him feel sick to his stomach.

He'd just given her more ammunition. More dirt to use against him.

You're such a moron.

Her failure to appear meant he'd missed going to the mechanic again, too. He needed his car back. Much as he'd enjoyed spending time with Audrey, he couldn't help feeling relief at the fact that Kayla would be back in a few days. He was quickly running out of ways to keep Audrey occupied.

"You sure Maddie wasn't planning on coming over?"

Cormac asked more pointedly, bringing him back to their conversation. "Audrey said she stayed for dinner yesterday."

Leave it to the four-year-old to rat him out.

He just needed to take the edge off again.

Relax, already.

Brooks shrugged, then made his way over to the liquor cabinet near the bar. The rental included all the liquor, of which there was a fantastic selection. "Want a drink?"

Cormac straightened with a frown. "You're not drinking."

"Why not?" Brooks gave a taut smile. "I'm fine. I don't have a real problem. Darren thought 'sobriety' would help my image. Lot of fucking good that did."

Cormac narrowed his eyes. "Is this about Maddie?"

The bottle of bourbon scratched against the marble bar top as Brooks slid it closer. "Maddie who?" He threw a sarcastic smile back.

Cormac set his pool cue on the table, then came closer. "You don't really want a drink. We're in our thirties now, man. Alcohol doesn't go down as smooth as it did when we were younger."

Brooks raised a brow, then poured the amber liquid into a glass. He set the glass to his lips, the potent scent filling his nostrils. Then he tossed back a mouthful, a warm feeling curling against his tongue as the alcohol evaporated in his mouth. He swallowed and topped off the glass again.

"I don't think you should drink, Brooks. Stupid idea of Darren's or not, you're a better man these days for not drinking." Cormac gave him a hard look. "I don't know what's going on with you and Maddie, but don't do this because of a woman. You've worked too hard."

"Don't be absurd. I've known her for a few days. Not to mention that she's a liar and a manipulator."

Cormac flinched. "I knew you were acting funny. What the hell happened?"

"Nothing happened."

Cormac's lips pursed, a spark of interest in his eyes. "Wow. You really like her, huh?" He spread his palm on Brooks's chest as he lifted the glass again. "But I'm serious. Don't do it, Brooks. Just throw it away. I like Maddie. But like you said, a woman you barely know isn't worth it."

Holding Cormac's gaze, Brooks tipped the glass to his lips and swallowed. "I don't need a reason for a drink."

"As your friend, I can't sit back and let you do this." Cormac snatched the glass and walked it over to the sink, then dumped it down the drain.

The heady feeling from those first sips burned through Brooks's veins. He clenched his jaw, his mind buzzing with anger.

Don't do it.

Listen to Cormac.

He's right.

"You got somewhere else to sleep tonight?" Brooks asked flatly.

Cormac jerked his head up. "You serious?"

"Get going."

"What about Audrey?" Cormac crossed his arms. "If you won't stop for your own sake, then stop for her."

"Leave, Cormac."

God, I hate the sound of my own fucking voice. The same voice that got me in trouble last night when I just didn't know how to shut up with Maddie. Just like I should shut up now.

"I'm not leaving you and Audrey—"

"Out. Now."

Cormac's expression darkened. He pushed past Brooks,

then left the game room. A minute later, the front door slammed shut.

Dammit, Brooks.

He should call Cormac back. Apologize.

Cormac had been a good friend for years—*one of the only people I truly trusted.*

But when had trusting people gotten him anywhere?

Maddie's face flashed through his mind.

"Fuck it." Brooks grabbed the bottle of bourbon from the counter, then headed outside.

17

MADDIE

MADDIE KILLED the engine of her car and stared up at the house.

She didn't want to be here—not after the evening she'd had confessing to Lindsay and Pops about Brooks, then getting grilled to death about the details of her arrangement.

Brooks's texts while she was talking to her family hadn't helped. Naomi had seen the one about *whenever I want* and flipped out, convinced that Brooks was using her for sex.

So she'd ignored Brooks and procrastinated, dealing with *that* problem.

She'd wanted to turn in for an early night, exhausted emotionally and confused as all hell.

But then Cormac had called as she was getting ready for bed.

She sighed, then went up to the front mat. Cormac had waited by the end of the driveway, waiting for her to arrive, and had handed her a slip of paper with the door's code. He hadn't said much, but from the worry on his face, she was glad she'd come.

Maddie typed in the code on the keypad. Opening the door, she blinked in the darkness.

Maybe Cormac was wrong. Maybe Brooks had just gone to bed, and a checkup wasn't necessary.

"Brooks?" she called out softly. Audrey was probably asleep, so she couldn't be too loud.

No answer.

"Brooks Kent, where are you?"

She checked the first floor, including his bedroom suite, then went upstairs.

Man, the bedrooms upstairs are bigger than my entire apartment.

Still, nothing.

Going to the basement, she looked around, then let herself out the back door to the yard.

There he is.

Brooks stood at the end of the dock, staring out over the lake.

Maybe he's fine. Maybe Cormac was worried about nothing.

But there was a half-empty bottle gripped in his left hand.

Maddie's heart pitched forward, then she started toward him. Her trek across the grass was noiseless, but the grass was already soaked with dew and cold, and she shivered. When she reached the dock, she slipped her soaking wet slides off her feet, then padded onto the wood.

Brooks turned at the sound of her footsteps.

Even in the dim light of the moon, his scowl radiated from his face. "What are you doing here?"

She slowed her approach. Cormac had called because he assumed they were something they weren't—that she'd had some right to be here.

Brooks wouldn't see it that way. Neither did she.

"Cormac said—"

"Of course he did."

She took another step, then took the bottle from him gently. "Did you drink all this yourself?"

He cocked a brow at her. "You here to parent me, too?"

"What are you doing, Brooks?" He oddly didn't *seem* drunk. Who knew what he'd had to drink?

A smirk crossed his lips. Had she never noticed the hint of a dimple in his cheek, or was it just the deep shadows from the moonlight? "I could ask you the same thing. I didn't call you to come over here, you know."

"Consider this completely off the clock." Maddie hugged her arms to her chest, the chill stronger by the water. Her feet were freezing too, the hems of her jogger pants damp.

She might not have Pops's experience dealing with people at the pub, but the last thing anyone liked was to feel judged. Setting the bottle to her lips, she took a small sip. "What are we drinking to tonight?"

Brooks continued to stare her down. "You didn't come today when you were supposed to. Or bother to text me back."

That couldn't be what this was about—could it? Maybe he was more of a celebrity diva than she'd realized.

"I told my sister about you. And the wreck." She'd already decided whether she was going to be honest, she was going to be honest all around. Lies made for a bad situation. "She was understandably upset. She asked me to tell my grandfather and my other sister, whose boyfriend towed your car."

He blinked at her. "So you broke your word?"

Was he angry?

She couldn't quite tell. If anything, there was a lack of emotion there that worried her.

"I did."

"Well, I guess that means I won't have to play for your town fair after all. Good."

His statement was flat. Empty. None of the anger she'd anticipated.

Yet I don't doubt he means it.

She set down the bottle and came closer to him. "I may have broken my word with you, but I broke it with them first. I like you, Brooks. But they're my family. I owe them my loyalty. You'd do the same if it were Kayla."

His chin jerked up. "Would I?"

"You know you would. You're a better man than you pretend to be."

Doubt shone in his eyes. "You don't really know me, Madison. Just believe everything you've heard about me. All those things you used as evidence against me that first night you showed up here. That's good enough for everyone else. And now you have a few more juicy details about my life to give the media when you decide you want to blackmail me again."

Oh.

Oh God, is that what's bothering him?

His behavior suddenly made more sense. He'd been incredibly vulnerable with her last night. Shared something deeply personal.

And I didn't bother to show up today.

Shit.

"Well, it's not good enough for me." She shivered again. "And I don't believe it. You're capable of being so much more than you give yourself credit for. I wouldn't be here tonight if I didn't think that. I didn't come earlier because I couldn't get away and then because I was overwhelmed by how upset my sister was with you."

She stepped a little closer as his face filled with doubt. "I *wanted* to be here with you, believe it or not. I'm sorry I didn't call or text."

"Why? You want to fix me?" A sardonic laugh left him. "What makes you think I do a single thing I don't want to do?"

His belligerence had to be a sign that he was more inebriated than he was letting on.

She set her hand on his. "You're drunk, Brooks. Let's go inside. Get you in bed."

His hand slipped around her waist, and he pulled her close. "Don't fucking tease me."

Leave it to a drunk man to take her words the wrong way. But as his fingertips pressed into the small of her back, he lowered his mouth to the sensitive spot on her neck, just below her jawline and ear, his lips brushing her softly.

"Why do you have to smell so fucking amazing, Madison? You have any idea what that smell does to me?"

Any other time, those words would have made her swoon. But he was drunk and didn't mean it. She set her hands on his chest, pushing back. He clamped her tighter still, his hand splaying across her back, pushing her against his hardened length.

Oh God . . .

She couldn't help the speeding of her pulse or the way the feel of him made her wet. He was attractive and sexual. And dangerous. *So, so dangerous.*

Right now, there was a chance that fact was turning her on even more.

"You think I haven't spent the day daydreaming about your mouth?" Brooks brought his thumb to her lower lip, dragging it across with a featherlight touch, then down so he could feel the wetness of her mouth. Almost involuntarily, her tongue darted against his thumb, a sensual thrill going through her.

"God, Madison." He held her chin with his forefinger and

thumb. "You should get out of here. Because if you don't, I'm going to kiss you. And if I do that, I won't want to stop."

Her heart pounded as his eyes locked on hers, her body powerless to move out of his grip.

Because I want him to kiss me.

I want to feel his mouth on mine.

I want . . .

She wanted to fuck him.

This was so, so bad.

"That's just the whiskey talking, Brooks," she whispered, struggling to get her voice out.

"Maybe. But I knew before I took a single sip tonight that I wanted to spread your legs and kiss that clit of yours. Taste you. See you come undone and then drive my cock into you and fuck you hard. That what you want to hear, Madison? That I can't stop thinking about you? That it drove me crazy you didn't come today?"

Her breath strangled, her mind racing.

Any more of this and she'd be a puddle ready to do just about anything to get some relief from the growing tension inside her.

Her face was burning as he lowered his lips to hers, an electric sizzle pulsed through her, and her clit practically twitched with anticipation. She was soaked and ready for him.

But she couldn't do this.

He was drunk.

A snap of a twig helped pull her out of the trance. She checked over her shoulder at the surrounding woods, then took a breath.

She pulled away, her body immediately hating the absence of him.

He took a stumbling step forward, reaching for her as she stepped out of his grasp.

He wouldn't try to force her, would he?

"Not tonight. Let's go inside." She held out her hand.

Brooks's face darkened. "You don't want to?"

"I do, actually. I want to kiss you. Maybe even make a few terrible decisions with you. But there's this little thing called consent, and you're too drunk to give it." She slipped her fingers into his and tugged his hand. "Let's go, rock star. I'm putting you to bed. In the completely nonsexual sense of the word."

Please, Brooks. Be the man I think you are.

He stared at her for several beats, his expression unreadable. Then he nodded, allowing her to lead him from the dock.

She grabbed her shoes but carried them in one hand, opting to walk barefoot through the cold, wet grass. Whatever miracle had gotten Brooks to listen to her and come along without protesting, she wasn't going to question it.

She led him in through the basement door, then locked it behind her. Taking him up the stairs, she fumbled in the dark through the unfamiliar house until she found the hallway that led to his bedroom.

Flipping the light on to his room, she held the door open and released his hand at last. In the light, she could see the glassy look in his eyes more clearly, the pallor on his face. He swayed, then made a face. "I think I'm going to be sick."

"Well, yeah, Romeo, you were trying to win the world-championship in bourbon solo drinking tonight." Maddie led him to the bathroom, flipping on lights as she went. Just as they reached the toilet, he lunged forward.

"Go on," he managed, falling to his knees in front of the toilet. "I don't want to be sick in front of you."

She nodded, then backed out, leaving him as the sound of his retching filled the space.

Maddie set her hand over her eyes, rubbing her temples.

"But I knew before I took a single sip tonight that I wanted to spread your legs and kiss that clit of yours. Taste you. See you come undone and then drive my cock into you and fuck you hard."

Good God, the man and his mouth.

Not one of her boyfriends had ever talked to her like that, which seemed to widen the gap between them. Her inexperience and his clear abundance of experience. This hadn't been an offer for some sort of relationship that could lead to forever.

He'd offered *sex.* Raw, feral, unattached sex with him. And he *obviously* knew what he was doing in that department.

Somehow, she'd narrowly dodged the temptation he'd offered. Like she'd passed some great test.

Congratulations, Maddie, you don't take advantage of drunk men.

Maybe it wouldn't matter to him, but she sure as hell knew how much it would matter in reverse. She sighed. "You okay? Want me to get you some water?"

"Just go!" Brooks hollered back.

Better to give him some space.

She went back out to the kitchen, poured him a glass of water, then brought it back to the bedroom. Setting it on the nightstand beside the bed, she sat wearily.

"Can you go check on Brooks, please?" Cormac had asked.

"What can I do? I barely know him, Cormac."

"You might be able to save him, Maddie. I don't know. But I know Brooks. And I've never seen him so out of it."

Saving a rock star was not on the agenda for her life.

But he wasn't just some random guy on a poster anymore, either.

She'd felt a tug between them. Thought about him all day, every day, since they'd met on Sunday.

And apparently, it's not so one-sided.

A small cry made her sit straighter.

Maddie frowned, then turned toward the door.

Was it some wounded animal?

She listened more closely.

"Audrey!" Maddie leaped off the bed, then rushed out of the primary suite toward the sound of Audrey's cries.

She found the four-year-old sitting up in the bed, tears staining her cheeks. "Mommy!" Audrey cried. "I want my mommy!"

Maddie picked her up. "Shhh . . . honey, it's okay. You're safe."

Audrey flailed against her. "Mommy, Mommy, Mommy!"

Lindsay used to have night terrors like this.

But that was a long time ago.

Bouncing her gently, Maddie carried Audrey out of the dark room and back down the hall toward the primary suite. Brooks was still in the bathroom, so Maddie turned off the lights, continuing to stroke Audrey's back while she rocked her little body.

When Audrey still didn't calm down, Maddie sang "Hallelujah." The Rufus Wainwright song had been one of her niece's favorites when Maddie babysat her.

Midway through the last verse, as Audrey continued to sob, Maddie switched to "Wildfire."

Maybe Brooks would hear her, but she didn't care right now. Audrey was crying so loudly that she had to sing loud enough so that she'd hear her.

Almost like magic, the tension in the little girl's body eased.

Maddie didn't have to question the lyrics—she'd listened to the song twenty times today alone.

Audrey's breathing softened and Maddie's arm ached, so she inched closer to the bed and crawled onto it. She didn't want to put Audrey near the edge of the bed where she might roll off, so she climbed to dead center and laid her on the pillow.

Audrey moaned, clinging to Maddie as she tried to pull away. At last, Maddie gave up and lay beside her, continuing to sing and stroke her back until she'd calmed and breathed softly, curled in her arms.

Then the darkness crept in, and, exhausted, Maddie drifted off to sleep.

18

MADDIE

THE SOFT CLICK of a door opening roused Maddie, and she blinked in the darkness, disoriented. A curtain opened, and she squinted one eye, then sat, recognizing Brooks's sister by the window.

Oh crap, I slept here.

Kayla stared at her, consternation on her face, then her gaze traveled to the little sleeping form beside Maddie. She held Maddie's gaze again as she crossed toward the bed. "Is she okay?" Kayla whispered with all the worry of a mother who'd just probably driven freaking herself out about the safety of her little girl.

Maddie nodded, swallowing hard. This whole situation was so bad, but hopefully, Kayla wouldn't be angry with her for snuggling with Audrey during the night. "She woke up with night terrors, I think. But Brooks was—"

"Yeah, I know. Cormac called me," Kayla answered, then bit her lip as Audrey shifted. She stepped away from the bed. "I don't want to wake her up."

Maddie took the cue to get up quietly. She went out of the

room before Kayla, tugging her hair out of the elastic she'd slept in and shaking it out.

I can't believe I slept here.

But what else could she have done? Brooks had been so drunk and sick. And Audrey had needed someone.

Brooks had needed someone, for that matter.

She sat on the couch, uncomfortable and unusually tired.

A few moments later, Kayla joined her in the living room. She sat beside Maddie and grabbed her hand. "I don't know how to thank you enough for being here," Kayla said earnestly. A flicker of annoyance filled her face, and she shook her head. "I'm so mad at Brooks right now I can hardly think straight, but I really owe you, Maddie. Thank you."

"It's not a big deal."

Kayla raised a brow. "It's a huge deal, actually. Audrey is my whole life. And that stupid man in the bathroom in there is the rest of it, but right now, he's on my shit list." Kayla released Maddie's hand, frustration on her face. "Do you have any idea what set him off?"

Oh great. This wasn't going to make Kayla like her.

Maddie cleared her throat, then ran her fingers through the tangles in her hair. "Uh, yeah, actually, I think it's sort of my fault."

Kayla stared at her in confusion. "How's that?"

She'd already admitted the truth to a few people. What was one more person?

Yeah, because telling Naomi went so well.

"Did Brooks tell you he crashed into my store Sunday morning?" Maddie asked cautiously.

Kayla's eyes widened. "Crashed? What? No. He didn't say anything. What happened?"

Dammit. She really didn't want to interfere with Kayla and Brooks, either.

Maddie combed her fingers back into a ponytail and tied it up again. She'd already said too much to backtrack now. "Brooks drove his car through my store window as he tried to dodge a deer. I live above the store, so I heard it, and uh, we ended up making a deal to handle the situation quietly."

Did she dare mention that she'd blackmailed him? Funny how it sounded so much worse to admit to someone who cared about him. If some random woman blackmailed either of her brothers, especially if they were rich and vulnerable to blackmail, Maddie would probably hate that woman.

Kayla gave her a hard stare as though she was already questioning Maddie's character. "What sort of deal? If he pays for the damage, what difference does it make if it's *quiet* or not?"

Maddie's face flushed. "I didn't know Brooks, Kayla. I'm sorry. I just assumed he was all these awful things that the tabloids seem to push, and I threatened to tell the press unless he played at the town fair for us in a few weeks. But I'm going to tell him never mind."

She said that last part without even thinking it through.

Yet it was the right thing to do, wasn't it?

How could she continue to blackmail him for a concert? She'd known the blackmail was wrong the whole time, but now?

The air was rife with tense silence.

Kayla didn't look at her.

"What changed your mind about blackmailing my brother?"

Ouch. It really sounded terrible.

What sort of person does that make me?

"To begin with, I'm realizing how much I hate myself for doing it," Maddie said, a lump in her throat. She needed a sip of water or something. "But also because Brooks has another side to him. He's . . . just really got a tough exterior. But he adores Audrey. And I think I was wrong about him."

KAYLA RUBBED HER EYES, not saying anything about what she thought of Maddie now. "But why would you blackmailing him make him drink? He's been blackmailed before. And Cormac said he thought you two were sleeping together. Brooks has had you over every day this week."

Maddie shifted in her seat, her knee bouncing. "We're not sleeping together. Brooks demanded ten hours of my time in our deal, and that's why I've been by. Mostly just running errands for him."

Kayla gave her a look of disbelief. "Cormac said you had dinner the other day."

Cormac has a big mouth. That wasn't entirely fair, though. She imagined Kayla probably had a thousand questions for him when he'd called about Brooks.

Maddie twisted the hem of her sweatshirt in her hands. "I did. And we got to talking afterward, and Brooks told me about your parents and how they died," Maddie admitted in a low voice. "I was supposed to come by yesterday, but I couldn't, and when I didn't show up, I think it must have triggered him somehow. Like he'd shared too much with someone he shouldn't have. Maybe it even scared him."

"He told you about my parents?" Kayla searched her face. Then added, "About Dad?"

Maddie nodded.

Letting a slow puff out from her cheeks, Kayla stood abruptly. "I need coffee. You want some?"

Coffee sounded magical right about now.

Maddie followed her into the kitchen.

Kayla pulled two mugs down from the cabinet. "I can't

believe he told you about Dad." She didn't meet Maddie's eyes as she started the coffee. "He never talks about him. *Ever*. And definitely not about his death."

That made Maddie's failure to appear the day before somehow worse. She turned on the sink, splashing some water on her hot face. Grabbing a paper towel, she dried off. "I don't know why he did—"

"He clearly trusts you, that's why." Kayla turned on the coffee machine. "Which is ironic, considering you blackmailed him. But yes, I can see why that would set him off. Not that it's any excuse. I'm still furious with him."

Kayla settled her weight on her hands, leaning forward on the counter. "To be honest, it's you I have my questions about. I like your brother; he's really sweet. I figured you were the same way. But I didn't expect to hear that you were blackmailing Brooks. That's . . . disappointing."

Hard to hear, but not undeserved, either.

"Except that you also told me about it. And you came over and took care of my daughter last night. And Brooks obviously sees something in you he likes. Telling you about our parents is monumental, Maddie. Like . . . I'm not sure he's ever told anyone about Dad."

"I get it, I really do." Maddie rested her weight against the counter. "It was a stupid idea to blackmail Brooks—I just . . ." She sucked in a deep breath.

"My ex-boyfriend, who basically cheated on me, has a cousin in the band River House, and I got them to play for the town fair next month. Except River House pulled out and is playing another night when my ex's new girlfriend's family is sponsoring the main concert stage. I needed a band. And who should come crashing into my store but Brooks? I don't know. It felt like fate in a way." Maddie cringed at the silliness of it. "But it was stupid. And Brooks doesn't deserve that. He's sweet, and this wounded soul that makes me want to hug him, and I'm so, so sorry."

"He's an ass," Kayla said with a smirk. She grabbed a bottle of half-and-half from the fridge, setting it on the counter. "But he has a sweet side, yes. I'm shocked he let you see it. He was an incredible big brother growing up—he still is—and he's an amazing uncle. You know he raised me, right?"

"Yeah, he said your mom died when he was eighteen."

"She did, but that's not what I meant. He *raised* me. Like almost entirely by himself." The coffee pot beeped, and Kayla pulled it out, then brought it toward them.

"After my dad died, my mom had to work a lot to keep us afloat. I never met my dad. The only dad I had was Brooks. He changed my diapers and took me to the playground. He got to school late every day because he insisted on walking me. Packed my lunch, too. Studied with me. Most girls go to their moms when they get their first periods, but I went to Brooks. Mom had already died. He did everything, Maddie. He raised me."

A deep, cavernous ache went through Maddie's heart.

My God.

She couldn't even imagine.

And she'd made some flippant comment about her wonderful family the other night.

What a privileged little brat you are.

"Why would your mom let him do so much? He had to have been a kid himself when you were little."

Kayla poured her coffee, then handed it to Maddie. "He was. But he grew up fast. Dad's death really sent Mom into a downward spiral. She was always sad, depressed, I think. We didn't have any extended family—both my parents were only children—and the only grandmother I knew died a few years after Mom. So Brooks didn't really have a choice. It was that or leave the state to handle me."

No wonder Brooks is the way he is.

He hadn't come from a life of love or happiness.

How in the world had he survived? Gotten so far?

That, by itself, was a testament to something great inside him. Determination. Grit.

Maddie's hands shook as she poured her own coffee.

I've been so wrong about him.

She set the coffee pot on the counter, as the warm scent was almost sickening her. "Thank you for telling me," Maddie said softly, tears stinging her eyes.

Kayla's face pinched, and she sipped her coffee, looking away. "He's a jerk to the rest of the world a lot, except when he's on stage. That's probably where Brooks is most himself, and that's why people fell in love with him there. Where they can see the person I've always seen and love. But it sounds like he let you in, too, Maddie. Just . . . don't take advantage of that, please."

Wow.

Maddie's head spun. "I won't," she promised.

Somehow, she was sure she meant it, too.

19

BROOKS

"Brooks August Kent!" Kayla's voice stirred Brooks from a deep slumber, and he jerked his face up.

Why does my body hurt so much?

His eyelashes felt stuck together, and he blinked one eye open, keeping the other one squeezed shut.

Fuck.

The cold tile of the bathroom floor pressed against his body.

Kayla stood in the doorway, and she flipped the lights on, making him wince.

She was furious.

"Kayla," he croaked, pulling himself to sit up. He balanced one hand on the toilet seat and closed the lid.

God, I'm a wreck.

Shame broke out over his brow in the form of sweat.

"Explain to me why Cormac had to call me first thing this morning and tell me you were drinking last night. Or that, when I got here, I found a woman I don't even know taking care of Audrey. Not that I'm mad at Maddie. I could kiss her, actually, and she's my new favorite person on the planet. But you? I'm going to murder you."

And she has every right to.

Brooks rubbed his eyes. "I'm a fucking mess, Kayla. It's unforgivable. You have every right to hate me and I'm sorry."

"What's going on with you, Brooks?" Kayla shook her head, disappointment and hurt in her eyes. "And why the hell are you drinking? I can't go through this again with you."

The smell of alcohol seemed to seep through his pores, and his mouth was acrid from a night of getting sick. He'd never considered himself that uncontrolled, but Kayla had been worried about his drinking, so he'd quit. Darren had heard about it and leaked it to the tabloids himself that time, wanting him to bring it up in interviews and other discussions.

Made him look like a raging alcoholic to the press.

Why do I keep allowing that? Because one day, Audrey's going to read all that shit.

Brooks struggled to his feet, then made his way to the sink. He turned the tap on and splashed water on his face, then took a long drink directly from the faucet. Putting toothpaste on the brush beside the sink, he looked at Kayla through the mirror. "Maddie's still here?"

Kayla nodded.

Double fuck.

He'd said some lewd things to her the night before. Tried to kiss her.

God, I owe her an apology.

"I'm sorry, Kayla," he said again. How could he explain?

He was a failure.

A fucking failure.

A disaster that just kept making his damn life worse.

Kayla's lips pursed as he brushed his teeth. The taste of the toothpaste turned his stomach, but he pressed on. No way in hell he had anything left to vomit.

"I managed to actually take tomorrow off, so I'm free to stick around until the rental is up. But . . . I don't want Audrey to see her beloved uncle with a hangover. She didn't deserve for you to put her in a dangerous situation last night, and she doesn't need to see that. So Cormac is picking me up, and we're going out for the day. Then he's coming back here, but you need to apologize to him because he's one of the few genuine friends you have. I also gathered up all the liquor bottles in this house and put them in a box. I want you to call the homeowner or the rental manager and have them pick them up this morning. Do all that, and I'll think about forgiving you."

"Consider it done," Brooks said, rinsing his mouth. *Holy fuck, I feel sick.*

"I'll consider it done when it's done. Get yourself cleaned up. Cormac will be here in ten minutes."

Without waiting for him to respond, Kayla left, shutting the door behind her.

Brooks closed his eyes, resting his weight on his hands as he leaned on the counter.

So this is what rock bottom feels like.

He'd finally done it. Pushed away the closest people to him, thrown five years of sobriety out the window, come onto a sweet woman while drunk . . . and that didn't even take into account the assault charges or the fact that he hadn't contacted Ava with any sort of plan for his image rebrand.

Or even really thought about it.

Because the truth was . . . *I don't want it anymore.*

Not the fame. Not the label. Not the control.

Music had long since lost its luster, and he could barely write what he wanted anymore. His well of inspiration was dry.

He didn't care about firing Darren *or* getting dropped from his label.

Because I have one foot out the door already.

All he wanted was to be left alone and live his miserable fucking life in peace with the few people who would tolerate him.

He couldn't believe Maddie had stayed.

Two awful nights in the past week. Both times, she'd been there. Hell, she'd even let him sleep on her couch without knowing him.

Because she's a good person.

A kind person.

And I've treated her like shit.

He owed her so many apologies he didn't even know where to start.

Meeting his gaze in the reflection of the bathroom mirror, he glared at himself.

Brooks, you're an asshole. You don't deserve to even talk to Madison Yardley again.

Self-loathing filled him and he tore his gaze away. He had no choice but to perform at the country fair. And he couldn't ask anything more of Maddie. *Fuck.*

He showered and got dressed, his stomach feeling weak the whole time, then left the bedroom for the living room. Audrey was watching cartoons, but she popped her head up as he came into the room. "Morning, Uncle Books!" She barreled toward him and threw her arms up with an innocent, happy smile on her face.

Lifting her, Brooks pulled her close, tears stinging his eyes.

Kayla's censure rang through his head. "*She didn't deserve for you to put her in a dangerous situation last night . . .*"

What the hell did I do?

"I'm sorry, baby girl. I'm so sorry," he whispered into the soft angelic curls that framed her face.

As he set her down, he saw Kayla and Cormac at the kitchen table. Maddie wasn't anywhere in sight, though.

Did she leave?

"You go on watching your cartoons," Brooks told Audrey. "We'll talk some more after breakfast."

Cormac stood awkwardly as Brooks approached, giving Brooks a once-over.

Brooks held out his hand. "I owe you, man. I'm sorry."

Cormac shook his hand, his eyes boring into Brooks. "It's all good. You okay?"

Brooks nodded. "Feel like shit, but yeah."

Kayla smiled tautly and stood beside Cormac. "Alcohol is in the dining room. Call the homeowner. Don't wait up for us for dinner, but we'll be back."

Brooks's gut simmered. She was still furious. She didn't hug him or offer any real consolation. *But I don't blame her, either.*

When they'd gone, Brooks went over to the television and shut it off. The silence was deafening.

He was alone.

And deserved it.

Big, fancy-ass house and not a single person to fill it with.

He plopped down on the couch and took out his phone. Firing off a quick message to the owner of the rental, he set his phone down on the empty seat beside him and laid his head back, feeling sick to his stomach.

He didn't know what was worse—that he was sitting here feeling sorry for himself or the fact that he'd made his own bed.

The sound of the back door opening caught his attention, and he glanced over as Maddie came inside, a mug in her hands.

She gave him a grim smile, then ambled over toward him. "Morning, sunshine."

Sunshine.

He couldn't have thought of a better description.

That's what she is.

"You stayed," he mumbled.

She sat on the coffee table across from him. "Someone had to take care of the toddler with night terrors. We ended up sleeping in your bed. Hope you don't mind."

Oh God.

The hazy memory of someone singing "Hallelujah" and "Wildfire" came back. *Maddie?*

"I owe you . . . so much more than I could ever owe anyone." He searched her gaze. "Consider the ten hours paid off."

"Oh, don't worry, I already did." She sipped the coffee in her mug, then set it down. "Are we going to talk about what happened last night?"

Brooks shook his head, leaning back against the pillow. "What happened is that I decided to torpedo the few good relationships I had left. I'm a piece of crap, Maddie. Just as wicked and horrible as everyone thinks. I put Audrey in danger, and I'll never forgive myself for it. And I'm exhausted."

"First, she wasn't in danger. I was here." Maddie reached across the space between them and took his hand. "And you need to stop repeating that bullshit. Repeat it enough and you're going to believe it, Brooks. You are *not* a piece of crap."

He gave a lifeless smile. "How would you know? You barely know me."

"You're right. I don't. But how many people really know you? How often do you give people the chance to know you?"

"There's nothing there worth knowing." Brooks brushed the back of her knuckles with his thumb. "You want to hear something? I'm about to get dropped from my label. My manager wanted me to check into rehab and go to sex therapy—he thought it would look good to the press as an image makeover—but I refused because even I won't pretend those are my issues for the sake of PR. The head of my label gave me a week's deadline to pitch a rebrand to her. I'm not going to. *Because I don't even care.*"

"Good."

He gave her a puzzled look. "Good?"

"Yeah, I think it would be good for you. You're clearly miserable. And if you're working with people who are asking things of you that you're morally opposed to, why continue?"

He gave her a jaunty smile. "What about my art? My fans?"

"Fuck them." She shook her head as he chuckled. "I'm serious. You don't owe people anything to the point of sacrificing your mental and emotional health."

She shifted. "Kayla told me about your mom this morning. How depressed she was all your life. How much time you spent helping babysit and cooking meals and being a parent when you were just a kid. And then how you took over and raised Kayla once your mom died. You went from that to being an international rock star, which may be great on the surface, but doesn't have a lot of depth." Maddie squeezed his hand. "I think it's time for Brooks to take care of Brooks."

"Not sure if I know how to do that." He didn't say it in a self-pitying way, but it sounded that way to his ears.

"Then start by letting your friends and family take care of you."

Brooks let his gaze drift over her. "Is that what you are, Madison?"

"You haven't scared me away yet, Brooks." She gestured to her messy hair, joggers, and sweatshirt. "I even came over here looking like this last night, all because Cormac wanted me to check on you. So yeah, I'd say I'm your friend."

How didn't I scare her away?

He hadn't always been nice to her. And the times they'd gotten along, he'd told her about the ugliest parts of his past.

He gripped her hand more firmly. "I owe you an apology. For being an ass to you all week and for coming onto you last night. I, uh . . ."

"Forget it, it's fine. I know you were drunk."

"I wasn't drunk all week."

She sighed and pulled her hand away. "You're hurting, Brooks. It's not an excuse for your behavior, but it is a reason. Even animals do it—hence the wounded dog metaphor. The important thing is that you recognize only you can fix it. That you need to work on healing. Besides, I owe you an apology, too. I never should have blackmailed you. It was wrong of me."

Now she's apologizing . . . to me?

That's unfathomable.

"Words of wisdom with Madison Yardley?" His lips curved in a smile. "You'd think I'm the younger one between the two of us."

She smiled and climbed to her feet. "Come on. Get up."

"Why?"

"Because you need to get out of this house. You need to work on being a *person* again, Brooks. So I'm going to show you around Brandywood, and I don't want to hear a word of complaint. I already told my sister I'm not going into the Depot today."

Why is she so . . . reasonable? Forgiving?

He didn't deserve the kindness she'd shown him.

Despite not wanting to do anything but lie on the couch, Brooks nodded.

He didn't want to disappoint Maddie. Not after caring for his family the night before. *She stayed so Audrey was safe.*

"Let me just grab some things." He left her there and headed back to the bedroom.

With sunglasses and a baseball cap in hand, he rejoined her a minute later, and they headed out the front door. "Is that your disguise?" she asked with a grin.

"Yup. Also, I'm driving, if you don't mind."

She gave him a quizzical look. "How are you driving?" She held up her keys. "I'm pretty sure I'm the only one with a car here. And a better accident record, as of late."

"It's just a habit I got into after my mom died." If he could control the method of transportation, he'd be safer.

Except Maddie was right. He'd wrecked right into her store the other day.

He released a tense breath. "You know what? It's fine. You drive."

A sports car approached and pulled into the driveway. Both he and Maddie turned as the car parked behind Maddie's, then the door opened, and a dark-haired man wearing a sweater and khakis climbed out.

"Hey, Jason." Maddie waved at him as the man pushed his sunglasses back.

That's a relief. At least Maddie knows him.

"Hey . . ." Jason gave her a curious look. "I didn't expect to find a Yardley here."

"Brooks is a friend of mine," Maddie said with an effortless smile. She opened her car door. "I'll just wait in the car."

As the door shut behind her, Brooks turned toward Jason, who approached with his hand out. "Jason Cavanaugh. I'm the owner of this property. I got your message and was in the area, so I hope you don't mind me stopping by."

Brooks shook his hand. *God, this is embarrassing.* "Yeah,

sorry to bother you. I . . . just would prefer to take the alcohol out of the house. My sister boxed it up and put it in the dining room."

"No problem. You finding everything else in the house okay?" Jason had an easygoing vibe, one that told Brooks he'd spent a long time in business. Or customer service. But considering the cost of this property, probably the former.

"Yeah, it's fantastic." Brooks glanced over his shoulder at Maddie's idling car. "I'm actually thinking of renting it for longer, if I can."

Jason pulled out his phone. "I think most of the weekends in September are booked, unfortunately. Sorry about that."

"Just the weekends?"

Jason nodded.

"I might be able to work around that."

What am I even saying?

Yet he didn't want to leave. Couldn't imagine it right now. Despite the night before, he'd felt a strange peace here. Like he needed to be here.

Jason glanced over his phone. "Getting attached, huh?"

"Something like that."

Jason gave him an amiable smile. "Brandywood has a way of doing that. I'm a transplant, actually. Grew up in Chicago, but I can't imagine living anywhere else now."

Brooks nodded politely. His eyes flicked to the beautiful blonde waiting for him in her car. The one he was going to allow to drive him somewhere.

He wasn't sure the town had anything to do with it.

20

MADDIE

Bunny's Café on Main Street was already crowded with diners for breakfast, as Maddie held the door open for Brooks. She grinned as he walked inside. "You gonna wear those sunglasses inside the whole time?" she whispered.

"Yes, ma'am."

"You'll probably draw more attention to yourself wearing the sunglasses." The funny thing was, the "disguise" was fairly effective. He was recognizable, of course, but no one was actively looking for him here. But while she wanted Brooks to experience some of Brandywood, she didn't want him feeling uncomfortable. "I might start calling you Clark Kent, instead. Change of glasses and hairstyle and *tada!* Superman."

He humored her joke with a practiced smile. "We'll just sit in a corner booth, and you can take the seat that faces out."

Maddie didn't answer as she grabbed them both menus and got in line. He'd clearly done this before, and it was a strange thing to get used to—worrying about who might be looking. But for him, it was just daily life. No wonder it had changed him.

And last night he'd seemed . . . haunted. It was the only

word that fit. It reinforced that he was just a man, like every other man. He wasn't perfect. He had scars that weren't on the surface, and he'd learned to hide them away so no one ever saw them. *He must be so damn lonely.*

All it would take was one person in Brandywood recognizing him and the whole town would know he was here. He had to know that was a risk, though, and he'd still come out here with her. Which felt oddly . . . *encouraging?*

Fortunately, there was also a level of civility that people in town had given Maddie confidence that they wouldn't harass Brooks. Brandywood folks might gawk and stare and whisper when his back was turned, but they would leave him alone.

"Why don't you walk around with a security guard?" she asked, the thought suddenly occurring to her. Didn't most famous people always have bodyguards with them?

He shrugged. "Too much attention. I have to have them sometimes, of course. But when I'm doing something like this, I skip it and just try to blend. I had a few stalkers for a couple of years that made that next to impossible, but they moved on thankfully."

Stalkers? As in legitimate people who hunted him down? That Brooks had a whole different life she couldn't even imagine was unsettling.

She didn't get the feeling he'd want to talk about that, though.

"What are you in the mood for?" Maddie asked, handing him a menu.

"Gatorade."

She rolled her eyes. "Eat something. And drink some water."

"Maaaaaybe some chicken broth."

"Serves you right," she said with a shake of her head.

"I forgot how much I hate hangovers."

"Well, here's to no more. Ever again." She leaned across him and pointed at his menu. "Bunny doesn't offer her chicken soup for breakfast, but she'll do it for me if I ask because I know she's already got it simmering back there."

"Sold." They got to the front of the line, where Bunny stood taking orders, a pumpkin-decorated apron over her plump figure. Some things in Brandywood never changed, and Bunny working the front register at Brandywood was one of those things that comforted Maddie.

Bunny's blue eyes lit as she saw Maddie. "Good morning, darling," she said, leaning across the counter and planting a kiss on her cheek. She looked over at Brooks and gave Maddie a questioning look. "Who's the dish?"

"Bunny, this is my *friend*." She purposely left off his name in case anyone close by was watching. "And this is Bunny Wagner Yardley . . . my step-grandma. Bunny is married to my grandfather. My friend would like a bowl of chicken soup, and I'll take the smoked salmon and avocado on a croissant, both of which are the most delicious in the world."

"Hello, friend," Bunny said with a knowing look. She chuckled. "You don't have to flatter me to get the soup, kiddo. I'm more than happy to get it for you." She directed her attention to Brooks. "I should warn you that you're in the hands of someone mildly exaggerating my talents."

"To be honest, your café was the first place I was recommended when I came into town—by someone else. So it's not just Maddie," Brooks said smoothly.

Really? Who else had he talked to in town? Maddie gave him a curious look.

"I'm not exaggerating anything." Maddie took her card out to pay.

Bunny waved her off. "You're family."

"But I want to."

"Family doesn't need to pay, sweetheart."

Brooks stepped in, slipping his card out of his wallet and sliding it over. "What if I pay? I'm not family. And I'd really love to treat Maddie to breakfast."

Bunny sighed reluctantly, then took the card. She swiped it and handed it back. "I'll bring the food out to your table, love."

Maddie turned to lead Brooks toward the table, then froze.

Josh and Gina were walking through the front door, hand in hand.

A squeal sounded from someone at a nearby table—one of Gina's friends—who stood, flapping her hands. "Let me see, let me see!" She rushed up to Gina, reaching for her hand.

Holy shit.

Is that a DIAMOND?

Feeling like the floor was opening beneath her, Maddie reached for the first thing to steady herself on, which happened to be Brooks's arm.

The whole café seemed to be watching Josh and Gina now, and a few people started clapping and handing out congratulations.

And there were the inevitable eyes on Maddie, too.

What the fuck?

They'd only been dating for a few weeks . . . *right?*

Maddie's throat quickly went dry, tears pricking her eyes as Josh met her gaze.

Brooks's smooth, deep voice was in her ear. "Someone you know, I take it."

She let his voice ground her, then tore her gaze away and nodded.

Brooks took her by the hand, then led her to the farthest corner booth. But instead of taking the seat that faced in, out of sight from the rest of the café, he plopped her in that seat and then sat beside her.

The familiar black-and-white-checkered pattern of the tabletop grew wavy in her vision.

Brooks said nothing but interlaced his fingers with hers. "An ex?"

A tear slid onto her cheek, and she brushed it away. "We just broke up four weeks ago." She swallowed hard. "He left me for her."

God, I'm so pathetic.

She'd told herself she wouldn't shed any more tears over Josh.

But it still hurt.

"Why, Josh? Why are you doing this?" she'd asked him the day they'd broken up.

"I just . . . we have so much fun together. She makes me feel alive, Maddie. I think we just settled into an ordinary, boring routine. Forgot to have fun anymore."

Ordinary. Josh Hawkins—the king of gray polo shirts and khakis. Who had oatmeal for breakfast, peanut butter for lunch, and baked chicken and rice for dinner—every day. Who had been voted in high school "Most Likely to Stay the Same."

He had called *her* ordinary.

"Maybe she gives him really good head," she muttered, barely realizing she'd voiced the snarky thought.

"Doubtful. Madison, if he went from you to her, he's an absolute fucking moron. Anyone with eyes can see that," Brooks said in a low growl.

If he'd said it another time, maybe it would have made her feel better, but it didn't right now.

Because Josh proposed to her.

After four weeks.

"Hey," Brooks tried again. He slid his arm around her shoulder. "Hey, look at me."

"I can't look at you," she complained miserably. "You have sunglasses on."

Brooks sighed, then pulled the sunglasses off, setting them on the table. "Better?"

"Yeah." Her eyes locked with his concerned gray ones.

My God, he smells good.

And he was close. Like, really, really close.

Her heart pounded as she remembered his words the night before, the feeling of his thumb and lips against hers.

She'd wanted to kiss him so badly.

Being the sober one in that situation had put her completely at a disadvantage now, though. Because she knew what she'd been feeling wasn't because of alcohol—it was real.

But what about Brooks?

Drunk people said many untrue things. Especially men.

"How long were you together?" Brooks asked softly.

"Four months. But we were living together, so I thought he was . . ."

"I get it." Brooks glanced over his shoulder at Josh and Gina. "Want me to punch him for you? I've been told my punches land so hard I should be in jail."

She laughed, despite the terrible truth to his joke. "That would be antithetical to my 'let's take care of Brooks's plan."

"Eh, fuck Brooks. Let's take care of Madison."

"You're ridiculous." But he'd made her smile.

A bowl slid in front of Brooks, then Bunny set Maddie's croissant sandwich down and sat on the opposite side of the booth. She wore a worried, serious look. "Want me to kick them out of the café?"

Thank God Lindsay and Travis stopped the feud between our families. I love Bunny.

Maddie smiled. "No, you don't have to do that."

"I don't mind doing it. Nothing would give me more pleasure than putting a Strickland in their place. I heard what they did to you—crossing your name out on the Applepalooza sign-up sheet. And also about that River Boat band. Your grandfather was livid."

Really? Pops hadn't displayed that level of emotion in front of her. Then again, she imagined there was a side of Pops that only Bunny got to see.

"River House," Maddie corrected. She felt Brooks's eyes on her, then remembered how he'd said the night before he wouldn't be playing at the fair. They'd have to come back to that topic eventually, but right now it felt like a hot-button topic to bring up amid a fragile truce.

Especially now that I've apologized for blackmailing him.

"Same difference." Bunny shrugged. Then she looked at Brooks. "You in town this weekend?"

Brooks nodded. "Yes, ma'am."

"You're a good-looking young man. You should sign up with our Maddie for the Applepalooza contests. Show those two up. You'll be the best-looking couple, that's for sure."

"Bunny, I'm sure Brooks has better things to do than go to Brandywood's Applepalooza. I'm not even sure *I'm* going."

"Hmph. Well, he should. And he should take you. Josh hasn't been able to take his eyes off your table." Bunny nodded in Josh's direction, then winked. "Just say the word, and I'll tell them to go somewhere else." She stood and headed back to the counter.

Shit. Is Josh really staring at us?

Maddie checked over her shoulder toward him. He *was*—but his gaze was fixed on Brooks.

Dammit.

Bunny might not know who Brooks was, but she didn't expect any of the older crowd in Brandywood to be familiar with young rock stars.

Josh definitely will, though. It appeared he already had.

And so had several other people in the café.

Maddie cringed. "Don't look now, but I think your cover is blown."

"I don't care," Brooks said, tucking his thumb and forefinger under her chin and lifting it so she focused on him. "Don't pay any attention to him. What's an Applepalooza?"

A smile curved on her lips. Tucked in the booth with Brooks, sitting on the same side, she could almost pretend they were in their own little bubble, even as the volume level dropped slightly and the whispers began.

"It's one of Brandywood's fall traditions. There are all sorts of different apple-themed contests throughout the day. Bobbing for apples, an apple pie contest, an apple-picking contest, apple barrel racing, Auction-a-Peck, a few other things . . . and then there's a singing competition at the end of the day."

"Singing competition?" Brooks furrowed his brow. "What does that have to do with apples?"

"Well, it used to be that you had to use a song that had the word 'apple' in it, but then people got bored with hearing one too many renditions of 'My Favorite Things,' 'You Are the Sunshine of My Life,' and 'Don't Sit Under the Apple Tree,' so they changed the rules a few years ago and just let people sing whatever they want. But the winner gets the Golden Apple trophy."

"I've officially left real America and entered New Christmastown on a romance movie set, haven't I?" Brooks snickered.

She dipped her finger into the collar of his dark gray T-shirt and tugged it out. "Don't worry, city boy. We'll have you wearing flannel and chopping wood soon—oh! There is a wood-chopping contest, actually. Apple wood, that then gets used in the following year's pork butt smoking competition."

"Of course there is."

"You laugh, but it is many a woman's favorite part of the weekend."

"The pork butt or the wood chopping?" Brooks raised a brow.

She shared a laugh with him, amazed at how well he'd been able to lift her spirits. "Both. But if you are still in town, consider coming. Audrey would love it. You don't have to do any of the contests, obviously. Most of them are for teams of two, so a lot of couples do them together."

Like Josh and Gina.

Then she made the mistake of glancing back toward the café. Everyone was staring.

Everyone.

Including Gina, who looked less than thrilled that Brooks's presence was supplanting her big news. All her friends, who had gathered at a table to celebrate, were looking at Brooks instead.

Maddie rolled her eyes.

Was this what his life was like?

God, this had to be annoying.

She pulled away from Brooks and stood on the seat. "Listen, people. Yes. It's Brooks Kent. He's here visiting one of our own—Cormac Doyle. And I'm trying to show Brooks around Brandywood today, so I'd really appreciate it if you'd all do me the favor of acting like chill human beings and treating him that way, too." Her gaze snapped to Henry Clayton, who had taken his cell phone out. "What are you taking a picture for, Henry? You going to stare lovingly at it night after night? I have a feeling you won't look at it again after today, so why bother take it at all?"

A couple of people snickered, looking away, embarrassed.

"Can I ask for an autograph?" another woman asked.

"For what purpose? Hanging it in your living room?" Bunny spoke up from behind the counter.

"Couldn't have put it better myself. So maybe let's show Brooks the side of Brandywood we all know and love and let him enjoy himself. Text your friends and family. Anyone who messes with Brooks will have Maddie Yardley's wrath to pay. And I am *not* as nice as the rest of my family. For that matter, you can count on the rest of the Yardleys giving you hell, too. Right, Bunny?"

"You got that right." Bunny crossed her arms in a no-nonsense look.

Maddie's face burned with a delayed sense of awareness as she sat again, but a moment later, normal conversation seemed to resume in the café. "That should take care of that."

Brooks was giving her an odd look.

"What?" She avoided looking at him, lifting her breakfast sandwich. She hadn't realized how hungry she was until now.

The package of oyster crackers beside her bowl crinkled as he opened it and popped one into his mouth. "No one has ever done that for me before," he said at last.

"Told people to stay away from you? Don't bodyguards do that?"

"I meant stand up for me when they didn't have to." He emptied the crackers into his soup and lifted the spoon.

Really? No one? Ever?

Sadness filled her. He wouldn't want her pity and hadn't been asking for it, though.

"Well, you had the good fortune of falling in with a Yardley." Maddie put on her brightest smile. "Everyone knows who my family is."

"So you're a celebrity around here." Brooks grimaced as he hesitated, then sipped at the broth. He gave a look of surprise. "This is better than I thought it would be."

"I told you." She took a large bite of her breakfast and tried to keep from groaning. Jen Cavanaugh, who had learned from Bunny, had some of the best baked goods in town, but *nobody* beat Bunny's croissants. "If you know what's good for you, you'll stick with me, Brooks."

He chuckled, then sipped his soup again. "You want to know a secret?"

She looked over her shoulder at him, batting her eyelashes prettily. "I'm a girl. Of course I do."

"I wouldn't want to be in Brandywood with anyone else."

Maddie smiled, but her throat clenched. Man, he had a nice smile. It was easy to forget how gorgeous he was when he was scowling.

Crap.

No. Don't even think about it, Maddie.

He's leaving. He's famous. His life isn't here.

So don't get attached.

But she had a feeling it might already be too late for that.

21

MADDIE

"Is THERE a reason we're crossing the street before we get to your family's store?" Brooks asked as they made their way down Main Street later in the afternoon.

Dammit, he noticed. Maddie winced, then peeled off her sweater and tied it around her waist. It had been cold when she'd headed out the night before to Brooks's place wearing a sweatshirt and joggers.

In fact, *this* close to her apartment, she could just as easily hop over there and change.

But she hadn't considered it because Naomi might see her.

She'd taken so much time off work this week. Devoted soooo much time to Brooks. After how hurt Naomi had been the night before—which was justified, really—she wasn't prepared for another run-in while *with* Brooks.

Maddie pulled her hair into a messy ponytail and met Brooks's awaiting stare.

"My sister—the one who runs the Depot with me—didn't exactly take the news about our arrangement with the accident too well."

His gaze clouded over some, his lips drawing to a line.

Right. He wasn't thrilled about me telling anyone, either.

"I had to tell her," she started, shifting her weight to her back foot. "She was suspicious anyway about the time I was taking from work, and then she suggested getting video footage from the shop across the street."

Alarm filled Brooks's face. "Does that exist?"

"Probably. I didn't really think of that. But I'm sort of hoping that as long as we don't say anything about what happened, they won't go looking for it."

Brooks crossed his arms, clearly unconvinced. "What sort of people are the shop owners across the street from you?"

Maddie looked around. Two o'clock on a Thursday in September wasn't exactly crowded on Main, but sometimes it felt like the walls and alleys had ears. She stepped closer to Brooks and sighed.

"Truthfully, they're terrible. It's an ice cream shop, and the owner, Fred Strickland, has had it out for my grandfather for a couple of years now. He claims that when Pops opened his shop, the town council promised him he'd be the only ice cream shop on Main Street. He has no record of that, of course, and nothing in writing, and until a few years ago, he took no issue with anyone else in town who sold ice cream in their stores. That all changed when my grandfather built the Depot across the street from him."

"Your Depot sells ice cream?"

Maddie nodded. "Gelato, actually. My grandfather is half-Italian, and he wanted to pay tribute to his mom with that. Fred started a campaign with a few rival families to get the Depot kicked off Main. It didn't go through the council, but he almost got half the town on board for a while."

Brooks scowled. "This is the bullshit that makes me loathe small towns."

Ouch.

"Also, his daughter is the one who just got engaged to my ex. So . . . yeah, we're not exactly friendly."

"Sounds like an understatement." He drew a sharp breath. "So how do we get that footage? I could try to get my lawyer involved, see if they'll sell it and sign an NDA."

Maddie shook her head. "I wouldn't trust Fred Strickland—or Gina. They hear you want money for that videotape, and they'll blackmail you. Might even shop it to the tabloids if there's anything worth seeing."

He gave her a dead stare. "Yeah, sounds pretty terrible, doesn't it?"

Oof. His words hit her square in the chest, her mouth going dry.

"I didn't—"

"Forget it. We're even at this point. And you apologized."

But his words fueled her guilt.

She never should have blackmailed him.

Or lied to Naomi.

God, I made such a mess out of things, and I have no idea how to fix it.

She could fix this—couldn't she?

"You know what? I have an idea." She grabbed his hand, tugging him down the closest alleyway.

"Where are we going?"

She didn't want to chicken out. "Almost no one locks their back door around here during the day. The Stricklands keep their storage room in the back, along with their security system, so if we're lucky—"

"You're not seriously suggesting we steal it, are you?" Brooks's voice belied more of his shock than his face.

"I mean . . . we might not be able to. I don't know if they've switched to something that uploads to an online server. But probably not. Fred isn't known for being a fan of modernizing. Or change, for that matter. Knowing him, he's got one that records to an SD card. I think he does. I've been in the storage room before."

Brooks grabbed her by the elbow. "But again. Breaking and entering. And theft."

Maddie rolled her eyes. "What choice do we have? It's just an SD card. Hopefully. We can wipe it and return it. No harm done."

Brooks removed his baseball cap, combing his fingers through his flattened, dark hair. "Jesus, Madison. And people think I'm a sinner. Meanwhile, you're a temptress who masquerades as an angel."

She didn't mind the sound of that. "I'll take that as a compliment. Are you in or out?" She crossed her arms. "It's the least risky way to get that video."

Then again, maybe it was Brooks who made her want to be daring. This was fun.

"And how is it you've been in their storage room?"

A slow smile curved on her lips. "One of my high school boyfriends used to work at the ice cream shop, and we used to make out in the storage room. There's also no security camera in there, which is why we chose that spot."

"I can't believe I'm actually considering this," he muttered.

She grabbed his hand again. "Just . . . don't overthink it. What's the worst that can happen?"

"We get caught. They call the cops. I get arrested. Again. Twice in one week would really do me in, you know."

"They're not going to catch us," she said with overconfidence. "Look, I'll go up to the back door, open it up, and see if anyone's in there. You can just stay outside. If someone comes,

I'll tap twice on the back door and you walk away. That way, there's barely any risk to you. But it is slow this time of day. It's probably just a bored employee sitting in the front scrolling through his phone."

He reset his cap and crossed his arms. "And you would do that for me?"

His words made her breath catch. *Yeah, I guess I would.* She nodded.

"Why?"

Why indeed?

Partially because she wasn't afraid of getting caught. And the bad consequences seemed easy enough to get out of.

But also . . . because he needs it. And he's never had someone on his team like this.

And after the conversation she'd had with Kayla this morning, she realized just how tough Brooks's life had been. He'd been a good big brother, one who had always put Kayla, and then Audrey's needs first. Last night had been a literal nightmare for him, and it was okay to show him some compassion.

"Because you're my friend," she said at last, tilting her head. "And it's worth a shot. You don't deserve to be blackmailed just because you had a car accident. Especially not by two jerks from this town." She winked.

"You're not a jerk." He sighed and was quiet for another beat. "All right, fine. I'll play your lookout. I can't really afford to get caught, though, Madison. People are pretty quick to jump to conclusions with me. That's why my manager thought he could sell a story about sex therapy and drug rehab to the press—even though I don't sleep around and have never touched a drug in my life. But people believe what they want to believe."

His words made her sad for him but also frustrated her. "I'm not saying this to be mean, Brooks, but you sort of let people believe that about you. You participated in toeing the line enough and didn't push back when you should have. And if you won't stand up for yourself, who will?"

He gave one stiff nod. "Send me your bill when I get back home."

Right. He's done with the life coaching. Still, she didn't entirely mind his smart-ass quips. It was a side of him she liked. Felt genuine.

"All right, fine. But I'm setting my watch. Two minutes. If you can't find anything, get the hell out of there. You don't need to risk anything with people who dislike you, either."

She waggled her brows. "Clearly, you don't know how smooth I am." Ridiculously, excitement bubbled through her. Life had certainly been . . . *more exciting* with Brooks in it. She couldn't remember the last time, since high school really, when breaking the rules had even been a realistic option. What was she supposed to do as a grown-up to break any rules? Eat dessert first?

. . . or move in with a new boyfriend after a couple of weeks of dating?

She hurried down the alley toward the Stricklands' ice cream shop, Brooks following her. Tracing her fingertips against the sides of the bricks, she drew closer to the back door and surveyed the alley.

No one in sight.

"Stay here," she whispered. "Like I said, if I tap twice on the door, get out of the alley, all right?"

Brooks's face was a dark mask, but he gave a curt nod.

Her heart skipped a beat, then she turned the knob and opened the door. "Mr. Strickland?" she called softly, just in case he was close by. He might think she was there for a reason, if so. She'd have to think on her feet and come up with a reason for being there, but that was doable.

Silence answered her. She didn't see anyone inside the small storeroom either.

Smiling to herself, she slipped inside.

The fluorescent lights were already on, and dust motes swirled in the air as she closed the door gently. This place hadn't changed a bit in the twelve years since high school—shelves of industrial-sized boxes of cones, cups, spoons, ice cream sprinkles, and more.

Her boyfriend in high school, Liam Kelly, had once suggested they get into the chocolate syrup and whipped cream while back here. She grimaced at the memory of her younger self, so eager. That was the time Fred Strickland had caught them back here, too. Liam had been fired, and they'd ended up breaking up over the whole thing since his parents were so pissed.

Her first real heartbreak.

Focus.

This wasn't a time to go down memory lane.

Especially bad ones.

Though the chocolate syrup had been fun.

She sidled up to a filing cabinet that housed the storage system for the security cameras on top.

Yes. Same old system. The thick layer of dust on top of the machine indicated how long it had gone without being moved.

The problem was, she was probably too late to get the SD card from the DVR. If she remembered right, Liam had needed to change the card every four days if he was locking up at night. He'd stored the cards in the filing cabinet . . .

. . . but it was locked.

Damn.

Jiggling it, she frowned.

Where in the hell did they keep the key again?

She couldn't be mad at her seventeen-year-old self for not

taking better notes of the Stricklands' security system. If anything, she was impressed she remembered as much as she did.

Turning in a circle, she scanned the shelves, searching for a key ring.

The back door to the alley opened, and Maddie's stomach clenched, her head jerking up. Brooks stepped inside, quickly closing the door behind him.

"What are you doing in here?" she hissed, closing the gap between them.

"Someone was coming down the alley. I heard people talking."

"So you jumped in here?"

He removed his sunglasses and gave her a sheepish look. "I didn't want to abandon you."

His words almost made her melt.

Dammit, Brooks. Don't be sweet.

"Yeah, but now you're stuck in here with me."

"You think I don't know that?" He rubbed his eyes with one hand, bringing his fingers slowly toward the bridge of his nose, stress written on his features. "What now? Shit, this was so reckless."

"The good news is that the Stricklands have the same security system they used to. Which means the only footage from last Sunday is on an SD card in this room."

He gave her a quizzical glance. "What's the bad news?"

"The card is locked in the filing cabinet, and I don't know where the key is."

"Fuck."

Maddie bit her lip, growing silent as the voices Brooks had referred to drew nearer.

Her knees nearly buckled as she recognized Fred Strickland's drawl.

Oh no, no.

"Make that double fuck." Maddie scanned the small space wildly. "We're about to get caught in here by the guy who owns this place."

A horrified expression filled Brooks's face.

Dammit. This was so stupid of me.

So dumb, Maddie.

Taking a risk that affected only her was one thing—but Brooks didn't need this.

Think.

She set her hand on his forearm. "I have an idea. You'll have to follow my lead, though."

"Whatever you say, boss."

"I'm serious," she hissed. "Brooks. I need you to kiss me. Like you mean it."

He gave her an incredulous look. "What?"

"Just . . . trust me."

"Trust you? Isn't trusting you what got us into this mess?"

Fred's voice was almost at the door. "*. . . you don't need sloppy seconds . . .*"

"Do it. Now."

Brooks reached over and plucked her toward him, lifting her almost effortlessly. As her legs slid around his waist, clamping around him, he pushed her back against the door. Her arms slipped around his neck as their mouths connected, as though they had practiced this thousands of times.

The feeling of Brooks's lips against her own sent a jolt of electricity spiraling through her, an involuntary moan curling through her throat as his lips claimed hers, unyielding in their pressure. She closed her eyes, her heart racing.

Their tongues collided, hungry, sensuously stroking.

Too real.

This feels too fucking real.

Oh my God, this man can kiss.

Heat flooded her face, her body taking over instinctively, as one of his hands slid up her back and cradled the nape of her neck, digging into her hair. Wrecking it. She didn't care, though. His mouth felt incredible, the taste of him making her suddenly desperate for more.

Fuck.

I'm so into this.

She tried to will herself not to get too wrapped up in the moment—*what the hell is taking Fred so long to open the goddamned door?*—but she also didn't want it to end. Her core turned to liquid, her body helpless as Brooks slid the other hand up the front of her shirt, his palm cupping one breast.

Yes. More.

A guttural sound came from her throat, and she swore Brooks chuckled—*damn him*—at the response.

Two can play, buddy.

She ground against his groin, twisting her hands into his short hair, his baseball cap falling off. At the feeling of his own hardening arousal, she almost moaned again.

Shit. Slow down, Maddie.

"*. . . and that's another thing. What's the rush? You got your whole life ahead of you,*" Fred Strickland was saying.

The throbbing rush of her pulse filled her ears. Brooks squeezed her breast. *Fuck it.* She moaned again, this time unashamedly.

The door opened, and they both went tumbling forward into the alleyway as Brooks tried to steady them from falling.

"What the hell?" Fred Strickland growled.

Face aflame, Maddie untangled her mouth and arms from Brooks, and he set her down. His neck was almost as red as her face felt.

Good.

She refocused her attention on Fred . . . and Gina, who stood beside him, both staring at her like she'd lost her damn mind. Which she probably had, let's be honest.

"Mr. Strickland!" Maddie straightened her messed crop top, wishing she had enough fabric to cover her stomach. She combed her fingers through her hair, her knees feeling unsteady.

Damn Brooks and his passionate kisses.

"Um, I was showing my friend around all my favorite spots in Brandywood. You know, a trip down memory lane." Her exit strategy no longer seemed like a great option, but if it got Brooks out of trouble, she'd take it.

Fred glared at her. "Yeah, you always were trashy. Get the fuck out of my store, Maddie. I ever catch you in here again for your perverted activities—"

Gina leaned in suddenly, eyes glued to Brooks, and whispered something in her father's ear.

"I'm so sorry, Mr. Strickland," Maddie said, taking the break to play nice. "We just got a bit carried away."

Fred stared Brooks down, his scowl etched deeply on his brow.

Brooks bent and grabbed his baseball cap from the ground, then set it on his head, giving Fred a disdainful look.

At last, Fred sniffled. He held out his hand to Brooks. "I suppose there's no harm done," he said gruffly.

Brooks set a hand on the small of Maddie's back, ignoring Fred's proffered hand. "I don't shake hands with assholes who insult my woman."

Maddie's heart squeezed hard, her eyes flying to Brooks's face as he replaced his sunglasses. Gina's mouth dropped open, and Fred's face reddened as Brooks steered them past the Stricklands into the alley.

My God.

She might not be his woman, but a line like that was enough to melt her panties off.

"Don't let me catch you back here again," Fred finally sputtered out when they were nearly twenty feet away.

A nervous laugh choked out of her, then Maddie grabbed Brooks's hand and ran.

22

BROOKS

Brooks didn't know how in the hell Madison Yardley had talked him into anything that had just happened. But as she led him up the backstairs of the Depot into her apartment, he also didn't question it.

His pride had almost screwed him with that dick, who could have easily called the cops on them.

But he also couldn't let the ass get away with calling Maddie a slur like he'd used.

For whatever reason, Maddie seemed exhilarated, a smile never leaving her lips as she turned the key to her apartment. Those fucking delicious lips had knocked him nearly senseless.

Then they were inside, and Brooks drew her to him.

Whether from the sheer adrenaline of the moment or the fact that they'd started something and now it needed exploring, they found their way into each other's arms in an instant.

Brooks pulled her long hair down from the messy ponytail, and it tumbled over her shoulders in waves.

So. Fucking. Gorgeous.

Her hands were on him, climbing up his back as he swept

her back against the wall again, his mouth devouring hers. She tasted better than any damn dessert she'd made him try today—his trainer in LA might kill him—and he kissed her like a starved man, unable to decide what part of the feast to start on.

Their bodies pressed into each other, his hunger for her damn near consuming him.

He was fucking turned on.

Wanted to flip her over and fuck her right against the damn wall.

Run his mouth over every square inch of her delicious body.

Fuck . . . he felt his control spiraling, raw sexual need taking over as his mouth widened against hers, his tongue dancing against her own.

Too many clothes were between them.

"You're so fucking sexy, Madison," he growled, yanking that crop top off her. She'd been tempting him all week with the low-cut tops and flat, perfect belly.

God . . . those tits. Perfect mounds of flesh quivering in a turquoise bra begging to be ripped off. His mouth practically watered at the sight, and her bra was off a second later.

Her pink nipples were tight, peaking for him, and he swept the nubs against his palms, wanting to draw them into his mouth. Suck her hard, feel her twitch against the swirling of his tongue.

Gaze locked with his, her hand slipped below his waistband, her eyes widening as she wrapped her hand around him.

Yesss. Fuck. Yes.

He drew a sharp breath, nearly losing control at the feel of her soft hand on his cock. He wanted her mouth on it. His mouth consumed hers again, hands squeezing her tits as she moaned with pleasure.

Fuck that.

He wanted to bury himself so deep inside her and fuck until they both couldn't walk.

"We should slow down," Maddie whispered between kisses.

He swallowed hard. "Your move, beautiful."

She wet her lips—*damn, that's going to do me in*—and he tried to steady his racing heart.

Returning her lips to his, she drew his lower lip into a soft, slow kiss. "I want to," she murmured, her breath warm against his mouth. "I want to so, so much."

"But . . .?"

Madison set her forehead against his, her chest rising and falling with heavy breaths, her breasts heaving under his hands.

"But you're leaving in a few days. And I—"

He closed his eyes, willing his pulse to slow.

She's not the one-night-stand type.

I already knew that, though.

"We don't have to do anything." He dragged his mouth to her temple and kissed it. "There's nothing to be ashamed of. It was natural. Our bodies just took over after that show back there."

Yeah, that's all it was. Except he'd done nearly naked modeling shoots for brands he'd worked with. Intimate photos with international models had never had the same effect that the kiss in that storage room had.

Raging unfulfilled lust.

Maddie nodded, then pulled her hand away and stepped back from him. Confusion showed in her eyes as she combed her fingers through her hair. Her lips were still swollen from their kisses. All he wanted was to reach down and kiss her again, but it was easier to stare at that delicious mouth than her tits, which might just kill him.

"I'm sorry," she said as she pulled her top back on. "My

body hates me right now, believe me. Because you're obviously incredibly hot. And it was a good kiss, Brooks. But I'm just getting out of something and neither of us is looking for anything. And I'm not good at casual anything, Brooks, let alone sex. I'm like that girl who guys dread because I start picking out curtains after a first date. And you're Brooks Kent, so we're not going to date. God, I think I just used your name like three times."

She was cute when she was flustered.

And she's also right.

"We don't have to overthink it." He smiled, hoping it looked genuine, even if he didn't feel it. "I'm just passing through town, and the last thing I want to do is hurt you. Especially after all you've done for me this week."

She guffawed. "Like what? Blackmail you? Insult you? Try to rope you into trespassing and theft?"

This time, he did smile for real. He came closer and pulled her into a hug that lacked all the heat of their previous embrace but still had warmth. "This has definitely been an interesting week."

She said nothing, and they settled into a comfortable silence. He set his chin on her head, breathing in her scent, wanting to memorize, catalog, and store it. Keep her with him forever.

Ever with me.

There was a lyric in the moment.

She was, by far, the first woman who'd made him feel . . . *anything* in a long, long time.

Maybe ever.

And somehow, admitting that to himself hurt like a firebrand going through his lungs.

Maddie sighed. "What's your life like after you leave here on Sunday?"

"Not sure." He couldn't get over how comfortable he felt just holding her, and he wasn't ready to release her yet. "I have to talk to my lawyer about my arrest and figure out what's going on with that. Talk to my label and quit. Hire a new manager. Sort my recording contract and see what impact it has on my international label. You know . . . all the boring legal things. What about you?"

"Same thing I do week after week for the rest of my life." She drew a sharp breath and pulled away. "I'm going to go change. I'm still wearing the same clothes I slept in. Maybe we can head back to your place after that, and I'll drop you off."

He nodded, and she went toward the bedroom.

Brooks glanced around the apartment, taking it in for the first time. The last time he'd been here, he'd been so exhausted and overwhelmed that he'd barely paid attention to the place.

He frowned.

For as warm and vivacious as Maddie was, this apartment was . . . the opposite. Spartan in decor and bland, it reflected nothing of her personality. He'd stayed in hotels that had more personal touches than this.

Maybe that wasn't the best comparison, considering the caliber of hotels where he'd stayed.

Still, these were the four walls she lived and breathed in. A life so vastly different from his own. He could remember what it was like to just exist in a town known only to a handful of people, every day beholden to the doldrums of the ordinary.

How hard he'd worked to break free of it—thinking that if he just worked harder, sold more, did more, he'd be able to escape. Only to find out that he could never outrun himself. He was too fucked up, too ruined.

Dad had ruined him, and nothing he could do would change that.

Was Maddie right, though? Did he perpetuate what people thought about him by *letting* them spread rumors?

Maybe it's about time I do something about that, too.

The door to the apartment opened, and a young woman—who looked eerily like Maddie—came in. She stopped short, hand on the knob, blinking at him. A look of displeasure settled on her mouth.

Thank God Maddie and I weren't having sex right now.

"You must be Brooks Kent. I should have known she brought you here." She didn't smile, didn't sound particularly welcoming.

"That's me," he said politely. "And you are?"

"Naomi. I'm Maddie's older sister." She came farther inside. "The *other* owner of the Depot whom you neglected to negotiate with after you wrecked the place. And the one who had to deal with most of the cleanup since you've been dragging my sister to . . . what is it again? Play servant for you?"

His old instinct to meet rudeness head-on flared, but this was Maddie's sister.

Holding back, he said, "No, not exactly."

Naomi crossed her arms. "Then what . . . exactly? Because I just got a furious phone call from Fred Strickland across the street, claiming that you two were using his storeroom for . . . fooling around."

That son of a bitch. He'd seriously ratted Maddie out to her sister?

When he didn't answer, Naomi's expression darkened. "Look, Mr. Kent. I don't know you, and I won't make any assumptions about you, but whatever you're doing with my sister, she's not without people who care about her. We will take you to task for hurting her."

He glowered at her. "Of course, the manner you're talking

to me contradicts the 'not making any assumptions' part, though."

The door to Maddie's bedroom opened and she came out, wearing a floral, long-sleeved minidress that hugged her curves. She stopped when she saw her sister. "Naomi!" A hesitant look crossed her face, and she came closer, seeming to sense the tension between them. "Hey."

"Hey yourself." Naomi raised a brow. "So Fred Strickland called."

Maddie's eyes darted to Brooks. "I can explain that." She went over to the kitchen and grabbed a glass from beside the sink. Her hand trembled as she poured herself a glass of water.

She doesn't deserve to be grilled by anyone—including her sister. "Whatever is between Maddie and me isn't really anyone else's business," Brooks said, crossing the room toward her.

"It is when you're making out like teenagers in the back of someone's store," Naomi snapped. She stared at Maddie. "What in the hell, Maddie? Why am I getting phone calls about stuff that Mom and Dad had to handle over a decade ago? To tell you the truth, it's worse that it's you two—you're grown-ass adults. And at the *Stricklands?*"

"It wasn't like that," Maddie said quietly, sipping her water.

"You swore up and down yesterday that you did *not* have a physical relationship with this man, even after he sent a skeevy 'whenever I want' text to you. Just another lie?"

Oh shit, Naomi saw that?

No wonder Maddie hadn't texted him back.

She must have been dealing with *this.*

"We don't have a physical relationship," Maddie blurted. "I was trying to get the security footage from last Sunday. Fred and Gina just happened to come by, and I told Brooks we should kiss as a cover since there was no logical explanation for us being there."

Naomi's eyes widened, and she set her hand to her forehead. "Oh my God, I didn't think the story could get any worse. You were trying to *steal* from Fred?"

He couldn't let Maddie take the blame for this. "It's my fault—"

"It was my idea. Brooks didn't even want to do it." Maddie set down the glass of water and moved around the other side of the island, closer to her sister. "I just got worried after what you said yesterday about the video."

"That didn't mean you should break into his storeroom and try to steal the footage." Naomi squeezed her eyes shut. "I can't decide if I need a Tylenol or a shot of tequila. What is even happening right now?"

When Naomi opened her eyes, they blazed at Brooks. "Why the hell are you still in this town? Haven't you done enough damage already? What, does Maddie need to go to jail, too, before you're satisfied?"

Funny . . . he could almost agree with her.

Guilt burned at his gut with an acerbic speed. "You're right, it was risky—"

"You're being incredibly rude," Maddie snapped at her sister. "Brooks had nothing to do with this plan. I dragged him over there. And he's my friend, so I'd appreciate it if you'd treat him with a modicum of respect."

"*Your friend?*" Naomi's expression pained, and she moved closer to her and set her hand on her elbow. "Honey, Brooks Kent is a megastar who has known you for a handful of days. Maybe I can buy that he's friends with Cormac Doyle—who I'm going to murder as soon as I see—but you? He's just using you. Whenever he leaves, and it can't come soon enough, Brooks is going to forget you even exist."

Maddie flinched. “I think you should go, Naomi.”

Naomi’s eyes filled with angry tears. “You’re my sister. I love you. I’m just trying to look out for you—”

“Right now, you’re being as bad as Logan was when he found out Lindsay and Travis were dating. Except worse, because you have no real reason to treat Brooks this way. What’s his big mistake? Having a car accident?”

“He asked you to lie about it! Set you up against your family from the start, without a single concern about how it might impact the rest of us. And then has some demented request to have you serve him for ten hours doing whatever he wants.”

No wonder Naomi was mad. Given the way she’d said it, she was probably imagining the worst.

She set her hands on her hips, glaring at Brooks. “And yeah, now I’m finding out it might be as bad as it sounds because apparently, you seem to have some sort of twisted Stockholm syndrome. ‘Fake’ or not, you certainly convinced Fred you were *his woman*. So I guess nothing’s off the table?”

The headache he’d been ignoring from his hangover all day roared to life, and he set his hands on the counter to steady himself. “She doesn’t owe me anything anymore. Anyway, our deal about the concert ended the minute she told you about it.”

Now it was Maddie who turned and stared at him, hurt flashing through her face. God, he didn’t want that. But he needed to walk away at this point anyway.

He wanted to do the concert for her, but his presence was damaging her life so much. He’d help her find another band. That was easy enough.

Breaking the deal was a good excuse to make sure anything tying them together—other than paying for the accident damage—would end when he left. He was in too deep with her and had spent the day letting himself get swept away by the notion that their connection might last beyond this week.

It clearly couldn't.

"Good." Naomi turned back to Maddie, setting her hands on her. "I'm not trying to hurt you, Maddie, but this guy is a creep."

He'd been called far worse. But somehow, he probably deserved this one.

"Leave, Naomi." Maddie tore herself away, swiping her eyes. "You have no idea what you're talking about. You clearly came here to say what you wanted to say and you've said it. I told you the truth and it still wasn't good enough for you—just like it wasn't last night. So please go."

Naomi appeared conflicted

The last thing I want to do is to come between Maddie and her family.

"I apologize for the damage," he offered in a low voice. "I fully intend to pay for it."

Naomi turned, shook her head, then was out of the apartment, closing the door behind her.

"That went well," Maddie said, her voice flat and defeated.

He'd wounded her when he'd said the thing about the concert, clearly. "Maddie, for what it's worth—"

"I'm sorry. She was insanely rude, and you don't deserve that. My sister—well, all my family, really—gets a little carried away with the protectiveness. The double-edged sword of being close, I guess."

"She's right not to trust me and probably to be worried. But this started as a business arrangement between us, Maddie. It's cleaner if we just stick to that, don't you think?"

Maddie blinked at him. "We left business behind at least one hangover and a few kisses ago, Brooks."

"But maybe we shouldn't have. Crossing that line only

confused things. Hell, I probably shouldn't have asked you for that time, either. It was stupid of me. It's better if we just go our separate ways and part as friends."

A few beats of tension-filled silence settled in the space between them.

Tension that had only been made worse by letting himself get carried away. Those searing kisses had clouded his judgment.

The sadness on her face was killing him.

She'd been let down by people, too. Her family, clearly, who wouldn't ever approve of him.

And that asshole in the café who had broken her heart. Brooks had really wanted to punch him, especially after seeing Maddie's crestfallen look at the engagement news. She didn't deserve that.

She deserves so much more. More than I can give her.

"I'm going to ask around and see who else can play at that concert for you. I don't want to leave you in a lurch." As though that could absolve him from walking away.

"Thanks." Maddie nodded at last. "I'll drive you back to your place, then."

When you do that, I'll be completely alone.

Can't we stay here? Together?

But he didn't voice the thought, pushing it away as quickly as it came. The outside world had already pressed in on the bubble of separation they'd existed in this week.

It was time for him to go.

23

MADDIE

Nothing sounded worse than going to family pizza night tonight, and as Maddie drove back from dropping off Brooks, she turned down the street for Pops's house instead.

Maybe she could catch him before he and Bunny left for her parents' house.

Pops's house had long been one of Maddie's favorite places in the world. After he and Bunny had married, the strangest part of going over there was how Pops's place no longer felt like *his* quite as much. They'd remodeled some, and Bunny's favorite furniture and decorations graced the space. Grace Wagner had moved into Bunny's old house and kept most of the furniture, and it made sense that Bunny and Pops have a place that was theirs.

. . . but that doesn't mean I don't sometimes get nostalgic about what it was before.

As it so happened, Bunny was on the front porch with her closest friend, Millie Price, when Maddie pulled up. Maddie smiled at both women as she approached the front door, genuinely happy to see them.

"Hiya, sweetheart," Millie said, jumping from her seat to give her a hug. "Bunny tells me you bagged yourself a fine-looking new man."

Oh gosh.

Not who she wanted to talk about right now. "Just a friend," Maddie corrected gently as Millie took her hand.

"I don't know, sweetheart. He seemed to watch you with a lot more interest than just friendship," Bunny said with a knowing glance. She gestured to her cell phone. "I was just showing Millie his picture online. Whole town is buzzing about him, you know."

Maddie leaned against the front porch rail and wrapped her arms around her stomach. "Yeah, I figured they would be. But he really is just a friend. He's leaving in a couple of days and going back to LA. I doubt he'll be back after that."

"Well, don't give up that easily. Brandywood had a way of charming those big, tough men into staying. Just look at Jason," Millie said with a shrug. No one had been happier when Jason Cavanaugh had fallen in love with Jen than Millie. She'd finally gotten one of her grandsons to move to Brandywood.

But life isn't a fairy tale. The conversation she'd had with Pops a few days earlier came hurtling back. Things didn't work out so charmed all the time. Even when the not-so-obvious arrogant prince with a secret heart of gold *did* roll into town.

Or crash.

Ugh.

Dammit. I really, really like Brooks.

Tears pricked her eyes.

Millie's face turned to instant alarm. "Oh no, honey, what happened?" She gripped Maddie's elbows.

"Nothing." Maddie shook her head, trying to blink the tears away. "Nothing at all. Is Pops here?" she asked Bunny.

Bunny watched her thoughtfully. "No, sweetie, he already

left for your parents' house. I'm staying in tonight on account of my arthritis acting up."

Oh. Damn.

She could really use his advice.

But, then again, what was she going to ask him?

"Hey, Pops . . . turns out I have a bad crush on a man I really shouldn't. He's leaving in three days and has no interest in Brandywood. Oh, also, Naomi might hate him. But I took care of him after he got plastered last night, and it turns out, he's not the terrible person everyone in the world thinks. What am I supposed to do here?"

Even Pops couldn't solve that one.

Because there's nothing to solve.

The decision not to get further involved with him physically and to part as friends was rational. *Maybe the smartest thing I've done all week.*

Sex would have been fun, but it was dumb. He wasn't offering anything else, either, and she didn't expect him to.

Hell, what was he supposed to offer? He was a rock star with a career. His life could never be here. And long distance? That would be ridiculous.

That's *if* he even wanted a relationship, which she doubted he did.

She swallowed back a breath, then looked back at Bunny. "It's fine. Tell him I dropped by. I'm skipping pizza night, too. I'm pretty exhausted."

"You sure you don't want to stay here with us and have some dinner? I'm cooking a frozen chicken pot pie," Bunny said, warmth in her gaze.

"Yes, stay." Millie squeezed her arm. "We need someone young to keep us entertained. Otherwise, we'll just keep talking about the same damn people over and over again."

Tempting as Bunny's chicken pot pie—and even their

company—sounded, Maddie shook her head. "I think I really need some sleep."

She said her goodbyes, then headed back to her car.

Tonight, she needed some time to settle back into her own loneliness. Get used to the idea.

Otherwise, she might be tempted into seeking comfort and company in the wrong place again.

She needed to be wiser. Learn her lesson and let go of Brooks before she got hurt.

24

BROOKS

THE SUN WAS BEGINNING to rise, the lake taking on a soft pink and gold tone as the sky above it changed. Brooks grabbed a coffee, then slipped out onto the back deck and started toward the dock. Even at home in LA, he often got up for the sunrise, taking his coffee on the beach.

Spending the day before with Maddie had almost been the perfect antidote to the worst hangover Brooks had had in . . . well, five years.

Even though he'd said they'd part as friends, there was a finality when she'd dropped him off that he couldn't shake. He'd wanted to call her back. Text her. Tell her to stay.

But he'd just let her drive off instead.

There was other damage he'd needed to turn his attention to.

He still didn't know how he would make it up to Kayla, though. Or Audrey. He'd let them both down, and even though he'd let himself get distracted by Maddie's company, the problem wouldn't solve itself.

Even now, he couldn't stop thinking of Maddie as he made

his way onto the dock. She'd texted late last night, apologizing for failing to get the wreckage video from Fred Strickland's ice cream shop. As though she needed to apologize.

She'd done more for him than most of his so-called friends.

Like the way she'd shown up two nights ago. Put up with him. Stayed with him. *Looked after my sweet niece.*

He didn't deserve that sort of kindness from her. From anyone, really.

Because that's all it was, too. She'd turned down anything more, even while amid a hot and heavy kiss. And before that, she'd maintained a distance when they'd been wandering shops on Main Street. Somehow, it still felt like she kept getting him to spill more of his guts, while keeping her own history tightly under wraps.

The only reason he'd even found out about her ex was because of that run-in at the café.

Prick.

How dare he humiliate Maddie like that? Even if Josh hadn't known Maddie was going to be at *her own step grandmother's place* for breakfast, once he'd seen her, he shouldn't have made a show of things.

To his surprise, he wasn't the only one who'd thought of coming out to the dock. As he neared the Adirondack chairs, he spotted Cormac, sitting low in one, scrolling through his phone.

"I didn't know you were up," Brooks said, taking the chair beside him.

Cormac stretched, slipping his phone into his pocket. "Right back at you. Am I in your way here?"

In your way. Because this was "his" place. And Brooks had made that clear by kicking Cormac out.

"Look, man, I really owe you a huge apology." Steam rose from his coffee cup, and he watched it dissipate in the soft light.

"Nah, you're fine. I mean it. I just wanted to make sure you and Audrey were okay. Sorry for getting Maddie involved."

"You don't have to apologize for anything." Brooks leaned back in his chair despite the dew there. "You were right to call her. And Kayla."

Cormac closed his eyes, leaning his head against the back of the chair. "You know I think of Kayla like my own sister. And my own sisters would have killed me if I did nothing in that situation." He gave a light chuckle. "Family. The best and worst pain in the ass on the planet, right? No matter how many times I think I'm happy I left, they reel me right back in here, too. And now that my dad is sober and Mom's happy . . . it's hard to remember why I wanted to leave."

"You think you could settle someplace like this? Move back here?" Brooks gave Cormac a skeptical look. "It's so . . . small, don't you think?"

"I don't know." Cormac sighed and stretched his legs out. "It's not about the size of the place. It's about who's there. Nashville makes sense for me, especially as a musician. God knows I couldn't get the same amount of work here. But I do sometimes wonder if I really want the life I've built there for forever."

Cormac's eyes reflected the hint of pink in the sky. "When was the last time you bothered to put up a Christmas tree?"

Brooks frowned at him. *A Christmas tree?* "I don't know. In my place, or when I've gone to spend Christmas with Kayla? I don't think I've ever put one up in my place."

"Exactly." Cormac shrugged. "Me neither. Because what's the point, right?" He turned his face toward Brooks. "But maybe that is the point. Maybe I miss it."

"Putting up Christmas trees?" Brooks raised a brow. How in the hell was this even a discussion?

"No, numb nuts. Having a *reason* to put one up." Cormac

stood, then stretched. "Like I said before, we're not in our twenties anymore. The hangover was bad, wasn't it?"

Brooks grimaced. "Worst damn hangover of my life."

Cormac nodded. "Yeah. Things change. We're changing. Even a fish that stops swimming still gets pulled by the current. Nothing you can do about that." He shoved his hands in his pockets. "Anyway. I'm gonna head on in and leave you to the sunrise."

Brooks watched him go, and he furrowed his brows, still thinking about the damn Christmas tree question.

I've never cared that I don't put one up. Hell, last year he'd "celebrated" Christmas in Cabo. Alone, despite Kayla's wishes. Started the morning off with a swim.

Not that it had felt like Christmas.

But Cormac's nonsensical thoughts bothered him, too.

When he'd started his career, he'd been in college. The world "ahead" of him.

Now he was thirty-four, and there was no *next thing*.

"Well, howdy. Looks like you found your way to the lake after all," a man's voice came from the side, just out of his peripheral vision.

Brooks whirled around, spilling his coffee. Peter, the old man who'd driven him to Cormac's place that first day, was trolling by in a small pontoon, fishing gear on the deck beside him. His blue eyes twinkled as he brought the vessel closer to the dock.

"Good morning." Brooks wiped the coffee that had spilled onto his hand on his jeans.

He smiled. "Did I sneak up on you? Sorry about that."

"Just a bit."

"So did you solve those problems yet? Gotta admit, you still look like you're walking around with a fifty-pound weight on your shoulders."

Brooks searched his memory. He *had* told the man more than intended, that's right. So much had happened since the beginning of the week that he'd nearly forgotten Peter and his chattiness. "Not yet. If anything, I might have made them worse."

Peter gave him a sympathetic look. "The offer still stands if you want to go fishing. I've got to pick up a friend of mine a little down the ways from here, but you're welcome to come along."

"Right now?" Brooks looked back at the still house behind him. Kayla and Audrey were still asleep. He couldn't just take off in a fishing boat impromptu—could he?

"No time like the present." Peter brought the pontoon closer to the dock. "Hop on board."

He could just say a polite no and be done with it. He'd thrown out the man's number already and hadn't felt an ounce of regret over it.

But now that Peter was here again . . . something about it felt a bit like fate, tugging him forward.

Brooks nodded. "Yeah, all right."

The smile on Peter's face widened, then he docked the pontoon. "You know, I didn't catch your name the other day," he said as Brooks left his coffee mug on the dock and climbed on board.

"Brooks." He held out his hand for Peter.

Peter took it between his own two hands, the palms of his hands rough and callused. "Nice to meet you. Officially. Glad we ran into each other again. Take a seat."

Brooks sat down on a bench and Peter started forward again, the lake smooth as they cut across it. Funny how he'd spent so long living near the water but had never been fishing out there or any of the many gorgeous places he'd traveled.

The last time he'd been fishing, he'd been a small boy and his father had taken him.

The memory had been soured by his father's choice to leave them—like all memories of his father—and it had been a long time since he considered himself to be "outdoorsy" in any genuine sense. He enjoyed being outdoors, of course, swimming and running, particularly. But all the other things that outdoorsy folk did—fishing, climbing, hiking, camping—were not his style at all.

He'd much rather eat the fish after a trained chef fileted and prepared it than to catch the damn thing.

He half expected Peter to talk his ear off as he'd done the other day, but he was quiet, his pleasant face scanning the water.

At last, he pulled over toward another dock, where another old man sat in a lawn chair. He frowned at Brooks, giving him a suspicious look. "Who's the straggler?"

"That any way to treat my guest?" Peter chuckled and met Brooks's eyes. "Brian isn't a morning person. Just give him an hour. He'll come around."

Brian harrumphed and climbed onto the pontoon. "You're ten minutes late."

"You keep complaining, and I'm gonna let you off, circle around a bit, and make it another ten minutes." Peter held out an old-fashioned lunch pail toward him. "Bernadette packed you some apple turnovers and a ham, cheddar, and egg bagel sandwich. You can give the extra sandwich to Brooks."

Brian gave Brooks the side-eye. "Now I'm sharing my food with him?"

"No, I'm sharing *my* food with him. You haven't eaten already, have you, Brooks? My wife makes the best breakfast sandwiches in the world."

"No, sir."

"Polite, this one," Brian said, still eyeing him with suspicion as he set the lunch pail on his lap. "Where did you say you were from?"

"Eat your sandwich before you say anything else, Brian. Your sugar is probably low—you're extra cranky this morning," Peter said with an eye roll.

Brian and Peter had an ease in their banter that spoke of a lifelong friendship. Maybe a case of opposites being friends, but sometimes that made for the best friends. Cormac was a lot more laid-back and friendly than Brooks was, come to think of it.

"You go fishing often?" Peter asked Brooks as he stopped the boat in the middle of the lake.

"Not really." He was regretting having come out here. *What in the hell possessed me?*

"We're not going to have to teach you how to bait a hook, are we?" Brian asked with a grimace.

Peter tossed an anchor from the back of the boat. "Everyone's got to start somewhere." He moved over to the front and set another anchor. "Don't listen to Brian. He acts like he's been doing this his whole life, but the man raised cattle. Retired to be a security guard at the local airstrip they like to call an airport. Wasn't until recently that we both found ourselves with more time in the morning and not a damn thing to do. Gets harder to sleep when you're our age. Those nighttime bathroom trips end up making four in the morning seem like a good time to get up. You a morning lark, Brooks?"

"Not really. My career requires me to stay up late a lot."

"What do you do for a living? Bouncer?" Brian looked him up and down, his arms focusing on Brooks's built biceps, then the tattoos.

"Musician, actually."

"I play the trombone," Brian said, chewing slowly. "Not a

hell of a whole lot I can do with the trombone these days, though. Kids don't appreciate good brass instruments in what they like to call music."

Peter took a parchment-wrapped sandwich from the lunch pail and handed it to Brooks. "Take a bite." He winked. "I promise there's not a better breakfast sandwich in the world. My wife makes her own bagels."

"I can't take your breakfast," Brooks protested, holding it back toward Peter. "I'll be fine."

"I already ate one before coming here." Peter took out a thermos. "Besides, a good cup of coffee is all I need in the morning to get me going. Want some?"

"I'm good. And thank you." He took a bite. *Damn.* It was good. Peter's wife was apparently a very talented cook. And the ham wasn't deli ham like he'd expected, but thick-cut slices of smoked ham.

Content to enjoy his sandwich in silence, he watched the breeze rippling through the trees surrounding the lake. So many more had changed color even since he'd arrived, and the whole place shimmered with one last breathtaking show before the coming of winter. He relished the peacefulness of it, the silence.

He couldn't remember the last time he'd started a conversation with a stranger . . . even when he'd met Maddie, their situation had forced them to talk. But to go out of his way to talk to someone he didn't know or wasn't introduced to? Not for ages.

Maybe that made him a snob. He'd always considered himself an introvert, but even he could see the pathetic side to his social skills if he gave it enough thought.

He just wanted to be left alone. Live and let live.

Which doesn't make me sound too different from a grumpy old man, come to think of it. "Have you lived here all your life?" he asked Peter.

"Where, the lake? Yeah, he's Brandywood's own Nessie," Brian quipped with a grin. Maybe the food *was* lessening his crankiness.

"Brian and I were both born and raised here. Got suckered into staying, I guess." Peter sat across from Brooks and lifted a fishing rod. "How're you liking our small town? Probably a change of pace from Los Angeles, yeah?"

"To be honest, I just made it into town yesterday for the first time. But I enjoyed it."

"Oh yeah? Where'd you stop?"

"More like where didn't we stop?" Brooks smiled at the memory. "The woman who showed me around seems to know every nook and cranny of the place. If I hadn't been feeling under the weather, I probably would have eaten my weight in pastries."

Brian shook his head, a knowing look coming to his eyes as his lips spread in a smile. "Oh, you did it now, sonny. Tasted our food. Spent time with our women." He ribbed Peter. "Did you see the way his face changed? He's a goner for sure."

A goner?

Brooks laughed. "How so?"

"Tell him. You saw that look," Brian said to Peter, taking out an apple turnover. He split it in half and handed it to Brooks.

"Brian, I'm never gonna be able to convince him to come fishing again if you keep yammering on like this." Peter opened his tackle box. He pulled out a tub of bait, then smiled at Brooks. "You met a woman, after all."

Met a woman. Maddie's flustered face after he'd crashed into the store came to mind. Then he saw her tentative smiles when he'd offered parts of himself. Her ferocity when she stood up for him when in that café.

Then her hurt when I told her I was done with anything to do with her.

"He met a woman."

What did that phrase even mean? The attraction was clearly there.

Tentativeness, too.

"I don't know if I'd call it that. We're friendly." Brooks finished the sandwich, then took the rod and bait Peter offered him. He didn't really know what he was doing, but he wasn't about to look like a moron either.

"Friendly is the first step. Is she a looker?" Brian asked shrewdly, still munching on his turnover. Brooks got the feeling he came more for the gossip and food than the fishing, but who was he to judge? *He had no reason to be here.*

"She's gorgeous. But it's not going to go anywhere."

"And why's that?" Peter asked him. He finished baiting his hook, then scanned the water.

"To begin with, I don't think either of us is looking for anything—that's if she's even interested. I'm not from here, she loves it here, and I've got a lot I'm currently dealing with. Life would need to slow down a lot more for me, and I don't see it happening." If anything, with the threat of lawsuits, trying to find a new label, starting over again with management, and making new contacts, he'd have to work even harder.

Brian gave a slow shake of his head. "Life doesn't slow down, young man. Ever. If anything, it just keeps going faster and faster until all of a sudden, you're creeping on eighty and you're not sure when in the hell you got here. You wait for the right time for anything, and that time'll pass you right by."

Now he sounded like Cormac.

"Have you asked the woman if she's interested?" Peter cast his line out into the water, then sat.

Ask her? What was he supposed to say? *Do you like me, circle yes/no/maybe?* They'd kissed in her apartment. She'd shut it down when things could have progressed. That was a clear enough sign.

She defended you to her sister, who she clearly loves very much.

"I can usually tell when a woman is interested," Brooks said with a chuckle. If anything, women made it a little too painfully clear to him. Did they usually talk this much while fishing? Didn't it scare away the fish?

"That's a no." Brian started in on the next apple turnover. "He hasn't asked her. Probably hasn't told her he's interested either. That's the problem with young people."

"I'm not that young," Brooks answered with a roll of his eyes. "And as a matter of fact, I did . . . tell her I was interested." The manner of his delivery had been less than ideal, though. Telling her he'd fantasized about sleeping with her probably hadn't been the best way. Fucking bourbon had screwed him on that one.

Brian gave a protracted sigh. "Listen, spring chicken. You have to a woo a woman. Bring her flowers. Make her feel special. You can't just offer her the sausage and think you've done your part. Most women think it's ugly anyway, so you got to give her the pretty things first."

Brooks had heard plenty of so-called locker room talk before, but this was . . . this was *something else.* He tried not to laugh. "I'll keep that in mind, Brian."

As though it could really be that easy. He didn't deserve a woman like Madison Yardley, and all the fame and fortune in the world couldn't make up for what he lacked. Bringing her into his problems and crazy life was unfair and selfish.

But if I truly had a choice, I wouldn't be walking away from her.

"Sorry about this idiot," Peter said with a shake of his head. "He's lost his filter."

Brian cackled. "You're assuming I had one in the first place."

Brooks looked back toward the shore, as though expecting to see the house he'd rented, which had long since left his sight. "What sort of advice do you have about how to handle an angry sister?"

"Oh, that's a rough one." Brian leaned back in his chair, relaxing. "Depends on what you did. I've had some friends who haven't spoken to their siblings in years. Those grudges go deep."

"I got drunk while watching my four-year-old niece."

Oof. Amazing how horrible that sounds. How had he ever thought it was a good solution to his problems in the first place?

Both Brian and Peter cringed.

"That's a tough spot to fix." Peter reeled his line back in, then cast it again.

"It doesn't make it any better that she was asleep and it was at night, does it?" He already knew the answer to that, though. He hated himself for it. *So much.*

"Circumstances matter." Peter gave him a sympathetic look. "And it sounded like you had a lot you were dealing with when you arrived in town. But your sister has every right to be angry. Have you talked to her about what you're going through?"

Nope. Because how can I complain to Kayla when she's dealing with her own bad news? Mike wasn't just a problem for Brooks, and Kayla didn't need anything else to worry about. She'd come to him before the concert because of that.

But he'd also never gone to Kayla with any issue. That wasn't the type of relationship they had.

"No, I haven't," he admitted. "To be honest, I don't think it's that simple."

"Simple is often the best. You never know. It might be worth a try," Peter said.

Brooks leaned forward, taking the bait, and letting the conversation lapse naturally into the comfortable silence of the water lapping against the sides of the pontoon. Could they be right?

Was straightforward conversation what he needed with Kayla?

After a lifetime of complexity, simple seemed so dubious.

Then again, what did he have to lose at this point?

If he didn't try, he might lose the only people in the world he cared about.

And then he'd really know the meaning of rock bottom.

Fuck. When did life become so complicated?

Scratch that.

When will it stop being complicated?

25

MADDIE

MADDIE GLANCED up from her laptop as her younger brother, Jake, slid into the seat opposite her at her favorite booth at Yardley's Pub. She'd come here for lunch and to get some work done —and because things still weren't any better with Naomi.

Their relationship had survived plenty of trials before—it was the nature of sisterhood—but Maddie wasn't sure if she'd ever seen Naomi hold on to hurt like this before. Normally, they were back to normal after twelve hours. *Max*.

Maddie broke her thoughts away from Naomi and caught Jake's stare as he drummed his fingers against the tabletop. "So *you* skipped family pizza night last night," he said at last. "Could it be because of a certain rumor I heard about a certain rock star who's hanging out with a certain sister of mine?"

"I can neither confirm nor deny the rumors," Maddie said, taking a break from the keyboard to grab a fry. She wasn't about to tell Jake she'd spent the night in her apartment, in bed, trying to process the past week. Then she cringed. "Mom wasn't mad that I skipped, was she?"

"No, but I was. Why the hell didn't you bring Brooks Kent

to meet us? That's not cool, big sis." Jake crossed his arms, his blue eyes narrowing to match his mock scowl.

That he *wanted* to meet Brooks was a good sign that Pops, Lindsay, and Naomi had probably kept their word not to say anything about the car accident. Maddie dipped a fry into some crab dip.

"Look, Jake, I love our family, but they're kind of a lot for anyone to meet, let alone a guy who's shy and insanely private."

"Brooks Kent shy? Come on, Mad. Then why did Logan get to meet him?"

Maddie looked over her shoulder to where Logan was behind the bar. In a similar way to how she and Naomi ran the Depot, Logan and Lindsay ran the pub. Jake did a lot of administrative work for her grandfather's brand and floated between the two locations.

Logan caught her eye and waved. Maddie made a face and turned back to Jake. "Cormac's the one who invited us over. Take it up with him."

"No, because according to the whole town, Brooks Kent seems to have taken a particular interest in *you*."

Maddie's fingers fumbled as she reached for another fry, hoping that Fred hadn't told too many people about that kiss.

She didn't want to think about the way that thought made her heart skip a beat.

She gave a patient smile to humor him. "Well, they're wrong. Brooks is leaving in a couple of days." *Back to a life that doesn't have room for a small-town girl from the middle of nowhere.*

He had a lot going on. Some of which, if she was honest, scared her.

Quite a lot of what had been printed in the media about him was extremely unflattering. And while she'd scratched the surface of some of those claims, only to find out that they weren't entirely true, it worried her.

And he'd gone back on doing that concert without batting an eyelash. The past few days were reduced to a simple business transaction—not that she could argue. She had broken her side of the deal. *I just didn't expect him to back out like that.* But it had never mattered to him. He'd only agreed to it because she'd blackmailed him.

I never should have done that.

Still, his offer to help her find another band was . . . unexpectedly kind.

He didn't owe her anything. Wanted nothing with her. So why bother?

Jake frowned and took a fry from her plate. "Listen. All I know is that if you don't introduce me, I'll resent and hold it against you for life. This is where siblings are supposed to pull through, you know. I'll never have an opportunity like this again."

"Aw, Jake. You have a crush? I have it on good authority that Brooks is straight."

Jake glared at her. "So am I." Then he tilted his head. "Wait, what do you mean on *good authority*?"

Maddie bit the inside of her lip, a shiver running through her as she remembered Brooks's hands on her hips, the hardness of his length pressed against her, his lips devouring hers. *Nope, don't think about that.*

"I mean, it's a fact. He *has* dated some famous women."

Jake shrugged. "Could be lavender setups. Celebrities use matchmakers all the time."

How am I the only person who didn't know about this? "Yeah, well, in this case, I'm pretty certain."

Jake eyed her suspiciously. "You didn't sleep with the guy, did you?"

"Give me a little credit. I'm not *that* easy."

"You moved in with your ex-boyfriend after two weeks, Mad," Jake deadpanned.

She couldn't argue with that, so she wrinkled her nose. "Don't remind me of that unfortunate fact. I can't believe I thought I was in love with that asshole."

"Weren't you just sobbing over him a week ago? Naomi and Lindsay said you were pretty torn up about him last weekend."

Huh. Had it only been a week since that had happened?

Yet . . .

Much as even finding out about Josh and Gina's engagement the day before had been like a punch in the gut . . . the same level of angst was just . . . gone.

Gina could have Josh for all Maddie cared. She didn't want him back anymore.

The thought brought such a profound sense of peace that she sat back against her seat, mesmerized by it.

I don't care anymore.

Josh no longer has a hold on me.

That relief quickly faded as Brooks's face flashed in her mind.

"Hello? Earth to Maddie." Jake dragged her plate of fries away from in front of her and closer to him.

"Hey!" She snatched it back. "Those are mine. Get your own damn fries."

An easy smile crossed his face. "I figured that would get your attention."

"What do you want?" She gestured toward her laptop. "Some of us have work to do, you bum. I have a thousand orders to place to make up for the inventory we lost when the store window was smashed."

"I was trying to get you to introduce me to Brooks Kent, remember? Are you bringing him to Applepalooza tomorrow?"

Ugh. She'd been avoiding thinking about the whole damned festival. "Nope. And for the record, I mentioned it to him, and he didn't seem remotely interested in going. I'm not even sure I'm going." *Or when I'll talk to Brooks again.*

Jake appeared appalled. "It's practically your favorite thing we do in Brandywood."

He wasn't entirely inaccurate, but . . . she was tired of it, too. The whole overblown . . . *everything.* "Maybe old Maddie was a basic fall bitch, but the new and improved version of Maddie is on to her grand millennial era. I think I'll stay home and crochet instead."

Jake squinted at her. "Are you even a millennial?"

"Don't care. What I'm not is someone who needs to show up to a day of apple-related fall festivities where her ex-boyfriend and his new fiancée are going to be. Josh and Gina deserve each other—they're both assholes—and I'm not interested in proving that I'm better than either of them in any arbitrary contest."

"Damn." Jake sighed. "I was hoping I could talk you into doing a few things with me."

"Like?"

"Apple picking. Pie eating. Bobbing for apples. Hard cider pong. You know—the fun stuff." Jake rolled his shoulders. "Plus, Millie Price made me sign up for the Auction-a-Peck and told me she needs more volunteers. I may have put your name on the list to auction off the Cortland apples."

Maddie's eyes widened. Of all the parts of the day she regularly avoided, it was the Auction-a-Peck. Volunteers would take the stage with various peck-sized containers of apples to be auctioned off to a crowd . . . but the top bidder of each auction also won a kiss from the volunteer. "I'm not doing that medieval contest, Jake."

"Come on." Jake put his hands together pleadingly. "It's for a good cause. And you're not currently dating anyone. What do you have to lose?"

"My dignity, for one. Don't you remember the year Laura Redding had to kiss Milton Hirsch? I swear the old man shoved his tongue in her mouth. And he bids on single women every year."

"But that's why they have rules now," Jake countered. "They always remind people that a peck means a peck. Some winners only kiss people on the cheek. Besides, people mostly bid on the apples, not the kisses. And the money goes to the senior center."

"The money could go to poor, starving orphan baby hedgehogs and it still wouldn't change my mind."

"Yeah, it probably would. You're a sucker for baby hedgehogs," Jake muttered. A glum expression crossed his face.

"Come on. You're not seriously bummed out because I won't do it, are you? Get Logan to do it. He's desperate enough for a woman to kiss him. He won't care."

"I heard that, Maddie," Logan called out. "I have more game than you think. And I'm not doing the auction."

The bar was empty enough that their voices were probably carrying louder than Maddie had intended. Maddie almost cackled. *Oops.*

"Please?" Then Jake's eyes lit. "If you don't, I'll go visit Brooks Kent—I know where he's staying, thanks to Logan—and I'll tell him you used to have a poster of him on the wall of your college dorm. That you once described his voice as . . . what was it again?"

Maddie's face heated. *No way he remembers that.*

"Oh yeah, that's right. *Liquid sin.* Not sure what the liquid part was all about, but it sure as hell sounds scandalous."

Dammit. "You wouldn't dare."

"Wouldn't I?" Jake gave her a devious look.

Maddie locked eyes with him. She didn't doubt he'd make good on that threat. *Come to think of it, we seem to overuse blackmail as siblings.* She made a mental note to bring that up for discussion at the next family pizza night.

"Fine. I'll do the stupid auction. With any luck, no one will bid on the apples. Cortland aren't that great." Maddie closed her laptop. "But just for that, I'm not doing the other contests with you. Maybe I'll do them with Logan."

"I already asked someone to the festival." Logan came out from behind the bar toward them. "So you're stuck with Jake. Sorry, hon."

Maddie feigned a look of hurt. "And who, may I ask, did you ask?"

"Kayla." Logan's eyes hinted with warmth. "I thought it would be fun for her little girl."

Nooooo. She knew that look. Logan got that look when he liked someone. "You can't date her."

"I like her. She's witty. Keeps old groucho on his toes. Cute kid, too," Jake said with a grin.

Maddie looked from Logan to Jake. "How do you know Kayla?"

Jake shrugged. "Logan invited her to pizza night last night. Maybe if you hadn't skipped it, you would know."

What? Kayla had met her whole family?

Maddie propped her elbows on the table and covered her face. "Ugh, no, Logan. Don't catch feelings for Kayla. That's so messy."

"And why is that?" Logan asked, sliding in beside Jake. He crossed his arms.

Jake copied his stance. "Yeah. Why *is* that, Maddie?"

"Because Brooks . . . is *leaving,* guys. So is Kayla. Neither are from around here." Not to mention that if Logan dated Brooks's sister and things didn't work out, it would . . .

Would what, exactly?

Make it hard for you to see Brooks?

Make family situations awkward? Only if she and Brooks were involved, which they weren't.

"Kayla lives three hours away. It's not that far. Besides which, it's a date to a fall festival, nothing more. I didn't ask her to move in with me like you would have done by now."

"Ouch, that was below the belt, asshole." Maddie shoved her laptop away, her appetite quickly fading.

Sincere regret filled Logan's face. "I was just teasing—"

"Forget it." That wasn't what she was upset about, anyway. And what she *was* upset about, she couldn't quite verbalize. Logan had every right to date Kayla if he wanted to, so what was the problem?

She stood. "I should go." She scowled at Jake. "You can sign me up for a couple of events with you. And maybe the singing competition by myself. I don't need any more grief about how much I suck."

Eyes burning, she hurried out of the pub.

She was already walking down Main Street when Logan caught up with her. "Hang on," Logan said, grabbing her firmly by the elbow. He hauled her to a stop, then faced her. "What's going on with you?"

Maddie swiped her lashes, blinking rapidly. "I don't know."

"I really didn't mean to hurt your feelings about the moving in comment, Mad. If anything, I think it's admirable how open you are to love. You jump in feet first, sure, but you jump. I've spent a lifetime hanging back and regretting it."

"Really, that's not it, Logan." She hugged her arms to her chest, the day chillier than she expected. They'd reached that point in Maryland weather when one day you'd wake up freezing and be boiling by noon, and the next, you'd dress in summery clothes and a cold front would move in by midday.

"What is it then, Maddie?" Logan set his hands on her shoulders. "You know you can tell me anything."

What am I feeling? Why am I this upset?

She pressed her lips together, then said at last, "I don't want you to fool around with Kayla."

He searched her eyes. "Why not?"

She gulped a breath. "Because I like Brooks."

There. She'd said it aloud.

To someone.

To herself.

Compassion dawned in his eyes.

Tugging her into his arms, Logan gave her a tight hug, which was just what she needed. *Big brother hugs.* No one hugged better than Logan, although her grandfather was probably a very close second. "I thought you might. I take it he doesn't return those feelings?"

"I have no idea. But he's a freaking rock star, Logan. I was googling him, and he . . . he's got a life I can't even imagine. The Met Gala, Grammys, red carpet appearances . . . even members of the Royal Family went to his last concert in London. *And then he met with them.* Why would he be interested in me?"

"Because you're real." Logan released her. "And you're wonderful. He'd have to be a dimwit not to see that. He probably *does* see that, considering he's been spending time with you."

"Not everything about him looks good on paper. Mom and Dad would freak. The press likes to present a rough side of him that isn't entirely accurate."

"Maddie, you're a smart girl. You can talk to him and judge for yourself if he's worthy of you."

Funny how different he was being about this than Naomi had been.

Then again, Naomi had been given reasons not to like Brooks from the start. *That's my fault, too.*

She hugged her arms in tighter. "Yeah, because I did such a great job judging that with Josh."

"You can't throw the entire crop out because of one rotten apple," Logan said, a smile in his eyes. "Forget Josh. If it's any consolation at all, Kayla and I have talked about Brooks, and she's told me how wrong the media is about him. Said there was a whole incident in Vegas last year after a concert where his band threw this party and some people ended up arrested. The media highlighted the prostitutes and drugs and made it a big scandal. Brooks wasn't even there, but he still got dragged for it, even after he released a statement."

"No, that doesn't make me feel better." *Poor Brooks.* He'd really had a rough go of it with the media. It made her want to take a flamethrower to all the powers that be on his behalf. Burn it all down.

Why doesn't he fight back harder?

Then again, the guy had been fighting all his life. Maybe he'd decided some things he didn't want to fight about.

"Brooks is one of those classic cases of walks and acts like a duck but is probably a goose. According to Kayla, anyway," Logan said with the kind of smile that recalled a conversation that had made him happy.

Dammit.

"When did you get the chance to talk so much to Kayla? Last night?"

Logan rubbed the back of his neck sheepishly. "Actually, I asked for her phone number on Sunday. We've talked and texted every day since then."

Oh. My. God. Logan must *really* like her.

Maddie's heart fell. "That's great, Logan. I'm glad you're

happy." She wanted to feel it as much as she meant it, but her own worries and disappointments ate away at her.

But what was she imagining anyway? Brooks didn't live three hours away—he lived on the other side of the country. And despite the attraction between them being mutual, the chance of them having any sort of relationship was ludicrous. Brooks didn't seem like a relationship guy.

Logan gave her a sympathetic look, as though he understood what she was thinking. "You should invite Brooks to come to the Applepalooza tomorrow. You never know, with Kayla and Audrey going, he might show up."

Maddie swallowed hard. Unlike Kayla with Logan, Brooks wasn't texting her at all. Or calling. She hadn't even heard from him after dropping him off last night.

And now that he'd said he wouldn't play at the fair, who knew when she would see him again? His rental was up on Sunday.

Lowering her shoulders in defeat, Maddie smiled sadly. "It doesn't matter if he shows up. I've got to put on my big girl pants and accept the situation for what it is. Brooks is just passing through this town . . . and my life. And my little crush won't change that fact."

She sucked in a deep breath. "I'll be fine, Logan. Don't worry, according to you guys, I'll find someone else to develop feelings for soon enough."

She walked away before he could respond, her heart aching.

Maybe they were right anyway. She could catch and lose feelings fast. She was already over Josh.

But she didn't want to forget Brooks so easily.

This was different in a way she couldn't say.

And that terrified her.

26

BROOKS

"You're not seriously going to that thing, are you?" Brooks asked from the couch as Kayla finished helping Audrey put on her pink cowboy boots.

Kayla gave him a sharp look. "Why? It's a fun fall festival. That below you or something?"

Cormac shifted in his armchair and shoved his cell phone in his pocket. "Hey, Audrey, you want to go see if we can spot some turtles from the dock?"

"You don't have to do that, Cormac. Logan's going to be here in a few minutes." Kayla straightened and pulled on a light jacket.

"But I wanna see tuttles," Audrey protested, tugging on her mother's jacket.

"No time like the present," Cormac said with a wink. He held out a hand for her, and she bounded over to him with a grin.

"Cormac . . ." Kayla gave him an exasperated look.

He grinned, then headed out the back door with Audrey.

"All right, but when Mr. Logan comes, we have to go. I don't want to hold him up," Kayla called as the door closed.

Brooks raised a brow at her as he took his feet off the cushion and sat straight. No wonder she'd stuck around even though she'd been mad and barely talking to him. *She has a date.*

"So you seeing that guy now?"

"Why, is there a problem? I thought you said it was none of your business," Kayla snapped.

Yikes. He tried to remind himself that her anger was justified and that he needed to stay humble. "It is none of my business. I was just wondering. He's not exactly local to where you live."

"It's an outing to a fall festival, Brooks, not a marriage proposal." Kayla checked her phone, barely looking at him.

"I just don't want you to get hurt."

Kayla arched a brow at him, exaggeratedly. "A little late for that, wouldn't you say? Besides, I've survived a lot worse. I can handle myself."

He stared at her quietly. *How do I fix this?* Peter's and Brian's words from the day before came to mind. "You're right," he admitted. His fingers curled into the palms of his hands. Funny how when his hands held a guitar, he'd always been able to come up with words that people liked so much they'd play them repeatedly.

And now, when he *needed* to speak, he could think of nothing worth saying.

"For the record, I'm sorrier about what happened the other night than I've ever been about anything, Kayla. I don't know how to make it up to you. I've always wanted to keep you from getting hurt, and I failed so massively and hurt you myself."

She was silent, then blinked rapidly. Swiping her eyes, she sat across from him. "Damn Cormac. I didn't want to do this right now. Logan's going to show up, and I'm going to have mascara running down my face."

Brooks looked around for a box of tissues, found one, then brought it over to her and sat beside her. "I don't know how to make it better. I just want you and Audrey to be happy. If I could give you every good thing in the world, I would."

"You already *have*, you idiot." Kayla sniffled. "But I don't need a better house, or clothes, or more money, and Audrey sure as shit doesn't need more toys. You don't get it, Brooks. You don't get why I'm so mad, do you?"

He furrowed his brow. "Because I was drunk?"

"No. It's that you're in such an awful state you felt the *need* to drown your sorrows in alcohol rather than just talk to the people who love you. I *need* a brother. Audrey *needs* an uncle. And you're struggling, Brooks. You think I can't see that? But my whole life, you have refused to ever tell me about anything that you're going through. Cormac says you haven't talked to him about it, either, so who the hell are you talking about it with? No one. Until it breaks you and you pull out a bottle to kill it, right? Why do you think I asked you to give up drinking years ago? You use it as your therapy."

I've just been trying to look after you and my niece.

Was that why he'd drunk? As his therapy?

He blinked, trying to process her words. *Why would she want me to give her any of the shit I deal with on the daily?*

"I just . . . don't want to burden you. How can I complain? I have a good life. People would kill to have my life."

"That's the absolute most pathetic excuse I have ever heard. So you're not allowed to have a bad day because you worked your ass off to get to where you are? I *saw* you working your ass off, you know. I saw the times when things didn't go your way. But you're smart and resilient, and yeah, maybe occasionally lucky, but mostly you have grit."

Brooks sighed, the truth to her words hitting him squarely in the chest. "It's not a bad day. Bad decade? Maybe. Maybe more. My life hasn't been a picnic, and I just never wanted you to go through what I went through. Especially after Dad. And Mom."

"So you shut me out."

Ouch. He squinted reflexively. "I never intended to shut you out."

"Well, that's what you did, though."

"You were just a kid. What else was I supposed to do? Tell you how hard it was working through college and trying to raise my little sister at the same time? I couldn't put that on you." *I don't even like to remember that.*

Mom hadn't left any money or life insurance behind. He'd gotten the only job with benefits he could find, working at a big chain hardware store, taking as many classes as he could online, making special arrangements with his professors. Getting Kayla the things she needed before himself. He'd even worn sneakers with a hole in them while he bought her new shoes for school.

And he'd do it all over again, too.

She didn't deserve that sort of guilt.

"Maybe not then," Kayla said in a quiet voice. "But I didn't stay a kid, Brooks. I'm not one now. And you still don't come to me when you have bad days."

She's right. I don't.

But then again, he'd never gone to anyone. In fact, he'd talked to Maddie more this week about the shit going on in his life than he'd told anyone—outside a therapist, years ago—ever.

"You really want me to?"

"Yes, you idiot. You're my brother. I love you. You need somewhere soft to land, just like you've given me all these years. And I'm never going to have as much money as you, so for God's sake, at least let me be your person. Or one of them. You should have more than one, really."

He pinched her arm gently. "You already are my person, but I'll try to do a better job talking about what's going on. I'm sorry I haven't. I didn't think about it from your point of view."

She sighed, then leaned against his shoulder. "Yeah, well, you're also a guy so you've got the emotional IQ of a five-year-old."

"Thanks?" He chuckled.

Kayla smiled. "You can always count on me to tell you the truth. Even if it's not my favorite news to deliver." The phone beside her buzzed, and she glanced at it. "Logan's here."

Normally in the middle of a discussion like this, Brooks would have been thrilled by the interruption.

But now . . . he regretted she had to go.

A corner waited to be turned, and he wasn't quite there yet, but it felt within walking distance.

"Have fun," he said. "I mean it. I hope it's a great time for you and Audrey."

"Cormac's going, too, you know." Kayla stood and stretched. "You should come. Logan told me that Maddie Yardley will be there this morning."

The thought of seeing her filled him with equal parts dread and anticipation. He hated that he'd effectively run away from her. *Yes*, he knew it was better for her in the long run. But even though he'd only known her for a few days, she'd left a rather large hole in his heart.

YET . . . *she's been on my mind constantly ever since.*

He smirked. "And why should that make a difference?"

"Don't play it cool with me, buddy. Cormac told me you two already slept together. Maddie tried to deny it, too, don't worry, but then I heard you two were caught fooling around in some storage room in town."

"That's . . . false. Cormac got the wrong idea because of a few incidents."

"You know, actually, I don't need the details of your sex life. It's one of the worst parts of being related to a celebrity—everyone speculating and talking about you in a way that just is super gross to me."

He couldn't even imagine what it might be like if the roles were reversed. He'd probably be in jail by now. "Either way, I'm leaving tomorrow. I have to call Ava and figure out a rental car situation because I never made it to the mechanic, but I don't think my car is fixed yet."

"That all sounds like a thrilling way to spend a Saturday and like stuff that would take a few minutes. You should still come. It could be fun for us to go out with you—we rarely get the chance."

Brooks scratched the stubble on his jawline. "You really want me to go?"

"I really do. I want you around all the time, you buffoon. But you keep running away. Skipping holidays with the worst excuses and then acting like a giant delivery of presents is the same thing as your *presence*."

He smirked. "I see what you did there." But her words hit him deeply.

Have I been doing that?

When did I become okay with allowing my schedule to impede seeing the only people I love?

Kayla blinked prettily at him. "Please come today. For me? And Audrey? You can even wear your sunglasses and baseball cap. Wear a burqa for all I care, but just come and be with us. *It's what family does.*"

A small-town apple festival sounded like one of those functions he'd avoid. But he sighed and stood. "Only if you promise to stop being so mad at me."

"Only if *you* promise to try to have fun. No one likes a stick-in-the-mud."

He got the feeling she was trying to ask for as much as she could out of him right now while she had the upper hand. And he was fine with letting her have it, too.

She deserved that and far more. *As always.*

"All right, fine. Lead the way."

27

MADDIE

"Dammit, Jake!" Maddie cried as her brother stumbled in the apple orchard. To keep himself from falling, he had grabbed her sweatshirt, almost causing her to fall over.

Usually, that wouldn't be a problem. But the apple-picking contest involved picking as many apples as they could from one orchard at the Pearsons' farm, where Applepalooza was held, and then racing them over to dump in a barrel before the five-minute timer went off.

Because the contestants could only take what they could carry, Jake insisted they both stuff their sweatpants and sweatshirts with apples to maximize each run into and out of the orchard.

A little trip would mean that Maddie, who could barely move from the apples stuffed into her clothes, wouldn't get back up again.

"Come on, Mad, we're almost there." Jake braced onto her elbow, sweat dripping down his temple. "Only like fifty feet to go."

"Thirty seconds!" Ben Pearson called out from his lifeguard chair into a megaphone.

Shit. "Oh God, we're never going to make it." Maddie pumped her arms as she tried to push forward, the weight of the apples holding her back. They had to get the apples into the barrels for them to count, and each barrel was on top of a scale, so every single apple counted toward the final weight.

"Come on, Maddie and Jake!" Lindsay cried from the spectator line. She and the rest of their friends and family who weren't in the race were gathered in a group near the end of their orchard lane.

Jake linked arms with her as best he could, hauling her forward. They were so close, but would they have time to transfer all the apples in?

Jake reached the apple barrel milliseconds before Maddie, then yanked his sweatshirt off, revealing his bare chest. He fought to keep as many apples as he could inside, but many fell out. "Come on, strip! Pants first, it'll be easier."

"Twenty . . . nineteen . . ." the crowd chanted.

Oh my God. Her sweatshirt was one thing, but her sweatpants?

She was going to kill Jake for this.

Maddie wiggled out of her pants, cursing the day she'd ever let Jake talk her into this—and her damn competitiveness—as the crowd hollered. She'd even worn apple-red panties, never expecting that all Brandywood would see them.

Still, she kept most of the apples in her pants. Cinching the waist, she sprang to her feet and dumped the apples from the pants into the barrel.

"Ten . . . nine . . . eight . . ."

She yanked the sweatshirt off as apples tumbled onto the ground. No time to think about how cold it was or the fact that all the spectators were staring at her in a T-shirt and underwear. She dumped the apples from the sweatshirt, then gathered some of the fallen ones from the ground.

"Time's up!" Ben called as the buzzer sounded.

The crowd cheered wildly. Maddie heaved deep breaths, her skin sticky, her clothes discarded somewhere on the grass. Before she could find them, Jake nearly toppled her with a bear hug. "You were awesome!"

She laughed into his chest. He still had apples in his pants—he hadn't been able to get his pants off as fast as she had—but somehow, they'd picked almost three hundred pounds of apples.

Despite her best efforts, she couldn't help but take a quick peek at Josh and Gina's score, since they were only two lanes away.

One hundred twenty-seven.

Gina looked pissed.

She'd flat-out glared at Maddie earlier, clearly angry about that interaction with Brooks and her father.

"And the winners of the apple-picking race are Maddie and Josh Yaaaarddley!" Ben called out from the lifeguard chair.

Lindsay's whoop broke through as the spectators left their roped-off section and raced toward them. Travis was only a couple of feet behind them, as well as Mom and Dad. "You guys were incredible," Lindsay said, wrapping them both in a hug.

Mom found Maddie's sweatpants and draped them behind her. "Great job, you two," she said with a laugh. "I'm not sure it was worth flashing the whole town for, but still. Very creative."

Dad shook his head. "You couldn't pay me enough money to do that nonsense." But his blue eyes shone with amusement, regardless of his words.

"Maybe next year, you and I should sign up. Give these two a run for their money," Lindsay said to Travis with a wink.

He draped his arm around her. "Maybe. I don't know if I have the same level of dedication as they do, though. Also, can we make sure they wash these apples before they make them into cider? Somehow Jake's sweaty apples don't have a ton of appeal."

"I resent that," Jake said, feigning offense. "I give them extra flavor."

"Ben's *your* friend. Talk to him about it," Lindsay answered with a shrug. "I still believe half the reason the Pearsons started Applepalooza is for all the free labor picking apples."

Maddie took the sweatpants from her mom, then wrinkled her nose at the streaks of dirt and smooshed rotten apples she'd stepped on while plunging into the orchard without care. "You have my backpack?" she asked Lindsay. "I don't think I feel like putting these back on again."

Lindsay nudged Travis, who lifted it. "The whole sweatpants look isn't the right vibe for Applepalooza anyway."

"Vibe or no vibe, put something on, for God's sake," Dad muttered. He frowned at Jake. "You, too."

"I didn't want my shirt to get dirty," Jake said. "You packed it in there, right, Mads?"

She pulled it out and handed it over. As she straightened, she glanced back toward the spectators. "Naomi and Logan didn't make it to see the race?"

She'd been keeping both eyes open for her older sister. They wouldn't go a whole weekend with this sort of tension between them, would they?

Then again, Maddie wasn't entirely sure she even knew what to say to Naomi at this point.

"Naomi's helping Pops and Bunny set up for the pie competition, and I'm not sure where Logan is. Haven't seen him all day," Dad said.

"I think he was heading for some of the kids' activities with

Kayla and her daughter," Mom said with a smile. "I might go over there and join them for a bit. It's a little less crazy than all this."

"Don't forget we've got Auction-a-Peck in ten minutes." Jake tugged his shirt on. "Don't you want to see if Milton Hirsh steals a kiss from Maddie?"

Mom grimaced. "I think I'll skip that one."

Maddie didn't want to think about that. The idea of auctioning off a kiss was the last thing she'd ever willingly volunteer for.

Secretly, she'd been hoping Brooks might turn up to it, though. Or just to the festival.

Of course, she wouldn't want him to see her standing in her underwear.

"I'm gonna go change. Be right back." She made a beeline down the orchard lane, farther from the crowd. She wanted to change her shirt, too, which felt just as sticky as her sweatpants had been. In fact, she would give anything for a shower right now.

When she was out of sight from anyone, she dropped her backpack and peeled off her shirt and sweatshirt. A stray apple tumbled from her sweatshirt and landed on her foot with a thump. "Dammit."

A footstep crunched from behind her, then a deep male voice chuckled. "We have to stop meeting like this."

Brooks.

She jerked upright, smacking the top of her head right into the branch of a tree. "Ow!" Her hair caught on a twig as she pulled away, and her eyes widened. *Shit. I'm stuck.*

And the bastard who'd caused this stood there with a smirk on his face, his thumbs looped into the pockets of his jeans, smelling like clean, manly soap rather than rotten apples and sweat.

"What the hell are you doing here?" she asked, tugging on her hair. She tried not to care that she was in a matching red bra and panty set.

"Enjoying the view," he drawled, turning his baseball cap backward.

Ow, ow, ow.

Her hair was really tangled.

"Help me," she snapped with wide eyes. She was already cold enough.

He stepped closer. "Is that any way to ask for a favor?"

He was enjoying this far too much.

"Help me, *please*," she gritted through clenched teeth.

Brooks removed his sunglasses, hooking them on the collar of his shirt. Now he was a breath away, so close that his thigh brushed up against hers, his arms on either side of her head as he deftly loosened the tangle in her hair.

When he'd finished, the tugging on her scalp eased, and she released a breath. "Thank you." Then she made the mistake of lifting her chin to look him in those deadly gray eyes.

"My pleasure, Madison."

Her heart slammed into her ribs painfully.

I've missed him.

He was so close now. All it would take was a slight lean from either of them, and they would be kissing.

His gaze flicked to her mouth, and one of his song lyrics floated through her mind. *"Drink my desire . . . honey on your lips. Back against the wall . . . and my pressure on your hips."*

God.

They'd actually done that the other day.

Goosebumps rose on her skin.

She didn't really care how he'd come up with those words, but she wanted that. Every inch of his sexual, seductive self.

That voice whispering her name. He was so fucking good at it, too.

A soft click tore her from her trance. "What was that?" She whirled around to look, stepping away from him.

Brooks frowned at her. "What was what?"

"Didn't you hear—"

"Dude, Maddie . . . what the heck?" Logan said as he and Kayla rounded the corner. They stopped short, and Logan turned around to block Audrey from seeing her.

The little girl popped her head around Logan's leg. "Hi, Miss Maddie!" She seemed oblivious to Maddie's lack of clothes, *thank goodness.*

"I—" Maddie grabbed her orange-and-brown-plaid flannel shirt and pulled it on.

Fuck. Heat flooded her cheeks. Logan was already walking the other way, lifting Audrey onto his shoulders.

Kayla smiled at Brooks, then Maddie. "Good to see you again, Maddie. We'll catch up in a few." She followed Logan, laughing as she hurried to catch up.

Maddie's fingers trembled as she buttoned the shirt. "Any chance they think that was a perfectly innocent encounter?"

"Is that what it was?" Brooks's eyes gleamed wolfishly. "Why the hell are you out here *only* in a bra and underwear?"

"I was *changing.* I have to go over to the Auction-a-Peck in a couple of minutes, and I didn't want to look like a crazy lady." She pulled on a long, flowy white skirt, then took out her boots.

"I have a feeling I'm gonna regret asking what Auction-a-Peck is."

Brooks's look of amusement hadn't faded.

"Laugh it up, Mr. Rock Star." She found her hairbrush and loosed her hair from her ponytail, shaking it out. "It's an auction. For apples. And kisses. The volunteer who comes out holding a peck-sized crate of apples—which is about thirty—also offers a kiss to the winner of each auction."

"A kiss?" Brooks appeared skeptical.

"Yes."

"Like on the mouth?"

"Yeah, but like a peck. Pay attention." She applied lip gloss from a tube.

"I am paying attention." He frowned. "So you're going to kiss some random person who bids on the apples you're holding?"

"I mean, I didn't *want* to volunteer for this. My brother Jake signed me up. He got roped into it by one of my step-grandma's friends. And the proceeds from the auction go to the senior center, so it's a good cause."

"Uh-huh." Brooks's frown deepened. "Well, good luck with that." He started down the lane in the direction Kayla and Logan had gone.

"You're not going to come bid?" She hurried to catch up with him.

"On you?"

"I mean, it doesn't have to be on me." She hesitated, then teased, "My brother Jake is volunteering, too, if that's more up your alley."

He guffawed. "Madison, there are far better ways to ask me to prove I'm straight, if that's what you want to know. In fact, I would have been happy to prove it the other day, but I wasn't the one who held back."

If she didn't know any better, he seemed . . . *annoyed* that she was doing this.

"So you won't bid?" she asked, setting her hand on his forearm.

Brooks stopped, then turned to face her. "If I kiss you, it's going to be because I know we both want it. Not because I won it in some auction, understood? I already crossed the line with you and regret it. You told me no last time. I accepted it and moved on. I won't do it again."

She gaped at him.

He really regretted the kisses they'd shared?

It wasn't that she hadn't wanted it. *Is that what he thought?* That she was holding back because she didn't want him? She'd told him the other day that she wanted to keep going . . . it just wasn't a good idea.

Of course, a man like Brooks probably wasn't used to rejection. Who in their right mind would reject Brooks Kent?

She tugged her hand back from his forearm, feeling like a scolded child. "Understood." Holding her head high, she hurried away from him.

"Wait, Madison," he called after her.

"I have to go, Brooks. See you around."

Maddie pushed forward without stopping, afraid that if she did, he might see her eyes welling with tears.

"I already crossed the line with you and regret it. You told me no last time. I accepted it and moved on. I won't do it again."

She knew, logically, this was for the best. But why did it sting so much more than she expected? *I've only known him for a week.*

She had to hold it together. Maybe, after the festivities were over, she'd have a serious talking to herself. It was time to keep her head held high. After all, *he'd* accepted there'd be nothing more between them and had *moved on.*

How, Maddie did not want to know.

28

BROOKS

FUCK.

Brooks's jaw clenched so hard, he practically had a headache as he sank into a metal folding chair on the lawn in front of a makeshift, roughly hewn stage.

He'd spent almost half his life on stages—they practically felt like home at this point.

This one, though . . . this one he wanted to run from.

But he had penance to do.

He'd hurt Maddie somehow—not on purpose. Considering how staunchly she'd stood up for consent the other night, he would have thought she appreciated knowing that he'd never kiss her if she didn't want it. She'd drawn clear boundary lines the other day when they'd been making out—he wasn't about to disrespect that.

Instead, he had somehow upset her.

He adjusted the hoodie he'd donned, using the sides of it to cover his face somewhat. His hat and sunglasses shaded the rest of his face. Being in the back row helped. No one appeared to have noticed him, but then again, the townspeople had left him alone on Thursday after Maddie had threatened them all.

The auction had started a full fifteen minutes earlier and still no sign of Maddie.

This is painful.

Brooks pinched right below the bridge of his nose, where his sunglasses had dug in. *Why do I care so much?*

He'd tried to keep his distance from Maddie as much as possible since Thursday. Even with Brian's and Peter's advice, well-intentioned as it had been, there were still too many hurdles.

His lawyer had emailed just this morning letting him know that Mike hadn't dropped the charges yet—and that Brooks's arraignment was scheduled for two weeks from now. And then there was the conversation he was still putting off having with Ava, where he needed to quit his job and put a temporary stake in the heart of his career.

Setbacks.

Maybe necessary ones, but setbacks all the same.

Then again . . . what more did he really want out of his career? He'd had the huge tours and played all the big venues. Put out all the songs he'd been inspired to write. His creativity had long since taken a nosedive, and in this industry, it was better to leave on top rather than hoping that the creativity would simply magically appear again one day.

I don't love it anymore, so it's the right time to walk away.

As Kayla had pointed out a few hours ago, he needed to spend more time with his family. *That was* what was important.

He had enough money to last him several lifetimes and had invested well. Set up a trust for Kayla and Audrey.

Any *why* he'd possessed to keep doing this had disappeared.

"Well, butter my biscuit, look who it is," Kayla's warm voice hissed beside him.

Brooks cracked an eye open. "Butter my biscuit?"

"Just trying out the country lingo. Feels good."

He rolled his eyes, fully aware she probably couldn't see it under his dark glasses.

"So . . . uh . . . you and Maddie caught up quick."

"Not what you think. I just bumped into her in the orchard."

"And her clothes fell off?" Kayla whispered.

"Don't make me regret letting you drag me to this thing."

"Oh, it's fun." She sat straighter. "Anyway, I just saw you sitting here and wanted to let you know I'm heading to the baking tent with Audrey and Logan. Cormac is already there, supposedly. I can't get my texts to work consistently here. Logan says his grandparents make amazing apple desserts—including apple fritters—and I want to try some. Meet us over there in a bit?"

Brooks nodded. "If I can find it."

"Would it kill you to ask for directions?"

"Probably." He smirked at her as she left.

Kayla was damn near glowing.

She looks so . . . happy.

Like she fits here.

And she had people welcoming her into their fold, which made Brooks happy.

"Next up to the auction block, we've got a pretty lady offering some delicious Cortland apples. A fantastic choice for baking and eating, Cortlands have bright red skin and white flesh, with a juicy and tart flavor . . ."

Brooks stood, ready to go after Kayla. He didn't really know what he was doing here. He wasn't about to kiss Maddie this way.

Of course, if he won, you could just give her a kiss on the cheek.

" . . . Maddie Yardley!" the emcee finished saying with a lift of his hand.

Brooks sat again.

Maddie came out on stage with all the confidence of a supermodel, carrying a wooden crate of apples in her hands. A megawatt smile lit her features as she displayed the apples and then stopped beside the auctioneer.

The thought of her kissing anyone else made him want to punch something. His fist curled reflexively.

"All right, the opening bid for this beautiful gal is fifteen dollars. Who'll start the opening bid?"

A few seconds of silence passed, the crowd shifting and exchanging glances.

At last, a man, probably in his fifties, lifted his hand.

"And look at that, an opening bid from Maddie's own father! Fifteen-dollar bid, now fifteen, now fifteen, will ya give me sixteen?" the auctioneer started.

More quiet glances.

What the fuck was happening?

Even Maddie's smile seemed frozen in place.

Why in the hell was no one bidding on Maddie?

At last, an old man lifted his hand. "Twenty!"

Brooks's gaze darted back to Maddie, his gut twisting.

The bidders were still quiet. Maddie's father raised his hand again. "Twenty-five."

Maddie had gone pale.

This didn't make sense. Maddie was gorgeous. She seemed to know everyone in town when they'd walked through it the other day.

"*. . . twenty-five, who'll give me twenty-six . . .*"

"Twenty-six!" the old man called.

"*. . . now twenty-seven, now twenty-seven . . .*"

Whatever the situation was, it was as though someone had purposely made sure Maddie wouldn't get bids. *Was someone really that petty here?*

This was the side of small towns he was familiar with.

The cutting, nasty side. Where one rivalry could make a person's life miserable.

Anger bloomed in Brooks's gut. "Two hundred," he called out, barely thinking about it.

Heads turned his way, including Maddie's.

Her eyes widened as she saw him, her smile long gone.

"Two hundred!" the auctioneer announced. He kept the chant going.

No way in hell someone is going to bid more. The highest Brooks had heard was a hundred twenty-five.

"Two hundred and one!" the old man called out. He turned toward Brooks with a mischievous gleam in his eyes.

"Five hundred," Brooks said in a voice that sounded bored.

"*Holy smokes, it's five hundred. Now five hundred, now five hundred, who'll give me five hundred one . . .*"

"Five hundred and one," the old man said, puffing his chest out.

Man, this dude really wants to kiss Maddie.

"One thousand," Brooks countered, giving the old man a cool look.

Gasps sounded from around him, murmurs breaking out as people stared at him.

. . . and now I probably look like the creep.

The old man grinned. "One thousand and one."

Then Brooks startled. The old geezer was driving up the bid.

And he'd fallen for it. *Hook, line, and sinker.*

He'd been betting that Brooks would continue to outbid him for any price.

Two could play at that game.

Brooks crossed his arms, raising his brow at the man.

" . . . *do I hear one thousand two? One thousand two, folks. Who'll give me one thousand two? Going once, going twice . . .*"

The man was good at this game of auction "chicken," but a bit of panic showed in his eyes now.

" . . . *sold!* To Milton Hirsch for one thousand one dollars. And I believe we've set a record for the highest bid ever placed at Auction-a-Peck, folks. Everybody give a great big round of applause for our Maddie Yardley."

The crowd—the same folks that had refused to bid on Maddie—clapped, though there were frowns on a few people's faces, who continued to look back at Brooks.

. . . *fuck.*

Brooks's gaze whirled back to Maddie, who stared at him with what could only be called a death glare as the old man wobbled over toward her, bewilderment on his face.

He'd gotten so caught up in the game of it, he'd forgotten that losing meant Maddie had to kiss the old man—who might not even be able to afford such an expensive bid.

And I basically announced I wasn't willing to pay over one thousand dollars to kiss her.

To her entire town.

Moron.

Maddie stepped off the stage and greeted the old man with a smile, then pressed a preemptive kiss to his cheek. Her face was bright red as she handed him the apple crate and hurried away, fleeing into the crowd that milled just beyond the auction.

Brooks bolted from his chair and followed, but he hadn't gotten far when Cormac seemed to appear from nowhere beside him. He put a hand out to stop Brooks. "Just let her go cool down, man."

"You saw that?" Brooks asked, slowing.

"Yeah. That was . . . interesting."

"Why the hell did no one bid on Maddie?" Brooks allowed Cormac to lead him away from the throng toward the back of a large, paneled tent.

"I asked a friend. There's a rumor going around that the Cortland apples were mealy. Sounds made up."

Yeah, that's bullshit.

"Also . . ." Cormac grimaced. "I heard Maddie was getting it on with a famous rock star in the back storeroom of Brandywood's oldest ice cream shop, and that the rock star then disrespected the hell out of the owner when they were caught. Depending on which folks you catch at an event, their loyalty might be with the shop owner."

Oh fuck.

"So no one bid on her?" Brooks nearly exploded. "Besides, the prick deserved my disrespect. He called Maddie trash."

Cormac's eyes widened. "It's true?"

"I mean . . ." Brooks let a slow breath out between puffed cheeks. *Shit, that sounds bad. Real bad.* "There were *reasons.* And anyway, I wasn't trying to leave her hanging out here. That people would try to embarrass her like that is crazy."

Cormac stopped and cringed. "I get what you were trying to do, but Brandywood has its way of dealing with things. You driving up the bid wasn't probably the best idea. If the Stricklands have it out for Maddie, they're not going to leave it alone. They'll just use this for ammunition. I doubt old Milton has the money for that sort of thing, and they'll paint him as one of your victims now, too."

"I wasn't driving up the bid, he was." Brooks searched

Cormac's face. "Wait. You think I was just trying to drive up the bid?"

"Weren't you?"

Brooks shook his head. "No . . . I just stopped because I realized that's what the old man was doing. I had every intention of outbidding him until then."

Cormac's brows drew together. "You were going to pay over one thousand dollars for a crate of apples and a kiss from Maddie?"

When you put it that way . . .

Brooks yanked his sunglasses off, his face flaming. "Look, it's complicated."

"Complicated? I thought you were hooking up. I didn't realize you actually liked her this much."

"I didn't actually *want* the kiss," Brooks tried to explain. "I just didn't want her to get such a low bid."

"So you *didn't* want to kiss her?" The confusion on Cormac's face was only increasing. "Not that it's any of my business, but this isn't one of those 'kissing is extra' arrangements between you and Maddie, is it?"

"For the last time, I haven't slept with her." This whole conversation sounded insanely juvenile. He couldn't remember the last time he'd had any sort of discussion about his love life—or lack thereof—with Cormac. Or any other friend.

"So you haven't slept with her, and you don't want to kiss her?"

"No, I want to. I just haven't."

"And she knows this?"

"That I want to sleep with her? Yeah, I told her. You know, when I tried to kiss her while I was drunk, thanks to a certain friend of mine that sent her my way when I was in no condition to make sound decisions. Anything else, Father Cormac?

Should I say five *Hail Marys* and come back tomorrow? I'm sure I'll have more to add to the list by then."

Cormac chuckled, his posture relaxing. "I wasn't trying for a confession, but I'll note your guilt for the file. Holy fuck, Brooks. Do you have feelings for Maddie Yardley?"

Brooks replaced the sunglasses slowly. "I don't know."

"You don't know, or you're just not ready to admit it?"

"What I feel is irrelevant. I'm not like Kayla, ready and able to date the first person I meet from this town. My life doesn't have room for a woman right now."

"Why the hell not?" Cormac's gaze traveled to the cornfield that served as a perimeter to the wide, open field where the festival was being held. "Look, I may not know a lot about what's going on with you in general or between you and Maddie, but I left this town thinking the world could offer me so much more. And the more I'm out there, the more I understand that meeting someone who makes you act as crazy as you just acted is . . . rare. The more people you meet, the rarer it becomes. The lonelier it gets."

"So you *are* planning on moving back home?"

"Not anytime soon. And don't change the subject." Cormac shook his head. "I'm not talking about me. I'm talking about the fact that you met a girl who makes you feel something. That's not something you should dismiss so easily."

Brooks didn't know what to say.

But it felt as though he was running out of chances.

Their lives didn't naturally intersect, and Brooks knew that. He had so many time-consuming and life-changing undertakings ahead of him, but he knew one thing for certain.

He didn't want to go through all of that alone.

He could share his troubles with Kayla and Cormac, sure, and he was going to work on that. But Maddie?

She'd cracked open the door to his past without trying.

He'd shared things with her he'd never felt he could share with anyone.

That was what was *rare.*

She calms me.

Her kisses consume me.

And her heart? It . . . *she* compelled him to be a better man, one who had more drive to do the right thing. *If* she'd consider giving whatever they could be a go.

He couldn't bear the thought of hurting her anymore. The look on her face just now had damn near crushed him. If she wanted something more, he'd be a fool to turn her away.

"Do you know where Maddie is heading later? She doing any more competitions?"

A slow smile spread over Cormac's face. "I know of one."

29

MADDIE

"I DON'T WANT to talk to you," Maddie said as she exited the luxury port-a-pots, where she'd been doing her makeup.

Jake had apparently been waiting for her, his face shadowed by the fading daylight. The Pearsons had plenty of patio string lights up in the area where their barbecue food truck was and over by the stage area, but here it was darker. "I'm so sorry, Maddie."

"Like I said, I don't want to talk about it." She brushed past him. She just wanted to put the whole humiliating episode behind her and for this fucking day to be over.

"You should know, I found out that someone started a rumor about the Cortland apples—folks just didn't want the apples, not you. I have a feeling I know who started the rumor—"

"Gina Strickland? Yeah, I figured." Maddie scowled. "I don't understand what the hell that girl's problem is. She won. She has Josh. And she's welcome to him. Why the hell does she have it out for me so badly?"

"You know the Stricklands never forgave Pops for selling

gelato at the Depot. Fred has been carrying on about how it has cut his ice cream business in half for the past two years. And then there's the fact that the whole town is going on about some incident in the Stricklands' storeroom. Slow down, will you?"

She didn't slow as she moved toward the tent serving as the "backstage" area. "First of all, the Depot hasn't hurt the Stricklands at all. With the influx of tourists in the summer coming to the Depot, lines were out the door and halfway down the block to the Stricklands this year. How often did that happen before Pops built the Depot?"

She drew a deep breath. "And the other thing? There might be some truth to it, but I doubt Fred Strickland mentioned he called me trashy, then tried to shake Brooks's hand. Of course Brooks didn't take to it too kindly."

"I'm not arguing. Just saying." Jake grabbed her forearm. "But it's the Stricklands. They want to humiliate you now. Don't let it get to you. You've always been good at letting this shit go."

Maddie almost paused, scanning Jake's face. The truth was, she was more upset for a reason she couldn't tell Jake: the crushing disappointment she'd felt when Brooks had let Milton Hirsch win the auction. Instead, she pressed forward, focusing on Jake's attention to the Stricklands instead. "What if I don't want to let go of it, though? What if I'm sick of how overblown everything has to get because we all constantly rub elbows with the same people? Brandywood just feels so . . . *small* lately."

Jake's steps faltered. "What're you saying?"

"Nothing." She tucked her long hair behind her ear. "It doesn't matter. Like I said, I don't want to talk about it. I have a song to sing and then I'm going home right after that. I wouldn't even do it if I hadn't signed up, but I don't want Gina thinking that she got to me."

"But she got to you and that's okay. It was a shitty thing to do. I'm not sure who I'm madder at—her and Josh or the people in town who cared more about not getting a bad crop of apples and want to take Fred's side every time he wants to bully people. But hey, at least Brooks made you look good at the end. Highest bid ever on record."

"Yeah, before giving up and letting Milton win," Maddie muttered, a fresh wave of embarrassment rising in her chest. Was that why he'd done it? She couldn't comprehend his motivation for driving up the bid like that and then abandoning it at the last second.

He couldn't have known that, with each bid, she'd felt a spark of hope and excitement she didn't dare dwell on for too long.

And then he'd just . . . stopped.

Why did he do it?

She squeezed her eyes shut, trying to stop the onslaught of thoughts.

It doesn't matter.

It doesn't matter.

It doesn't matter.

"I have to go," she snapped. "I'm gonna sing and get the hell out of here. See you later, Jake."

She hurried to the backstage area. The competition had already begun and, even from here, she could hear Millie Price doing her infamous rendition of "Don't Sit Under the Apple Tree." The familiarity of it was sweet, but Maddie almost rolled her eyes.

Normally, it would have brought at least a smile to her face.

When had she become such a curmudgeon?

"Maddie?" Samantha Doyle came into the tent, holding a clipboard. "You're almost up. Right after Millie."

Garrett's wife had her long dark hair tied up, looking fresh-faced and stylish. When she'd moved back into town after living in New York for years, Maddie remembered how often she'd tried to memorize Sam's outfits, hoping to go online and find something similar. They'd never been close—Sam was older by several years—but Maddie liked her a lot.

"Okay, thanks," Maddie said, a flutter of nerves gripping her stomach.

"You're going to do great," Sam said with an encouraging smile. "You always do."

Maddie nodded distractedly. As Sam turned to go, Maddie said, "Hey, Sam—"

Sam turned back and waited.

Maddie drew closer to her. "I know this is super random, but . . . do you ever regret coming back to Brandywood? Or miss New York?"

A faint look of surprise lit Sam's eyes. Then understanding.

"I don't regret coming back. Brandywood is home now—for real—and I'm happy here." She stepped a little closer. "But do I miss New York? Yeah, I do. I didn't leave New York because I didn't love it. Living there was fun. Exciting. I had a life that checked all the boxes for my career as a photographer. Giving that up wasn't easy; but it forced me to be creative in other ways that I might not have allowed myself to if I'd stayed there."

Her pulse quickened.

She'd never really allowed herself to go down this line of thought too much. Like Sam said, Brandywood was home.

"It's a hard decision to make," Sam said softly. "In my case, I didn't have the same relationship with my family that you do. But I regret the time I lost with them. Especially after my mom died."

Maddie blinked, feeling strangely exposed. "Yeah, I just . . . wonder, sometimes. It was easy not to let myself think of anywhere else because of that. And anyway, I have the Depot to run."

Sam pursed her lips and hugged the clipboard to her chest. After a beat, she leaned closer still. "If I can give you any advice, Maddie, it's this. If you're not happy with who you are when you're home, you won't be happy with who you are away from it. That doesn't mean you can't leave. It just means you'll need to find your peace somewhere along the journey."

Why am I even thinking about this? I love Brandywood. It's my home.

She didn't really want to leave . . . did she?

Applause punctured her thoughts. Time to go.

Her gut churned. She'd sung in front of people from town dozens of times. It wasn't her most comfortable place, but she'd do it for the fun of it. But somehow, today wasn't fun.

She'd chosen "Wildfire" because she'd been listening to it so much the past week that she was certain she knew the lyrics by heart.

But if Brooks is there . . . especially given she'd chosen one of his songs . . . would he walk off mumbling about amateur hour?

No, Maddie. Just get this done so you can leave.

She wouldn't think about the possibility of him hearing her, or that everyone in town knew she'd been hanging out with him.

Whatever. I can only go up from today's lovely apple auction. Or the apple picking. Or the orchard incident with Brooks. In fact, the whole day had been one embarrassing episode after another.

She headed up onto the stage, blinking in the blinding light. The lone spotlight was operated from behind the chairs set up in front of the stage, beside the sound booth.

Her pulse went faster.

This is stupid.

Why did I say I would do this?

Yet she had done it so many times before. Most of these people had heard her sing.

But usually the town wasn't mad at her, with the Stricklands gunning against her.

Then again, she was from this town, too. She knew how to charm them. How to get people back on her side.

She grabbed the mic, thankful that she couldn't see the audience because of the spotlight. "Hey, Brandywood. Everyone having a good night?"

A few tepid cheers sounded, including a familiar whoop from Jake. *At least I know he's here for me.*

Time to be vulnerable. She hadn't practiced saying anything, so she didn't know what to say, but these were *her people.* They also knew an apology when they heard one. And like it or not for Josh and Gina, the town also knew what had happened with that relationship. Maybe Brooks had offended Fred Strickland, but she'd been hurt first.

"So the man who wrote this song came into my life recently . . . when I really needed it. He helped me get my feet back on the ground on a night when I was having a tough time and needed a friend. He's a pretty amazing person and musician, so I'm sure you'll recognize the song, and I promised to show him a side of our town that would help him see why Brandywood is the best. A place of warmth and forgiveness. Where when someone makes a mistake, we do our best to extend the hand, make things better. Work to settle our differences. We support our own, but we also welcome strangers. So this song is for you, Brandywood. I love you."

More applause this time, stronger than before.

She drew a shaky breath. *Here goes nothing.*

The familiar music began from the speakers, and she put the microphone back in the stand, trying to relax.

You can do this, Maddie.

Somehow, the words came, as though her voice knew what to do, even if her brain was going into overdrive. Singing had never felt like she had as much on the line, and she loathed that the Stricklands and their ilk were out there, probably judging her.

And then there's Naomi, who avoided me all day again.

Don't think about that.

The easier the words and melody came, the more her body relaxed into it. Her voice wasn't perfect, she knew that, but it was strong and she could carry a tune without being pitchy.

Crack.

The music and spotlight went out.

Maddie froze, blinking as her eyes adjusted to the hanging string lights.

What the hell just happened?

Her stomach plummeted, her eyes scanning the face of the audience that grew clearer by the second. The guy handling the sound booth and light was on his hands and knees in front of the booth, scrambling for an unplugged cord . . .

No.

It wasn't possible. The Stricklands wouldn't sink this low, would they?

The audience was looking back at the sound booth now, exchanging glances. She saw the faces of her family in the audience, near the front row . . . Mom and Dad, Jake, Naomi and her husband, Lindsay and Travis . . . Logan, Kayla, and Audrey . . .

Brooks stood up from beside his sister, no sunglasses this time. He'd taken his hat off, too.

In a few fluid steps, he snatched a guitar that was set up on stage. Throwing the strap around his shoulder, he came closer and whispered, "Just start from that verse again."

Her heart throbbed as he played, the guitar's sounds bright with a confidence that his expert hands evoked. Not like the quiet strumming from the other night, but someone who knew this melody like the back of his hand.

Because he does.

Her throat thickened with emotion, then she cleared it and sang, trying to keep her voice steady.

A cheer went up from the audience, bolstering her confidence.

Brooks stayed in the background, not intruding as she continued. She'd heard acoustic versions of "Wildfire" before, but for him to be her accompaniment? *Sheer. Magic.*

She could barely process it.

It wasn't just that he'd rescued her from a situation meant to humiliate her.

Or that she might sing this better than she'd been before.

But . . . Brooks Kent, rock star, celebrity, whatever else he was . . .

. . . *might actually be her friend.*

When the song ended, the audience collectively seemed to hold their breath.

She stared out at the crowd, her heart pounding loudly now. *Please.* She sent the message out to them all. *Please be the people I know you are.*

Then the entire audience climbed to their feet, shouting and cheering more loudly than they'd done for anyone. The spotlight popped back on, and Maddie squinted against the harsh light as Brooks set the guitar down and came toward her. "Take a bow," he said with a wink, then started for the edge of the stage.

She grabbed his hand. "Take one with me."

His fingers slipped against hers, interlacing hers with gentle pressure. Her chest squeezed, his touch sizzling with a fire that jolted through her. He lifted their hands up and then took a bow together.

The crowd continued their boisterous, standing ovation.

Rather than releasing her hand, Brooks tugged her closer to him. "I cheated myself of a kiss earlier," he said in a low voice against her ear. "But not because I didn't want to pay one thousand dollars for it, Madison. Or because I didn't want to."

What is even happening right now?

He cupped her face softly as though there wasn't a loud crowd continuing to clap. His eyes searched hers. "A kiss from you is priceless. But I won't ever force you."

Is that what he thinks? That I don't want to kiss him?

Before she could overthink it, Maddie wrapped her arms around his neck and stood on her tiptoes, her mouth colliding with his.

She didn't care that everyone she knew was watching.

She cared about the way her body fit against his, his arm curling around her upper back. His hand slid to the small of her back, tugging her closer as the soft pressure of his mouth molded against her own.

Cameras flashed, but she closed her eyes, ignoring them all.

Her body heated with desire, her head spinning as she forced herself to break away before a simple kiss turned into a full-on make-out session in front of her parents. And the town. And his niece and sister. That wouldn't do anything to win anyone over.

But *damn,* she wanted him.

Okay, Maddie, calm the fuck down.

Her breath was ragged as she stepped back, heart slamming hard in her rib cage. She didn't venture a look at her family.

Brooks held out a hand toward the crowd to settle them.

When they were quiet enough, Brooks used a voice that was clearly well-practiced on stage and said, "Not sure what happened with sound there, as a plug has never simply come out of its socket for me before, but let's get it fixed. In the meantime, I'll be back in town for the festival in just a few weeks to headline the Saturday night concert. Looking forward to it, Brandywood."

Wait. What?

The crowd cheered again.

"I thought you said the deal was off?" she whispered to him.

He shrugged. "I'm not doing it because I owe you. I'm doing it *for you*. Because I want to."

She searched his gaze. "What are you saying?"

"I'm not ready to walk away from this, Maddie. From you. And I'm sorry I didn't tell you sooner."

As though he hadn't already practically melted her into a puddle.

She was tempted to kiss him again.

Brooks leaned his lips close to her ear. "Want to get out of here?"

"I can't think of anything I want to do more," Maddie whispered back.

They hurried off the stage, hand in hand, heading for the back. Maddie pulled Brooks forward, away from the noise and chaos of Applepalooza. Her family would want to come celebrate *and* rage with her, but right now, she just needed this man in front of her.

"I'M NOT DOING *it because I owe you. I'm doing it for you. Because I want to."*

He was complicated, but his simple statement told her

something important. He was loyal and kind, and she wanted a man like him in her life. *Even if I don't know how to make our very different lives fit together.*

Moonlight illuminated the way, the crisp scent of burning wood fires filling her soul.

Brooks Kent was only here for one more night.

But maybe he had something else in mind.

Going back with him didn't hold any guarantees. No matter what, she wasn't ready to walk away either.

30

MADDIE

MADDIE HAD TAKEN Brooks back to his place, but now that they were here, the weight of expectation choked her. Fortunately, they'd arrived before Kayla and Cormac, which meant they had the house to themselves—but for how long?

And what was the plan, really? Have sex with Brooks, go home . . . and then?

Rather than going to the main living area, Brooks had taken her to sit on the balcony of the master suite, which felt more private despite its sizable nature. A chimenea provided them with warmth—Brooks had lit a fire in there as soon as they'd arrived—and he came back from the kitchen now with a bottle of wine and a single glass for her, as well as a bottle of sparkling water for himself.

"Miss me?" he asked with a grin, setting the glass down on a small table beside her chair. He poured the glass for her.

"You sure you don't mind me drinking wine?"

He nodded. "It's not that alcohol is something I can't quit. It's that I don't like—and neither does Kayla—who I become when I drink. Kayla asked me to sober up when she thought it was becoming a problem. I was always more of a binge drinker than anything."

"And the sex and drug addictions?" She sipped her wine. They needed to clear some things up before things went further.

"Complete fabrications. What else do you want to know? I graduated Summa Cum Laude from Duke—straight-A student all my life. Valedictorian in high school. I was a huge nerd. There wasn't time for dating and sports, so I played the guitar."

"A nerd with the body of a supermodel," she said with a laugh.

"That didn't come until later. I filled out in my twenties. My manager got me a personal trainer and a dietitian . . . and I've been on a program ever since. Turns out sex really does sell."

"Oh, I never doubted it." Sex did sell, and Maddie couldn't help thinking that he had definitely gained some skills in the kissing department over the years of his "transformation." That also could be the wine talking since wine instantly made her hornier. "Can I make a confession? About you and my secret crush on you in college?"

His gray eyes lit with amusement. "Go on."

"I had a verrry sexy poster of you on my wall. I used to talk to it occasionally, too. And the sound of your voice . . . has definitely made me wet." *Oh God, did I just admit that out loud?*

Brooks's lips curved in a devilish smile. "What was all that nonsense about not being a creepy groupie when we first met then? How you hadn't listened to my songs in years?"

"I was wearing a towel when we first met. I was embarrassed enough. And it's not like I fantasized about *you* specifically. Well, maybe once or twice this week, but that's different."

He raised a brow. "Only once or twice?" He chuckled.

"You are painfully honest sometimes, you know that? Here I've been thinking about you all week."

"I didn't mean that." She bit her lip, suddenly nervous again. But speaking of being honest . . . "I just—I'm not sure what I'm doing here. What *we're* doing. It's been a weird week and I feel like I've been all over the place emotionally with you."

He studied her for a few moments. "What do *you* want this to be?"

On stage he'd said he wasn't ready to walk away from her. But what did that mean?

She certainly wasn't going to demand a relationship with him. That would be crazy—they hadn't ever even been on a date.

But something like a date didn't really feel important somehow now either. They'd spent the last few days getting to know each other. Letting the other in.

Yet she'd also already told him she didn't do one-night stands.

"I don't know, I'm . . . scared about what happens when you leave, Brooks. Because it's not an *if.* You're leaving. You can say you don't want to walk away, but I don't know what that means. And I don't want this to be a one-night-only situation, either."

"I know that." Brooks reached out a hand for her. She swallowed a large mouthful of wine, then set the glass down and interlaced her fingers with his. He drew her over toward his chair, and with a smile, she stepped out of her boots, then straddled him.

"Better?" he asked.

Shockingly, being close to him like this calmed her. "Much."

His lips skimmed her jawline, drawing a seductive line to her earlobe, which he nipped. "I don't have all the answers,

Maddie. This is new for me, too, believe it or not. But I respect and like you too much to sleep with you and then walk away. I have a lot on my plate right now and just as many unknowns and maybe it's better if I get all my ducks in a row first, but damn if the thought of that doesn't make me miserable."

She rested her cheek against his jaw, closing her eyes. "It makes me miserable, too."

Brooks trailed his hand up her back, gently. "Can we just take it a day at a time for now? Adjust as we go along and . . . figure it out together?"

That didn't sound unreasonable.

And it was honest, too.

Neither of them knew what they were doing. A day at a time wasn't forever, but it wasn't a one-night stand, either. Or, worse still, nothing.

And maybe thinking about *forever* had been part of her problem in the past, too.

She'd gotten so caught up in getting on with the rest of her life that she'd forgotten to enjoy the present. That was what Brooks was ultimately offering. *Right now with a path forward.*

She pulled back and searched his gaze. "I think I can handle that."

Warmth lit his eyes. "Good. Because I have a question for you."

What now? "And what's that?"

His thumb skimmed the bare skin at her waist. "How wet?"

She swallowed. "How wet what?"

"How wet did you get when you were fantasizing about me?" His lips continued a slow path down the side of her neck to her collarbone, making her pulse throb.

Trust him to return to that topic.

She laughed lightly, her eyelids growing heavy with the

allure of his kisses. "Not as wet as you've made me when we kiss."

"Wet enough to touch yourself?"

Her breath rasped in her throat, and her head spun with desire. Maddie's fingertips brushed against the stubble of his jaw, then made a slow path down to his chest, where she steadied herself as his tantalizing kisses continued down her shirtfront.

He undid the top button of her shirt, and she sucked in an unsteady breath.

"Maybe."

"Madison, tell me the truth." Another button came undone, and her breasts felt heavy with the anticipation of his touch.

God, I want him so much.

"Occasionally."

"Tell me about it." The silken command was enough to make her shiver. He clearly carried that demanding, bossy presence into the bedroom, which didn't surprise her. Brooks was in charge, and she liked that about him.

"Brooks—"

"Tell me." Another button opened deftly, enough so that her bra was exposed now. Her nipples were growing hard. "I want every single dirty detail, Madison. Don't pretend you're shy now."

"I'd uh—" She struggled to think as he quickly undid the other buttons and pushed her shirt off her shoulders. "I'd slip my hand between my legs . . ."

He unhooked her bra, his gaze locked in on her breasts. "My God, your tits are fucking perfect." His hands skimmed them gently, then he arched her back against one hand, lowering his lips to one nipple.

A brush. A flick of his tongue. The gentlest pressure of his lips around the nub. She drew a shattered breath, trying to think straight.

His breath was against her breast. "Go on . . ."

"God, I'm so wet." She moaned as his lips enclosed around her nipple. "So wet for you, Brooks. I'd slide my finger against my clit, and my pussy was dripping."

He groaned in response, taking her nipple into his mouth harder.

His sucking was fucking incredible, drawing deep electric currents from deep within her.

"More." He moved to the other nipple, his hand palming the one he'd abandoned. "Don't hold back now, sweetheart."

Her back arched more as he drew her into his mouth.

"And I'd use the other hand to push deep inside my pussy, stroking myself . . . sliding in . . . and out . . ." She released a strangled gasp. "Brooks, I need your mouth on mine."

Brooks lifted his lips from his feast on her breasts, then smiled. His mouth crashed against hers obligingly, a need there that had a frantic edge to it.

No restraint.

No holding back.

Just the pressure of the softness of his lips against hers, his tongue tracing against her lips, urging her mouth to open for his.

She closed her eyes as his hands claimed her, taut against her back as he pushed her into the front of his jeans, where his cock bulged against her.

Fuck. Yes.

I needed this.

She'd spent all week trying to keep herself from touching him and failing. Besides being the most gorgeous man she'd ever been around, his grouchy disposition made her want to kiss those smirks and sarcastic quips away.

He took his time delving into her mouth, his tongue softly circling hers, stroking her desire for him from a quiet low burn into a deep, seductive conflagration. *Wildfire.*

"Holy shit, I'm so wet," she moaned as his hands slipped onto her ass. He shifted her better onto his hips, and she wrapped her arms around his neck, the kiss deepening as she ground against him, aware of the distinct disadvantage she had wearing a skirt. She had just the flimsiest fabric of her panties between them—which were now soaked through.

She wanted him in a way she'd never wanted any man. Wanted to touch him. Feel him inside her. *Right now.*

With her arms wrapped around his neck, the softened peaks of her nipples brushed against his shirt. "Your turn. Don't make me tell you all my secrets."

He laughed lightly. "Is that how you think it is between us? You know the things I've never told anyone, sweetheart. Got me down to the marrow. A little taste of your sexy fantasies is hardly going to tip the scale."

His words made her feel like putty in his hands. *Dammit, how does he keep doing that?*

"But if it makes you feel better, I wasn't lying when I told you the other night I've dreamed of burying my cock in your pussy, Madison. I want it. And if I take it, you should know I'm a greedy son of a bitch. I don't intend to share you with anyone. You still want to be mine?"

Mine? I'm not sure what that really means, not to a man like Brooks Kent, but I'll take what he's giving me tonight.

She ground against him, her lips against his ear. "I still want you, Brooks."

"You have no idea how much effort it took not to kiss you in that orchard. If I'd had known you wanted me to, it would have saved us both a lot of trouble."

"Are you planning on torturing me as a punishment?" She

moaned, her knees pressing together reflexively as his hand moved down between her legs and pushed the fabric of her panties to the side.

"God, Brooks. Please," she panted in response.

"Please what?" He gave her a wicked grin as he slid his fingertip into the wetness between her legs.

He made a slow figure-eight around her clit and she jolted against his touch, her clit throbbing with pleasure.

"You *are* wet, baby. So fucking wet it makes me want to take you right here."

"I want you to," she said, groaning as his fingertips went deeper. He slid one finger inside her and her eyes closed with the heady pleasure, her head dropping back.

She'd never had foreplay like this . . . or had a man talk to her like this. A gulf clearly existed between his level of experience and her own, but he didn't treat her that way, either.

"Tell me what you would do." He licked his lips, his voice like silk. "If my cock was stroking that wet pussy, baby. You want me bare? I want to feel every inch of you, coat that pussy with my cum."

Bare?

That was just as dangerous as he was.

But it also showed something deeper, too.

Trust.

That he didn't just want her for a night. He wasn't just opening a path for them, he was telling her he wanted this to turn into *something.*

"God, Brooks . . . that feels so . . ." Her words drowned as he slid another finger inside her. "Is it safe?"

"I wouldn't offer if it wasn't. What about for you?"

She nodded. "Yeah." She'd gone to the doctor after her breakup. That he'd asked was undeniably hot, too, in a way she couldn't quite explain.

"Good."

Her cheeks flooded with heat, her lips still wet from his kisses as she moaned, breathing harder as he slipped his fingers against her wetness, curling them against that tender spot past her entrance that throbbed to his touch.

The man knew where to touch her with a skill that made her want to cry.

Waves of pleasure came over her as he stroked her, drawing back to make circles around her clit, every inch of her feeling consumed by his touch.

He's so fucking good with his hands.

Raw, intense arousal built within her and her hips pressed against him. "Brooks," she managed. "I need you. Bare. Inside me. Now. I want to come with you."

He lifted her, wrapping her legs around his waist. Carrying her as though it took no effort, he made his way toward the back door to his room.

The room was lit by the faint glow of a gas fireplace and he set her on the bed, laying her back, gently. Without taking his eyes off her, he pulled her skirt and panties off. She slid her feet onto the bed, her feet cold from having been outside, and focused her gaze on him.

Brooks pulled his shirt off, the taut muscles of his body rippling as he did. *My God, he's gorgeous.* The deep tan, the chiseled muscle, the tattoo sleeves . . . was it really possible that a man this insanely hot wanted her?

Then he kicked off his shoes, as his fingers unbuttoned his jeans. He stepped out of them, then the black boxer briefs he wore under them.

The man was fucking hung.

Her eyes widened as he set one knee on the bed, parting her knees. "You're so huge," she said, her stomach lurching as he drew closer.

Brooks smiled, returning his thumb to her clit, where he made a slow figure-eight. "You want me, Madison?"

"Please."

"I'm not going to hurt you," he said, pushing the head of his cock inside her. She gasped at the feel of him, a feral moan building as he inched forward.

"God, you're so fucking tight, Madison. Never gone bare before. Feels fucking amazing."

Never?

Holy shit.

She panted, her chest rising and falling fast now as he set his hands on either side of her and dipped his mouth against hers once more. She clung to his neck, her legs falling open more widely as he gained another inch, her heart slamming harder into her chest, her face and lips on fire.

He pulled her hands back from his neck, pinning her arms above her head with one hand. "Relax, sweetheart. Just relax."

She nodded, needing him to fully insert himself in a way that was indescribable and also terrifying. He kissed her once again, gliding his tongue against hers, taking his time to deepen the kiss, pushing inside her inch by inch as she relaxed against the hardness of his cock.

One final kiss and he pushed himself to the hilt, eliciting a cry of pleasure that ripped through her entire body as he groaned loudly.

"You okay?" he breathed against her temple. His heart was pounding against her chest.

"Incredible," she said with a nod, her breath ragged.

She found his mouth again, kissing him as they found a rhythm together, her hips rising to meet each thrust of his length.

"Fuck, Madison. God, you feel good."

The deep drive for satisfaction that had started to build out on the balcony now took over, her hand clamping into his hair, her body taking over.

Yes. My God, yes.

Brooks Kent was the best sex she'd ever had . . . and she hadn't even come yet.

"Brooks," she gasped out, the pressure of a building climax growing stronger within her. "Brooks, I need . . . oh God, Brooks. Feels . . . amazing."

He thrust harder now. Faster. *In and out . . .*

"I want you to come. Come apart for me, Madison, baby."

Him saying her name like that.

That was all it took.

A cry left her as her climax ripped through her, her body slackening against him. Her legs trembled, her head light as he shuddered a loud groan. His cock throbbed inside her as he poured out, emptying himself—as though he'd been waiting for her to let go.

Oh. My. God.

He had given her the most incredible orgasm. Ever.

She opened her eyes as he pulled out from between her legs. A devilish smile curled at his lips as he kissed her temple. "Fucking best appetizer ever."

"Appetizer?" She cocked a brow.

"You better believe it, sweetheart. The night is just starting."

A slow smile spread across her lips. She might never recover from a night with Brooks.

But she didn't want to, either.

31

BROOKS

THE RINGING of his cell phone roused Brooks from sleep and he blinked groggily in the early morning light, lifting his head from his pillow.

Beside him, Maddie groaned, her eyes squeezed shut. "Who in the hell is calling at this hour?"

Brooks shook his head and silenced the damn phone on his nightstand. Whoever it was could wait. A beautiful woman had slept in his arms, and he wasn't about to spoil the morning with a damn phone call.

"Morning, gorgeous." He wrapped his arms around her waist, pulling her against him, then kissed her bare shoulder.

"How in the hell are you hard again?" she asked with a laugh, her eyes still closed.

"Good question. But I think I know how to fix that problem."

She shook her head sleepily. "You already spent the entire night between my legs. I'll be lucky if I can walk today. If that didn't fix it, I don't know how."

"I'm pretty sure your mouth has magical powers, too."

"Best I can do is a hand job," she said, reaching back and wrapping her hand around his length.

Can't complain about that. In fact, with her hand on him, he couldn't think about anything else, anyway.

How he'd ended up going from a horrible start to the week last week, to an incredible night of sex with a woman he couldn't get enough of . . . he wasn't quite sure.

But he had.

She'd somehow brought him back from the brink.

Seen him.

He didn't want to question how they'd gone in a week from forced interaction, to blackmail, to tenuous friendship, to . . . *whatever this is.*

But he felt more sure about continuing this than anything. *One day at a time, for now. Until we can figure out where this is heading.*

Being with her felt the closest to normal he'd felt in forever. Like he could be completely himself and she wouldn't run away.

As her slow rub continued, he reached around and dipped his hand between her legs, returning the favor. He smiled, finding her already wet for him.

Fucking delicious woman.

"You're not playing fair, you know. How in the hell are you ready to go again?"

Good question. He didn't want to really know how little they'd slept. But they'd taken turns waking each other up, pressing against each other, kissing.

Hungry.

Brooks smiled, then pushed her onto her back. "Then feel free to relax." He trailed his lips from the nape of her neck, tracing down the length of her back. As he did, goosebumps rose on her skin.

"What are you doing?"

"Taking care of my woman. I told you I was greedy." He reached for that gorgeous ass and flipped her onto her stomach.

"Brooks . . ."

Pushing her legs apart, he cupped her ass cheeks and dropped his kisses lower. Her full body shuddered as his tongue stroked her wet pussy, then darted inside.

"Oh my God," she gasped.

"You taste incredible, Madison."

As his tongue made a trail down to her clit, flicking against it, his fingers slipped inside her. Didn't matter how many times they'd had sex last night. He wanted more. *Can't get enough.*

"So unfair," she panted, then pulled away from him.

Crawling toward him, she pushed him back into the middle of the enormous bed, then straddled him. One quick, fluid motion and he was sheathed inside her. "This how you wanted to wake up?"

"I mean, I'm not going to complain." He lifted his hands and squeezed her breasts, her head dropping back as she arched into his touch.

"You poor sex-starved man. Went a whole—what—twenty minutes without it?" She rocked against him, lifting, then lowering herself.

"Fuck, you feel so good." Her pussy clenched around his cock at his words, and a smile spread across her face. "And I'm not the only one who kept waking up last night."

"You've ruined me, you know. I can't spend my life in bed with you in a luxury lake house. And from now on, all I'm going to think about is how much I love fucking you."

He'd never believed in fate or destiny before, but dammit if that deer jumping in front of his car didn't come close. Crashing into her store might just be the best thing that had ever happened to him.

Release came quickly this time and as he left her on the bed to grab her a warm washcloth, he memorized the sight of her there, flushed, satiated, and beautiful against his bedsheets. She murmured and smiled at him, reaching lazily across the bed to grab her cell phone.

We've ruined each other.

He was just in as much risk of not being able to recover from this night with her. But at least he had a plan. No way he could walk away from her yet.

He washed up quickly, then squeezed out a washcloth for her.

"Oh, I just wanted to tell you. I saw Jason Cavanaugh yesterday, and he extended my rental to this coming Friday," he said as casually as he could as he started back to the bedroom. "And then for the remaining weekdays in September. Weekends were unfortunately booked."

Maddie was seated on the bed, frowning at her phone, her expression frozen.

A thunderclap of alarm went through him. *I know that look.* "What?"

"Uh . . . don't freak out." She turned her phone toward him and held it out as he approached.

The screen had a picture of the two of them kissing on the stage the night before.

A tabloid article.

He blinked at it and pulled on a pair of boxer briefs, a knot of tension growing in the pit of his stomach. "What does it say?"

"Bad boy rocker Brooks Kent finds love with a small-town sweetheart . . . but will he break her heart?" She looked up at him anxiously.

Thank goodness. His shoulders relaxed. "That's not actually so bad."

"W-what do you mean?"

He sat beside her and handed her the washcloth. "There are a hundred ways they could have spun that photo, Maddie. Believe me when I tell you that's tame by comparison."

"And . . . you just live like this? With your every move being torn apart by people who make up whatever they want about you?"

"Pretty much. Yeah."

She shook her head in disbelief, the wide-eyed innocence of her questions cute. "Doesn't it ever get to you?"

"I can't do anything about most of it. So what's the point of worrying about it? I can practically see the next headline they make about us: Saint and Sinner." He winked. "Little do they know the truth about you."

"Har-har." She shook her head and climbed down from the bed, heading to the bathroom. "It's crazy to me. How did that picture get in the news so quickly? What, they work overnight?"

"Yup." He grabbed his own phone. *Shit.* He'd missed a phone call from Ava.

About the pictures?

Probably.

"Wait—" Maddie popped her head out from the bathroom door. He loved that she was still naked. Her eyes went wide. "Did you say that you're extending your rental?"

He smiled. "Took you long enough to hear me."

She let out a cry of happiness and came racing out of the bathroom toward him. Throwing her arms around him, she held him tight, nearly knocking him backward. "Why didn't you tell me this sooner? I was ready to cry thinking you'd be packing up in a couple of hours."

He tugged her to rest against him and lay back on the bed. "I mean, I've been a little busy since I made the arrangement.

But it turns out I'm going to need to be close to Baltimore anyway for my arraignment. And I met someone. She lives here, so I don't want to exactly take off just as things are getting started with her."

She ran her fingers against his chest. "And what happens on the weekends when you're not able to stay here?"

"Well . . . maybe the girl could take me in. Or, if not, I could fly her to Paris. Abu Dhabi. Banff. You know, anywhere she wants to spend a romantic weekend with yours truly."

"Can you fly internationally while on bail?"

"It's a misdemeanor, so I sure as hell hope so." He kissed the top of her head. "Any place you want to see? I'll get us tickets for next weekend. I probably would advise against Abu Dhabi since it's like a thirteen-hour flight, but my jet has a bed so it could be a fun one."

She propped her chin on his chest. "You know, I had almost forgotten you're like insanely rich until you said that. Now I just feel intimidated." Leaning up farther, she searched his eyes, her hair draping his face. "And does this mean . . . we're dating?"

Funny how, with her, this conversation didn't come with the level of stress that it had in the past. Despite their conversation the night before, he understood her need to put a label on their relationship. But "defining what we are" had always had such a weightiness to it, usually involving official confirmations and press releases. Especially when the match was a setup.

With her, it meant giving her whatever title made her feel more comfortable with their arrangement. He just wanted to make her happy.

"It means we can be whatever you want to be. I'm completely at your mercy. But if the role of boyfriend is open, I'd love to apply."

From her expression, it was clear he'd given her the right answer.

A knock on the door pulled their attention away. "Uncle Books! Uncle Books!"

Brooks smiled at the sound of Audrey's voice. "One sec," he called out.

Maddie pressed a quick kiss to his lips. "I'm going to shower. Make me some coffee, will you?"

"Anything for you, babe."

She grinned, then headed back to the bathroom, closing the door behind her.

Damn. Much as he loved Audrey, he was tempted to tell her he was still sleeping and go join Maddie in that shower.

Instead, he got dressed and went to the door, where Audrey stood patiently waiting for him. She threw her arms around his leg, nearly hitting him in the junk, and he winced. "Hey, kiddo. Have a good time at the festival yesterday?"

"Uncle Books! Logan is gonna take me for a pony wide today."

Brooks picked her up and carried her down the hallway toward the kitchen. "Really? A real live pony or one in a merry-go-round?"

Her eyes were giant, her eyebrows with the wide exaggerations of childhood innocence. "A live one! Wight, Mr. Logan?"

Brooks jerked his head up in surprise as he reached the living room, where Logan and Kayla sat beside each other on the couch, drinking from matching coffee mugs. Logan had clearly spent the night.

Cormac gave a jaunty wave from the kitchen, where he was frying bacon. "Morning, sunshine. Good night for the Yardleys and the Kents, I see."

Awkward.

"Morning, Cormac." *Jackass.* Brooks avoided Logan's gaze

as he set Audrey down. Whether the man was sleeping with his sister, he had to know that Brooks was banging Maddie. Her car was parked in the driveway, and that kiss on the stage had likely confirmed any suspicions.

Hopefully, the walls were soundproof. They hadn't exactly been quiet the night before.

They had to be—he hadn't heard anyone even come in last night.

"So I hear you're heading for a pony ride?" Brooks asked Kayla.

She smiled, setting her hand on Logan's knee. "Yeah, Logan has a friend who owns a horse farm. We figured it would be fun for Audrey before we have to drive back to Virginia tonight."

"Well, just so you know, I'm extending the rental. We don't have to be out of here until Friday. And then I can continue renting the house for all the weekdays in September."

Kayla's eyes widened. "Are you serious?"

Cormac let out a low whistle. "I don't even want to know how much that costs. You still keeping the chef?"

Brooks shook his head. "Nah, I'll figure the food part out. But you all are invited to stay as long as you want."

Cormac turned off the burner and set a plate of bacon on the table. "I would, but I have to get back to Nashville. I'm in the studio this month doing some recording for my friend Elle Winnick."

"Oh, I love her," Kayla said with a grin. "She's got such a great voice. Maybe you can introduce us. Logan likes country, too, right, hon?"

Wow. The ease with which she'd said that caught Brooks off guard. He liked that Logan made her happy—he just wasn't sure any of this should be happening so fast for them. Especially with Audrey involved.

Logan seemed to sense the direction of Brooks's gaze, and

his eyes darted to him. "Yeah, country's great. Not that I don't listen to rock, too."

"I'm not offended if you hate it. Music is personal." Brooks crossed the room toward the plate of bacon, which was calling his name. "Any coffee left? Maddie was asking for some."

"Miss Maddie is here?" Audrey asked, looking from Kayla to Brooks.

Amazing how quickly old, generational guilt could come back. Mom wouldn't approve. In all Mom's time as a single mother, she hadn't once brought a man back to the apartment to spend the night. She'd said she didn't want to introduce anyone unless it was forever. She didn't want them to get attached to people she couldn't guarantee would stay in their lives.

Even though Brooks wasn't Audrey's father, he still felt the weight of the example he needed to set for her weighing on him heavily. His eyes met Kayla's, and she looked away as though she knew what he was thinking.

"Um, well, much as I'm going to make it a point to come back here in the next month, I have work. So Audrey and I have to go back tonight. But we can come visit occasionally."

He hadn't really considered the idea that it might just be him up here in this giant house for most of the month. Alone. Maddie had a life to live, too. And while he was determined to spend as much time—and nights—with her as possible, she couldn't always be here.

Brooks was about to grab a piece of bacon when his phone rang.

Ava.

Dammit.

He needed to deal with this sooner rather than later.

Excusing himself, he went out to the back balcony and shut the door behind him.

"Brooks, imagine my surprise when I saw you in the news again today." Ava's voice was startlingly warm.

"That so?" His eyes flicked out toward the lake. Despite the sun today, it wasn't exactly warm out. He'd need to get more clothes if he was going to stay here.

"Well, I think it's an excellent strategy. You, settling down in a small town with a slice of American pie? Absolutely. The public loves those star meets girl-next-door arrangements. Makes them feel like if they dream hard enough, it could happen to them." Her laugh was caustic. "So when do we meet her? We need to brief her on her role, of course, and get her to sign an NDA. We'll need a new single release on the books for you in the next few weeks, roll her into the press junket."

Of course.

He almost laughed.

Of course.

Ava would think this was staged.

He'd promised her a well-thought-out plan to deal with his problems and had no idea he hadn't given it the slightest bit of consideration.

"Yeah, that's not going to happen, Ava."

She cleared her throat. "Excuse me?"

"I'm not feeding Maddie to the wolves. Ever. This isn't some *scheme* on my part. I care about this woman."

"Oh, for Pete's sake, you have got to be joking. Are you going to tell me you're in *love*?"

In love? No. But well on his way to falling for Maddie?

He closed his eyes, letting out a slow breath.

Absolutely.

"She's my girlfriend," he answered simply.

"So you mean to tell me you've been holed up in the middle of god-knows-where, playing house with this woman? For real? This isn't for your image? What about your career?"

"You know what the thing is, Ava? You wouldn't be freaking out about how to solve my problems if I didn't make you a lot of fucking money. So maybe you hold all the cards and maybe you don't. But it doesn't matter anymore. Because I'm done. I'm terminating our relationship, effective immediately."

"Now listen to me, Brooks—"

"Anything further you have to say can go through my lawyer." He hung up before she could continue.

Damn, that felt good.

He drew in a deep breath, setting his hands on the railing.

Maybe it had been because he'd spent the night with Madison Yardley.

Or that he wasn't going back to LA yet.

But for the first time in a long time . . . Brooks felt free from everything crushing him under a merciless heaviness, dragging him under the surface.

He could finally breathe again.

32

MADDIE

Lindsay opened the door to her apartment with a wide smile on her face. "Yay, you're here!" she said, throwing her arms around Maddie's neck. "I was wondering if I'd ever see you again."

Maddie rolled her eyes and handed her the bottle of wine tucked under her arm. "I missed *two* family pizza nights. It's not like I went to Timbuktu." She was determined not to feel the slightest shred of guilt for spending every night after work this week with Brooks. He was all alone up there at the lake house—and they had a lot of catching up to do as soon as she walked through the door.

Which had been fun.

Sex in every room of the lake house, on multiple surfaces.

She'd never felt so close to being a sex goddess in her life before.

"Two is too many, which is why I called this emergency girls' night." Lindsay tugged her in through the door, nearly knocking them into Travis, who was pulling on a black leather jacket.

"You leaving?" Maddie asked Travis with a wry lift of her eyebrow.

"Are you kidding? I'm not about to hang around and watch *Thirteen Going on Thirty* with you all. I have manly stuff to do. Like poker nights and playing with cars—"

"Don't forget to pick up the dry cleaning while you're out, please. Also, the groomer said to pick Ratchet up at seven. And tell the girls at the senior center bingo night that I promise I'll come by next week, and I miss them." Lindsay planted a kiss on his cheek and winked.

Maddie chuckled.

Travis muttered a grumble. "I'm only going because my grandmother likes for us to go occasionally."

"And we all love Bunny. I get it."

"Oh, by the way, tell your new boyfriend that his car will be ready next Tuesday. I finally got the windshield in."

"I'll let him know," Maddie said with a wave as Travis backed out the door.

Lindsay shut the door behind him and squealed. "Okay, now that he's gone, you have to *spill.*" She dragged Maddie into the living room, where Jen Cavanaugh was setting out charcuterie. "Is Brooks Kent as yummy as he looks? We need every sordid detail."

Maddie's face flushed. "Jen does *not* want to hear about my sex life."

Jen's blue eyes lit with interest as she sat on the sofa and grabbed a piece of prosciutto-wrapped melon. "Jen *does* want to hear about your sex life. I had twins a year and a half ago, Maddie. Action in my house in the middle of the night is Jason or me getting up to walk someone around until they fall back asleep again. And because there are two of them, they like to take turns on being awake."

"Does he have stamina?" Lindsay asked, pouring a glass of

Riesling. "He looks like he would have stamina. All those ab muscles."

Maddie covered her face, chortling back a laugh. "You guys are ridiculous. What the hell do ab muscles have to do with stamina?"

"I don't know. He clearly works his core muscles."

"The hell with stamina. Who needs long-drawn-out sessions anyway? Wham, bam, thank you, ma'am, can be pretty great. I want to know if he sings to you," Jen said, lifting her brows. "Because *that* would probably make me fall completely in love."

Maddie looked at their eager, expectant faces and shook her head. *I'm not seriously considering telling them anything about my love life, am I?*

Then again, it was fun to be with Lindsay and Jen. She had missed their company despite her time with Brooks. And Jen had always been like the fourth Yardley sister because she'd only had two older brothers and had been best friends with Lindsay her whole life.

Maddie chewed on her lower lip slowly. "He's very—"

The doorbell rang.

"Hold that thought. I'll get it," Lindsay said, popping up from the couch again. She crossed back toward the living room and opened the door. Naomi stood there, holding a plate of brownies.

Maddie's heart lurched.

All week long, she and Naomi had done a decent job of avoiding each other. They didn't both need to be on the floor of the Depot at the same time, and most of Maddie's work was behind the scenes anyway.

Naomi locked eyes with Maddie, a frown settling on her lips. "I didn't know Mad—"

"Oh, cut the crap and get inside," Lindsay said, dragging

her by the arm. She shut the door behind them and pulled Naomi into the living room.

"Hey, Jen," Naomi said, setting the brownies on the coffee table.

"You can't ignore Maddie, Naomi. We all know what you're doing, and she was just about to tell us all about Brooks's skills as a lover, so don't ruin it for us."

Naomi made a face. "I'd really rather not hear about that."

"You know what? Maybe I should go. I don't want to kill Naomi's fun. She's the one with kids who doesn't get to get out for girls' night as much." Maddie glanced back at the exit.

"No." Lindsay stamped her foot. "What, are you guys just not going to talk anymore?" She turned to Naomi. "So Maddie lied. She fessed up and told the truth. Apologized. She made Travis lie to me, and I'm not still mad at her. Can't you forgive her already?"

Naomi crossed her arms defensively. "I'm not the only one who's mad, you know. Maddie kicked me out of her apartment."

Lindsay backed away slowly, heading to the sofa and the safety Jen offered there.

Maddie sighed. "After you insulted Brooks and were incredibly rude to him—"

"Well, what was I supposed to think when Fred Strickland called me to tell me you were having sex in his storeroom?"

"Oh, Brooks *does* sound like fun," Jen whispered to Lindsay as she sat.

"He *is* fun," Maddie said pointedly. "And a good person. One who doesn't deserve to be judged by my older sister—who doesn't know a thing about him—yet assumed every bad thing people say about him is true." *Now* she was getting mad. "Logan said you practically rolled out the red carpet for him when he introduced you to Kayla. Why can't you do that with the man I'm falling in love with?"

Naomi flinched. "Because I'm the one who has to be there to pick up all the fallen pieces of Maddie when the breakup happens. When was the last time Logan brought someone he cared about home? Never. You've met the 'love of your life' a half dozen times."

Lindsay drew the gasp that Maddie felt deep in her own heart. Her eyes pricked with tears.

The room seemed to freeze, the four women staring at each other tensely.

Lindsay stood. "Okay, Naomi, I love you, but that's probably the meanest thing I've ever heard anyone say. Ever."

She turned to Maddie. "And please don't hate me when I ask this because I completely believe you know your own heart better than anyone, but could you tell us how Brooks differs from what the internet says? And why this is different for you?"

Maddie swiped her lashes. "I don't think I need to defend what I feel, Lindsay. So what if I catch feelings easily? Just because I'm not afraid of falling in love doesn't mean I should be an object of Naomi's mockery."

"I'm not mocking you," Naomi said softly. "Haven't you ever considered how hard it is for those of us who love you to see you go through that? To know that you're suffering, even if it's for someone who doesn't deserve your tears . . . like how it was with Josh? Do you know how much it fills me with incandescent rage to know that Josh dumped you like he did and then got engaged to Gina? Gina, who doesn't hold a candle to you, Maddie. I may be the quiet one of the three of us, but that doesn't mean I don't want to scream at that prick for hurting you. And when I see someone like Brooks, where there doesn't appear to be a single green flag in sight, I *worry*."

Naomi stepped closer, her own eyes shiny with tears. "I

love our parents, but it's always been us Yardley siblings watching out for each other. Mom and Dad are sweet, wonderful parents, but they don't get involved in this stuff, even if it bothers them. Even if they should. No, I don't think it's a great idea for Maddie to hop into bed with Brooks after . . . I don't even know how many days of knowing him. Especially not when she's rebounding from a major heartbreak, and the guy practically has 'love them and leave them' as a tattoo."

Jen cleared her throat. "If it helps, Naomi, I slept with Jason after knowing him for only a few days. We turned out all right."

"And I had multiple one-night stands with Travis for *years* before we admitted we loved each other," Lindsay chimed in.

"I'm not sure if they count as one-night stands if it's with the same person," Jen said wryly.

Maddie gave them a sad smile, thankful for their efforts, then glanced back at Naomi. "Not everyone gets together the way you and Jeremy did—friends, then college sweethearts, marry, and have a family. Some of us have a different path to take. That doesn't mean it's the wrong one."

Maddie hugged her arms to her chest. "To be honest, I don't think you've earned the right to know about Brooks just because you want me to prove he's a good guy. But if you don't believe me, ask Kayla. Ask her about the sacrifices he made for her. He didn't grow up rich with a silver spoon in his mouth. Hell, Naomi, he would probably kill to have our good, sweet, *detached* parents. He doesn't have any parents, and that much you can find out online if you look. He's had to work really hard to get where he is in life. A life I don't even fully understand the difficulties of. And he's attacked constantly, his privacy violated repeatedly."

She didn't mention that all week long they'd been finding

themselves getting photographed. Since their picture at Applepalooza had gone viral, the paparazzi had found him in Brandywood. Making out on the balcony was no longer an option. Neither was any sort of intimate time in the hot tub.

Splotches of color formed on Naomi's face. She stiffly sat on the loveseat perpendicular to the sofa, her shoulders falling with defeat. "I'm sorry," she said at last. "I'm not trying to be a jerk. I just don't want Brooks to hurt you, Maddie."

"He's not going to hurt me. There's a much higher chance that I'll hurt him anyway if I fall in and out of love as easily as you think," Maddie said with an eye roll. She sat on the loveseat beside Naomi. She'd hated the distance between them over the past week and a half.

"I want my best friend back. It's been killing me not to be able to tell you anything about Brooks. Why do you think I confessed so quickly? Meanwhile, I have Tweedledee and Tweedledum over here begging for all the details of my sex life and I'm strongly considering telling them incredibly NSFW stories because I don't have my big sis to dish to."

Lindsay's jaw dropped with mock horror. "I resent that."

Jen sipped on her glass of wine. "Long as you're Tweedledum, I can live with the nickname."

Naomi's lips twitched with laughter. "God, I've missed your sense of humor. Family pizza night is boring without you." She turned and slipped her hands into Maddie's. "I'm so sorry. I *have* been an asshole. And honestly, it's kind of impressive that you not only blackmailed Brooks into a concert but also bagged the man himself."

"What's that about blackmail?" Jen asked, looking from Naomi to Maddie.

"It's a long story." Maddie laughed and hugged Naomi. "I'm sorry for kicking you out of my apartment. And for breaking into Fred Strickland's storeroom. It was stupid, and you're right, if he'd caught me stealing that SD card, it all could have been much worse."

"What!" Lindsay reached for a brownie. "I feel like I should have made popcorn. Y'all are gonna have to back up because clearly, Jen and I are completely out of the loop."

"You guys don't even want to know." Maddie poured herself a glass of wine.

"Um, yeah we do." Lindsay leaned forward eagerly. "*Nothing* even remotely interesting happens around here, Maddie. It's Brandywood. Gossip is all we have."

Maddie smiled to herself, dropping back against the couch and curling her legs under her.

Somehow, in the past couple of weeks, Brandywood had felt . . . smaller.

But right now, she didn't mind. Right now, she was with some of the people she loved the most. Including Naomi.

33

BROOKS

"Much as I've come to like your Brandywood," Brooks said as he walked into the bedroom from the adjoining bathroom of the room they'd booked in the Serendipity Lake Lodge, "I'm still not sure how we ended up at this bed-and-breakfast when Paris was on the table. Or Quebec City, which might be one of my favorite places in the world."

Maddie stood at the full-length mirror, applying her makeup, and she smiled at him. "Because it's my grandfather's birthday. My whole family wants to meet you. It's not going to make a great impression on them that they've met Kayla three times and you not at all, considering she's going to be there."

Maddie had been unusually happy since she'd returned from a girls' night with her sisters the night before. She'd suggested that they stay here at the Serendipity rather than at her place for the weekend, citing the nosiness of Main Street citizens.

He wasn't about to question her good mood—she'd gotten straight onto her knees the night before when she'd entered the bedroom and given him the best goddamn blow job he'd ever had—but the idea of meeting her entire family terrified him.

He came up behind her, wrapping his arms around her waist. "Impressions are overrated. You know what's not overrated, though?" His lips grazed the side of her neck. "The sound you make when you come for me."

She turned her face toward him, and her freshly glossed lips found his. "Mmm . . . you know how to tempt me, babe, but I'm going to go with no. Even if you met no one else in my family, I'd want you to meet my grandfather. He's my favorite person on the planet."

He feigned a wounded look in the mirror.

A slow smile spread across her face, and she kissed his cheek. "Don't worry. You're my second favorite."

"Hey!" His arms tightened around her waist, and he lifted her. She squealed, trying to get away as he carried her a few feet over toward the bed, where he dumped her. Laughing, she squirmed in his arms as he held each of her wrists down to the bed, his mouth crushing hers with a kiss.

She melted into his arms, the kiss slow and lingering, their tongues delivering well-practiced strokes. One week of nonstop sex had been exhausting—let's face it, he wasn't eighteen anymore—but her body felt familiar in his now, each curve and plane explored. She was ticklish behind her knees, and her chest flushed after an orgasm. She had a light smattering of freckles across her cheeks—mostly hidden by makeup—and an even cuter patch of freckles on her left shoulder.

And he didn't have to question what he was feeling.

He'd never felt so content in his life. She was such a breath of fresh air. He'd never met someone so genuine in her affection, attentive to how she listened to him . . . and kind.

Gorgeous. Funny. Sweet. Sexy.

He was falling in love with her, harder and deeper each day.

When he broke away from the kiss, she moaned. "Not fair taking me horny to a family party."

"We can do something about that, you know." God knows he was ready to go again.

"Not unless we want to be really late." She closed her eyes as though it pained her to push him away, then climbed out from under him. "I'm officially banning you from the room while I finish getting ready. Go on. I'll meet you on the front porch. If you're a good boy, I might even let you drive again."

He chuckled, stealing her keys from her purse with a wink. She'd actually been good about letting him drive them anywhere this week—not that they'd gone many places. But while she still had the privilege of being one of the few people he knew that had ever driven him in years—because he couldn't control when he needed to go by a chauffeur—she'd also explained that she understood his path to healing from the trauma of his mom's fatal car accident was something he had to do on his own time.

Which he appreciated about her.

She didn't look at his darkness and shame him for it. Somehow, she made him feel safe to speak about it.

He left the room and went down the hallway, then the stairs of the old house. A converted Victorian mansion, the Serendipity was owned by the cop who'd taken the police report that first day—Dan Klein—and his wife Avery.

As he stepped out onto the front porch, he bumped into them sitting there, each of them with mugs of coffee that steamed in the frosty morning air.

"Morning," Dan said, standing from one of the chairs on the wraparound porch. "Sorry, people usually end up on the back porch in the morning. You want a seat?"

"No, feel free to sit. I'm just waiting for Maddie. Sorry to interrupt, actually." He imagined they probably took this space as their little haven from the guests, considering they lived here.

"You didn't interrupt at all," Avery said, warmth in her green eyes. She swung back on a hammock swing. "We were actually just talking about you, Mr. Kent."

"You can call me Brooks." He turned and leaned his back against the railing, his hands on it. "Hopefully nothing bad."

Dan's face became more serious. "No, not about you. But I've had to chase a couple of photographers off the property this morning. I don't have a lot of tolerance for stalkers. They're parked across the street on the side of the road, though. Not much I can do about that, I'm afraid."

Damn paparazzi. They'd been hounding him all week, trying to get pictures of him and Maddie. "That's good to know." He frowned. He didn't want them following them to Maddie's grandfather's party and pestering them the whole time. By now, he was sure they had memorized Maddie's car's make, model, and license plate.

Dan seemed to read his expression. "You going somewhere this morning?"

He nodded. "Maddie's grandfather's having a birthday party."

"You need a lift? They won't know my car."

The offer was tempting despite his dislike for being driven. But it seemed like since he'd arrived in Brandywood, it had been one person after another doing it.

"I don't want to pull you away from the Serendipity," he said.

"Dan can drive you," Avery said, stopping the swing. "If you don't mind. I've got it covered here without him." She stretched, revealing a slight baby bump. "When I first moved out here from California, I couldn't handle the constant curves on the roads. They made me so carsick."

"You're from California?" Huh. He wouldn't have pegged her as anything other than a local. She seemed to blend seamlessly with everyone he'd met. "How'd you end up here?"

"I'm from Florida, actually. Even more reason for the roads to make me sick. Flat, flat, flat, there." She gave her husband a loving grin. "But my family used to take summer vacations here at the lodge. I met Dan when I was a teenager, fell madly in love, and many years later, found my way back here."

"There are more transplants to Brandywood than people realize," Dan said. "Especially in the last few years. The whole town revitalized after Peter Yardley's businesses took off."

"Maddie's grandfather?"

Dan nodded. "The man is a legend around here now."

A chilly breeze rippled past them, carrying with it a swirl of yellow leaves. "So Maddie's like . . . Brandywood royalty?"

Avery laughed. "I couldn't have put it better myself. The Wagners and the Yardleys are probably some of the best-known families in town. They used to be rivals, but then joined forces when Bunny and Peter married."

Brooks could hardly keep a straight face. "When you say 'Bunny and Peter' all I'm picturing is that Beatrix Potter character."

"You know, I've never thought about that, but you're right," Dan said with a chuckle.

"Right about what?" Maddie asked as she pushed open the front porch screen. She sidled up to Brooks and set her hand over his.

"The names Bunny and Peter conjuring illustrated visuals of rabbits wearing blue jackets," Brooks said dryly.

"Hey, don't make fun of my grandparents," she said with mock indignation. She squeezed his hand. "I'll be sure to tell my grandfather. He'll get a kick out of it. He hates the nickname Bunny anyway—he never called her that. It's a nickname her late former husband gave her."

"I'd forgotten about that," Dan said, lifting his light-colored eyebrows. He smirked. "Anyway, I was a fierce Yardley loyalist, thanks to Lindsay, so I never liked Mr. Wagner. Bunny, on the other hand, she always gave us cookies."

"Our little sisters are best friends," Maddie explained to Brooks, and gave Dan a warm smile. "And Dan and I basically played in the sandbox together."

A strange stab of jealousy went through him. Not because he felt like Dan was a threat in any way—but that connection. That feeling of belonging to a town and people you'd known your whole life . . . he'd never experienced that. Not like this. Fountain Springs had made him want to flee and never look back.

His parents were buried in the Presbyterian church's graveyard, and he'd never even gone back to visit their gravestones since he'd left. Not once.

"If it makes you feel better," Avery said, giving Brooks a knowing look, "these two play up the glamour of living in Brandywood pretty hard. If the Yardleys are royalty, the Kleins are like dukes." She rolled her eyes. "Don't let them fool you. There's plenty of drama, small-town gossiping, little old men and ladies being outraged about inane things. Some people—like your friend Cormac—leave town and don't move back."

"Still, it seems like many people stay."

"Because they make a home here," Avery said, and snuck an affectionate glance at her husband, her hand curving over her bump. "If you find the right people, then all the petty things are easily overlooked. The good outweighs the bad."

Brooks didn't glance Maddie's way, as a troubled feeling arose in the back of his mind.

Whether he wanted it to be, for now, his life was centered around LA. He might be wealthy enough to play house with Maddie at the lake house, but soon enough, he'd need to go back.

He didn't want to think about that yet.

"Ready to go?" Maddie asked, holding the keys out to him.

"Apparently, we have paparazzi waiting for us, and Dan offered to drive us. It might be a good idea, so they don't follow us to your grandfather's house."

"We can take my truck or my police cruiser. Windows are tinted in the back of the cruiser, but it might look suspicious," Dan said.

Brooks had no desire to ride in the back of a police car. "Truck is fine."

They said their goodbyes to Avery, then headed around to the detached garage off the driveway. "I noticed you don't have a security detail," Dan said as he unlocked the garage. "Have you given any consideration to one while you're here?"

A cop would notice that. He had to give Dan credit, though. He clearly kept a close eye on his property. Knew who was lurking. *Also probably a cop trait.* "I'm just trying to fly under the radar here for a while. It worked for the first week anyway."

"Well, it looks like they found you now." Dan flipped on the light to the garage. "Just something to think about. Brandywood is about as safe as you can get, but it's not people from here I'm worried about. And we don't really have a ton of resources here like the big cities might to handle someone of your profile."

Once again, Dan would have thought about that—and know the reality of the situation here—because of his background.

"There something we should worry about?" Maddie asked with a laugh as they climbed into the back of Dan's truck.

"I'm just being cautious," Dan said as he shut the door.

"We'll probably want to just sit on the floor until we get past where the paparazzi are parked or this is pointless," Brooks told Maddie as she buckled up.

Maddie raised a brow at Brooks and climbed to the floor. "Is this how you live? Constantly looking over your shoulder?"

Brooks shrugged, trying to relax as best he could onto the floor mat. She looked cute sitting there—and actually fit, unlike him. His knees were by his face. *Damn, this is cramped.* "Sometimes. I live in a gated community and I have bodyguards when I need them. Mostly, I just drown out the noise when I'm in public and avoid going out."

Light flooded the garage as Dan opened the garage door.

"Isn't that lonely, though?"

Dan opened the driver's side door then and climbed inside. "All set?"

"I think so," Maddie said and laughed. "I feel like I'm sneaking out of the house or something."

She's laughing now because she hasn't had to live this way for years. In a way, he envied her naivety. The first time someone had asked for his autograph while he'd been out to dinner with Kayla, he'd walked on a cloud for the rest of the day.

Now he didn't bother to eat at restaurants if they didn't give him a private room or close off a section for him.

Somewhere along the way, all the attention had stopped being fun.

Maybe it had been the first time his life was threatened.

Or when a fan had broken into his hotel room.

Or when the paparazzi had mobbed his car and made it impossible for him to leave a parking garage in New York City.

He didn't complain about it—*poor, poor rich and famous boy, so sad, how tragic*—and many people withheld sympathy.

But it *was* lonely.

He might not have even realized how lonely he was if not for Maddie.

Reaching a hand out, he interlaced his fingers with hers.

As if you get to keep her if you just hold on tight right now.

When would that wide-eyed innocence and laughter about riding on the floor of a truck fade? Would she come to hate him for it eventually?

"I think you all can probably sit on the seats now," Dan said, breaking into his thoughts.

They climbed back onto the seats and Maddie took the middle, rather than the one a seat away. "Hi," she whispered, snuggling into him. "You were too far away."

He wrapped his arm around her. "This is perfect."

"Have you met the full Yardley clan before this?" Dan asked, meeting his gaze through the rearview mirror.

"Not all of them. Just Logan and Naomi," Maddie said with a grin. "And don't scare him off, Dan. I already warned him they can be a lot. At least they're not like the Klein brothers. You should see the hell Dan and his older brother put Jen through when she was trying to just be a normal teenager and date. Guys practically shit their pants if they talked to her and Dan or Warren happened to see."

"Yeah, well, it's no walk in the park to witness your baby sister get knocked up by an asshole, then leave her to fend for herself," Dan said grumpily.

Brooks's gaze flicked to Dan's again. *Interesting. I do, actually, know what that's like.*

Maddie winced. "Don't worry, Dan, I never bought the story that you were a huge bully. I knew why you stood up for her."

Maybe he and Dan had more in common than he realized.

The topic changed again to something more pleasant, and within a few minutes, Dan had pulled into her grandfather's street and dropped them off at Maddie's grandfather's driveway.

Brooks reached for Maddie's hand.

When was the last time he'd met anyone's family?

The normalcy of it was more intimidating than anything else. He was just a guy, dating a woman, about to meet her family. That was how it went in the movies, right? A family barbecue was tame enough.

"You look like you're holding your breath," Maddie teased, poking him in the ribs. "Don't worry, they're not going to hurt you. Naomi is the most likely to give you a grilling, and she's too repentant right now to say anything."

"I'm fine. I'm just not the biggest talker, you know." They drew closer to the back gate. A white picket fence. *Of course.* "Give me the rundown. Who's here?"

Maddie tucked her arm into his, her breast curving against his arm. *Dammit, woman.* Was she doing that on purpose? "Well, you know Naomi. She's over by the swings with her husband, Jeremy, and her two daughters, Emily and Olivia. And that guy over there by the grill is Jake, who is talking to my dad, Larry. You've met Travis. He's playing corn hole with my sister Lindsay—the one who looks like me—and his sister, Grace. And Bunny is right next to my grandfather—"

"Peter." Brooks jerked his chin up with surprise.

Maddie's grandfather was Peter—the old guy from the fishing boat.

He let out a chuckle of disbelief.

Maddie drew her brows together as she studied his profile. "You've met him?"

"Yeah, he—uh . . ." Brooks rubbed the back of his neck.

"Drove me out of Main Street the first day we met. Then he took me fishing a week ago with his friend Brian."

"You've gone fishing with my grandfather?" Maddie's jaw dropped open.

"He's . . . a good listener."

It all made sense.

No wonder he felt he could bear his soul to the chatty man.

Maddie *was* just like him.

Peter saw him and raised his hand in a greeting. "Brooks!" He crossed the yard, ambling toward them with a wide smile. "I was wondering when I was going to meet you officially." He kissed Maddie on the cheek, then shook his hand. "Looks like you solved that woman problem, eh?"

"*Woman* problem?" Maddie crossed her arms. "Did you talk to my grandfather about me?"

Brooks laughed. "I didn't know I was talking to your grandfather."

"Don't worry, Maddie, it was nothing bad."

"You know, I don't even want to know. If that old letch Brian Pearson was there, all bets are off on what could have been said." Maddie lifted her hands and started to walk away.

Brooks caught up with her and grabbed her by the waist, dragging her back against him. He kissed the side of her neck as she laughed. "Mostly, we talked about how I shouldn't offer you any sausage, but I didn't listen," he hissed in her ear. "And you're not abandoning me to meet everyone on my own."

"Oh my God!" Maddie's cheeks predictably grew red, but her eyes danced with amusement.

"Awww, you guys are so cute," Lindsay cooed and left her game of cornhole. She extended her hand to Brooks. "I'm Lindsay. Maddie's nice sister."

"Hey!" Naomi gave a shocked look. "Just because I was a jerk one time doesn't mean you're the nice one. I was protecting my sister." She joined them. "But seriously, I'm sorry about my behavior, Brooks."

"Wait, you women can't hog Brooks all to yourself. I'm Jake." Jake came jogging over. "And—"

Jake scanned the laughing expressions of his sisters. ". . . and I'm going to immediately go shotgun a beer and burp to prove my masculinity."

"Oh, honey," Lindsay said with a laugh, "it's going to take a lot more than a beer to prove that."

Jake feigned a hurt look, and his gaze dropped to Brooks's forearms. "Maybe a tattoo? Or three? Can you recommend someone, Brooks?"

"Hey, what about asking me?" Travis hollered from where he stood. "I actually live in town and have tattoos."

A woman who appeared to be in her mid-fifties came out of the house then, carrying a tray of appetizers. "Young people and their fascination with marking up their bodies. I just don't understand it. When I was a teenager, the only men with tattoos were in the military or in jail." She stopped in front of the group and smiled warmly at Brooks. "No offense, Brooks. I'm Maddie's mother, Susan. That's my husband, Larry, by the grill. Maddie's dad, I mean."

Larry waved. "He looks perfectly normal. Like an actual, real-life person. Don't know what everyone was making such a big fuss over."

As the group bickered with embarrassment and laughter, Brooks caught Maddie's eyes.

They *were* a lot to take in at once.

But she looked in her element.

Completely, totally happy and herself.

And she was beaming with pride at him.

Because this is her home. And she never wants to leave.

A lump formed in his throat. As Dan intimated, Maddie

was practically Brandywood royalty, but she was also blissfully content. *Brandywood has more implants than I thought, but it seems rare that people leave.* Here, she had a good, predictable life, but away from here? Would she survive the harsh reality of the real world outside of here?

Witnessing her here made one thing clear—there was no way he could ever ask her to leave.

34

MADDIE

"ARE you sure it's not a problem?" Kayla's face was anxious as she looked out from the passenger side window of Logan's car.

"It's fine. I'm here. And even if I wasn't, Brooks is never, ever going to do anything to put Audrey in danger again. You can trust him. And my grandfather is taking us fishing," Maddie said. She wasn't about to tell Brooks that Kayla had displayed such a high level of concern—he'd be hurt—but she understood it, too.

Maddie leaned forward and smiled at her brother. "Have fun on your date, you two. And don't worry about being back early. I can put Audrey to bed in my room if she gets tired."

Logan grinned. "Thanks, Mom."

She blew him a kiss and straightened as the window rolled up.

Flicking her gaze across the street, she frowned at the familiar sight of a paparazzi photographer parked across the street. Maybe Dan Kline had made her more aware of it, but in the week since they'd come back from staying at the Serendipity, she'd started seeing more of them.

Everywhere she and Brooks went.

Often, they seemed to arrive minutes after they got somewhere, like someone had tipped them off.

When they'd come to stay at her apartment for the weekend yesterday, they'd already been waiting in the parking lot. The more paparazzi arrived, the more Brooks seemed to grow agitated, too.

Whatever small semblance of peace Brooks might have felt in Brandywood before was clearly gone.

So when Pops suggested taking Audrey out on his fishing boat, Maddie jumped at the opportunity. She'd adored going out on the lake as a kid and had occasionally joined Pops on his morning fishing trips while she and Josh had been dating since Josh loved fishing.

Maddie headed into the Depot, glancing through the large store toward the darkened stage in the back. These days, they mostly used the stage area to display more retail items, but Pops had first built it as an area to film his home cooking show. Since he'd slowed down a year ago, he hadn't been doing a lot of shows, but he had an annual Christmas special to film soon.

The energy that filled the Depot on filming days was unmatched. The crew came in from out of town, the store was abuzz with excitement, and ticketed guests waited in a line to get into the store early.

She missed the days when Pops filmed more. Partially because he'd lost a bit of bounce in his step the last couple of years despite being happier than ever married to Bunny.

Pops was showing his age more, and that worried Maddie.

She weaved her way through the displays toward the back of the store, passing a pine- and holly-scented section that reminded her of her favorite holiday.

Even though she and Brooks hadn't talked about Christmas

yet—it was too far off—hopefully, she'd have the chance to show him the magic of Brandywood around the holidays.

But don't get too far ahead of yourself.

He'd only booked the lake house until the end of September, after all. And if he had plans to stay for any longer than that, he hadn't said so.

Climbing the stairs in the back, she went into her apartment, where Brooks and Audrey sat on the floor. The room smelled like nail polish, and Audrey was dutifully painting Brooks's fingernails black.

Maddie laughed. "What are you guys doing?"

"She found it in your bathroom," Brooks said, his mouth twisting wryly.

"Uncle Books said black was asseptable." Audrey's brow furrowed in deep concentration, her mouth opening and closing with each stroke of paint—which was all over Brooks's fingers.

She plopped down beside them and kissed Brooks's temple. "Well, you'll be the prettiest fisherman out there."

"If Brian says something, remind me to show him pictures of a long line of musicians who paint their fingernails black."

"You know, you could beat him to the punch and just wear thick kohl eyeliner. Brian would be so distracted by that, he wouldn't even notice the nail polish." Maddie leaned toward Audrey. "You ready to go fishing?"

Audrey shoved the nail polish brush into the bottle and hopped up. "Yes! I get Mr. Fluffy!" She raced toward the bedroom, clearly having made herself at home.

"You're just going to leave me like this? Half finished?" Brooks displayed the one hand Audrey had painted. His pinky finger remained untouched.

"I think it looks good," she said as seriously as she could muster.

Reaching a hand over, he smeared a line of wet nail polish across her forearm with his pointer finger.

"Hey!" She jerked her arm back with a giggle. "Audrey is going to be very offended that you ruined a lovely manicure like that."

"Oh shit, can you throw more paint on it for me?"

"Polish, Brooks. Nail *polish.* Geez, what sort of C-lister rock star are you?" She retrieved the bottle of nail polish and leaned down, fixing the area he'd ruined. "Although, in reality, I'm going to go out on a limb and guess that you've probably had way more professional makeup jobs than I've ever had."

His lips twitched. "How many have you had?"

"Um . . . two. One for Naomi's wedding and one for Jen's wedding. Oh no, three. I also got one when Pops and Bunny got married."

He held her gaze, his eyes amused. "Yeah. Same. Three for me, too."

"What, three thousand?" She capped the bottle as Audrey's footsteps approached. "Audrey, you did a beautiful job painting Uncle Brooks's nails. Think you can paint mine when we get back?"

Audrey beamed proudly and nodded, the ringlets in her pigtails bouncing.

She is such a little doll. Maddie had initially felt inept at entertaining Audrey, but she was such a great kid. She loved her Uncle *Books,* and it seemed Audrey loved Maddie as an extension of that.

Brooks stood. "What do we need to bring with us?"

"Nothing. Knowing Pops, he'll overpack food. He'll have towels, too, even though we won't need them. Lake's too cold this time of year."

Brooks took Audrey by the hand and they headed out the door. This time, when they got to the bottom of the stairwell, they went toward the back, rather than through the Depot, to where Brooks's car waited in the parking lot. They'd switched the car seat he'd bought from Maddie's car to his after he'd gotten it back from Travis a few days earlier.

Brooks scowled as they stepped outside, confronted by a handful of paparazzi. Flashes blinded them, and the photographers did not bother to step out of the way.

Brooks lifted Audrey into his arms and grabbed Maddie's hand. "Get the hell out of here," he snapped at one of them as he took Audrey's picture repeatedly.

Maddie had a feeling he'd restrained himself because of Audrey.

They pushed their way toward the car, then Brooks loaded Audrey in as Maddie climbed into the passenger side.

Audrey's eyes were wide. *Terrified.*

"Hey, honey," Maddie said, leaning back from her seat and grabbing the little girl's hand. "Hey, look at me." She yanked her phone out of her purse and clicked on one of her favorite social accounts. "Have you seen this guy before? He makes the most incredible things all out of chocolate. Look at this. This is a train he made."

Audrey's gaze refocused away from the outside, where the paparazzi had continued taking pictures, to the video playing on the screen. Slowly, her little face relaxed as she got sucked into the video, mesmerized.

Brooks shut her door and then hopped into his seat. "Jesus," he muttered, raking his fingers through his hair. "They're fucking relentless. How many pictures do they need of me putting my niece in her car seat?"

"I don't know." She took his hand with her free hand. His half-polished fingers were trembling.

She'd figured he was used to this by now. "They do this all the time, though, right?"

He met her gaze and flexed his fingers. "It's one thing if it's me, Maddie. I invited this sort of attention into my life. But you? Audrey? Kayla? That's another thing entirely. They should have the decency not to harass the people I care about, but they don't."

"They should have the decency not to harass you, either, Brooks."

He released a slow, deeply held breath and started the engine.

"I see more?" Audrey asked from the back seat.

Maddie smiled and scrolled to another video. "Here. He makes a big banana out of chocolate in this one."

"Thanks," Brooks said as he drove. "You're pretty good with kids, you know that?"

"It's because of Emily and Olivia. I have practice. It does *not* come naturally." Truth was, since Brooks had come into her life, she hadn't seen much of her own nieces, and she felt a little guilty about that. Naomi hadn't complained yet, thank goodness, but she'd have to make up for lost time soon enough. Before it became any more obvious.

"Where are we headed?"

"Pops keeps his pontoon on a little slip near the Serendipity, actually. So just head in that direction, and I'll give you better directions as we get closer."

"Shit, they're fucking following us," Brooks said with a growl, his eyes focused on the rearview mirror.

"I take it you don't normally go out with Audrey in public?"

"Rarely. And never when these assholes are around."

"Mommy said that's a no-no word," Audrey said without taking her eyes off the phone.

Maddie put another video on for Audrey and handed her the phone. Reaching over, she rubbed the back of Brooks's neck, which was knotted with tension. "Relax, it's gonna be okay. Don't let it get to you."

Brooks didn't respond, his gaze continuing to dart with annoyance at the mirror.

By the time they'd arrived at the pontoon, his mood seemed to have soured altogether and Maddie could hardly wait until they got on the water. At least the paparazzi couldn't follow them out there.

Pops was waiting for them with a tiny life jacket for Audrey, and Maddie helped her put it on, then handed her over to her grandfather to seat her on the boat.

"Hold up," she told Brooks as he moved to follow his niece. She caught his hand.

Brooks gave her a steely-eyed look.

"Let this go, or this won't be fun for anyone," she whispered. Wrapping her arms around his neck, she stood on her tiptoes and kissed him slowly as though no one else was around.

He didn't return the kiss, and she pouted. "Come on, babe." She searched his gaze. "Can't you just *try* not to let it get to you? Yes, they suck, but they're keeping their distance now. And once we're on the lake, they'll stop following."

He chuckled bitterly. "Yeah, I've had them chase me on a boat before. More than once. Not that I think they'll do it here, but that's not the point."

"The point is that your niece is here. I'm here. And we want you to have fun with us."

Brooks gave a stiff nod after a moment, then climbed onboard wordlessly.

This was not going well.

Even the weather seemed to be against her. The sun had been shining in the blue sky but was now stuck behind increasingly thick clouds, everything a lot grayer in appearance.

Maddie sidled up beside Pops, glad for his presence. "Have any chocolate in your picnic basket?"

"For cranky pants?" He smiled at Brooks.

"No, for me. I'm going to need it to survive his mood."

"You know I can hear you," Brooks said, setting his arm around Audrey, whose feet swung from her seat.

She tossed him her best smile. "Oh, can you? Good. Maybe you'll work on cheering up." Unable to admit that it bothered her he wasn't putting any effort into making the most of an unpleasant situation, she looked away from him.

Yes, he could be grouchy.

But why did it also feel like sometimes he just dug in his heels about things that had other solutions? He seemed to make up his mind about some things and only increase in inflexibility if he was questioned.

That side of him . . . scared the shit out of her.

A determined Brooks was a force to be reckoned with. The negative side of that might have consequences she didn't want to consider.

Then again, while they continued to be in this "one day at a time" situation, who knew if she would even *have* to consider it? The label had been easy enough to accept at first, because she didn't want to lose him. As more time passed without them really figuring out what they were doing together, though, the more it weighed on her.

So far, she'd been doing what had been the easiest—avoiding thinking about it. She had a feeling he was doing the same.

That couldn't last, though.

They were soon cutting across the lake, speeding toward the dock where Pops always met Brian. She'd put her sunglasses on to shield her eyes from the wind, and the cool air stung her face. With her hair whipping past her cheeks, she glanced over her shoulder to look at Brooks and Audrey.

She was holding on to his arm but eagerly looking out over the water, her face radiating her excitement.

He . . . *clearly needs to cheer up.*

She knew something that might help, actually.

Pops seemed completely at ease as he approached the dock, but Brian didn't appear to be there yet. "Want to hop out and see if Brian is up in the parking lot?" The dock was a community one near the state park. "We're early, but sometimes he beats me up here and then sits in his truck listening to the radio."

Maddie nodded and started toward it. "Hey, come with me. I want to talk to you," she said to Brooks. She glanced at her grandfather. "You have Audrey for a minute?"

Pops smiled. "Sure. I can show her some lures or something but tie me up on the dock." He handed her the dock lines.

After tying the boat off, she tugged Brooks off the boat. At least here there weren't any paparazzi. With it being September, they also had the advantage that the park was empty. Few people were on the water this time of year. They checked the parking lot—no Brian—and then Maddie started into the woods.

"Where are we going?" Brooks asked with a frown. "This the part of the movie where you leave me in a shallow grave for being an asshole?"

She gave him a sly smile, then stopped and got to her knees. "No. I just thought you might need some relaxing. And we're completely alone . . ."

A devilish smirk came to that kissable mouth of his. "Oh really?"

Unbuttoning his jeans, she pulled the zipper down. The hardening head of his erection was already peeking through the top waistband of his boxer briefs, and she leaned forward and kissed him right there. He groaned softly. No matter how many times they'd been together the past two weeks, the sight of him instantly aroused her. But this wasn't about her.

"I want to take care of you," she murmured as she tugged him free, her hand wrapping around his length. "And considering I can't stop dreaming of fucking you . . ."

"That dirty mouth of yours is gonna get you in trouble," he growled.

She trailed the tip of her tongue down his length, eliciting a sharp intake of breath from him and a shiver from herself. She wanted to savor him, this freedom she had with him.

I'm his. He's mine.

That's all that matters.

But they didn't have time to draw this out the way they might if they were in a bedroom and the uneven surface of the forest floor was digging into her knees.

Taking the head of his length into her mouth, she swirled her tongue around him, then slowly drew him into her mouth fully. His size meant that he hit her throat and she drew deep breaths, her lips locked in a perfect circle around him.

"God, Madison. You're fucking incredible."

His hands wound their way to the back of her head, his fingers slipping into her hair as she pulled away, using one hand to stay completely wrapped around him, the other to grab his balls and squeeze.

"Fuck," he breathed.

As she drew him back in again, she tried to ignore her own growing need for him. Maybe just a few minutes of having him inside her . . .

Focus. Just him right now.

She wanted his cock inside her so badly that she threw her efforts into stroking him more fully, deeply, increasing her pace.

He *could* last for a long time, and that would only work to make her insatiable.

Drawing her mouth to the tip of him once again, she sucked lightly. "I need you to come soon, baby, or I'm gonna have to push you down and climb on top of you," she said.

He got the hint. "Open that dirty mouth and take me."

Dammit. I want you so much, Brooks.

He thrust into her mouth, and she slid her hands around his hips to grab his ass as he fucked her mouth, her body warm with desire for him. She moaned as she took him.

"I'm gonna come, babe. I'm gonna shoot my load right down that throat. Swallow it." He throbbed into her mouth, then she tasted him as he let out a deep, low groan.

She pulled back slowly and swallowed, then stood, her knees shaky. Smiling at him, she met his gaze. "Better?"

His face had visibly relaxed and he simply nodded in response.

She kissed him gently. "See you at the boat."

"Yeah, I'm gonna need a minute."

Leaving him there, she found her way out of the woods, her heart bubbling. She'd always enjoyed sex, but something about being able to bring a man like Brooks to his knees made her . . . giddy. Maybe it was the dynamic. He truly could have his pick of women in the world.

And he wants me.

He's mine.

Brooks Kent is my boyfriend.

For now.

That was a startling thought when she dwelled on it for longer than a second.

She was more content with him than she'd ever been with anyone. Wanted him more than anyone. The sexual energy between them was insatiable sometimes. She never would have done something like what she'd just done for another boyfriend.

But.

She'd also never had as little discussion about being in a committed relationship, either.

What are we doing here? Such a simple question with everyone else.

She'd let herself be complacent with the boyfriend and girlfriend titles . . . but that didn't *mean* long-term anything. And she was starting to *feel* long term for this man.

Don't lie to yourself, Maddie.

She wasn't *starting* anything at this point. The last few weeks, she'd been oh-so-casually falling for a man she was in a *one-day-at-a-time* relationship with. A man who treated their relationship as anything but *casual.*

They needed to talk about this.

When she was almost at the dock, she saw that Pops and Audrey appeared to be eating cream puffs—because Pops always fed people and usually started with sweets if it was a kid. Bunny worried about his health, but Maddie thought it was cute. *Same old Pops.* Always sneaking sweets and salty snacks.

Maddie almost didn't see a woman jogging from the parking lot down the narrow path toward the dock. The woman caught up to her just as she reached the first wooden plank.

"You Madison Yardley?"

Maddie turned back toward her and smiled. "That's me."

The woman's eyes narrowed. She shoved Maddie, hard, with both hands.

Maddie went flying backward against the dock, her butt and head smacking against the planks, sending spots into her vision as she cried out.

What the hell?

"Stay away from my boyfriend!" the woman screamed, hovering over her.

What? She stared at the woman, frozen with confusion.

"Brooks is mine, you hear? You keep your bitch hands off him."

What the hell?

A shiny flash of metal glinted against the cloudy sky as the woman pulled a knife out from under her jacket.

"I'll kill you. I'll fucking kill you!"

"What? No!"

Suddenly, Pops appeared beside Maddie, and without an ounce of hesitation, he reached out, snatched the knife from the woman's hand, then pushed her over the dock and into the water. The woman continued to scream, thrashing in the water, as Pops tossed the knife off the opposite side of the dock. It sank instantly.

What is happening?

Brooks came into sight.

Thank God.

A younger, more heart-breaking scream punctured Maddie's horrified mind.

"Maddie!" Brooks cried. He bolted toward them.

She turned to get to Audrey, who stood screaming and clearly terrified in the boat.

Please don't fall out of the pontoon, Audrey. Oh my God, what if that woman gets to her first?

Thankfully, the woman was swimming away and toward the shore, away from them. Maddie leaped into the pontoon, which rocked violently, knocking Audrey into her arms. Audrey wailed, trembling. *But I have her.*

Maddie attempted to scramble to her feet. Then she saw the dock, her heart slamming into her ribs.

Blood. *Oh God, Pops.*

Pops held his wrist to his shirt, but there was so much blood already dripping from his wrist. *Did the knife nick him in the scuffle?* She refused to believe it could be anything else.

"Maddie," Pops said in a low voice. Brooks wasn't far from them now, but Maddie scooped up an inconsolable Audrey and stood on wobbly legs, then climbed onto the dock. She hurried toward Pops. She could only hope that it was the adrenaline keeping the pain in her back and head subdued.

"What the fuck happened?" Brooks yelled as he reached her, grabbing Audrey from her arms. His face was reddened with rage.

"Pops!" Maddie turned toward him. *Please be okay.*

"Tell me what happened," Brooks demanded again.

"Stalker," Maddie managed, then pointed at the woman, still swimming away. She'd need to get out of the water soon—it had to be freezing cold. "Came at me with a knife."

Pops had gone ashen, and he clutched his chest, taking one stumbling step forward. Brooks caught him by the arm.

No.

"Pops!" Maddie grabbed his arm. "What is it? Are you okay?"

Distress crossed his features. "Heart attack."

"Call an ambulance," Maddie said to Brooks. "And the cops."

He took out his cell phone immediately, turning away from them to talk.

Shit. Keep it together, Maddie. How in the hell is this happening? How did that woman find us here?

The sight of Brian Pearson coming over the hill nearly undid her.

Thank God, thank God, thank God.

"Can you walk?" she asked Pops. No way they could carry him.

He nodded shakily.

"Grab Audrey," Maddie ordered Brooks. She didn't wait for him as she started off the dock toward Brian.

Brian stopped. "What happened?"

"Pops is having a heart attack. We need to get to the hospital." The sound of her own voice was strangely distant, as though her mind and body were disconnected somehow.

Keep going, Maddie. Keep going.

Pops's face looked more ashen, his footsteps unsteady.

Brian hurried to his other side. "All right, buddy. It's all right. We're gonna get you taken care of."

Please don't die, please don't.

Please, God, help me!

"Ambulance is on its way." Brooks came up beside her. Audrey had stopped screaming, but her eyes were wide, her cheek plastered into Brooks's shoulder. "What happened to his arm?" He nodded at the line of blood.

"The woman pulled a knife on me."

"What now?" Brian looked aghast.

"Motherfucker." Brooks's jaw clenched, his eyes lit with fury.

And guilt.

Guilt she shared.

She'd been horny and stupid and hadn't listened to him.

Left herself exposed, not paying attention to her surroundings. Tears stung her eyes.

But that didn't matter now because Pops was all that was important. Getting him to the hospital.

Brian led them to his truck. "I can take him. Maybe meet the ambulance if necessary."

"We'll all go. None of us is staying out here with that lunatic," Brooks said in a voice that left no room for argument. Not that she disagreed.

Pops looked back toward the dock. "The boat—"

"Don't give it another thought. It'll be fine." Maddie held the passenger side door open for Pops, and Brooks helped him in.

As Brooks closed the door, their eyes collided. "You okay?" He scanned her face, his expression anguished.

"Yeah, I'm fine. Bruised and sore—she shoved me—but I'm fine."

"I'm sorry." His gaze held an intensity to it, a level of pain that she didn't know how to interpret.

I can't handle this right now.

Maddie shook her head. She couldn't talk about this right now or she'd start crying. Opening the back door to the truck, she slid inside, then Brooks followed with Audrey.

No car seat, but it didn't matter.

Nothing mattered but getting Pops to the hospital.

Please, you can't die.

35

BROOKS

"HE'S OUT OF SURGERY, and he's stable. He's resting now, and we can let his wife in to see him once he's out of recovery, but everyone else will have to come back tomorrow during normal visiting hours," the nurse said.

Brooks stood at the fringe of the group waiting in the hospital—Maddie's parents and all her siblings had come.

Kayla had already left with Audrey *with* an armed security guard.

And even though she'd said it wasn't his fault . . . *she's wrong.*

Everything was his fault, from start to finish.

He should have been there, not off in the woods getting a blow job.

He shouldn't have left Audrey for that.

Kayla would kill him if she knew that part of it.

The guilt ate through his soul, searing his gut with acid. He'd failed to protect Maddie, Audrey, and Peter.

Peter had a massive heart attack and needed to be rushed in for emergency bypass surgery.

Maddie had a concussion.

Audrey had been terrified and sobbed when her mother showed up.

All my fault.

Not to mention that the stalker had been there because of him. *His stalker.* Who had gotten away.

The police had taken a report at the hospital, and he'd barely been able to contribute. He hadn't been there.

Later, Dan Klein showed up at the hospital and reiterated that he really needed to get a bodyguard out here.

Done already.

But not in time to save Maddie and her family and his niece from this.

Because of me.

"I can't see him?" Maddie said to the nurse, her face pale. "Please let me see him. I was there when it all happened. I have to see him."

The nurse gave Maddie a sympathetic look and shook her head.

Susan Yardley sank onto the bench beside her daughter and pulled her into her arms. "It's fine, sweetie. It's okay. You're not to blame for this. We all have known for a long time that Pops was having heart trouble."

"He won't listen to me," Bunny said somberly, her tired face filled with sadness. "I keep telling him to stop eating those damn potato chips."

"But it is my fault." Maddie laid her cheek against her mother's chest. "Because he was protecting me. He shouldn't have exerted himself that way."

Her words made Brooks's heart hurt in a way he couldn't describe.

Thank God for Peter.

But it should have been me there.

"Dad would take a bullet for all of us," Maddie's father said. "That's who he is, Maddie."

Naomi came up beside Brooks. "You should probably take her home," she whispered. "I'll get everyone else to leave so she doesn't fight it. But she needs to rest."

Brooks nodded, peeling himself away from the wall where he'd been leaning. "Thank you."

I'm sorry, he almost added. *I'm sorry for hurting your sister. For exposing her to this.*

He pressed his lips together. Naomi might not forgive him anyway, and surely, she already knew. The rest of the family might have been welcoming, but Naomi had seen right through him.

He didn't deserve Madison Yardley.

True to her word, Naomi got the other siblings going, which left Bunny with Maddie's parents. Brooks squatted down in front of Maddie. "Let's get you home."

She closed her eyes as though she couldn't look at him.

She'd been avoiding looking at him.

"You need to get some sleep, sweetie," Susan said, gently pulling away from her. "You're all banged up."

"I'm fine," Maddie said and sat up straighter. She looked around for her purse, which the police had fetched from the pontoon and brought to her.

"I'll bring you back first thing tomorrow morning." Brooks slipped his hand into hers.

After a moment, she sighed, then stood. "Fine. But first thing."

The car ride back was just as quiet and painful. A bodyguard waiting in the corridor escorted them to an SUV with fully tinted windows, where more armed security waited. They'd be parked behind the Depot the rest of the night. One bodyguard would remain outside the apartment door.

Once inside her apartment, Maddie went to shower, and Brooks did his best not to pace. The black nail polish Audrey had used on him was still on the floor and he picked it up, then scraped some paint off the floorboards.

A stab of pain went through him.

This day had started so normally. Or what he'd fooled himself into believing could be normal. Playing with his niece. A boat ride with his girlfriend.

But this was no longer the quiet lake house he'd sought when he'd come here with Cormac. Paparazzi were following his daily movements.

Then the stalker.

He'd stayed in Brandywood too long.

He needed to go.

Three weeks of being here was long enough to prove that this fantasy he'd let himself indulge in wasn't sustainable. This was becoming dangerous for him and for Maddie.

Maddie found him packing when she got out of the shower.

"What are you doing?" She wore a towel around her, water droplets still glistening on her skin.

"I should go—"

"You're fucking leaving?" She wasn't hurt, like he'd expected she might be.

She was angry.

"It's for the best. Things are getting out of control."

She marched up to his bag and grabbed a fistful of his clothes, then brandished it at him. "So this is your answer? Pick up and leave? What the fuck, Brooks?"

His brow furrowed. "You weren't even able to look at me all day today, Maddie. You think I don't get it? I'm supposed to protect you. I failed you—and Audrey—*and* your grandfather. I wasn't even there! And the only reason that bitch attacked you was because of me."

Astonishment crossed her features, and she crossed her arms, keeping her towel from slipping down, his clothes still gripped in her hand. "That's not why I couldn't look at you. Don't you have any idea how guilty I feel? I dragged you into the woods and gave you a blow job. I distracted both of us and was reckless, even after you warned me."

How can she even remotely blame herself?

His shoulders drooped. "This isn't your fault. Not in the slightest. It doesn't change the fact that I have to leave, but you need to know that. I'm gonna go shower, and then I'll get going. I'll leave a bodyguard with you here tonight and then make arrangements for you until the noise here dies down."

He started toward the door.

A shirt hit his back. He turned and looked at her with surprise.

"Asshole! How fucking dare you walk out on me tonight?" Tears shone in her eyes. "Don't you think I went through enough today? Don't you know how terrified I was?"

His mouth went dry. "I'm sorry about your grandfather, Maddie, I really am, but it doesn't change the fact that I'm putting—"

"I'm not talking about me. Or Pops. I'm talking about you! I'm terrified for *you*, Brooks. I can't believe you live like this." She swiped her tears away with the back of her hand. "Just think about what could have happened to you if that woman had found you instead of me. You were distracted and vulnerable. This is your life?"

She was worried *about* him? He couldn't be mad at that.

And I can't help think about how differently Darren and Ava would react here either.

They'd see it as an opportunity for more free advertising.

He nodded slowly. "It is."

"But you drive yourself places. You hate people driving you."

"As much as I can, yes. But it's not always possible. I do loathe being driven, but sometimes I'm forced to let my bodyguards take over, especially when there's been an incident. Or when I have to use a chauffeur in another country. That woman got away today, and I'm not taking any chances."

She shuddered. "How often are there incidents? Tell me the truth."

"Enough." He didn't want to scare her. "Most are online threats that I don't know about. People trying to hack me. But as soon as I leave my house, any freedom I have goes away. The global scale of harassment is . . . intense, at times."

That's putting it lightly.

He picked up the shirt she'd thrown. "My house was broken into a few times before I moved to a gated community. My guards have dragged me away from meet-and-greets or in the middle of concerts. I did a talk show once where a fan charged the stage. It happens, Maddie. It's a reality of my life. The sunglasses and baseball cap seem ridiculous, I know, but you have no idea how much that helps give me a smidge of privacy back."

She looked away. "That doesn't sound like living to me. It sounds like prison. Like the world has become your prison."

Exactly.

"I couldn't have put it better myself. Which is why I have to go. I'm not about to drag you into that prison with me. You deserve the sun on your face, to live your life with complete, uninhibited joy, free of scrutiny. I refuse to take that from you. We said one day at a time and time's up. Today proved that."

She didn't respond and he took that as his cue to leave.

He showered quickly, trying not to think about what it was doing to his heart to leave her tonight. *It has to be done.*

Better now, before I'm in any deeper.

But when he arrived back in the bedroom, he found her curled up in bed, wearing his shirt. His bag was unpacked, his clothes folded neatly in the top drawer of the dresser she'd cleared out for him.

He sat on the edge of the bed. "Maddie . . ."

"Just get in bed, Brooks. I can't deal with this tonight. It's been a long day and I don't want to fight with you. I don't deserve to be alone right now." She reached up to her nightstand and flipped off her lamp, plunging them into darkness.

His shoulders sank and he crawled into bed beside her but didn't get under the sheets. Setting a hand on her waist, he said, "We don't have to fight, but I don't want you to get your hopes up."

"Are you my boyfriend or not?"

"What?"

She turned toward him and even though he couldn't see her face, he knew she was looking at him. "If I'm your girlfriend, and not just some woman you spent the last two weeks fucking, then you don't get to leave without us talking things through. I mean, I guess you could, but that would just make you a complete and spineless asshole. I don't know what your plan was here, Brooks, but the moment you started a *relationship* with me—even if it was a *one day at a time* cop-out—you should have thought about what happens next."

"What do you mean?"

"I mean, you can't meet my family, and spend time with me, and call me *yours* and then treat me like I'm just someone to be discarded the second something goes wrong. You're going back to LA? Fine. But what does that mean for us? We break up? Never see each other again? Or does that mean we're dating long distance now? Or do you want an open relationship? Because it sure seems like you're thinking option A, and that pisses me off. Plus, the fact that I was *attacked* today, and you're even considering leaving. Now lay the fuck down and go to bed. I'm not doing this tonight."

Us.

There is an us here now, you jackass.

He dropped his hand from her side. Unbuttoning his jeans, he took them off, then pulled his shirt off and got under the sheets. Anger and tension radiated from her side of the bed and he lay on his back, staring at the ceiling.

He'd spent so long alone.

Not just single, but alone.

Every decision he made was about him, for him.

No *us.*

But she'd come into his life like an unexpected storm, breathing life into the darkness, a beat into his heart. Yes, maybe he'd let the initial raw and sexual attraction control the start of their relationship.

Two weeks in, though, and they were at a crossroads.

Was she just someone he was fucking?

The thought turned his stomach.

Not a chance.

But if he got any more involved with her, tearing himself away would be impossible. Just a little farther down the tracks and this train would pick up unstoppable speed. Did it make him a coward if he pulled on the brakes now? Wasn't that the wiser choice to avoid more situations like today to occur in Maddie's life? He'd never forgive himself if Maddie got seriously hurt.

Never.

He could walk away now.

He *should* walk away.

It would be better for them both if he left.

. . . wouldn't it?

Maddie was a dream. A dream he hadn't let himself think about for a very long time. Someone to love and be loved by.

A dream that would never be realized if he let her go even though he was already half in love with her.

Her smile did painful things to his emotions. Her intelligence and wit challenged him. Her ferocity . . . *her loyalty.*

She wasn't afraid to look him in the eye and tell him the truth—but she knew when to be gentle, too.

A sniffle intruded into his thoughts and he was a goner.

Turning toward her, he found her still facing him. He slid his arm under her, then curled her into his chest. Her tears wet his skin.

He palmed her shoulder, stroking her hair with the other hand. "It's all right. I'm not leaving, Maddie."

"I just . . ." Her words dissolved into tears, her shoulders shaking with sobs. "I can't get her voice out of my head."

Shit.

He hadn't paid enough attention to her, either.

You complete and total prick, Brooks.

She needed him. He'd failed to protect her earlier and now he'd failed to offer her safety, too. He kept messing up and she still wanted him, despite that.

"We're safe here, Maddie. I'm here. Both of us are safe."

Her hand slid up to his neck and she clung to him, her tears growing stronger.

He knew what she needed to hear. And it terrified him.

"I'm not leaving," he whispered at last. "I won't leave you. I promise."

If only I can work out how to keep that promise, when it doesn't feel at all achievable.

Fuck.

36

MADDIE

THE BED beside Maddie was cold when she woke up.

Is he gone?

Sitting up with a gasp, Maddie tossed her sheets to the side. Her feet hit the soft rug under the bed, and she'd didn't bother putting on socks or slippers as she headed out of the room, her heart pounding.

Brooks was in the living room, though, laptop open in front of him, phone at his ear.

Thank God.

Her footsteps faltered as he looked up, then held up one finger toward her, his gaze falling to the side.

He's still here. He didn't leave.

She swallowed hard and went into the kitchen. Pouring herself a glass of water, she took a few sips, watching him.

They hadn't had sex last night, which was the first time they hadn't since they'd started a sexual relationship. It was weird, in a way. They'd *actually* just *slept together*. That was it. No physical expectations.

He'd held her, and they'd slept.

Somehow, that feels oddly intimate.

"Email me a contract as soon as possible, then. All right. I look forward to it," Brooks said into the phone. He hung up a moment later, closed his laptop, and stood.

Stretching in his sweatshirt and pajama pants, he looked . . . comfortable. "Morning."

Almost at home here.

Her heart throbbed, and she remembered his attempt to leave the night before.

Maddie set the glass down on the counter, then hurried toward him. She slipped her arms around him, laying her cheek against his chest as his arms tucked her in. "I thought you were gone."

"I promised I wouldn't leave, Maddie. I just needed to make some better security arrangements for us both." He kissed the top of her head.

They stood in the still, quiet apartment for a few moments, and Maddie listened to his heartbeat, her eyes closed. Drawing a long breath, she pulled away, then tugged him back onto the couch. "You still want to leave, though, don't you?"

Brooks scrubbed his face with his hand, sighing. "It's not about *want*, Maddie. I don't want to leave you, no. I don't want to hurt you, either. But I'm not going to lie and say that I'm entirely at peace with staying, either. When I think about how many people got hurt yesterday, though, it fucking terrifies me. And it could have been much worse, too."

"I know," she said quietly.

Because he was right, yesterday had been horrible. And that woman who'd come after her could have stabbed her.

She interlaced their fingers. Was she being selfish? Was it selfish to ask him to stay when he wanted to leave? To put his fears to the side?

The longer they spent together, the more she realized she

had no clue *at all* what his life was like. Celebrity life seemed so charmed on the outside. But, then again, they'd always been in her world. Not his.

"It's not working, Maddie, you have to admit that."

She gave him a sharp look. "I'm not working out or one-day-at-a-time isn't?"

"God, you know I don't mean you." He looked away, his hand tightening against hers. "I'm trying, Maddie. Trying to come up with any and every solution to keep you safe. But we've been together for two weeks, too. I can't ask you to give up your friends, family, and world and come be with me in LA, where we might be safer. And I can't stay here shuttling between a long-term rental and your place for forever. I don't know *how* to make it work. I'm open to suggestions."

The irony of her having moved in with Josh after two weeks wasn't lost on her.

And what I feel for Brooks is so much more intense than anything I ever felt for Josh.

But he was also right. She wasn't ready to leave her friends and family and go to LA. She had to have learned *something* after that experience with Josh.

"Would you consider long distance?" she finally asked. "I think defining what we're doing would help a lot."

"Is that what you want?" Brooks studied her. "To have a long-distance relationship?"

"It's better than *nothing*." She turned her body toward him so she could face him better. "You're right. I'm not ready to move across the country and live with you. But you're making security arrangements for me here, right? And really, I'd imagine the threat to me is nothing compared to the threat to you. But who knows . . . maybe we can reevaluate our living situation after a while and figure out where to go from there."

He scanned her face, a skeptical but hopeful look in his

eyes. "So you want to go all in? Plane trips back and forth, talking on the phone, you know, the whole bit?"

"Yeah, I do." She gripped his hand. "I want to be with you, Brooks. And if that's the way we have to do it for now—even if it means more time apart than together in the meantime—then so be it."

He brushed his thumb against her knuckles, clearly considering the idea. "What happens when the tabloids posts pictures that worry you, though? I've seen it happen so many times in long-distance situations. Tabloids love a good salacious story, especially where one doesn't exist. It will get to you, Maddie. Wear on you. Even if you trust me. Because other people—like your family and friends—might be the ones coming to you with news before I even get a chance to explain myself."

"Then how about I promise to never make a judgment before I give you a chance to explain yourself?" It sounded naive, even to her, but what else could she offer?

"That may be easier said than done." He lifted her hand to his lips and kissed the back of it. "But it's a start."

"So is that a yes?" She scooted closer to him. "Will you consider dating long-term *and* long distance?"

He held her gaze, then nodded. "Right now, I'm willing to consider anything to keep you in my life. I'm serious. But your safety is the most important thing to me, too. And I have to admit that, after yesterday, this town doesn't feel like the haven I hoped it would be."

She ignored the latter part of his statement, focusing instead on the fact that Brooks had just said he wanted a long-term relationship with her.

Long-term.

Her heart fluttered, emotion overtaking her.

God, I really, really care about him.

Love him.

She slid her arms around his neck, dipping her forehead against his. "Maybe that's the part we figure out a day at a time, Brooks. Because I'm not willing to compromise on the *us* part of this, okay?"

He kissed her gently. Cautiously. "Okay."

She sank against him, resting her head against his shoulder. "There's one more thing we have to do today, though," Brooks said, tracing his palm over her thigh softly.

"What's that?"

"I need to go apologize to your grandfather. Make sure he's all right. Because he's not out of the woods yet, and if something happens to him, I'm not sure your family will be as forgiving as you are."

She kissed his neck. "They will be, Brooks. I promise. My family is the least of our worries, but I want to go see Pops too."

She tried to relax into him, taking comfort in his arms. His presence.

A voice in the back of her head told her she was being naive, though. Her family *might* have more to say about what had happened with Brooks than they had. Naomi's reaction to Brooks in the first place should have taught her that.

But if we're together, we'll figure it out. We can make it work.

She had faith in that. *In them.*

And he was willing to take the leap with her.

That's all that matters.

37

MADDIE

"WHERE's that handsome fellow of yours?" Pops asked as Maddie walked into his hospital room.

She glanced over her shoulder at the empty space behind her, then back at Pops and raised a brow. "What am I, chopped liver? Brooks has to come with me now?"

Pops chuckled, waving her comment off with one hand still connected to plastic tubing. "No, but you've brought him for the past four days. I just assumed he was coming."

She sat in the chair beside his hospital bed and set a food storage container beside him. "He's on his way to Baltimore for his arraignment."

"Arraignment, huh?"

"Audrey's deadbeat dad is suing for custody and showed up at Brooks's concert at the beginning of the month to taunt him. He threw the first punch, but Brooks punched back and the as—*jerk* is pressing charges."

Pops smiled. "You don't have to pretend you don't swear in front of me, kiddo. Believe me, whatever you say, I've heard worse."

"Yeah, but you're my angelic grandfather. Although, what was up with that sausage talk with Brooks?" She shook her head. "You didn't know he was talking about me, did you?"

"That was all Brian, first of all. And of course I knew Brooks was talking about you. He got here and holed himself up in Jason Cavanaugh's rental place, and the only person he could have met was you. I knew who he was the second I met him. He's a good-looking kid. Old soul. Needs to figure some things out, but so do you. I like him for you."

His approval meant more than Maddie could say, but she just smiled.

Since her discussion with Brooks the other morning, they'd fallen back into their routine before the attack. Nights together, days mostly apart. Except with bodyguards, now. And Brooks had been busier than ever trying to sort his contract with the label in online meetings with his lawyer.

But she was happy. Brooks seemed more relaxed, even, now that their security had increased.

Pops reached for the container. "What'd you bring me?"

"Um, they're dark chocolate-covered dates filled with natural peanut butter. As close to healthy as I could get. They won't be sweet enough for you, but Bunny's been on patrol. She even checked my bodyguard's pockets to make sure he wouldn't sneak you something."

"Depriving an old man of his favorite foods isn't going to make him want to live any longer," Pops said, wrinkling his nose at the container. "Dates remind me of roaches."

"But they're *not.*" She nudged the container closer to him. "Just try them. Doesn't have to be now. You can wait until I'm gone so you're free to spit them out if you don't like them."

"You know, I'm glad you're here without Brooks," Pops said, settling back against his pillow. "Because I have an important discussion to have with you."

Maddie tried not to show her alarm. "How important?"

"Eh, pretty important. To me, at least. And the future direction of my company." His blue eyes searched hers. "I wish I'd had this talk with you a few months ago, but I didn't, and I worry this isn't a good time for it, but I'd like you to take over as the face of my operation. You do too much behind the scenes. I think going from me to you makes the most sense, but it's a lot of responsibility."

Pops wants me to step into his role?

The revelation was astounding.

Her face must have expressed shock.

"I know any of you kids could carry the torch, but you're the most like me. Jake has the personality for it, too, so he'd be a good backup if you don't want it, but I want you to think it over. Seriously. I'm not sure if I'll be up for filming in a few weeks or not—maybe—but I'll have to talk it over with the doc. But either way, I want whoever is stepping into my position to be there so we can start the transition."

Wow. They'd all talked around what would happen after Pops passed, but never made a solid plan because, well, none of them wanted to even really think about life without Peter Yardley. She was tempted to tear up now, even considering it.

"I—" She stared at him.

How could she ever fit into his shoes?

She couldn't. *Plain and simple.*

Her grandfather was irreplaceable.

"Pops, I-I don't know what to say."

He set his hand over hers. "You don't have to answer now. I've already talked about this with my production team and your father, by the way. Just to make sure that my wishes were known. But I know there's a lot to consider, especially because your heart may just take you elsewhere."

Her heart.

She blinked, his full meaning dawning on her.

Brooks.

Being the face of her grandfather's company didn't just mean taking on more responsibility. It meant even more permanency here in Brandywood.

Her grandfather filmed here. He was available to his fans here. Brandywood was a huge part of Peter Yardley's brand.

Pops squeezed her hand. "I don't want you to decide based on what you think I want to hear, Maddie. You need to do what's best for *you*. Brooks is in your life now, and he doesn't live here. I don't know what his plans are or where he's heading, but as much as I would love for life to be a fairy tale, I can tell you from my minor exposure to fame—it's not all it's cracked up to be. Living in a small town would be very difficult for a man like him."

Standing, Maddie crossed the room to the small sink and turned on the faucet. She needed a moment to collect her thoughts, especially since Pops was discussing significant issues. She splashed water on her face and gulped down a mouthful of water.

Brooks's voice filled her memory. *"I'm not about to drag you into that prison with me. You deserve the sun on your face, to live your life with complete, uninhibited joy, free of scrutiny. I refuse to take that from you."*

Unable to face Pops, she asked, "Why would it be so hard for him to live here?"

She set her hands on the counter, her shoulders sagging as the water swirled around the drain, emptying slowly.

"It's not impossible, just difficult. Not a lot of privacy, for one. Just think about how easy it is to be found here. He'd be recognized constantly, unable to blend in when tourists are around. And remember how half the town started hating me because of the Depot? People would do the same to him eventually. Complain about the circus he brings into their lives. Not a lot of opportunities for rock stars in a small town like this, either. He'd have to travel constantly, and we don't even have a good airport nearby."

"Why are you telling me all this?" she whispered. She'd asked the damn question, but the answers weren't what she wanted to hear. She turned to face him, her heart breaking.

The person she loved the most in the world—her pops—was giving her an impossible choice to make.

"You have to consider all of this, Maddie. It's all got to factor into your decisions with Brooks *and* with my offer. Your family, too. You're a smart girl, and I know you'll make the right decision."

"You think I should break up with Brooks? Is that what you're saying?" She studied the wall of devices and plugs behind him, unable to look him in the eye.

"Gosh, no. I see how happy he makes you. You know me, I'm a romantic."

"Then why offer your role to me at all? Why make this so much harder on me?" She didn't want to be mad at her grandfather, especially while he was in the hospital recovering from a heart attack and bypass surgery—*from protecting her* . . . because of Brooks.

His face filled with regret. "I was hoping I might have a few more years in me before I had to hand the reins over. But I don't. This heart attack proved that time is something I'm running out of. Besides, if things don't work out with Brooks, and you found out I didn't offer you the job because of that, you probably wouldn't like me very much. If it's something you wanted, of course."

His logic was sound, but still . . .

. . . what am I supposed to do now?

38

BROOKS

"Charges are dropped. Case dismissed."

Brooks's lawyer, Christine Lewis, looked pleased. An immaculately dressed, elegant Black woman, she was one of the top lawyers in the country—and she was a killer in the courtroom.

"You're the best. As always," Brooks said with the hint of a smile. He didn't bother looking at Mike, who groused loudly at his lawyer. "What now?"

Christine's dark eyes lit with pleasure at his compliment. "Well, he can still try to sue you civilly, but I don't think that will happen, considering the judge wouldn't entertain the charges. But it's Mike. He's unpredictable."

That's putting it mildly. But today, at least, he'd been neutralized.

"You're not kidding. What about the contract with the label?"

"I'll call you when I get back to my office, and we can talk about the next steps. In the meantime, I think we've made some good progress on your contract with the label. And Ava is more open to negotiations now that she's cooled down a bit. We'll have you releasing music soon, I'm sure."

Mike, slimy prick that he was, continued to complain as his lawyer led him out of the room. Brooks's eyes darted back to Christine. "Sounds good. Look over the international label contract, too. I might be ready to enter my indie era."

"Anything you want."

Brooks shook her hand, loosened his tie, then headed out of the courtroom with his bodyguard in tow.

Well, this was a complete fucking waste of my time. But at least he'd gotten to see the judge wipe the smug smile off that asshole's face. And he'd see it again if Mike kept up with his plans to sue Kayla.

He started down the hall, then headed to the restroom before the long drive back to Brandywood. All he wanted was to get back to the lake house and pull Maddie into his arms.

He walked over to the urinal and had just started to piss when the toilet in the stall flushed.

Mike came out of the stall. He stopped with a scowl, then his face darkened. "Think you're a pretty tough piece of shit, do ya, Brooks?"

If he hadn't been in the middle of going to the bathroom, he would have walked out. Brooks clenched his jaw.

Mike, taking advantage of the situation, came closer. "Want to see something interesting that came my way recently?" He pulled out his cell phone, scrolling through it.

"I have no interest in the dick pics that get you off, Valders." He flushed and started toward the sink.

"Funny. Real funny." Mike held up his phone. "What about video footage of you crashing into a storefront? What happened, Brooks? Have a bit too much to drink that night?"

Brooks froze, his unwilling eyes darting to the screen of Mike's phone.

Fuck.

How the hell had he gotten hold of the video from Fred Strickland's store?

"How much do you think the tabloids are offering for this one?"

A few tense beats of silence passed, and Brooks struggled for calm. He'd just gotten the case dismissed for punching this asshole in the face—he wasn't about to get arrested again today for the same damn thing.

Brooks straightened, his eyes narrowing. Sure, maybe he didn't want the video to get out. But the press already said whatever it wanted about him. Now that the case was dropped, he had less to worry about with public perception.

He held his hands under the automatic faucet. "Fuck off, Mike. I don't give a shit who sees that video. If they look closely, they'll be able to tell that I was dodging a deer. And I worked out arrangements with the owner of the shop to pay for the damages. She'll back me up."

"Yeah? How many more fucks do you owe her until your debt is paid off?"

Now Mike's words truly sent a chill down his spine. Brooks held his breath, his pulse pounding. *Calm the fuck down.*

But how the hell did Mike know so much about this?

He could see himself grabbing Mike by the throat, slamming that spineless, brainless moron's body into the wall and beating him to a pulp.

Because he's clearly been digging.

The thought of him even knowing about Maddie was excruciating.

But he couldn't let Mike know he'd gotten to him. That was even more dangerous.

"I said fuck off." Brooks grabbed a sheet of paper towel and headed toward the exit.

"You'll change your mind about cooperating with me, Brooks. I have more videos. Better ones."

Brooks slammed the bathroom door open and walked out, never more relieved to see the bodyguard waiting for him. He was going to have to ask them to follow him into the bathroom at this point. He'd had to do that before and hated it, but this was getting out of control.

More videos. Better ones.

What the fuck had Mike been referring to?

He didn't want to know.

But he had a feeling Mike would show his face again soon enough.

And even though he'd only just beaten the son of a bitch, he had a feeling that had only made Mike more dangerous. *And I have no idea how to fight that.*

39

MADDIE

THE SOUND of a car in the driveway came, and Maddie was at the door of the lake house, barefoot despite the cold. The SUV parked, and Brooks climbed out, wearing a finely tailored suit and tie.

Damn.

When she'd left for work in the morning, he'd still been sleeping.

She didn't even know where he'd gotten the suit from. He hadn't had one in the closet, so likely someone had met him with it—but he looked freaking incredible in a suit.

As though he needs the help.

He met her gaze and, despite the serious expression on his face, a smile lit his eyes.

She didn't wait for him to come to the door, running out to greet him instead.

As she threw her arms around his neck, he caught her and hoisted her up and onto his waist. "Hi, baby," he whispered in her ear, then caught her lips in a deep, thorough kiss.

Maybe there were paparazzi there.

She didn't give a shit right now.

She pulled back, searching his gaze. Sunset was well on its way and his eyes reflected the golden hue of the sky. "Hungry?"

"Depends on what's for dinner. You?"

Maddie bit her lip, throwing a glance at the blank faces of the two nearby bodyguards. It was one thing to have them be in their shadows, but these intimate conversations were hard to have in front of them. "Um . . . maybe. I was going to say I made you something."

Brooks gave her a questioning glance, then threw his head back and laughed. He set her down, then swatted her on the ass as they moved toward the door. "I meant, *are you hungry?* But now that I know having you for dinner is on the table, I'll take you up on that." He held the door for her.

"Having me for dinner *on the table* sounds much better than what I made," she murmured in his ear, then kissed his neck.

He closed the door and pushed her up against it, his hand palming the bare sliver of skin between her crop top and her skirt and sliding to the small of her back. "If you're going to play sexy housewife, you should think about dressing for the part," he growled, then nipped her earlobe as he squeezed her breasts, hard.

She pulled the knot on his tie down, her lips inches from his. "Maybe I am. Or maybe I'm not wearing anything at all under this skirt."

His eyes glimmered with pleasure, then he slid his hand from her back, down her waistband and over her bare ass. He groaned, his knees buckling ever-so-slightly as he pressed into her. "God, I love you."

She didn't mean to freeze at the words, but she did.

What?

He loves me?

He drew her chin between his thumb and forefinger, searching her gaze as though it had just dawned on him he'd said what he'd been thinking out loud.

I love you.

I love you.

"I love you, too," she whispered.

Their mouths came together in a kiss, slow and lingering, her heart racing as his arms swept her against him tightly.

Brooks loves me.

But she knew that.

He'd been so worried a few nights ago after the fishing trip, ready to leave everything and make himself miserable because of his fears and need to take everything on himself.

Yet he'd stayed.

She'd needed him, and he'd stayed.

And then he'd agreed to her long-distance plan, which meant *forever* seemed like a possibility now.

I love this man so much.

Lifting her into his arms, Brooks carried her into the bedroom. He slowly disrobed them both, then made love to her, lingering over her body, his mouth and hands caressing her, his gaze and words worshipping her. Not frantic, or hot and heavy, but sweet yet soul-achingly sexy, their fingers intertwined, bodies consumed with one another's.

And absolutely perfect.

As she recovered in his arms, she practically purred and stretched. "I'm never leaving this room again."

He smiled and kissed her forehead. "It was good for you, then?"

"Good doesn't even begin to describe it. Much better than the dinner I—"

She sat bolt upright.

Shit.

Taking the sheet, she ran from the bedroom to the kitchen. The burned smell reached her before she reached it.

"Dammit," she cried, flying over to the oven. She threw the door open and found her pot roast smoking.

Using potholders, she pulled it out and carried it over to the stovetop, where she banged it down against the grates.

"Is it ruined?" Brooks asked, coming into the kitchen. He'd pulled on a pair of gym pants but remained shirtless.

Why does he look so amazing, no matter what he's wearing?

Men liked to talk about women's beauty using terms like "natural" while referring to women with ridiculously expensive hairstyles and precise makeup.

Brooks, on the other hand, was naturally, ridiculously beautiful. Maybe not effortlessly—she was certain those muscles took a lot of work—but still.

"Huh?"

He caught her staring and grinned. "Dinner? Is it ruined?"

She gave a sheepish nod as she lifted the lid. The roast was black. "Yeah, I'm afraid so. Damn you and your hot sex. I hope you're satisfied."

He came up behind her and set his arms around her waist, then lowered his chin onto her shoulder, glancing over it toward the pot. "I *am* satisfied. But still hungry."

She gave him an incredulous look. "For sex?"

"For dinner, Miss One-Track-Mind."

"I can't help it. My boyfriend just told me he loves me, so I'm kind of on cloud nine."

"We might save some from the middle of the roast if we cut off the edges. Make street tacos out of it."

"Explain."

He whistled softly as he went over to the knife block, then pulled a chef's knife out. "Get a cutting board, then a head of cabbage out of the fridge."

Maddie raised a brow. "You have *cabbage?*"

He shrugged. "I eat a lot of tacos. They're the perfect food."

He *would* say that.

"You really are the perfect man, you know." Smoothing the sheet over her front, she was distinctly aware that she was still buck naked. "How about I go clean myself up and get dressed? Be back in fifteen minutes?"

"I'm beginning to think this was a trap to get me to satisfy your sexual fantasies and then make you dinner." He winked at her. "But I'm happy to oblige."

She almost skipped back to the bedroom.

Pausing for a moment, she reflected on the fact that she'd never felt that happy with Josh. *Or with anyone else.* In some sense, she could be thankful Josh dumped her as she never would have had this had they still been dating.

Huh. And Naomi was right. Josh had never deserved her.

She had never, ever been so deliriously in love in her life.

When she was with him here at the lake house, it was almost possible to pretend they lived inside a bubble, just the two of them versus the world.

No paparazzi looking in.

No bodyguards staring out.

No rapidly approaching end of rentals or town fair concerts in four days—*how in the hell has Brooks already been here almost a month?*—or court dates that meant he no longer needed to stay.

No Pops asking her to take over his role at his company to be the face of his business.

But as each of those thoughts pressed in, she found her heart growing heavier and heavier, the clouds encroaching once more.

She got ready quickly, eager to be near him again, and as

soon as she stepped out of the bedroom, she heard the soft strum of a guitar.

Brooks sat on a stool in the kitchen, a pencil tucked behind his ear and his guitar in hand. His brows were furrowed in concentration, his jaw held slightly slack as his fingers slid against the neck of the guitar in a barre chord, and there was an exquisite sound of strings against the surface of his skin.

She tiptoed in farther, but he didn't appear to have noticed her. It was as though he was deaf to the world around him when the guitar was in his hands.

"You're still whole and you are worthy . . ."

His deep voice was just a shade above a whisper, and she hugged her arms to her chest, leaning against the wall.

Brooks stopped, wrote something down on a sheet of paper on the counter, then slid the pencil behind his ear again.

Brooks Kent was writing a song.

Maddie's hand slid up to her throat as she swallowed a lump there.

Maybe he did this in front of people all the time. Maybe not. But for all the times he'd stripped himself down in front of her—physically or emotionally—this felt different.

Like watching a master at work.

He continued as though in a trance for a few minutes, then frowned and looked up. He smiled when he saw there and set the guitar down. "I was wondering what happened to you. I left you a glass of wine on the counter."

She slipped into the kitchen and found the awaiting glass. "I was enjoying listening to you. You didn't see me?"

He shook his head as he closed the guitar case. "I had a sudden jolt of inspiration to write down something floating through my head. Everything is ready for the tacos, though. All we have to do is grill the tortillas and heat the shredded beef a bit. The potatoes and carrots in the roast were, sadly, not salvageable."

"You're officially my favorite person ever." She picked up the glass of wine as he moved into the kitchen. "Is this what living with you would be like? Because I'm *this* close to quitting my job and being a kept woman."

"I don't have many references, but I am happy to make lofty promises of being an amazing roommate." Brooks lit a burner and slid a tortilla onto a grill pan. "Do you want your tortillas soft or a little crispy and charred?"

"Ooo, option B." She studied the stem of her glass, memories of the heaviness from when she'd been getting dressed pressing against her chest. "Um . . . so I have some news. News that might have a bit of an impact on you. On *us*, really."

Brooks looked over his shoulder, the color from his face draining. "Don't tell me you're pregnant."

Her eyebrows lifted. "No! I mean, I don't think I am. I haven't gotten my . . . I mean, I wouldn't know yet, but . . ."

He'd grown even paler. "You're scaring me."

"I'm not pregnant, Brooks. I wasn't even *thinking* about that, so you completely caught me off guard. I mean, with the amount of unprotected sex we've been having, it's always a super remote possibility even on the pill, I guess, but—" She clearly wasn't making him feel any better.

Maddie put her hands out in front of her. "Okay, let me start over. I'm not pregnant. But my grandfather asked me today to take over his role and be the face of his company, which *is* what I wanted to talk about. Not about pregnancy or future babies. Although, maybe we should so that we get that talk out of the way and know where we stand since you'd clearly be miserable if I *was* pregnant."

Why did she always do this when she got flustered? She needed to learn when to stop talking.

The corners of Brooks's eyes narrowed, and he gave her a thoughtful stare, then flipped the tortilla with his fingers.

"I wouldn't be miserable. I don't want kids . . . or never have wanted them before. But I'm open to discussion. It's . . . just not a great time in my life for any other stressors, especially after the day I had today."

She tilted her head. "I thought today was a good day? Didn't you say in your text that the judge dropped the case?"

He nodded and spooned some meat into the grilling tortilla. "She did."

"Then what?" She approached him slowly, worry creeping in.

"Um, you know what? Why don't you go first? You had news and I railroaded it with the pregnancy stuff. Your grandfather wants you to be the face of his company?" He started on another taco, not meeting her eyes. "Is that what you want?"

"I—" She had the sudden, urgent need to sip her wine. Swallowing back a large mouthful, she then set the glass down. "I don't know, Brooks. It's a lot. His business is based here. People come to Brandywood to see him. The whole show is set here. There's just . . . a lot to consider."

"You'd be great at it." He took one taco off and set it on a plate. "Add some shredded cabbage, avocado, and lime juice to that, will you?"

She took it from him and went to the island, where the remaining ingredients had been placed on a cutting board. "You don't know that I'd be good at it. I'm not really sure my grandfather knows that either. He just likes that we're similar in personality."

"No, he knows. So do I. I watched you on stage that night at the apple festival. You have good stage presence. You're comfortable there. And, of course, you're beautiful and smart."

"So you think I should do it?" A wave of disappointment

crashed through her. He had to know how much that would tie her to here.

He brought a couple more tacos over to her. "I didn't say that. I just said you'd be good at it. Doesn't make a damn bit of difference, though, if it's not what you want to do."

She kept her gaze focused on filling the tacos. "There's a lot of distance between LA and Brandywood, Brooks. I know a lot has happened between us in a short amount of time, but I can't pretend that's not going to factor into my decision. Long distance is one thing, but taking this job means even more permanency here for me."

He was silent at her side, helping her, and she counted the seconds as they passed.

Not knowing what he was thinking was driving her crazy.

"Brooks?"

"I heard you, Maddie." He wiped his fingers on a damp cloth. "I just don't know what to say."

Not the answer I was hoping for.

"We can't put off a conversation about what happens with something like this, babe." Frustration brimmed from deep inside her. "A handful of days ago, you were ready to pack up and go back to LA. Now the arraignment is over, the concert is in four days, and your rental here ends in three days. We talked about long distance, and I'm happy with that, but what if I can't move so easily?"

His shoulders fell. "I don't know. You don't want to leave Brandywood anyway, do you? That's what I always understood. You love it here. And now your grandfather—"

"I don't want to leave, at least right now, but that's less important to the discussion than me being able to understand what happens if I *can't* leave. I mean, I don't even know if you want me to leave and go to LA someday."

He prepared two plates and carried them over to the table. "Coming?"

Her anxiety grew despite his calm demeanor. That he was *this* calm made it worse, actually.

Carrying her glass of wine to the table, she sat opposite from him. "All I want to know is what you want. Do you even want me to be a part of your life in LA? Or would you consider moving here?"

The tacos he'd made looked mouth-wateringly delicious, but she'd also lost her appetite.

Brooks lifted his gray eyes, his expression guarded. "I love you. Of course I want you to be a part of my future in LA. Or maybe here, if we could make it work."

Once again, what he hadn't said was louder than the spoken.

He might not be able to live here.

"But . . ."

Brooks took a bite of a taco. "Eat something."

Because he'd made it, she lifted a taco obligingly. It tasted as good as it smelled. "Wow," she admitted, taking another bite. "These are really amazing. I didn't know you could cook anything outside of hot dogs and mac and cheese."

"Unless I wanted Kayla eating McDonald's every night, I had to learn how." He chewed slowly, scanning her face. "But you're the one who made the roast. So really, it's me who should thank you."

"Nice try. Don't worry. You're on track to get lucky again tonight without the fake schmooze." She finished the taco, mostly because it was delicious and she didn't want to hurt his feelings, but she really didn't want any more. "Now finish your previous statement. You love me, but . . ."

Brooks slipped his phone onto the table and clicked it open. Sliding it across the table, he drew his hand back.

"A YouTube video?" She frowned.

"Just watch."

Tapping the play button, she leaned toward it. A grayish video, as though taken at night, came into focus. The front of the Depot . . . and Brooks crashing through the front window.

Fred Strickland.

The taco sat heavy in her stomach now as her gut clenched.

"Mike threatened me after the court case today. Said he was going to release this to the tabloids—I think he wanted money. I told him to fuck off. Sure enough, the video hit the tabloid sites about an hour ago, and I'm sure it will be on the entertainment cable shows soon."

"Dammit." Her failure to retrieve that video stung even more now. "How the hell did Fred figure it out? *And* give it to Mike?"

"I don't know. But Mike's clearly been digging. And he says he has more damaging material." Brooks finished his other taco and took a sip of water.

"What does that mean?"

"I don't know." His gaze grew distant. "But I sure as hell won't allow him to threaten me or Kayla or Audrey . . . or you. And I'm worried that he's going to threaten all three of you. I will protect the people I love."

"What about you, Brooks? Who protects you? Because you're ultimately the person he's threatening."

"I have bodyguards and security teams and lawyers. I'm not worried about me."

His words didn't make her feel any better.

"So what does that mean for us? Sure, Mike is a threat, but there will always be threats."

"I won't let you be threatened."

"You can't control everything, Brooks. You can't stop every

threat. Not for me or Kayla or Audrey. Or any other person you might fall in love with in the future."

He lifted his head sharply. "You're it for me, Madison. I love you. Only you. Always. But I will rip out my own heart if it means protecting you."

The intensity of his words stole her breath.

She shut off the looped video, reached across the table, and took his hand. "I know you would, but so would I. And if it's you and me now, then we have to start making these decisions together. Even if it means hard talks and scary unknowns, all right?"

Brooks's shoulders tensed. At last, he nodded. "All right."

40

BROOKS

For all the times that Brooks had played in local fairs at the start of his career, as he twirled Maddie on the dance floor of the Brandywood fair, it occurred to him that he had never once actually attended one. Especially not with a date.

But then, *I've never had a date with a woman I'm in love with.*

Being in love with her was every single thing he'd written about in a song, but never fully lived in the flesh.

Mesmerizing, intoxicating, surreal, and petrifying.

He pulled her into his arms as the song a local country band was playing ended, then kissed her. His own band members had arrived the night before, which had been a reunion he'd been unexpectedly glad to make. He'd also brought Cormac in to play with them for the evening, considering this was his hometown.

All of it made him feel sickeningly normal. Like life was finally getting back on track, but better than ever.

He'd moved out of the lake house for the last time and simply shifted his belongings to Maddie's apartment, where he'd stay . . . indefinitely. They'd been talking around the next step still, because she was clearly torn about what she wanted to do regarding her grandfather's offer and he wanted to avoid the topic as much as possible.

Someone bumped into them and Brooks pulled away from Maddie to see an "apologetic" fan who held out a pen and a pad of paper for him. She hadn't been lying about the size of this fair. The place was crushed with people from out of town, and it wasn't even noon yet.

"Sorry, I don't do autographs in blue pens," Brooks told the fan, who pouted and went her way.

Maddie gaped at him. "Is that for real?"

He nodded, and they started hand in hand toward the apple fritter food truck he'd promised her they'd visit next. He gave her a mischievous grin. "Don't know how true it is, but that's the advice. I always figured it was one less autograph to do."

"You're a rat sometimes, you know that?" She cringed at the line for apple fritters as they drew closer, then stopped. "You're not going to want to stand in that line, are you?"

He followed the direction she'd pointed out. The line had to be at least thirty people long and looked to be crawling.

A long-ass wait meant he'd be a sitting duck for fans to ambush him.

The disappointment in her eyes was palpable, and he squeezed her hand. "I'm sorry, babe."

"Ugh, it's fine. Maybe I can get one of my siblings to grab me some and bring them backstage with you later or something. I just wanted you to try one since you don't eat that stuff normally."

"I've spent the last month eating stuff I don't eat normally." He nodded toward one bodyguard. "But if you don't mind waiting in the line, Trent can hang out with you and I'll head over to the petting zoo with Ryan and meet Kayla and Audrey. Just meet me over there with your apple fritters when you're done here."

Maddie's face brightened. "Okay." She stood on her tiptoes and kissed his cheek, flipping his baseball cap backward. "I like this better like this, by the way, Clark Kent."

He rolled his eyes, then switched it back. "You're cute when you're annoying."

She sauntered off toward the line, bodyguard in tow, and he started in the opposite direction.

She'll be fine. She has a bodyguard.

But, shit, this place was crowded. Too crowded. Too exposed. His own bodyguard, Ryan, had to remain practically at his elbow not to get separated.

He was halfway to where the petting zoo was located when he got a text message from Maddie.

Maddie: Trailer. Right now.

Maddie: P.S. leave the guard outside ;)

He smiled to himself. They'd started the morning in the shower together—after waking each other up a few times during the night. Damn woman was going to exhaust him.

Brooks: Yes, ma'am.

He couldn't help wondering if the need for her would ever diminish. It had to, right? He'd have to be naive not to think so. But all it took was a flash of those tits or a sly grin, waking up with her ass pressed against him and he was a goner.

Peter Yardley had delivered the trailer, a rental, to the fairgrounds the night before—a place for him and his band to hide away. He was grateful for it, and it was large and luxurious, with several beds. One of his band members had even used it rather than rent a hotel room while here.

Due to its size and function, the trailer was parked off the beaten path, in the far corner of a field that was being used for parking for vendors and the amusement ride trucks and trailers. A good five minutes from the main fairground.

"I'll check inside and make sure it's secure, Brooks," Ryan said.

Maddie had Trent with her, so he wasn't worried. "Nah, it's fine. Trent's with Maddie inside, so just make sure no one else comes in," he said, eager to get to his girl.

"Of course, sir," Ryan said.

When Brooks stepped inside, he locked the door and called out for Maddie.

"Madison?" Brooks glanced around the empty living room and kitchen area. The television was still on, the volume low, and he found the remote and turned it off.

Maybe she was in the primary bedroom waiting.

The door was closed, and he tapped on it twice, then turned the knob. Stepping into the darkened room, he flipped the light switch.

The bed was empty.

The door closed behind him. "Ready to get lucky?" a familiar male voice said.

Brooks startled, readying a punch as he turned—then he froze.

Mike stood just off to the side. His hands were wrapped in latex gloves, and there was a gun in his hand.

Oh fuck.

His throat went dry, his heart pounding hard in his chest.

"If you use that, your source of money will quickly run dry, asshole."

"I'm aware. I only brought it to make sure you didn't call for your armed brawn." Mike held out an open Ziploc bag. "Cell phone. Take it out, send one message to your girlfriend. *I'm sorry. I had to go. Don't try to reach me.* Then drop it in the bag. No alarm. Nothing else or I'll shoot. I'm watching."

Brooks's jaw clenched.

Goddamn motherfucker.

He did as Mike directed, then dropped the phone in the bag.

Please do your Maddie thing and demand we talk. He sent the silent prayer out, hoping somehow, she'd get it.

"Watch, too. Anything that has Wi-Fi."

After Brooks had complied, Mike shoved the bag into his jacket pocket.

"How in the hell did you hack into my messages?" Brooks snapped. He was going to have to fire the people he had handling that. Change his number. *Fuck.* A whole annoying cascade of changes. But if a "normal" guy like Mike could hack into his messages, they clearly weren't doing their job.

Mike smiled. "Wouldn't you like to know? Guess you'll have to keep wondering. Sit on the bed."

Brooks sat, his eyes trained on the gun. That was one of Mike's smarter moves. If not for the gun, which he didn't doubt Mike would use if he wanted, Brooks would have tried to rush him by now. Mike wasn't much smaller than him, though.

"You get one minute to decide. I'm gonna show you on the TV screen in here some things I have, and if you don't want them out, you're paying up. Today. Something happens to me, I have a friend on standby who'll release them. I get arrested, same. You make a phone call, talk to anyone, same deal. You talk only to me, deal only with me. You have one move, Brooks, and it's to pay. Once we leave here, you're gonna be my best buddy and you're gonna act like it and not one person is going to know a damn thing or these will get out."

Sweat broke out on Brooks's forehead.

What the fuck does he have? And how does he really believe this will fly?

. . .

THEN MIKE LIFTED the remote and turned on the television and a montage of images started across the screen.

Him and Maddie in the orchard after Applepalooza—with her in a bra and underwear. They got progressively more explicit from there.

The first time they'd had sex on the balcony.

Sext messages they'd sent each other.

Footage from inside the damn lake house.

Oh my God.

Brooks almost vomited at the idea of all of this in Mike's possession.

He shut the TV off. "You get the idea. I'll post it to every porn site out there, Brooks. And I'm a man of my word."

"How the hell did you get all this?"

"You were out of that rental house every weekend, Brooks. It wasn't hard."

Dammit, dammit, dammit. How in the hell had that never occurred to him?

Brooks's chest was wound so tight he could hardly breathe. "How much?"

"One million, in cash. And that's me being generous."

He swallowed. "There isn't a bank around that can get me that in cash today."

"Well, we're not going to a bank. We're going to Vegas. Right now. They'll give you a big line of credit, you'll cash out, and then hand it over to me."

Vegas?

Going there meant he wouldn't be here to do the concert for Maddie.

Although, maybe that would worry her enough that she'd sound the alarm.

Stupid piece of shit. "You think you're so smart, don't you, asshole? I'm just going to turn around and sue you for extortion. Put your ass in jail."

"No, you won't. Because if you do this, I'll also drop the custody case with Kayla."

"You never would have won that anyway."

"Really? You think I won't tell the judge about Kayla leaving Audrey with her drunk uncle? Or the time a stalker tried to attack my daughter on a fishing trip with that uncle? Kayla was on a date, right? Audrey drove to the hospital without a car seat, too."

How the fuck does he know all this?

How the fuck did he get so close?

His astonishment clearly showed. "You made this so much easier for me than I ever could have imagined, Brooks. I had a good source, and damn, you made it easy."

A good source? What the hell did that mean?

Someone in town?

Mike checked his watch. "Your minute is up."

He wanted so badly to punch him.

Brooks met his hard stare. "I need a guarantee in writing that footage will be destroyed."

"I'm keeping a copy in a bank safe for five years. Once the statute of limitations for you pressing charges expires, you get the code."

"That's not good enough. What's going to stop you from coming back when you run through your money? You always do, Mike." Brooks glared at him. "No way in hell I'm giving you a cent without a written guarantee you will destroy that footage and stay away from Kayla, Audrey, and Madison for the rest of your sorry, miserable life."

He was talking out of his ass at this point. He had no way of being sure he could make that happen. But maybe Christine could come up with an ironclad contract that Mike could sign online. "I'll need one email to my lawyer."

"You think I'm stupid enough to give you your phone?"

"Didn't you say you'd release the footage if you get arrested?" Brooks raised a brow, a strange sense of calm coming over him.

Breathe, Brooks. Mike's actions spoke of desperation. He couldn't afford not to take anything Mike said seriously. Stupidity on his part could get him killed. "One email. You can point a gun at me and watch me type the whole time if it makes you feel better."

A bead of sweat ran down Mike's temple. "Fine. Once we get to my car. Let's go. Out the back door."

Brooks stood, his head spinning.

What else can I do?

How can I beat this prick at his own game?

How can I make sure that Maddie doesn't believe what this asshole made me send her?

Could he code the message that only Christine would understand?

If I relent today, will he really leave Kayla and Audrey alone? And who the hell was this "buddy" and what was the guarantee that he *wouldn't simply choose the same path as fucking Mike?*

But he came up empty.

For once, Mike had him by the balls in an iron grip.

Fuck my life.

41

MADDIE

"Calm down." Naomi set a paper cup of water beside Maddie, then took Maddie's trembling hands. "Calm."

"I just don't get it. Why would he leave? Why turn off his phone? Something must have happened." Maddie met Kayla's eyes on the other side of the trailer sofa. "Everything was fine. We were happy." She appealed to Dan Klein. "Isn't there any security footage at all?"

"We're looking for aerial footage," Dan said with a frown. "But you know how it is. It's a field in the middle of nowhere. We don't have resources like they have in the cities, Maddie." He and the two other police officers in the room made the space feel crowded. God love her parents—they'd taken Audrey to their house for safekeeping.

One of the other officers cleared his throat. "Is it possible he left on his own? That's often the case with something like this. Especially when it's only been four hours. And his text message to you indicates that's what happened."

Cormac, the other person in the room, shook his head. "Brooks wouldn't just leave when he's got a concert to play, and definitely not without telling anyone and evading his bodyguard. That's not like him at all."

"What about Mike? Was his mom able to get in touch with him?" Maddie asked. Her gut instinct had been to worry about him, considering he'd threatened Brooks earlier in the week.

Kayla nodded. "Yeah, she just texted me back. She doesn't know where he is. They don't talk too often."

"You really have to cut her off, Kayla. She's a nice lady, but that link is toxic," Cormac fumed.

"I'm not discussing that right now," Kayla shot back. They acted like brother and sister sometimes. Maybe because Cormac was the closest thing Brooks had to a brother.

Maddie looked away from them both, thankful that Naomi was here. She was always steady in these situations. "Brooks didn't just leave. I'm certain of it."

"Okay." Naomi squeezed her hand. "What do you think his text message meant then, Maddie?"

"I don't know." Maddie met Naomi's gaze, searching her eyes frantically. "I don't know. But I'm sure he wouldn't leave. He loves me, Naomi. He wouldn't just walk out without talking to me. He wouldn't leave the whole town high and dry with this concert. Humiliate me. He wouldn't."

"We can take a missing person report if you want, Maddie," Dan said gently. "But the text message is a crucial piece of evidence here."

Maddie closed her eyes, trying to think straight.

No way in hell Brooks would leave like this.

Kayla wasn't saying much, but Cormac appeared to be on Maddie's side.

Everyone else, it seemed, thought the text message was damning.

Because it is.

"I'm sorry. I had to go. Don't try to reach me."

What the hell was she supposed to make of this?

Had the fair freaked him out? He'd been worried about waiting in the apple fritter line, but they'd been wandering around the fairgrounds before that. Dancing. He'd signed a few autographs.

Maybe she'd misjudged how much he enjoyed it?

But then why hadn't Brooks taken his bodyguard, Ryan, with him? Ryan had said that Brooks had told him not to bother sweeping the trailer before he'd gone in. Maybe it was just Ryan's way of protecting himself and not be blamed for failing to do his job—but then why had Brooks slipped out without telling Ryan?

Brooks was worried about security. He'd insisted on the bodyguards this week, everywhere they went.

"Dan, can you and your friends step out of here for a couple of minutes? We'll call you back," Naomi said.

Maddie didn't open her eyes but heard them go.

Naomi settled on the couch beside her. "It's your move, Maddie. If you want to file a missing person report, I get it. But there exists a small possibility that Brooks . . . just needed to get away from this."

Maddie gave her a doubtful look. "Without a bodyguard?"

"I don't know. He came to Brandywood without a bodyguard, didn't he? Maybe he doesn't like them around all the time."

"He doesn't," Kayla said quietly.

"Maybe so, but what happened at the lake terrified him. I don't think he'd go anywhere right now without Ryan—even if he doesn't like bodyguards."

"The concert is the biggest sticking point for me," Cormac said with a frown. "His last concert got canceled because of his arrest. I don't think he'd walk out on the next one. Some people here tonight probably came from Baltimore because they missed the last one. The fair is never *this* crowded."

Thank you, Cormac.

"I agree," Maddie said quickly.

"You're agreeing because it's what you want to hear," Naomi said. "You never know, he might come back in time for the concert. Maybe he just needed some air."

Cormac's eyes were troubled. "We need to come up with a contingency plan in the meantime. There are going to be a lot of disappointed people out there otherwise."

Maddie stood, feeling like her head was going to explode. "I don't care about the damn concert. I'm telling you, I know Brooks. He wouldn't leave the concert. He wouldn't leave . . . me."

She met three sets of pitying eyes and her heart broke.

Maybe none of them were as sure as she was.

But she was right, wasn't she?

They had talked. They were in a relationship. Doing things long-distance.

He wouldn't leave without talking to her.

. . . except he'd tried to do just that once before. *Only a week before.*

She stood there, a scene from just the weekend before playing in her mind. He'd packed her bags in her apartment. *"You're fucking leaving?"* she'd asked him.

"It's for the best. Things are getting out of control."

The slick, miserable hand of doubt wrapped its way around her throat, choking her.

Then she dissolved into tears.

42

BROOKS

As THE AIRPLANE's wheels touched down in Baltimore, Brooks stared stonily into the darkness. He'd caught the red-eye out of Vegas and hoped to sleep on the plane.

Sleep hadn't come.

"Pleasure doing business with you."

Mike's slimy voice when Brooks had handed him the cash rang through his head.

I just want a shower to wash off the stench that is Mike Valders.

Blackmailed. The son of a bitch actually successfully blackmailed Brooks. His fury was palpable.

For what it was worth—*possibly little*—Christine's contract would provide some legal recourse to keep the man out of his life.

Who the hell am I kidding? Valders is a narcissist.

Brooks couldn't protect them. That was the bottom line. Mike didn't give a shit about the law.

Neither did any person who would try to harm the people he loved.

He had no real way to protect Maddie.

With enough determination and ingenuity, like Mike had displayed, the people determined to hurt the woman he loved would get through. No amount of money or bodyguards or security teams or gates could keep them out.

For the thousandth time, Brooks asked himself why the fuck he didn't have Ryan check the trailer. This would be a very different last sixteen hours.

Brooks pinched the bridge of his nose, his eyes burning with tears.

He hadn't cried in years.

He could love Maddie—would love her—until the day that he died.

But as long as she's with me . . .

I *am a danger to her.*

His existence was the threat.

An aching, hollow feeling rose in his chest, where Maddie had brought life to him once again.

He had just one move—and it might kill him.

But it had to be done.

43

MADDIE

THE SOFT CLICK of her bedroom door opening roused Maddie from a relatively sleepless night filled with fitful, awful dreams. She blinked, her eyes swollen and burning from the tears she'd been shedding.

Brooks stood in the doorway, his figure barely visible in the early morning light.

With a cry, Maddie leaped out of bed. A startled Naomi, who'd spent the night with her, jumped and sat. "What the hell?" Naomi grumbled.

Maddie didn't bother to glance back, running toward Brooks. She flung her arms around his neck, and he caught her, his arms tight around her as she clung to him. A fresh wave of tears burst from her eyes, and she inhaled his scent, molding her body to him as her shoulders shook with sobs. "I was so worried," she cried. "My God, Brooks. I was terrified."

Brooks said nothing, but his arms crushed her, his hands stroking her back and hair, soothing her.

"Let me give you two a moment," Naomi said in a soft

voice, then slipped past them, into the hall. The door shut behind her.

"Are you all right? Are you hurt? What happened to you?" She assailed him with a thousand questions at once, searching his face.

"I'm fine. I'm fine now. It's a long story, but I'm here, and I'm safe, and I'm so sorry."

He's safe.

His words filled her with regret and worry.

Something had happened. *Of course it had.*

Tearing up again, Maddie laid her cheek against the soft fabric of Brooks's shirt, listening to his heartbeat. *God, I missed him. This heartbeat.*

So much.

I never want to be away from him.

She wiped her cheeks and pulled away, swallowing hard as she gave him a half-hearted smile. Crossing to the window, she opened it to let in some early morning sunlight. "You have some serious explaining to do, Mr. Kent. I was this close to filing a missing person report."

"Mike—" A pained expression crossed Brooks's face, his own eyes looking glossy.

It was all he needed to say.

Her heart constricted. "Did he threaten you? What happened?"

Brooks shook his head, then sank onto the bed, covering his face. "Well, yes, but more importantly, he threatened you. He had pictures, Maddie. Of us. Damaging ones he was going to upload to the internet. Apparently, he's had a private investigator following us for a while."

A chill ran through Maddie, and she hugged her arms to her chest. "What did he want?"

"What do you think?"

"Money?"

"In cash. Only place we could get the amount of cash he wanted, though, was in Vegas. And it had to be yesterday because he wouldn't let me out of his sight until the money was in his hands. If I used my phone, called you, the police got involved, he got arrested—any of it—he said he'd have the files transferred instantly."

"So you paid him?" Maddie gaped at him and sat beside him, her brain spinning. "Brooks, that's extortion."

"You think I don't know that? He had me by the balls, Maddie. What was I supposed to do?"

"Let the damn images be released. I don't care." It wasn't true, of course, but what else could she say? It was better than extortion.

Brooks gave her a sharp look. "Maybe you don't, but I do. I love you, Madison. I'm not going to allow the world to view our private moments. I don't *want* other people looking at you that way."

"Brooks, I hear you, but all you did is open yourself up to more of this. You think Mike won't come back again? Haven't you said he keeps doing it? And what if other people try to do similar things? You can't protect me by constantly paying people off."

"I know," Brooks said miserably. He closed his eyes, his jaw clenching hard. "I know that."

Tense silence crept in, and Brooks stood. "Which is why this has to be over between us, Maddie. I wanted to call you as soon as Mike let me go, but we needed to talk in person. You deserve that much. And I wanted to get my guitar. I don't care about my other things, so you can throw them out."

What?

Maddie's heart ripped at his words, and she stared at him in disbelief.

She didn't know whether to be angry or devastated.

He'd tried to do this before, and now he was doing it again.

"Absolutely not." She stood and grabbed his hand. "No. You aren't walking out on me, Brooks. I won't allow it. We love each other—"

"I do love you, Maddie," Brooks said, his voice a low growl. He cupped the sides of her face and kissed her forehead. "I love you more than I've ever loved anyone or anything, but I can't protect you. Over the past week, you've been attacked and threatened in ways that made me go crazy. I chose this stupid lifestyle, and there's no going back for me. I can't stop being who I am. But I won't have your life and reputation put in danger because of me."

"So you hire security! We live in your gated community—"

"That would mean you having to leave Brandywood. You don't want that."

"I . . ." She hesitated, swallowing hard.

For the past week, she'd ignored the thought. What if Brooks needed her to choose between him and her home? Her family? The place where everyone knew her, and she knew everyone?

And now, with Pops stepping back even further, her family needed her more than ever.

"I know you're not ready for that. And you haven't even decided about your grandfather's business."

"I-I'll tell him no. That I won't do it."

"Do you have any idea how massively unfair that would be for me to ask something like that of you? Something you've barely had a chance to think about? You might hate me for it later."

She hated him for being the voice of reason right now.

"Couldn't we get security at a house here? Maybe build a gate?"

"Around Main Street?" He stepped back, his shoulders slumping in defeat. "Or the lake, where you were attacked?"

"That wouldn't have happened if I'd had a bodyguard with me."

He nodded. "You're right because I got careless. I got so comfortable being here, where no one knew how to find me at first, that I forgot I don't get that privilege all the time. Mike implied he gained access to the lake house to put cameras in during the weekends when I wasn't there. And your life was threatened, your grandfather was hospitalized, my niece traumatized. Enormous price to pay for my carelessness, wouldn't you say?"

She shook her head. "Brooks, I know it won't be easy, but I—"

"You don't know, though. You don't know the half of it." Brooks shoved his hands in his back pockets. "You have no idea what it's like to be chased by the paparazzi in LA. To go out to dinner and be mobbed. To have the people you love threatened when they're completely innocent. Mike pulled a gun on me . . . what if he did that to you?"

She gasped. "Mike held you at gunpoint?"

Oh my God.

Brooks could have been killed.

Brooks nodded, the strain on his face clear. "Why do you think I didn't do more?"

He looked so tired, so *sad.* "I can't show up anywhere without being photographed. My life isn't *normal.* And for a few weeks, you gave me normal again, Maddie. Fall festivals and making out in storerooms and getting breakfast at Bunny's. Family parties. Almost enough for me to forget who I am."

Her throat thickened. What scared her more than his descriptions of his life was that she didn't seem to be changing his mind. "Brooks, listen to me. I'll admit that I don't know what any of that is like, but I'd still rather live that than be apart from you."

"You could barely look at me after what happened to your grandfather, Maddie. Hell, I could barely look you in the eye—I was so ashamed. What if something like that happens again? It's not just you and me involved. It's your family. Any future kids that you want. Kayla and Audrey have the unlucky position of being my family and look at what happened there. Mike has been a plague to them both. Getting him to go away this time came at a high cost."

"So we take him on legally—"

"He still has access to those images. If I take him on legally, he'll release them. I got him to sign a contract saying it's a one-time deal and that he'd stay away from you, Kayla, and Audrey in perpetuity."

"He'll come back. He'll continue threatening to release them."

"Not if he's convinced I don't care about you. Those images will lose their power then."

The weight of his statement made her want to throw up. To convince Mike of that . . . Brooks would have to convince *the whole world* that he no longer had any interest in her.

"I'm changing my phone number after I leave. Getting rid of this one because it was hacked."

"What do you mean? How? Didn't you say you had a team to stop that?"

He nodded. "I did. They clearly didn't do their job. I got a text that I thought was from you—it even went into our exchanged texts—asking me to meet you in the trailer alone. I thought you wanted a quickie, so I went. But it was Mike waiting there for me with a gun. He demanded I text you and tell you I was leaving."

She gasped, horrified at the idea. *A message from her?* Mike lured her with a fake text from her? And she'd been right. *Dammit, I was right. I knew it.* The message from Brooks hadn't been real, either.

"He needs to be arrested, babe. If not for what he did to you and me, for Kayla and Audrey's sake."

"I'm already working on security measures for them. Please don't make this harder on us both."

"Brooks, no." Tears flowed down her cheeks, and she reached for him as he turned away. She rushed up behind him and clung to the back of his shirt. "No, no, no. Don't do this. Please. I love you." She wrapped her arms around his waist, her tears soaking through his shirt. "Please."

"It's over with us, Maddie," he whispered. "It has to be. I won't risk you. Find someone who can give you everything you deserve. I can't give you that here in Brandywood, where you can have everything you've ever wanted. And you deserve *everything* you've ever wanted."

But I want you.

He peeled her arms from his waist, a resolve in his face that frightened her. "Thank you for loving me."

Tears clouded her vision.

How in the hell was this happening?

He was breaking up with her. Really, truly breaking up with her.

She couldn't order him back to bed this time. Convince him to talk about it when they'd had some sleep. Nothing would change his mind.

"I love you more than I've ever loved anyone or anything. But I can't protect you. I won't have your life and reputation put in danger because of me."

Maddie understood that from a cerebral point of view, but what about his heart? *Our* hearts? She wanted to rant and rave, to scream for him to stay, but his determination to protect those in his life was fierce—something she couldn't fight against.

He's leaving.

He came for his guitar.

He made up his mind before he came here.

She sank onto the floor, covering her eyes as he slipped out of the room, tears flowing down her face.

Why hadn't he given her the chance to change his mind?

Yet . . . the last time he'd tried to leave, and she'd changed his mind, things had only gotten worse. As he'd been worried about.

A murmur of unintelligible voices from the living room sounded—he must be saying something to Naomi—and then she heard the door open.

He was gone.

Brooks.

The man she loved with all her heart.

The man she'd sworn would never hurt her.

He's leaving.

She scrambled to her feet.

What am I doing? I can't let him go like this.

Grabbing a sweatshirt, she yanked it over her pajama top and ran through the living room.

"Maddie!" Naomi called out as she went past her.

She ignored her. Hurrying down the back staircase, she went out the back door.

Brooks was on his way to the front of the building, heading toward Main Street, guitar case in hand.

Maddie ran, her bare feet stinging against the pavement. "Brooks! Brooks, stop!"

Brooks slowed as he reached the front sidewalk and turned to look over his shoulder at her.

"Brooks! Please don't go. Please," she called out.

She didn't care that anyone who might be on Main Street would hear. Or see her running, barefoot, in her pajamas, with swollen eyes and tears on her face.

She didn't care if she looked pathetic.

Brooks turned toward her, just slightly, his hand lowering the guitar case to the ground slowly. His expression was tortured, his face filled with grief.

Then a flash went off.

Two flashes.

Three.

The damn paparazzi were already waiting for him.

Whatever momentary hesitation had come over him vanished. Brooks turned and headed straight for an awaiting black sedan.

"Brooks, no," she cried out as he climbed in, and the sedan swiftly pulled away from the curb.

Then he was gone.

Maddie sank to her knees. She covered her face with her hands, sobbing uncontrollably.

Oh, Brooks.

Please . . . no.

Why can't there be any other option? This isn't fair. He wants to be with me.

She heard more camera flashes, then strong arms enveloped her.

"Get the fuck out of here!" Naomi yelled toward the paparazzi, her arms tight around Maddie. "Out! Before I call the cops for trespassing." She pulled Maddie against her chest, cradling her head. "Come on, sweetie, we have to get up. Get away from the bloodhounds."

"I don't care," Maddie sobbed, her shoulders shaking. "He was blackmailed, Naomi. He's leaving because he won't risk me getting hurt."

Why is there no other way to be together?

Naomi shielded her with her arms and body, and Maddie felt her sister's tears splash onto her neck as she drew a shaking breath.

Thank God for Naomi.

Thank God she's here.

Then Maddie drew a hard sniffle, desperately in need of a tissue. "We can go inside," she managed.

"It's over with us, Maddie. It has to be. I won't risk you."

Brooks wasn't coming back.

44

BROOKS

THE MOMENT the sedan pulled away from the curb, tears stung Brooks's eyes.

I don't want to leave her.

I can't leave her.

She was there, on the sidewalk, crying. *Sobbing.*

And he was the one who'd hurt her.

His hand fisted, and he pounded it against the panel of the door, so hard that his hand throbbed.

Fuuuuuuuuck. But the pain wasn't from his hand.

He wiped the moisture from his cheek, staring out the window.

The last time he'd left Maddie's apartment this early had been a month ago. To the day, actually. He'd slipped out thinking he'd never see her again.

His first impression of the town—of her—had been so wrong.

Where once he'd seen bleak storefronts filled with fake charm, life now brimmed instead.

The grocer where he and Maddie had walked to get food to make dinner the other night.

The bakery where he'd bought Audrey a cookie.

The mechanic shop where his car had been fixed, with the dog that slobbered all over your shoe while you waited.

The café where the love of his life had stood in a damn booth and told the whole town to leave him alone.

Every inch of the town filled with the memory and fingerprints of *her* and their time together here.

How can I leave her?

He had to. He had to protect her.

This wasn't like fleeing Fountain Springs. And it certainly wasn't anything like any other breakup in the past.

This felt more akin to tearing his soul from his body.

Goddamn Mike Valders.

He'd taken *everything* away.

His sense of security, his hopes, his dreams.

Maddie.

Everything.

Bitter, acrid bile stung his throat.

I love her so much.

He would be damned if Mike ever hurt anyone he loved again.

Brooks picked up the phone and dialed Christine.

She picked up after the third ring. "You should know you're one of the only clients who has the privilege of waking me at six on Sunday. What the hell is going on?"

Brooks cleared his throat, his voice sounding as raw as it felt. "Still have that friend at the FBI?"

Mike Valders may have won for now and taken everything good from his life.

But he will never hurt my family again. I'll make sure of it.

45

MADDIE

ONE MONTH LATER

"The window looks fantastic, Garrett," Maddie said as she surveyed the outside of the Depot. She wrapped a thick shawl around her shoulders, the icy chill of autumn getting stronger each day. The foliage had peaked already—most of the trees had lost their leaves.

Winter—and Christmas—would be around the corner. It was usually her favorite time of year.

These days, though, even the allure of the holidays had lost its luster.

"It *does* look fantastic," Naomi said, smiling at Garrett Doyle as he packed up his tools. "And I'm thrilled we'll have our best display window up in time for the Christmas season."

Garrett straightened, a gentle smile on his handsome face. "Sorry I couldn't do it any sooner. But thanks for being patient with me." He searched Maddie's face. "How are you doing these days, Maddie? Sam and I have been worried about you."

"Hanging in there." She gave a taut smile. "You know, getting inducted into Brandywood's Most Notoriously Dumped Women's Club this week."

Naomi shook her head. "Only Maddie could joke about something like that."

"At least I'm joking." Maddie shrugged. There was truth in that statement, even though she'd delivered it as lightheartedly as possible. She'd cried into her pillow for three weeks straight after Brooks had left. Called him, despite the number not being in service, and sent text messages that were never delivered.

Then, about a week earlier, she'd finally stopped crying at night. But the pain of heartbreak pervaded every single day. Rom-coms didn't make her happy. Parties and family events seemed overwhelming.

She didn't want to go anywhere or do anything.

Yet here she was, struggling along because—what else could she do?

Garrett leaned over and gave her a hug. "Just let me know if you need anything at all. We're here for you. All Brandywood is on your side."

Yeah, I doubt Gina Strickland is. Then again, she'd been fortunate not to really run into Gina lately.

She nodded, swallowing a lump in her throat. His words were kindly meant, but she didn't want there to be a side. Even if her family was mad at Brooks—if everyone in town was mad at Brooks—she still loved him. Every kindly meant barb in his direction hurt.

She'd wanted to explain to the town that Mike had kidnapped him and exhorted him for money, and that was why he didn't perform at the fair, but that would affect Kayla, so she couldn't do that either. *It all just sucks.*

As Garrett left, Naomi wrapped her arm around Maddie's shoulder. "You okay, or are you done peopling for the day?"

"I can handle it," Maddie said with a sigh. "If I need a break, I'll just head up over to Pops's for a bit. See how he's doing." She'd been staying at Pops's house for the past few weeks anyway. He needed a hand around the house after surgery while Bunny was working, and she didn't want to sleep at her apartment anymore.

Everything there reminded her of Brooks. Even his clothes were still there, his razor still on her bathroom sink. As though he was coming back for them. She couldn't stand it.

A tug at her skirt made her look down, then Audrey popped her head around her hip. "Hi, Aunt Maddie! Aunt Nami!"

Maddie looked around, surprised, then saw Kayla and Logan coming down the sidewalk. Kayla had been making plans to move here recently—she'd even gotten a job at the local hospital—but as far as Maddie knew, she was still living in Virginia.

She was happy for Logan, but the idea of eventually running into Brooks again because of his sister being in a relationship with her brother was exactly what she'd feared.

How in the world am I going to handle that?

"Hey, Audrey." Maddie bent to give her a fierce hug. It still took her breath away sometimes when she looked at Audrey and Kayla—they both resembled Brooks enough that it hurt—but she'd grown to love Brooks's sister, who had been calling and texting her daily. "How are you?"

Kayla and she had also bonded over the fact that Brooks was avoiding Kayla, too. He'd sent more security measures to her house, sure. Just like the bodyguards stationed outside Maddie's apartment despite her asking them to go.

But Kayla had talked to Brooks only once, she'd said, and only for five minutes.

"Mommy said we had to check on you," Audrey said, then put a hand on Maddie's forehead. "Are you sick, Aunt Maddie?"

"Nope!" Maddie kissed her soft, chubby cheeks. "I'm

good." She stood as Kayla and Logan reached them. "I didn't know you were coming into town today," she told Kayla after exchanging a hug.

"I wasn't." Kayla searched her face. "Have you been offline today?"

Oh no.

Dread formed in the pit of Maddie's stomach as she nodded. "Why, what happened? Tell me."

"Audrey, Mr. Logan and Aunt Nami are going to take you to get some gelato, sound good?"

Naomi took the hint and scooped Audrey up. "What's your favorite flavor? Chocolate? Mint chocolate? Oh, I bet you'll love pistachio."

"Ewwww . . . pishtachtio is yucky," Audrey said as Naomi carried her off into the store.

Logan gave Maddie a backward glance, worry in his eyes.

This has to be about Brooks.

Maddie felt the blood drain from her face as she looked at Kayla. "What is it? Did something happen to him? Or is he dating someone?" Nausea roiled her stomach, every bad possibility assailing her imagination.

In some ways, the latter would be worse than the former.

The idea of Brooks moving on and falling in love with someone else was probably the worst thing she could imagine happening. It would certainly put a pin in Mike's plans to exhort more money from Brooks with pictures of them . . . *but it would break my heart even more than it's broken now.*

Kayla gripped her shoulders. "No, no, nothing like that." She released a slow breath. "He put out a new single today. It's called 'Ever With Me.' I'm pretty sure it's about you. Logan thinks so, too. He was asked about it, and then released a statement that it has nothing to do with you."

Relief sank all the way through her, replacing her fears with instant tears.

No, no. Don't cry.

Not now.

She blinked them away and nodded. A single. She could handle a single. He was a musician, after all—new songs would be inevitable. "Oh, thank God. And that's good, right? It means he figured out a way to get around the contract stuff. Good for him."

Kayla hugged her again. "Sorry, I didn't mean to scare you like that." She sniffled and pulled back. "Don't worry. If he was dating already, I'd go find him and punch him in the face. I've been tempted to do that a half dozen times, anyway. But that would put me over the edge."

Maddie swallowed back a tearful laugh. She sounded so much like Brooks sometimes, too.

"So I shouldn't listen to this song, I take it?"

"I don't know." Sadness filled her eyes. "It made me cry, so I can only imagine what it would do to you. I think he's still really in love with you, Maddie. And I'm so mad at him for doing this to you. To all three of us. Audrey misses Uncle Brooks so much. She doesn't understand why he's not Face-Timing as much as he used to."

"He'll probably let you in soon enough." If Maddie knew Brooks and he'd really loved her as much as she believed, he had to be hurting. She hated he believed he needed to walk away to protect her, but there was no way he'd shut Kayla and Audrey out forever. "I doubt he's ready to talk yet, that's all. He wouldn't have called you and given you his number if he wanted to cut things off with you."

She'd been tempted to ask Kayla for that number—but Brooks had been clear, too. She wouldn't intrude on his privacy just because she knew his sister.

Kayla scrunched her face. "You're not supposed to be trying to make me feel better. It's the other way around."

"Like it or not, you're like a sister to me now. Logan loves you, and so do I."

Kayla laughed. "Like it? Getting into your Yardley sisters' girls' club is one of the things I'm looking forward to the most about moving to Brandywood. If there's room for a fifth sister."

"There's always room for a fifth sister. Maybe even a sixth if Jake ever gets around to finding a girl."

Maddie stepped back from Kayla, her gaze going farther down the sidewalk. If she didn't know any better, that man with the slick camera . . .

Shit.

The paparazzi.

Not just photographers, either. A few men and women hurried toward her, giving her flashbacks of the days after the breakup, when reporters had hounded her.

"Madison Yardley?" one woman called as she drew closer, waving her hand in the air.

They seemed to come out of nowhere, as though the reporters and paparazzi had all descended on her in a surprise attack. "Miss Yardley? Can we get a statement from you about Brooks Kent's new song? Is the song about you?"

"Are you in touch with Mr. Kent?" another man called out.

Kayla and Maddie shoved their way toward the door of the Depot, but more reporters blocked them.

"No comment," Maddie managed, unable to move past them.

The sound of a familiar truck roared, then stopped on the curb beside them.

Josh.

He sat in the driver's seat of his truck and leaned over, opening the door. "Maddie," he called. "Get in."

She exchanged a helpless look with Kayla. It would be easier to make a fast getaway with Josh, but what about Kayla?

"Go on," Kayla said with a light push. "They're not interested in me."

Despite her reservations, Maddie climbed inside the truck and closed the door behind her. Josh pulled away from the curb, giving her a worried smile. "You okay?"

"I'm fine, thanks." Ironic, finding herself here. Only a handful of months ago, she'd felt so comfortable in the passenger seat of this very truck. So sure that Josh was everything she'd ever wanted.

Now, as she looked at him, she couldn't quite remember what she'd seen in him. "I'm just glad I was passing by. That's quite a throng of people out there. The reporters been bothering you?"

"Sometimes." She glanced back. Maybe she should have tried her luck and stayed out there. Here in the truck with Josh didn't feel any safer.

The Depot was quickly moving out of her line of sight. Why hadn't he just taken her to the back of the Depot?

"How're you doing, Maddie? I've been thinking about you a lot these days."

She frowned at him. Josh wasn't the smoothest—never had been—but back when she'd believed she was in love with him, she thought he was kind and honest. After what had happened with Gina, she knew he wasn't honest. Kind was questionable, too.

"I'm good."

Josh gave a slow nod. "If you ever need anything, a friend to talk to, someone to drink with, whatever, I'm here for you."

She stiffened, her brow furrowing.

Josh pulled up to a stoplight, then leaned over toward her, his hand sliding onto her thigh. Then he gave it a squeeze.

She didn't wait to think it through. She just unlocked the door and climbed out of the passenger seat.

"Hey, where are you going?" Josh called after her.

"You're not my friend, Josh. You never were, asshole." She slammed the door and turned to walk away.

A stream of curse words started from his open window, but Maddie ignored him and fled onto the sidewalk. She kept running, crossing the street and going back toward the Depot. Jumping into the alleyway that ran behind the stores on the street that faced the Depot, she ran until the heel of her boot snapped.

Dammit. Just my luck.

Then again, high-heeled boots weren't meant for running.

She took both pairs of boots off, then made her way down the alley in her socks. This day was spinning into a shit show, one she wasn't sure if she was emotionally prepared to handle.

As she drew closer to the stores that were across from the Depot, she slowed. The reporters were still probably out there, waiting for her to return. Who knew how long they'd be there?

She sank against a brick wall, tightening the shawl over her shoulders. Her mind spun, trying to process the events of the last few minutes, which felt chaotic.

Jumping into the car with Josh had been stupid, but she couldn't have foreseen him hitting on her like that.

He's engaged, for goodness' sake.

She hadn't seen that coming.

More importantly, Brooks might have written a song about her and now she'd need to figure out a way to deal with the press again until that settled down.

How long would it be like this?

She really didn't *want* to care about Brooks anymore.

Didn't *want* to love him as much as she did. At times, she

even let herself be mad at him—but it didn't last long. Mostly, she just felt sad.

Lonely.

Because she understood why he left the way he did. She still recalled the absolute devastation on his face as he thanked her for loving him—*as if that was a hard thing to do*—and told her that the only way forward he could see to keep her safe was to separate himself from her. It just didn't make things hurt less.

Of course she knew he could be cold and detached—that how he'd gotten through life. But even when they'd been strangers . . .

Ugh, who am I kidding? Dealing with Brooks hadn't been a walk in the park at the beginning. He was arrogant, difficult, and sometimes rude.

But he was *her* arrogant, difficult, and rude man. Or he had been. And when he had been, he'd treated her like a queen.

Those were the moments that were so hard to forget.

She'd forced herself not to listen to his music, but the sound of his voice stayed with her no matter how hard she tried to forget it.

"You're it for me, Madison. I love you. Only you. Always. But I will rip out my own heart if it means protecting you."

He'd meant it, too. But he'd ripped hers out in the process.

Her eyes welled with tears.

She drew her knees up and hugged her arms around them, sighing. She didn't even have her cell phone out here with her—it had been in the Depot when she'd gone out to talk to Garrett.

"Psst."

The whisper came from farther down the alley.

Maddie lifted her head. She didn't expect to see Gina Strickland standing at the back door to her father's store, but there she was. She waved Maddie forward. "In here. You can hide here, Maddie."

Maddie hesitated. After her run-in with Josh, Gina was the last person she wanted to talk to.

What's she up to?

Gina held the door more widely. "Truce. I promise, Maddie. I have no agenda."

She'd never really trusted the Stricklands, but Gina also had no reason to offer her shelter right now. She could have just kept the door closed.

Unless she has reporters hiding in there with her.

Maddie rolled her eyes at her own ideas. *That's ridiculous.*

She stood and hurried down toward the Stricklands' place, trying to forget the last time she'd been in here.

The first time Brooks and I kissed.

Gina closed the door to the storeroom behind her.

No one in here. Whew.

"You okay?" Gina asked. "Can I get you some water or something?"

"Actually, water would be great."

Gina nodded and pointed at a metal folding chair. "Feel free to sit. It's not super comfortable back here, but you know that." She went over to a shelf and pulled a bottle of water from a package. "Here you go."

"Thanks." Maddie took it and popped it open, her eyes roaming the space. She hadn't given thought to the comfort of the storeroom before. Gina was right, though. Their back storeroom was a far cry from the Depot's. In fact, the Stricklands hadn't updated anything—including the front—for years.

She knew little about them, but she didn't get the feeling they had a ton of money. Gina didn't dress well and worked part-time at the front desk of the accounting office where Josh was a partner. Fred drove a ratty old station wagon that Travis swore was held together with duct tape.

For the first time, Maddie felt a wave of shame go through her.

Maybe she'd never considered the Stricklands point of view.

She loved her grandfather and the Depot, but she'd gotten so caught up in their *right* to sell gelato and how much business they brought to the town that she'd never considered the hurt they'd inflicted regardless of their intentions.

Just like Brooks hurt me, regardless of his intent.

"Gina, I'm sorry." Maddie took a swig of the water, thirstier than she thought. She capped it and looked up at her. "I'm sorry that my family hurt yours. That I disrespected your father and your store by fooling around with guys in here. I've been a brat and I'm sorry."

Gina's eyes clouded. "You don't have to apologize."

"I want to." Maddie set the water down. "There's enough petty drama that happens in town, and I don't want to be a part of that anymore. My family isn't better than anyone else's. And gosh, the Stricklands have been here as long as the Yardleys. I think I was even best friends with your sister Hannah one summer after camp. I don't want to have enemies. Do you?"

Gina pulled her dark hair into a ponytail and leaned back against a wall. "No, I don't." She sighed. "By the way, I never cheated with Josh. I swear it. And if it makes you feel any better, Josh dumped me. He's dating some girl from a few towns over now."

Wait, what?

Josh had dumped Gina?

Ugh. I can't believe I ever thought I was in love with him. Or lived with him. He was despicable.

"It doesn't make me feel better to hear Josh dumped you.

Having recently had my heart destroyed by a man, I don't wish that on anyone. But at the risk of sounding like my family, you deserve better than Josh, Gina."

"God, that phrase sucks when you still love the idiot, right?" Gina unfolded a chair and sat beside her. "I was so jealous of you. First, when you were dating Josh. Then, when I realized Josh still was hung up on you even though we were dating. But then you were fine and happy and dating a rock star and I just kept thinking to myself, *how does she get so lucky?* Guess Brooks Kent wasn't as great as it seemed, either."

Maddie lifted her water bottle in a mock cheers. "Here's to my *luck*." She let out a sarcastic laugh, then rubbed her eyelids. "Brooks was great, though. And I know I sound dumb. You know why he broke up with me, right?"

Gina shook her head.

No, of course. How would she know?

"Well, first a stalker of his showed up and attacked me, tried to stab me with a knife. My grandfather shoved her into the lake, but he had a massive heart attack as a result." She didn't know why she was telling Gina any of this, except for the fact that they were both heartbroken women. "That was in addition to the paparazzi showing up everywhere we went, making our lives impossible and losing all privacy.

"Then someone threatened me and extorted Brooks. He was terrified of me getting hurt. Felt like he couldn't protect me, especially here where he lacked resources, and he didn't want me to have to leave Brandywood for him. So he left."

Gina blinked at her for a few moments, then stood and grabbed her own bottle of water. She shook her head. "Well, shit."

"Yeah."

Gina chugged some water back. "And why are you still in Brandywood?"

"Well, he didn't give me a choice, either. Not to mention, my family—"

"Yeah, but . . . look, even I know that deep down Josh is a scumbag, but it sounds like Brooks actually loves you. If a man loved me like that, I would have packed my bags and left this town a long time ago. And I love my family, too."

Maddie studied her hands. She'd had the same thoughts. *Just go to Brooks.*

And what?

Ask him to take her back?

He'd left her sobbing on Main Street.

Changed his number.

Made it clear they were done.

Brooks left no room for a relationship with her, now or ever.

"It's not that easy, unfortunately. And he *did* hurt me, Gina. If I had found him today, I couldn't guarantee we weren't walking right back into the same situation as before. Besides, I have family obligations here."

Gina appeared conflicted. She took another sip of water, then said, "Did you know Josh sold information to the paparazzi about your whereabouts? He figured out that you'd come into the storeroom for that security tape, too, so he sold it to someone for a lot of money. Then he was hooked. Kept looking for people to sell more information to about Brooks. I told him not to," she added quickly. "But he wanted the money."

Josh?

It was Josh?

This whole time, she'd been furious with Fred Strickland about that tape.

"Your dad didn't know about the tape?"

Gina shook her head. "Josh didn't give him a penny from the money he made, either."

But . . . *how? How did Josh figure so much out?*

"Did someone tell Josh about the video? And how did he find out about where I was going to be to tip off the paparazzi?"

Guilt flashed in Gina's face. "No." She cleared her throat. "Turns out you'd signed into your text message app on his laptop and never signed out. He knew your password anyway. So he'd lurk on your messages, find information, then pass it along."

Oh my God. No wonder the paparazzi knew where we were all the time.

Gina's fingertips trembled slightly. "The guy he sold the video footage to, his name was Mike. They had a lot of online meetings. I thought he was a reporter. They didn't talk in front of me, but I knew his name because I'd ask who he was talking to, and he would just say, 'Mike.'"

Mike?

As in Kayla's ex, Mike? It had to be.

Maddie stared at Gina, astonished and sick. The sheer violation of her privacy was overwhelming. She'd sent so many intimate text messages to Brooks. And other things, too—like texts to her sisters about how brokenhearted she'd been about the breakup with Josh. And all the while, he'd been reading her messages?

How mortifying.

It's so gross.

Fury ignited inside her. "Why are you telling me all this?"

Gina twisted her hands together. "About a month and a half ago, a woman showed up at my apartment to talk to Josh. I don't know what her name was, but there might be video of her on the Ring camera to my apartment still. I confronted Josh about it because I thought he might be cheating on me with her. He said she was just an actress he'd hired for a job with Mike."

Oh. My. God.

"She showed up at the apartment the day before your grandfather had his heart attack, Maddie. I'm not sure if it's the same woman who came after you, but . . . I swear I didn't know. I didn't connect the two things at all. I knew nothing, but—"

Maddie stood bolt upright from her chair. "Fuck," she breathed, her gut twisting.

Josh and Mike.

What a perfect asshole pair.

"Josh sold information to the paparazzi about your whereabouts . . ."

Well, that explained the way the press had just descended on her. And Josh's "stunning" rescue at the same time.

Piece of shit.

Josh must have seen it as one more opportunity to make some money from a well that would soon go dry. He must be desperate for more if he'd pulled that stunt.

Maddie pulled out her phone, knots forming in her shoulders.

Hadn't Brooks said he'd gotten a text from her the day Mike had extorted him?

A text from *her*.

What if he hadn't been hacked?

What if he'd *actually* received a text from her account? Josh could have sent it, then deleted it. She'd deleted texts off her laptop app before—it would delete it from all connected devices, including her phone. She would have never seen it as having been sent.

But those deleted messages usually disappeared after thirty days.

Heart pounding, Maddie swiped to her recently deleted texts, her thumb shaking. After recovering all her deleted texts, she went to her thread with Brooks and scrolled back to the morning of the fair.

. . .

MADDIE: Trailer. Right now.

Maddie: P.S. leave the guard outside ;)

Brooks: Yes, ma'am.

Oh my God.

She covered her mouth, horrified.

Josh *had* worked with Mike to extort Brooks.

And this was the evidence.

Maddie's head spun. "Thank you for telling me all this, Gina."

Thick tears trailed down Gina's face. "You see, you don't owe me an apology at all. I owe you one. I felt horrible about Josh spying on your texts the whole time, but mostly, I was just jealous because I was sure it meant he was in love with you. I convinced him we should get engaged instead. I should have said something to you. I didn't want Josh to get in trouble, but I should have anyway. It was wrong of me not to. I never should have looked the other way. You didn't deserve it."

Maddie turned to Gina, scanning her face. Forgiveness was a moot point. The amount of processing that she would have to do to figure out how to move past this was . . . ridiculous. Brooks's desperation for privacy no longer felt extreme. "Gina, would you be willing to go on record with any of this?"

Gina sucked in a deep breath, then gave one curt nod.

Brooks had said he'd made a deal with Mike to make him go away forever, but that wasn't good enough. The man needed to pay for what he'd done to Brooks and see the inside of a prison for a long time.

"I have an idea."

46

BROOKS

"NEWS FROM SMALL-TOWN AMERICA TONIGHT, where rock star Brooks Kent has once again been spotted with his former flame, Madison Yardley—"

Brooks jerked his head up from where he sat at the small beachfront bar. The place was quiet and clean, a great spot to stop after his run and to grab tacos for lunch when he didn't feel like eating another bite of quinoa salad, and, most importantly, not open until dinnertime.

Fortunately, the owner, Jose, who was currently working behind the bar, always accommodated Brooks.

"Can you turn that up?" Brooks asked, gesturing to the television on the wall. He usually avoided the entertainment shows, but this one caught his attention. "Volumen," he added in Spanish. Sometimes he wasn't sure if Jose spoke any Spanish.

Jose smiled and turned the volume up.

The screen switched from the newscaster, a pretty blonde with a well-practiced smile, to a montage of still, somewhat blurry shots.

Brooks didn't have to look closely to recognize Main Street in Brandywood.

His heart constricted, and he leaned forward.

"We've all been following the riveting love story between the rock-star legend, who had a hot and heavy romance with Miss Yardley in September only for things to come to a devastating conclusion in October . . ."

The screen switched to a photograph of Maddie on the ground, sobbing, Naomi holding her.

Brooks's stomach lurched.

Yeah. You did that, asshole.

" . . . but now, it appears there might be a reconciliation in sight after all. As Brooks's new single 'Ever With Me' continues to climb the charts, smashing records, it's raised speculation that this budding romance may not quite be as concluded as we thought. What's more, we've had a steady stream of Brooks sightings in Brandywood, Maryland, where the happy couple appears to have picked up right where they left off . . ."

The video cut to footage of Bunny behind the counter of her shop. "Yeah, they were in here yesterday. Like regular lovebirds," Bunny said, a smile on her face.

What?

Brooks stood, inching closer to the television, his appetite vanishing.

"It's disgusting, really." The footage switched to Fred Strickland, who shook his head. "I went to the drive-in last night with my wife. Those two? All over each other. This is a family town. There needs to be some respect for the kids, you know?"

"I think it's great." Brian Pearson's voice came in, and the footage switched to him and Millie Price, who were seated on a park bench in the middle of the town square. "Brooks brings business. People want to see him, and they stay and spend their money here. And our girl gets a happy ending if you know what I mean." He winked lewdly.

"Schtooping. Lots of schtooping," Millie added with a laugh.

If the interview had been about any other topic, he almost would have laughed.

Except none of this made sense.

Why would all of them lie like this?

"Not everyone in town is as happy with the return of Brooks Kent, though. A few concerned citizens have started a petition to *ban* the star from the town. We'll report directly from Brandywood's town hall, where the issue will be voted on at noon. So happiness for Brooks in Brandywood may be short-lived. But he sure looks happy for now."

Another montage of still shots and Brooks felt the floor drop out from under him. The woman in the photos was clearly Maddie—he'd recognize her in a second—but the man in question was less clear. He had dark hair, wore a baseball cap similar to the one Brooks had left in Maddie's apartment . . . *holy shit, those are my clothes.*

The photos weren't particularly over-the-top, though there was a lot of intimate embracing, maybe even kisses—their arms blocked a good view—which made Brooks's blood boil.

The camera froze on one last photo of Maddie wrapped up in the man's arms, standing near the window of the Depot. As the camera zoomed in, he couldn't get any clearer look at the man's face.

But he'd recognize the tattoo on the hand, just above the wrist, from anywhere. He had the same damn one on his left hand, and it unironically read "Lefty" in a fancy script. He'd gotten it at the same time as Cormac Doyle one night when they'd gotten drunk in New York City ten years earlier.

They were both lefties, so they'd both gotten one.

Because they were like brothers.

What. The. Fuck.

Why in the hell was Cormac making out with Brooks's woman?

She's not your woman. You let her go, you moron.

I need to get out of this bar before I make a mistake.

He paid for his tab, then left the bar, feeling like the walls were going to cave in on him.

A sheen of sweat broke out on his forehead.

Cormac had made a move on Madison?

Nausea burned a hole in his gut.

Was she doing this to punish him?

You deserve it. You should be punished. You don't deserve her after what you did to her.

But what about Cormac? Why would Cormac do this? Sure, he hadn't answered his friend's calls or texts the last month, but surely, Cormac had known he just wasn't ready to talk yet.

The weeks after returning to LA from Brandywood had been the closest to hell he had ever lived.

He had lost everything.

His heart had been completely shattered.

And in his attempt to protect the woman he loved, he'd taken a flamethrower to both their hearts.

Your fault.

Your fault.

Your fault.

Brooks whipped out his phone, gripping it tightly.

Madison.

He headed onto the sand, straight toward the water, the need to drown himself in *something* encapsulating him.

She'd moved on.

Already.

Maybe to injure him.

Maybe not.

But the townspeople had to know it was Cormac, not him. So why would they all lie?

Why tell the reporters he had come back?

Unless they wanted to protect Cormac. He was one of their own, and maybe they didn't want to share the truth because the lie was easier to explain. Brooks and Cormac shared dark hair, a similar height and complexion.

But why the fuck was Cormac wearing my clothes?

Brooks couldn't prove it was his clothes, of course, especially not from the blurry photos, but that baseball cap was identical to the one he'd left. And why would Cormac wear clothes that were like the ones Brooks wore?

He dialed his so-called friend.

It all felt like a sick, fucked-up prank.

The phone went straight to voicemail.

"It's Brooks. Call me." He hung up, seething.

Maddie had every right to move on if she wanted. He'd told her to.

Walked out on her.

But that didn't mean he had to like it.

And if she had moved on with Cormac . . . it was damn near unforgiveable.

Not to mention that Cormac had wanted to leave Brandywood in the rearview mirror and never settle there again. *What the fuck?*

Unless this was what he meant when he'd hinted he was thinking of putting down roots again.

For weeks, Brooks had teetered somewhere between crushing depression and the urgent need to keep moving forward. He'd regretted leaving the instant his feet had hit the tarmac in LAX. Not a single day had gone by without him regretting hurting her. Wishing he could be with her.

But he'd tried to tell himself he'd done the best thing for her. That he loved her enough to let her live a happy life in the town she loved, with the people she loved, free of the danger and chaos he brought to everything.

Every damn day he told himself it was better in the long run.

And every damn night, he woke up tormented and unable to sleep, his peace completely and thoroughly fucked.

He'd written more music in the past two weeks than he had in years—to the point that his fingertips had bled from playing the guitar so much.

Fortunately, Christine had come through for him. She'd renegotiated his contract with Ava for a better deal that gave him more control over his music and rights and a shorter term on the contract—just eighteen months.

He'd been right all along: Ava couldn't afford to lose him on the label.

To keep her happy, he'd promised a single, then put out "Ever With Me" because Maddie was all he could think about. She consumed him with a fire that had branded his soul.

Then, of course, he'd regretted *that* decision because the press had started the reporting about her all over again and it felt like he'd reset the clock on trying to convince Mike that he didn't care. The easy thing would be to set up a few high-profile dates, but he couldn't do that to her.

And now he may have lost her forever.

"You idiot, you already lost her forever." Brooks breathed in and out as slowly as he could.

Madison. The only person who had ever seen him.

"I can't live without her," he breathed.

The thought pressed into every fiber of him, pulsing into his brain with a reckless thrum.

Was she Cormac's now?

Would she even forgive him?

Would anything he did make a difference to her after he'd hurt her the way he had?

He had to know what the hell was going on in Brandywood.

And then punch his former best friend's face.

47

MADDIE

THE BRANDYWOOD TOWN hall had been full for two hours before the council meeting was even supposed to start, because almost everyone had turned out. In fact, she hadn't seen it this packed since the Wagners had tried to kick Pops off Main Street.

But this time, the town wasn't there because they were divided on an issue.

A few strategic secret meetings with key members of the community was all it had taken.

Her family was in the front row with her—all of them, including Pops—and Maddie had never been more grateful for them. They were the first people she'd gone to after what Gina had revealed, and Dad had taken a sworn statement from Gina that same afternoon. Having a lawyer for a father felt like such a blessing.

TJ, who happened to be a private investigator, found the cameras that had been installed in the lake house. Jason had asked the other weekend renters if they'd let anyone into the property and learned that someone, probably Mike, had shown up in an electrician's uniform claiming he was there for service the weekend they'd been at the Serendipity.

TJ had also recovered the Ring camera footage of the woman Gina believed might have attacked Pops. He'd found her online, too. She was from Frederick, Maryland, and the cops were waiting outside her work to arrest her after this meeting was over.

As soon as the meeting started, Mike would be arrested. Turned out the FBI had already been investigating Mike.

Thanks to the nonexistent cell phone service in the town hall, Josh—who'd taken a seat with his family a few rows away—had no way of being alerted.

TJ, who'd been working with Dan Kline and the local police, as well as Dan and Jen's father, who worked as a consultant for the FBI for financial crimes, all believed that Josh and Mike had probably been working alone. They'd gotten lucky—access to Brooks through Maddie's foolish mistake of leaving her messages account logged in.

For sharing her password with her ex-boyfriend when she lived with him and then forgetting to change it.

The guilt Maddie still felt over that was enormous. She'd felt so stupid, so naive.

She'd been so naive, honestly.

And it had cost Brooks dearly.

Josh had been foolish by breaking up with Gina, but he'd probably also been certain that Gina and Maddie would never put their heads together and talk.

And Josh's cockiness would be his downfall. Today.

"Ready?" Dad asked from beside her as Bill Mackintosh, the mayor, went to the podium.

Maddie nodded.

"All right, folks. Should be a quick one today, but I'm glad to see we're all as eager to get this matter resolved. An emergency petition brought to the council this weekend, the town of Brandywood versus Brooks Kent, needs to be voted on. Would you like to take the podium and say a few words, Fred?"

Maddie's throat went dry as Fred ambled up to the podium. Never in her life would she have put so much on the line with the Stricklands, but Fred was the best man for the job. The only one that might get things rolling before Josh panicked and took off.

Would Fred do what he'd promised?

Fred smiled at the crowd. "I'm the one who brought the petition to the council. Enough is enough. The Yardleys and their ilk have ruined our town. And now Maddie and her boyfriend are up to their disgusting behavior all over again. I won't be bullied by them anymore. I'm sick of seeing photographers outside my store windows. Reporters milling around our town. I want things to go back to normal."

Bill picked up another microphone. "Do you have any witnesses to these new sightings of Brooks Kent that you've mentioned? Some people aren't even sure Brooks Kent *has* returned."

The bookstore owner, Annie, stood up. "I talked to Maddie three days ago. She told me she and Brooks were heading to the drive-in theater."

Fred nodded emphatically. "See?"

"Thank you, Annie."

Mr. Wong from the deli also stood. "Maddie told me she and Brooks were going to Pearson Creek for a picnic on Tuesday."

Grace Wagner also stood. "Maddie booked a private hour at my art studio for her and Brooks."

Laura Redding joined the group that was standing. "Maddie also booked my best cabin for a few nights for her and Brooks."

One by one, people joined them until nearly a dozen people stood, issuing similar statements.

Fred grinned, setting his hands out. "See? And what's more, the paparazzi showed up at every single one of these places and took pictures of them there together. The two of them, all over each other every time. A picture's worth a thousand words, Bill. And I witnessed with my two eyes the two of them going at it in my storeroom way back in September. It's out of control."

Maddie lowered her gaze, her cheeks flushing. Most of the town already knew that, but it was still embarrassing to have it announced.

And God, do I hope this works.

Bill nodded gravely and thanked the people who continued to stand. He looked at Maddie. "Madison Yardley? Do you have anything to say for yourself?"

She took a deep, calm breath in through her nose, then nodded and went over to the podium. "Excuse me, Fred."

Fred stepped to the side.

Maddie scanned the town hall, the faces of the people standing, the press in the corner of the room.

She swallowed hard.

Brandywood had turned out for her.

I love this town so much.

Her voice wasn't as strong as she wanted it to be, but she said, "A few quick questions to the people standing." She leaned closer to the microphone. "Grace, I texted you about that booking, right?"

Grace nodded.

"Did you tell anyone I was going?"

"No, Maddie, you know I'd never do that."

"How about you, Laura? Same thing, right? I texted you and asked for your discretion?"

Laura nodded. "And you got it. I wouldn't ever tell people you were going to be there."

"But the paparazzi still found out somehow." Maddie frowned and looked at the other people in the standing group. "What about the rest of you? Did *you* tell anyone?"

"One person. Josh Hawkins," Annie said.

Josh shifted in his seat.

"Only Josh," Mr. Wong said.

The same answer came from the rest of the group.

Josh's face had reddened by now, his eyes dark.

Maddie looked straight at him. "Funny how they all only told you, Josh, and still the paparazzi were waiting for me every time." She leaned forward, hands on the podium. "Because you know what, I only told one person where I was heading each time, too. Annie was the only person who knew I was going to the drive-in. Mr. Wong was the only person I told about Pearson's Creek. But you know the really weird thing? I didn't tell anyone about Grace's studio or the Redding Cabins. I *only* texted them."

A projector turned on, illuminating the wall behind her. A screenshot from her deleted texts sent to Brooks. "Look familiar, Josh?"

Josh stood so quickly in his seat that his chair fell backward. He was sweating now. "I want my lawyer."

"I'm sure you do. I do, too. Because you violated my privacy, used the text messaging app I had downloaded onto your computer to log in to my messages, and then used those private messages to threaten Brooks Kent and sell the information you found to the paparazzi. You and Mike Valders hired a woman to stalk and threaten me, and my grandfather had a heart attack as a result. You didn't just betray me, you betrayed this whole damn town. Every one of us missed out on Brooks's performance at the fair because he had to fly to Vegas to pay off the extortion you participated in, Josh. At. Gunpoint."

Gasps came from the people in the room, and photographers took more pictures from the press side.

The back doors opened, and the uniformed police officers strode down the center aisle, heading toward Josh.

"You're lying!" Josh yelled, his face filled with fear.

"Gina has already signed sworn statements, and she's happy to cooperate. I guess you didn't think the Stricklands and the Yardleys might come together to take down a douchebag like you, did you?" She smiled at Fred, who nodded while glaring at Josh.

Dan came up behind Josh and yanked his hands behind his back, handcuffs at the ready.

"Oh . . . one more thing. That 'Brooks' you've been so worried about in town this week?" She nodded toward the side door, which opened.

Cormac sauntered through with a grin, wearing Brooks's clothes, including the baseball cap. The effect had been remarkably effective. Maddie might have had to snuggle and pretend to neck with Cormac Doyle more than she'd ever wanted to, but it hadn't been too hard to fake kisses with well-positioned arms and hands.

She didn't need to explain that part of it to the town, though. The truth would get out soon enough and spread through the rumor mill. The press could think what they wanted.

Maddie turned back toward Bill Mackintosh as Cormac joined her and slung his arm over her shoulders. "This is the so-called Brooks I've been hanging out with this week. We're not going to ban one of our own from the town, are we? And anyway, since when did public displays of affection become a crime here?"

Bill nodded. "I'm going to dismiss the petition, then. The town hall meeting is adjourned."

The townspeople clapped as the police led Josh away.

Turning toward Cormac, Maddie hugged him tightly, relief pouring through her. "Thank you. Thank you so much for everything."

"There's a mountain of evidence against Josh now. I guarantee you he'll sell out Mike in one second flat. You did good, Maddie."

Maddie nodded and pulled away. "I owe you, Cormac. I really do. If you get around to calling Brooks anytime in the next couple of days, maybe explain to him . . . actually, never mind." She sniffled, determined to stay dry-eyed. "Let him think what he wants."

Cormac chuckled. "He called me yesterday, but I didn't pick up. Didn't want to risk him actually showing up here and messing up all our well-laid plans. I'm probably going to have to tell him, you know. He won't forgive me otherwise."

The news was bittersweet. Maybe Brooks had called Cormac because he'd seen the newscasts, and it had bothered him. Perhaps that meant he still cared.

On the other hand, he hadn't called *her*.

"Yeah, I guess so." She stretched, looking around the town hall as it emptied. It was loud, and her father had given the press instructions on where to meet for a briefing. He would be handling it himself, thankfully.

"I'll see you around, Cormac. Call me when you come back to town next time. If I'm here, we'll meet up." She gave his hand a last squeeze, then headed back toward her family.

"You were amazing, Maddie," Naomi said, giving her a hug.

"I think Josh officially takes the cake as the worst blackmailer this town has ever produced," Lindsay said, then poked Logan in the ribs. "And that's saying something."

Travis snickered behind her.

"Hey, I'm not the only one in our family known for blackmail. This whole thing started when our *sister blackmailed* Brooks Kent," Logan said, giving Maddie a wry look.

Maddie covered her face with her hands. "I'm officially retired from blackmail. Forever."

Jake shoved his hands in his pockets, a satisfied and impish look on his face. "Bet you're wishing we hadn't stopped being roommates when you moved in with Josh. I never did you dirty."

"No, but you *are* dirty. If I had a nickel for every time you didn't do the dishes, I wouldn't ever need to work again."

"Cheap shot," Jake muttered with a shake of his head. "You going back to the Depot this afternoon?"

"Actually, I wanted to take Maddie out to celebrate. You know, sister to sister." Naomi linked arms with her.

Lindsay frowned. "You didn't invite me."

"You can come if you want, but I figured you'd need to get back to the pub."

Lindsay groaned. "Fine, fine. Remind me why I picked working at the pub instead of the Depot? Logan isn't nearly as much fun as you guys."

"Keep saying that, and one of these days, I'm going to believe you," Logan shot back.

Maddie laughed, then set her arms around her two sisters. "Come here, you guys. Yardley sibling group hug."

They all joined in, and Maddie closed her eyes, her throat thick with emotion.

Damn my stupid need to cry.

She blinked rapidly, and as she did, she met Pops's light blue eyes from where he sat, watching them several feet away.

He nodded just slightly, his face beaming with pride.

They were Yardleys. His grandkids. His legacy.

And she couldn't have been luckier to have been born into such an incredible family.

She and Naomi made their way out the back door, then crossed the street to the parking lot beside Bunny's Café. It had always been Maddie's favorite place to view Main Street. From here, you could see all the way down to Yardley's Pub, practically the whole length of the strip.

Her heart gave a throb at the storefronts, the people walking on the sidewalks, and the kids playing on the playground in front of the town hall.

The place she'd loved and lived in her whole life.

In a month, it would glow with twinkle lights for Christmas. The Christmas Carol play would be on the street, the smell of apple cider and cinnamon would permeate the air, and Brian Pearson would bring some of his horses to town for carriage rides in the snow.

For Valentine's Day, reds and pinks would take over, then flowers would sprout everywhere once spring hit, and the cherry trees planted near the sidewalk would bloom.

Summer would bring hot, sticky days filled with tourists visiting the lake and the Depot. Ice cream dripping down faces, and pit beef and barbecue wafting through the air. Fireworks for the Fourth of July. Days at the lake.

But now, they were in that brief season between the end of fall and the beginning of Christmas, when the trees were bare, but not everything was decorated for the holidays quite yet. When people were starting to think about holidays and family but still felt like they had time on their hands.

The in-between two seasons. *Like me.*

Maddie tore her gaze away and hurried to Naomi's car. As she settled in, she smiled, determined to be happy. *Today is a good day.* "Where are we headed?"

"It's a surprise."

They started forward, and Naomi put on a song. Something about it felt familiar, but it wasn't until the vocal part started that Maddie sat straight with recognition.

Brooks.

She turned to Naomi and gave her a shocked look. "What?"

"I thought you should listen to it. It's his new song, 'Ever With Me.' It's a beautiful song, Maddie."

Maddie's jaw quivered, and she stared down at her hands.

That voice would be the death of her.

" . . . *I'll be forever with you. You'll be forever with me. . . ever with me.*"

She reached across and slapped the button on the radio.

"I can't," she said. *Not yet.*

She needed to brace herself first. Get herself ready.

They drove straight out of town onto the curving roads of the woods. Maddie frowned at Naomi. "Where are you taking me?"

"You'll see."

At last, Naomi pulled off the main road onto a dirt path. Her car bumped along it, but she pushed forward. Even from here, Maddie could see the lake through the trees in the distance.

The car drew to a stop as the trees thinned and the path ended.

What in the heck?

"Um . . . Naomi, I'm not sure what you had in mind when you said celebrate, but this isn't quite what I was expecting."

Naomi smiled. "Will you just trust me? Get out of the car and go that way." She pointed toward the lake. "It's all set up there. I'll come join you in a minute. I just have to get some stuff from the trunk."

With a skeptical look, Maddie opened the car door and climbed out. She hugged her arms to her chest, wishing she'd brought something thicker than a light jacket. She hadn't expected to be outside.

As she pushed through the trees, the leaves crunched against her boots.

When the lake came into view more clearly, she stopped short.

A picnic was set up on a small field in front of it, complete with candles and flowers. Lots of them.

And standing in the middle of it all . . . was Brooks.

48

BROOKS

MADDIE STOPPED WALKING at the edge of the woods, her face frozen with shock.

God, she's so beautiful.

So beautiful that he couldn't breathe for several seconds, his chest tight.

How did I ever walk away from her?

Maddie checked back over her shoulder in the direction she'd come from and didn't come any farther. "What are you doing here?"

"I saw an interesting news segment yesterday. Tried to call Cormac, but he didn't answer. So I got Naomi's number from Kayla." He looped his thumbs into his jean pockets and took a few steps forward. "She told me everything."

Maddie crossed her arms. "She shouldn't have. I swore her to secrecy."

She isn't happy to see you.

"There may have been some begging involved. Of the variety where I literally said, I'm begging you." Brooks's shoulders sagged, a hopeless feeling settling in him.

She's never going to forgive you.

"For the record, she made it clear she doesn't think I deserve you. And she's right. But . . . I had to try."

"Try what?" Maddie came closer, her eyes guarded. "To surprise me with a picnic in some random woods and say you're sorry?" She stopped an arm's length away, close enough to touch but far enough that he felt the distance between them.

"Actually, it's not just random. It's forty acres of secluded property . . . that I just bought from Jason Cavanaugh."

Her eyes widened. "What?"

"It'll take a while before I can put a house on it. There are permits and then building the thing. I thought about just buying the lake house at first, but I didn't want anything that had memories for us—good or bad. You know, a fresh start."

Brooks came closer, longing to touch her. "I have ached for you with my every breath, Madison. Leaving you was unforgivable, and I'm still terrified. I know I can't protect you perfectly, and that scares me down to my core. But living without you scares me more. So I'm begging you, please forgive me. I want to be with you and only you, Maddie. Forever. You're branded in my soul."

Her eyes shone with tears. "I just—" She swallowed and squeezed her eyes shut. "And you think it's possible for us to be together now?"

"Naomi told me about the case you were mounting against Mike . . . so I called my lawyer's friend at the FBI, who filled me in on the rest. He just sent me a message and let me know Mike's been arrested. Anything Mike had on us will be destroyed."

That, by itself, was a victory they should celebrate, but she didn't appear happy about it. Or relieved. She just nodded, blinking a few tears away.

"I know that's your win, Maddie. You did it. I can't promise there won't be other threats, but that one, at least, won't be hanging over us anymore. And that's a huge deal to me."

Somehow, nothing he said seemed right. Or good enough.

Will she ever forgive me?

After another moment, she looked at him more directly. "You hurt me in a way I didn't know I could hurt, Brooks. I've had my heart broken before, but never like that. Never. When you walked away, it felt like the world went dark. And then your silence . . . that hurt me the most of all."

"I wanted you to be safe. I didn't want Mike—or anyone—thinking you were a weakness in me to exploit. To hurt you."

"I know why you did what you did." She clasped her hands together. "I understood it, and you made that much clear. But what I didn't understand—what I still can't understand—is why you thought you needed to keep sacrificing everything. Why you *insisted* on doing it all alone. You had me, Brooks. You *had me.* And you still did it all alone."

He couldn't take it any longer and reached for her, tugging her toward him. "I'm sorry, Maddie. I'm so sorry. Please forgive me. I love you. I promise, I'll never try to take everything on by myself again. Please let me make it up to you and make a home with you here, to start over again."

She stiffened at his touch, her eyes pained, filled with hurt.

Shaking her head, she whispered, "No."

His hand dropped, stunned.

No.

He'd worried that she might not forgive him.

But considered it as an actual possibility? That he'd leave here without her . . .

"Maddie, I love you." Tears stung his eyes, and he squeezed them shut. "I—"

She set her fingertips to his mouth. "You can't build a home with me here. Not yet. You're not ready, Brooks. We'd be setting ourselves up for failure again because you were right . . . I love Brandywood, but it's not the right place for you, for us, right now."

She drew her hand back and stroked his cheek. "Which is why I bought a one-way ticket to LA tomorrow morning. I guess neither of our sisters are good at keeping secrets because Kayla gave me all your information, too."

He let out a strangled breath, his lips parting in shock.

. . . *what?*

Maddie came closer and wrapped her arms around his neck. "I love you, Brooks Kent. Of course I forgive you. You have to swear to me you'll never be so stupid again, of course, but—"

He cut her off with a kiss, his hands cupping her face, fingers splayed across her jaw.

She cried softly, then kissed him back, her mouth crushing to his deeply.

"I love you," he whispered between kisses. "I love you, Madison. I'm so sorry. So sorry."

Their tears mingled as she returned his kisses, clinging to him with her entire body.

"It's you and me, Brooks, you understand? Together. I won't survive you ever doing something like that to me again. I love you too much to live without you."

"What about your grandfather?" he asked suddenly, scanning her face. "He offered you a job—"

"I talked about it with him this morning, actually. He's going to ask Jake, instead. While I love the Depot and his business, it's not what I see for myself right now. To tell you the truth, I'm sort of fascinated by the idea of being an entertainment manager. Maybe for a musician or something . . ."

He cracked a smile at her. "So long as you don't mind sleeping with your boss."

From the tree line came the sound of a car radio turned all the way up.

"Ever With Me."

Maddie pulled her face away and laughed, sniffling as she wiped her tears away. "That's Naomi reminding us she's still there."

Brooks chuckled, wrapping her tightly in his arms. His chin rested on the top of her head. "She probably doesn't want to be witness to anything else."

"I'm pretty over witnesses, too. Maybe we could go somewhere else, though?"

Brooks nodded and pulled back. "We don't have to stay here. Where do you want to go? Paris? Abu Dhabi?" The corners of his eyes crinkled.

"Someday you're going to learn . . . I don't need to go anywhere fancy, Brooks." Maddie reached for his hand and interlaced their fingers. "Let's go home."

Home.

Home was wherever Maddie Yardley was.

He knew that now.

EPILOGUE
MADDIE

One Year Later

MADDIE COULD FEEL the crowd's energy from the side of the stage. She usually stayed here so she could greet her husband first when he finished a set.

She would never, ever tire of watching Brooks Kent play his guitar.

"This is amazing!" Lindsay shouted in her ear. Even standing shoulder to shoulder, they could barely hear each other up here.

Maddie grinned, then wrapped her arm over her sister's shoulders. Naomi, on her other side, did the same thing. Kayla and Jen soon joined them. Their five Yardley sister group.

All of them had been slightly miffed with Maddie and Brooks when they'd eloped the previous June. Not because they thought it was too soon—all of them knew Maddie well enough to know she didn't do love on a schedule—but because the elopement had been a secret.

Just Brooks and Maddie on a remote mountaintop in Banff. One by one, they'd been checking off all the places Brooks had wanted to take her, but that trip had been Maddie's favorite by far.

They'd come back and done a big, family-style barbecue party to celebrate with everyone in Brandywood, of course, but every now and then, Naomi would grumble over the phone, "I still can't believe you didn't invite me to your wedding."

Applause and screams erupted as Brooks finished a song, then he grabbed the microphone free from its stand. "Thank you, Brandywood!"

More screaming. The fall town fair was on *fire* tonight.

While Brooks hadn't been on tour this year, he'd still been busy playing concerts and releasing music, which meant they'd spent a lot of time on the road. Not that Maddie minded. Managing his career had been fun—and she'd even started taking on other clients.

And with Mike behind bars and Maddie and Brooks's relationship becoming less *interesting* to the press, the paparazzi had been more muted, too. That had all helped Brooks lower his guard some. Feel safer.

They'd even broken ground on the property here in Brandywood, which made Maddie's heart happy. She'd been religious in watching Pops and Jake in any special the Happy Home Network produced and loved seeing Jake as the new face of the company. He was a perfect fit.

"This concert has been over a year in the making," Brooks said as the crowd quieted. "And I'm so glad I can officially say I owe you all nothing. My debt is paid off."

Laughter followed, then the lights dimmed. "I've got one last song, with some special guest appearances for you. It's not one of my own. In fact, it's not even a rock-and-roll song. This little medley was put together by some country greats a few years back, so, with some minor changes, here's my love letter to you all."

The familiar notes of "Take Me Home, Country Road" started, and Brooks's deep voice began the first verse. But when he got to the chorus, he swapped out "West Virginia" for "Western Maryland". . . and the crowd went wild.

As the song continued, Cormac came out from stage left . . . and then Maddie left her spot with her sisters, microphone in hand.

The cheer from the crowd was deafening, their exuberance radiating through her.

She joined Cormac and Brooks, the song flowing through her with ease. She couldn't see anyone in the crowd, but she knew her parents were there. Her brothers and Audrey. Her nieces.

Pops and Bunny. The Doyles. The Wagners. The Kleins and the Cavanaughs. The Stricklands. The Pearsons. Millie Price.

The community that she'd always be a part of, no matter how far she traveled.

When the song ended, the applause went on for several minutes, the crowd clamoring for more.

She would always love them.

Maddie turned toward Brooks, and dripping in sweat, he wrapped her in a hug.

She laughed as he rubbed his forehead against her neck. "Oh my God, you're disgusting!" she shouted in his ear with a squeal, knowing he probably wouldn't hear her with his in-ears in still.

The cheering continued as Brooks led her off stage. They

got backstage, and he smiled boyishly. Her handsome devil of a rock-star husband who still made her panties melt.

Maddie kissed him then.

"What's that for?"

"I'm just happy," she said as his arms tightened around her waist.

"Happy to be home?" He searched her eyes.

"No, silly man. Happy with you. I could be anywhere, and as long as I'm with you, I'll be happy. I love you."

"I love you, too, Maddie. Always." He kissed her again, then pulled his head back and frowned, a teasing glint to his eyes. "Does that mean I should tell the builders to stop that house by the lake?"

She grinned. "No, I didn't say that."

"Ahh, so you do want to move here now?"

Maddie drew in a deep breath of cold, country air. The fair and all its familiar scents of hot frying oil, apple fritters, smoked meats, and warm fires. The smell of dozens of childhood nights.

Then Maddie looked back at her husband and smiled, lifting the back of his hand to her lips.

"Brandywood will always be here. It will always be a part of me. And maybe someday—when we're ready—we can come back here. But my home is with you, Brooks. Forever. And today's a good day to live wherever you are."

As the sounds of cheering started to die, Brooks held her close. "Forever, Madison. You and me."

NEWSLETTER AND NEXT BOOK

Want to keep up with me and hear what's going on in my world? Join my newsletter on my website! I have freebies and giveaways, exclusive content and, of course, you get to hear all about upcoming book news, my life, and my small army of children.

I hope you enjoyed Maddie and Brook's story! Thank you so much for reading; my readers really are what make this possible and I am so grateful for you! If you enjoyed this book, I'd love it if you took the time to leave a rating or review at your favorite book retailer. It truly goes a long way.

While the Brandywood series has wrapped for now, there's more small town romance on the horizon. Or, check out the Wanderlust Contemporary Romance series, in *See You Next Fall* and *He Loves Me Knot.*

ACKNOWLEDGMENTS

Brandywood was a place I **needed** to escape to in the winter of 2021, when my own mother faced a cancer diagnosis that sent my world into chaos. It was a home, a place to shed tears, new joys, new friends, and it will always be a part of me. For now, my journey to visit that lovely spot in the mountains is over but I'm grateful to each and every one of you that made it possible.

Huge thanks to Marion Archer for always being a top notch editor and so wonderful to work with. Many thanks also the rest of my team—Jenny Simms, Amanda Coleman, and most especially to Julie Deaton (I"ll miss you!!).

Patrick Knowles, thank you for the fantastic illustrated cover to complete the set.

To Kari March, thank you so much for all the gorgeous covers—paperback, ebook, and hardcover—they are absolutely beautiful and I'm so thrilled with them.

To my Bookstagram lovelies—you're the best. You keep me going with your encouragement and messages. THANK YOU.

And to anyone who has ever sent me a note to tell me how much Brandywood has impacted them, this one is for you. You made this dream a reality and I couldn't have done it without you.

ALSO BY ANNABELLE MCCORMACK

The Windswept WWI Saga:

A Zephyr Rising: A Windswept Prequel Novella

Windswept: The Windswept Saga Book 1

Sands of Sirocco: The Windswept Saga Book 2

Whisper in the Tempest: The Windswept Saga Book 3

The Brandywood Small Town Romance Series:

All This Time

I'll Carry You

Once We Met

Until Forever Ends

Ever With Me

Winnick Contemporary Romances

See You Next Fall

He Loves Me Knot

One Time in Paris (Coming Soon)

Don't Forget to Write (Coming Soon)

To find out the latest about my new releases, please sign up for my newsletter or Facebook Reader's group! I love hearing from readers and have some great offers lined up for my subscribers.

ABOUT THE AUTHOR

Annabelle McCormack writes about timeless love and unforgettable journeys. She is a graduate of the Johns Hopkins University's M.A. in Writing Program. She lives in Maryland with her husband and five children. When she's not busy writing, she's probably overwhelmed by laundry and . . . *let's be honest.* She's always busy writing. But she wouldn't have it any other way, either.

Visit her at www.annabellemccormack.com or http://instagram.com/annabellemccormack to follow her daily adventures.

www.ingramcontent.com/pod-product-compliance
Ingram Content Group UK Ltd.
Pitfield, Milton Keynes, MK11 3LW, UK
UKHW022341210225
455360UK00010B/48

9 781960 883230